Asher and Erik are getting married, but Asher isn't happy about the pressure being put on him by their families and unwittingly by Erik himself. Issues that have plagued him for a long time come bubbling to the surface and threaten to overwhelm him. Although he cries out for help, no one hears; instead they write it off as Asher throwing a tantrum again. Only Angel sees the cracks, but it's too much for him to handle on his own, although he tries.

The pressure builds, and even though there are breakouts, still no one sees the extent of the problem until the night before the wedding, when Asher is confronted by Erik in front of all their family and friends, and bolts.

Fortunately, Asher is rescued by Vince's Uncle Tony, who makes him an offer he can't refuse.

The Band heads off to London for a three-month tour, and not everyone is happy about it. Vince is stressed out and worried that Angel is not being entirely faithful. Should he say something? Then Connor meets an old friend, just when he starts having doubts about his relationship with Angel, and the fur starts to fly.

Will any of the couples survive?

Aria
Copyright © 2019 S.L. Danielson and Cheryl Headford
ISBN: 978-1-4874-2522-7
Cover art by Angela Waters

Published by eXtasy Books Inc or
Devine Destinies, an imprint of eXtasy Books Inc

Look for us online at:
www.eXtasybooks.com or www.devinedestinies.com

ARIA
UPSTAGED BOOK 4

BY

S.L. DANIELSON AND CHERYL HEADFORD

DEDICATION

To anyone with a mental illness who thinks no one hears them.
Keep shouting.

CHAPTER ONE

V ince smiled to himself, thinking how the past year had seemed to fly by. He and Billy were doing great, which was the best. It had taken a while, but they'd finally found a great house and were enjoying every moment. Several months ago, they had talked Daisy into being a surrogate for them, and Joey was constantly by her side for support. Angel was back in the States, attending the art school of his dreams while Connor was still in Ireland, working on completing his schooling for construction. Then, of course, there was Eric and Asher. Poor guys had been living the wedding planning nightmare, but only had a few more days to go.

Dripping fat hissed on the brand-new barbecue, and Vince moved some of the hamburgers over so they wouldn't get singed. The grill was full of meat of all kinds—chicken, burger, even a couple of steaks. Erik had a huge appetite, as did Daisy, ever since her pregnancy.

Vince had cut back on his own food intake, and the proof was in his new wardrobe. He'd lost 30 pounds since the marriage a year ago. Amazing, since he was a chef, with only a year to go to complete culinary school. He wondered whether Billy saw him any differently now he'd lost the weight but decided not. Billy loved him just as he was, and that was the key to everything.

As if he knew Vince was thinking about him, Billy appeared at his side and draped his arms around Vince's shoulders. Vince shivered as his husband kissed his neck. "Hey, baby. How's it going out here on your new toy?"

Vince hooked Billy with one arm and held him close. "Just great. Love this thing. It's perfect on this huge patio. Beats the old house of ours hands down."

"Yeah, but we had lots of memories there, didn't we?" Billy's playful tone made clear which memories he was thinking about.

"That we did, my love." Vince kissed him softly. "How's everyone doing? Dinner's almost ready."

"Meh, doing pretty good. Daisy's eating everything in sight. Our children will be well fed. Course, with you as their awesome daddy, they will be anyway."

"Look who's talkin', Billy Caliendo. You'll be the best daddy, too. You've got such a sweet demeanor—funny, smart. You can teach them the drums."

"Oh, definitely! Watch them pick up Mommy's guitar skills, though. Uncle Erik can teach 'em how to sing. We've got a band in the making. Connor and Angel can show them how to build toys, then paint them. Asher, too."

Vince stifled a laugh. He flipped the food a final time and put it on the serving platter. "All right, let's go eat. I'm starved."

They brought the food into the house, and everyone stood in a somewhat orderly line to fill their plates. There were multiple salads, meats, and other dishes, most of it handmade by Vince himself.

They all strolled outside to the patio table. "So, a toast to our new house!" Billy offered.

"Hear, hear! It's awesome, guys!" Erik agreed. "Love this view."

"Love the peace," Asher sighed, with a pointed look at Daisy.

"We wanted a good chunk of land, not to be crowded into housing lots," Vince replied. "Eventually I'd love a few acres and a ranch style. By then I'll be an old man."

Billy laughed. "Old man. Listen to you. You're all of twenty-one-years-old, baby. If you're old, I'm old . . . and so are all of us, so let's not even go there." He glanced up at Erik. "So, six days to go! Are you so excited you can't sleep? Gettin' married? The ol' ball and chain?" He kicked Erik's chair.

"Ha, ha, I'm fantastic. I'm really stoked about this. Life's good, The Von's doing great, and we've got our new house. Once it's fixed up, it'll be the talk of the neighborhood." He took Asher's hand. "Best of all, it's ours."

Asher smiled and squeezed Erik's hand. "I can't wait to move in. Can't believe those stupid rules and regulations. Who the fuck cares if there's electricity, or a floor in the kitchen, or walls in the studio? We've got candles, and there's running water. It's fucking nuts that some official in an office somewhere gets to decide when we can move into our own house. It wouldn't happen in the UK, and you think *we're* crazy."

"Those are the rules. Gotta be safe and livable." Joey waggled a finger at him. "Oy, Connor told me half of what he had to learn was all the building codes. Although, to be honest, I think he can't wait to get hands-on with the building again. The business course is driving him crazy. He's about ready to rip his hair out." He laughed into his glass.

"Better not, Angel would kill him!" Billy joked. "They come in when, Wednesday? I can't wait to see them again. Thank goodness for email and Skype."

"Amen to that one," Erik added. "Anyway, I love your house almost as much as ours. It'll be boss for you and the kids."

"Thanks, Erik. Yeah, we looked at what, twenty before we chose this one? It had to be kinda changeable, but not a wreck either." He looked at Daisy. "How're you feeling, Daisy? You know we're indebted to you for the rest of our lives for this amazing thing you're doing for us."

"Hey, I couldn't think of two people who deserve children more, and I'm absolutely made up that I can help you. If I'm honest, if you'd asked me a year ago whether I'd ever consider being a surrogate, I'd have laughed in your face." She laughed. "Actually, I did laugh in your face when you first brought it up, but it didn't take much thought to change my mind."

Daisy sat back and patted her stomach where, at just under four months, the twins she carried were already making her tummy swell. Joey rested his head on her shoulder and his hand over hers on her belly. "I wish they were ours, and I hope one day this beautiful little body will be carrying our child, but I can't begrudge you guys. Like Daisy said, you were made to be dads. These little ones are so lucky." There was a wistful note in his voice as he patted Daisy's rounded tummy, but the smile he gave Vince and Billy was open and bright.

This last year had given Vince an entirely new perspective on Joey. He had always been the quiet one, the one who was happy sitting in the background while the bigger characters—principally Erik if he were truthful—took the spotlight. Sure, that was true, but there was a lot more to his personality. How many men would be prepared to support their girlfriend without restriction through carrying children for not one but two other men? Of course, it hadn't all been sunshine and rainbows, and Joey sometimes got upset, or even angry, but it never lasted long. It was clear to see how much Joey and Daisy loved each other, and that love shone through everything, even this.

"Eew," Asher said, screwing up his face. "Do you have to talk about that? It's gross. The whole baby thing creeps me out, and the fact it's my sister . . . Just don't go there."

Erik laughed and shook his head at Asher. "You crack me up. You don't like little babies, my hubby-to-be? You're gonna be an uncle soon. You should get used to that idea, at least. I'm thrilled for you guys."

"Thanks, Erik," Vince answered. "Joey, I know you guys will have a lovely child of your own someday, too, if you ever get around to getting married."

"After the band and school, I'm giving it top priority," Joey said. "My parents are having a tough time of it lately, taxes and all. I've been helping them out a lot, now we're making good money with the band, but we're not exactly superstars yet, so it's going to take a while to get everything sorted. I want to get us a house first, like you guys, and that's next on the list now my folks are out of trouble. Once the babies are born, we'll go house-hunting, then start saving for a wedding."

Billy clapped Joey's shoulder. "You're a good guy, Joey. You've got it all figured out."

He smiled at them. "Thanks, Billy. Ugh, I need some more to eat. Daisy's pregnant, but I'm eating almost as much, I think." He got up and went inside to a round of laughter.

"So, how're the final touches on the wedding coming, guys?"

Erik waggled his eyebrows in mock horror. "For heaven sake, Vince. Don't say the *W* word in front of Asher. He might explode . . . or kill someone."

Asher punched him in the arm, none too gently, and scowled. "I told you from the very start this would get out of hand and we'd have been better off eloping. But no, Mr. Von Nordgren had to have his day in the spotlight. Not as if he doesn't have enough of them. I knew damn well as soon as the women got their hands on it, things would get out of control." He said *women* as if it was a swear word. "I feel like I've been catapulted into hell and surrounded by she-demons, constantly beating me over the head with seating plans and menus and flowers." He shuddered. "Can you believe my mother actually believes she's going to get me into a suit?"

"And so she will," Daisy said, firmly. "It's your wedding. You have to be smart."

"What's smart about wearing a suit? When have you ever seen me wearing a suit?"

"At Grandma's funeral."

"It wasn't a suit. It was black slacks and a vintage jacket with silver buttons and—"

"It was close to a suit," Daisy snapped, "and this time it's your wedding." She sat back as if the point was decided.

"And, because it's my wedding, how about cutting me a bit of slack?" Asher growled back. "You've already blown every idea I've had about the stupid wedding right out of the water and if you really think—"

Daisy huffed. "Your ideas have been ridiculous. Who gets married at midnight in a cave with the officiant dressed as death?"

"I do," Asher said grimly. "Or rather, I don't."

"We've reached compromises—"

"Compromises? You mean you've thrown me a few scraps, like agreeing to have the wedding in the evening, putting some black serviettes on the table, and going for red roses instead of white ones. Big deal. Well, I'm warning you, keep pushing me and you'll be sorry. If you force that fucking suit on me, I'll walk down the aisle in a dress."

Vince nearly dropped his drink. "Oh gawd, Asher. I shudder to think what else you'd wear. You're at the very least—er, how can I put it—shocking with what you choose to wear."

Billy nodded. "Truth there, baby. You looked smokin' hot at our wedding, but I can't fathom what you'd wear to yours if you had the chance. Something toeing the line of legality, I'm sure." He laughed. "Aw, Ash. You're setting a bad example for Angel. That boy looks up to you, you know."

"Tsk, tsk. Must behave now, mustn't we?" Vince joked,

catching the scowl Asher sent to Billy. Thankfully, Asher smiled and relaxed back into his seat. He was such a powder keg lately, and the last thing Vince wanted was a stand-up row. "You're not the only ones, you know. Our mothers took over our wedding, and the hens clucked so damn much together over it they became best friends." He chuckled, lost in memories.

"Sure did. How are yours getting along? Have you had much of a chance to help out, Daisy, or have the moms just hoarded it all?"

"Are you serious?" Asher said, still hyper. "She's a fucking woman, of course she's doing her bit to *help*. And as for our mothers . . ." He shuddered. "You'd swear they were twins separated at birth."

"Whoa, there. Just simmer down, Asher." Erik laid a hand on his arm.

Asher shook it off.

"Hey, in the end, it's our day. Let the women take care of the details. It's what they live for. My mom's always pestering me with questions, and I tell her to just run with it. So far, it all sounds good to me." He ran a hand over Asher's hair. "Besides, whatever you wear—I don't care if it's a suit or a dress, whatever—you'll look fabulous. It'd be more interesting if you did wear a dress, then you and Con would match better." He laughed.

Joey joined the chat. "What about a dress? What'd I miss, Daisy?"

"My ridiculous brother is threatening to turn up in a wedding dress if we keep trying to persuade him to wear a suit."

"Connor's wearing a skirt," Asher grumbled, scowling at his plate as he systematically shredded a bread roll.

"It's a kilt. It's different. You know it is."

"Whose wedding is this anyway?" Asher snapped. "I don't want to wear a penguin suit and sit around pretty white tables with bowls of roses under a flower arch and play with the fairies on the way down the aisle. I want black roses and candles and a cake with a skull on top. And I *know* it's not *traditional*, but neither am I."

He threw his napkin onto the table and stood up, scowling. "I'm going to sketch the sunset over the paddock. Call me when it's time to go. No, call me after the wedding." Tossing his hair, he slouched around the corner of the house and disappeared.

Vince took a long drink. "Wow, never a dull moment, huh, Erik? You sure about that ball of fire?" He shook his head. "I'm really worried about Angel. You know how he is with Asher now they're going to school together. I don't want him picking up Asher's temper, and it's not fair to expect him to deal with Asher when he's like this. I dunno if he can handle it."

"Connor will help him. If Asher gets too nasty, he'll put a stop to it for sure."

"Aye, that he will," Billy smirked.

Erik looked over his shoulder. "Well, as moody as he is, I love him, and he agreed to this, so he's gonna have to grit his teeth and deal with it. I'm not putting up with this level of drama forever, that's for damn sure." He stood up and stomped off indoors.

"I'm worried about them." Daisy's gaze remained locked on the door through which Erik had passed. "The stress is showing on them both, but Asher's a nightmare. You know what he's like ordinarily. Talk about moody . . ." She gave a thin smile that didn't fool Vince for a moment. "I know this has been rough on Ash. He hates all the attention, and they never let up. My mother's on the phone just about every day, and when it's not her, it's Mrs. Von Nordgren. Then there's the house. He was really pinning his hopes on being able to escape there. We had no idea the law would be so different here, about houses having to be finished before you can live there. It was a big blow. And I know the exhibition is a good thing, a great thing, his biggest yet, but it's a lot of stress. He's been doing a lot of storming off, and I think Erik's getting fed up of it."

"I'm worried too," Billy added, then shook his head and smiled at Daisy.

"Now, you be careful with your health, Miss Daisy," Vince cut in. "You've got your own health, and the children to worry about, too. Oh hey, didn't you have a gender test the other day? Did you get the results back yet?"

Daisy dragged her eyes away from the house and smiled. "Damn, I forgot to tell you." She grinned at them, her eyes lighting up. "I know you'll be more than happy no matter what gender they are, but I think you're going to be so pleased. I was." She grinned. "It's one of each. A girl and a boy. Just like me and Ash."

Vince beamed. "How awesome! It'll be cool to see what traits they pick up from each of us. Will one be a blond and the other a redhead? Maybe get your dark blue eyes or . . . omigod. Those lilac eyes of your brother's."

Vince paused and rubbed his beard. "Now wouldn't that be interesting? A blond with lilac eyes. It'd look like Erik and Asher's child."

"Oh gawd it would, wouldn't it?" Billy said. "Well, I hope the red comes through, with your hazel eyes. At least we know how to decorate the nursery now . . . or is it two rooms?"

Joey smiled. "Sounds awesome. I'm sure they'll be adorable. Look at their mother. Oh, and your two mugs of course," he joked.

"Very true," Vince said, chuckling. "They'll be modeling before they're one." He sobered and sighed, gazing at Daisy's belly. "One thing's for sure, they'll be loved and wanted no matter what they're like. And not just by their daddies. These kids will have quite the support system."

Billy glanced over his shoulder to the house. "That they will. I'll be back . . . gotta go say something. It's my duty as best friend and best man . . . if there's gonna be a wedding at all, not a funeral."

Vince smiled at his husband. "Be careful. Billy. They're both powder kegs, I'd hate to see you get caught in the cross-fire."

CHAPTER TWO

The sunset over the fields was a breathtaking sight. Asher couldn't help but appreciate the wonderful view of the surrounding countryside, such as it was, from Vince and Billy's home. Three sides consisted mainly of houses with large gardens. On the fourth side, however, there were woods and fields all the way to the horizon, and over them, the sun was going down.

He had never watched a sunrise or sunset and failed to be moved. He loved everything about those times. There was a different quality to the light that appealed to his artist's eye, and a feeling of clarity that calmed his mind. Tonight, however, he wasn't calm. Not even the drawing pad on his knees and the charcoal pencil in his hand could bring him the peace he usually felt when he was immersed in his art.

Truth was, he hadn't been able to find peace for a long time — weeks, maybe more. He was blaming it all on the wedding, convincing himself that when it was all over the peace would come again, but the truth was, he didn't know if it would. Another clearer, more honest corner of his mind was telling him the wedding wasn't the problem at all.

Asher sighed and put down the pencil, hugging the book to his chest, and stared out into the gathering dusk. He thought about his other sketchbook, the one he always left at school. He thought about all the sketches he'd been working on so feverishly, more and more and more. What was he thinking? What the hell was he thinking? He was playing such a dangerous game, and sooner or later he was going to get caught. Then what? He should stop. He knew he should stop. He should never have started, but—

Erik coughed to announce himself. "It's gorgeous out here, isn't it? They chose the perfect spot. The yards are so manicured . . . the meadows, the woods . . . a beautiful backdrop." He stepped closer. "Billy and Vince make such great decisions together . . . they always have. Do you know what the best decision I ever made was, Asher?"

"No, but I know what the worst one was." He looked up at Erik, taking in the tall figure with his broad shoulders and long blonde hair. Erik was his Viking, his Nordic god. He was too good for him, way too good. Asher was nothing but a screwed up emo freak, with a mind so twisted it was only a matter of time before it imploded. What the hell was Erik even doing with someone like him? "We should never have got together in the first place. You're too good for me. You deserve someone who isn't a fucked-up nutjob."

Erik shook his head and sat down next to him. "Wrong. The correct answer was asking you to marry me. As for you being a fucked-up nutjob and me being too good for you, are you kidding me?" He laughed and picked at the grass. "Asher, you've driven me crazy since the beginning, and granted, I didn't know how to handle a lot of it, but we got through it. We survived the insanity in London all on our own. Look at me." He tipped Asher's face to look at him. "You're the love of my life, and nothing you say will persuade me otherwise. Do you even realize that? You can't get rid of me."

"I don't want to get rid of you," Asher said, jerking his chin out of Erik's hold and turning away. He was gazing at the sunset, but he didn't really see it. "I just . . ." He sighed deeply. "This wedding is driving me crazy, Erik, and I don't mean just frustrated crazy. It's all been building up, and I've been . . ." No. He'd been about to tell Erik, to get everything out in the open. Should he have? Should he? If it blew them apart, maybe it was better it happened now. But the fact was he really wanted this. He desperately wanted to be Erik's husband, to have someone to take care of and to take care of him. He needed it. And if he told him, if he told Erik the truth . . . Well, he didn't think Erik would stick around. He had to manage it on his own. He had to find some way to push it all down again, bury it deep. It would be easier when the wedding was done. All he had to do was wait for the wedding. When it was finished, things would settle down again. They'd be okay. He'd be okay.

"It'll all be over soon, I promise. By the end of the week we'll be done with it all and get back to our lives, our house, and have fantastic memories. Things will calm down." Erik took Asher's hand. "Do you believe me at least a little bit? I'm not pulling your leg. This is not worth going batshit crazy over, okay? It's a wedding. If I could, I'd marry you right here, right now, but I don't have the ring with me." He tried to garner a smile at least. "It'll all be over soon, baby. I promise you."

Over soon? I don't think so. I don't know if it will ever be over. "It's not that I don't believe you, Erik. Things will get better after the wedding. I know they will. But I don't think you understand. The stress is making me crazy, really crazy. And after the wedding, there's the tour with the band, which you know is going to catapult you right up there with all the craziness that'll bring. Then there's the exhibition. It's the biggest thing I've ever done. It's unbelievable, and yes, it's exciting . . . yes, it's career-making . . . yes, it's going to make us enough money to get the house properly finished but . . . It's all stress, Erik. There'll always be stress, and I don't know if I can—"

"I know it's all stressful, I hate it too. I'll be here for you every second, Asher, you know I will. We got through the shit in London, I know we can do this." He kissed Asher's hand.

"You have a support system here, you know that. We need to lean on each other, not dig into each other, or your sister either. This makes me nuts, too, but I just think of the big picture. We will survive. Just . . ." He let out a sigh and looked out over the yard. "Just talk to me. Don't shut me out. We can do this."

Asher took a shaky breath. His hand shook as he moved the charcoal over the page absently. Maybe this was the time. Maybe he should stop shutting Erik out. "I want to. I really want to, Erik. It's just—"

Footsteps made Erik look up and Asher followed suit.

"Hey guys, I thought I'd check in on how things were. Got pretty heavy back there at the table. You guys all right?" Billy knelt down next to them and put his hands on their shoulders.

Asher closed his eyes and exhaled. He'd been about to tell Erik, to finally open up and tell him, shit or bust. Ah hell, it was probably just as well. A lucky break that he was cut off just before he opened his mouth. *Just batten it down again, Asher. You know you can do it, you've done it before. I don't need Erik to help me with this. I don't need anyone, I can do it by myself. I can make it go away . . . until the next time, the next dream, the next sketch. But it's okay, it's okay, I can do it. It's getting better. I can put it all in the sketches now. No more dreams . . . almost. No more waking in the night and almost . . . almost calling the wrong name. It's all going down on paper, and it'll stay there. I just have to keep putting it down on the paper and making damn sure I hide them better.*

"I'm fine," he said, surprised by how calm he sounded.

Billy cocked a brow. "Wow, you must've really chilled out. You were all fire and brimstone back there. I'm glad you're calmer now. Erik, I'm shocked you finally figured out how to talk to him without sticking your foot in your mouth first." He stuck out his tongue.

"Ha ha, I learned that a while back, thanks to you. You should be a relationship counselor, what with yours being so perfect, an' all." He whacked Billy in the arm and glanced at Asher. "You wanna stay here and watch the sunset, or go back? We're being rude to our hosts, ya know."

"Yes, you are. We have dessert, Strawberry shortcake. Vince made the cake himself. It looks so damn good."

"Vince or the cake?" Erik teased.

Billy blushed. "Both." He offered a hand to Asher. "Come on, let's just enjoy a quiet night, all right? No more talk of the *W* or anything else of the kind. Maybe politics instead. Something soothing."

Asher was shaking internally. All the way down inside, where it didn't show on the outside. In the deep, black hole where he buried all the scary shit he'd been feeling and thinking. Down there, he was shaking so badly he could barely think, barely function. But it didn't show on the outside, so he smiled and took Billy's hand, letting Billy help him to his feet.

It was probably better that he hadn't spoken to Erik, that he didn't speak to anyone. Yeah, if he didn't speak to anyone, didn't open up the hole, maybe it would be big enough to take all the craziness, and when everything was over, and calm again, he could let it out little by little and deal with it . . . just like he'd been dealing with it up to now. Yeah . . . everything was going to be okay. He just had to plaster a smile on his face, keep calm, and get through it, and on the other side, everything would be okay.

Angel was still half asleep. It had been such a long day of traveling, and having Caitlin, Connor's niece, with them didn't help. She just never stopped talking. Was that the way all thirteen-year-olds were? To be fair, she was a lovely kid, with bouncy copper curls, beautiful green eyes and lots of freckles. She was a heartbreaker, and she knew it. She flirted with everything and everyone like it was totally natural. She just couldn't help it. Angel sighed. She'd tried with him, but he'd put his foot down. Nora, Connor's sister, had not been impressed with her and had not held back in her scolding. Not that it had the slightest effect because, as soon as her mother's eyes were off her, she'd sidled up to him with a sly smile and wink again.

Angel sighed once more as he tagged along behind the other three, dragging his feet. Connor was full of bounce. He was so excited to be here, finally. It had been a long winter for both of them.

Last summer had been magical. He and Connor had spent pretty much all of it in Italy. A warm smile crept over his face from deep inside at the memories. There'd been nowhere he hadn't taken Connor, no one he hadn't introduced him to. It had taken no time for the entire village to fall in love with him, just as Angel had.

The dark swarthy Italians had taken to the bright Irishman instantly. The dancing glitter of his shamrock-green eyes had pulled them in, and his sharp wit and charm had kept him close to their hearts. Angel was so proud of him, so very proud.

But their time in Italy couldn't last, and the summer had ended. Over the fall and winter, he'd seen very little of Connor, other than a few weeks over Christmas when both he and Connor had flown to America to celebrate the holidays with his father and their friends.

That holiday was one they wouldn't forget in a hurry. Never mind the shock of Daisy deciding to be a surrogate for Billy and Vince—which had turned out to be twins—but then there was the house Asher and Erik had bought. Well, a *house* only in the loosest sense of the word. *Typical Asher.* It was an old church with its own graveyard. It had a bell tower—without bell—and the living room had enormous stained-glass windows and a real wood floor. It needed a lot of work, but hell, it was going to be superb.

Connor was going to help them with the construction work until he started with Angel's father's business in a couple of months. Connor was going to devote himself to the project, with everyone else pitching in, in the hope the house could be finished, at least enough to pass inspection, before he had to abandon it.

Thinking of Asher, he sighed. There was still tension between them. Not like before, but it still hung in the air, and Connor didn't help. Angel loved the way Connor protected him, but sometimes he was a little overprotective, especially when Asher was near. He was often cold toward Asher when Angel was around, and that just made it even worse.

As it happened, he didn't see much of Asher at school, and he'd made his own friends, but it was like another world there. Asher seemed different when he was in the art rooms or workshops, more relaxed, more like he used to be. They could laugh, chat about art and school and all kinds of things, without the slightest stress. As soon as they were out of school, though, it seemed as if a shutter would come down and Asher locked himself away behind it. And it wasn't just from Angel.

Ah well, Erik and Asher were getting married in less than a week, so Angel was very hopeful they would both be happy and more like their old selves. He missed the easy camaraderie that had suffused the group at the time of Vince and Billy's wedding, and he was hoping this wedding would be a new start.

"Got yer head in the clouds again, *a chroí?*" Connor took Angel's hand and walked them to the baggage claim area to get their suitcases.

Angel spotted a familiar group, with a sign that read *The Italian / Irish Combo*. He laughed aloud as they grabbed their suitcases and ran to their friends.

After a round of hugs, Connor stood back and put an arm around Nora, who was the female version of him, minus the beard, and with much shorter hair. "This is me sister, Nora, and a grand one at that, hi. Saved me life more than once for her sins, eh? And this little cracker is me niece, Caitlin. Watch this one, boys. She's a heart breaker, so she is."

Nora smiled warmly at everyone in greeting, but Caitlin looked up at Erik, Asher, Billy, Joey, and Vince and curtseyed to them all, batting her long, copper lashes. "Ah, ye're all fair grand, so ye are. Enough to make a nun wet her knickers, and no lies." She focused on Asher, then Erik. Her flirting seemed to be fluid. Her accent wasn't nearly as harsh as her uncle's, although it was more pronounced. Her voice was almost melodic.

"Caitlin," Nora snapped, but it was clear she was trying to hide a laugh. "Don't ye be rude to Connor's friends now."

Connor put a hand on her shoulder. "She ain't doin' no harm, are ye, macushla? But don't ye go flirting with me boys here. Brothers of me heart, so they are. Begging yer pardon, Daisy, me darlin'. This is Asher, Erik, Billy, Vince, Joey, and Daisy."

Nora smiled at Daisy. "Congratulations, Daisy. I see yer expectin'."

"Yes, twins. I'm not four months gone yet, so I'm going to be the size of an elephant by the time we get to the serious end."

"Aye, ye're big for four months." Nora gave another warm smile, and Daisy smiled in return.

Angel had never doubted the two of them would get on well.

Daisy patted her stomach contentedly. "I found out the other day they're a girl and a boy. A perfect starter family, for my favorite daddies."

"Aye, our Connor told us what ye were doin'. A fine thing

it is, too. A true friend is a treasure over all the gold in creation." Nora patted her arm. "Lucky boys."

"Oh, they deserve it," Daisy gushed. "They're wonderful. So much in love, and with so much more love to give. They were made to be parents, and I'm so happy I could make their dream come true. It's not as if I'm not going to see the babies. They're going to know I'm their mother even though I don't live with them, and we'll see them every week. Erik, Angel, and Connor are all going to be uncles or at least honorary ones. Asher, of course, will be a real one."

Vince and Billy put their arms around her. "That's right, and we'll be the happy daddies taking care of our little darlins." Vince glanced at Caitlin. "How old are you, sweet Miss Caitlin?"

"Don't ya be callin' me that now. I'm no wee babby. I'm thirteen, so I am. A woman grown, and dontcha be forgetting it." Her pointy little chin jutted, and her green eyes flashed at Vince in warning.

"Come away now, missy," her mother growled. "Keep your flirtin' for boys yer own age."

"Yeah . . . and maybe you should try pitching for ones who are actually interested in girls," Asher drawled.

Joey gulped. "Uh, dude, that'd leave just me."

Caitlin put her hands on her hips and gave Asher a calculating look that was strange to see on a little girl, then she tossed her bouncing curls. "Well you're a fine thing, fer sure, but the amount of shite that comes out of your mouth . . ." She shook her head and ignoring her mother's reprimand for swearing, turned to Joey. "But you, me darlin, are boss. Here, I'll let ye take me arm, so I will." She reached out and linked her arm with Joey's, bouncing along at his side, each step a neat little dance.

Joey glanced helplessly at Daisy over his shoulder. Daisy shrugged and stifled a giggle.

"Can we go home now?" Angel whined. "I'm so tired I don't know if I can stay upright much longer, so we're either gonna have to head home, or I'm going to lie down on the floor right here and go to sleep."

"Then I'll carry ye, ye know that." Connor started to pick him up, but he stopped when the others laughed.

"Angel! I didn't notice your hair before, cous. Wow, it got long just since what, Christmas?" Vince ran his hand through the black hair which now almost touched Angel's shoulders. "Very pretty. Con, yours too! You need to wear it in a ponytail when you're working with machinery."

"That I do, Vince. Don't need it to be ripped out o' me head." He caught Angel's arm. "Come on, let's get home. Ah, now isn't that a fine thing to say. A home at last!" He wore a grin a mile wide as he led the pack out of the airport and into the stretch SUV Tony had sent for them.

Wearily, Angel climbed into the back of the car, glad to have the chauffeur take care of the luggage. Connor sat next to him, and he rested his head on his boyfriend's shoulder gratefully. The rest of the friends spread themselves around the spacious interior, and they set off. Angel was glad everyone was going to be spending the night at his father's house. It meant he could spend time with all his friends but not have to actually go anywhere.

There was only one thing Angel was worried about. Erik and Asher were going to share the small house with him and Connor tonight, and he really wasn't sure it was wise. It could go two ways. Either it would clear the air and help things get back to normal again, or it could just make the whole situation worse. Could he really be dealing with the drama on the first night? Ah, well, too late now.

"Here we are, the grand Caliendo estate, where Angel's father lives, with some servants, too," Connor informed his sister and niece. "This is the most incredible house ye'll ever see in yer life!"

The group followed him inside and filed over to the living room, where food and Tony were waiting.

He stood, dressed in black pants and a navy-blue shirt with a pipe in his hand. "You are looking tired, Angelo. Is that boy of yours not taking care of you?"

"He's taking care of me fine, Papa. It has been a very long day." Angel turned to Nora and held out his hand, which she took. "May I present Nora Hollaran, Connor's sister, and her daughter, Caitlin."

Nora blushed as Tony took and kissed her hand. Caitlin smiled until her dimples showed and totally charmed Tony. From that moment on, she stayed close to his side, her arm linked through his.

Chapter Three

The laughter continued out the door as Erik opened it to say goodnight to Billy, Vince, Joey, and Daisy. It was late, and Daisy looked tired.

"Good night, guys! See you in the morning. You get some rest, Miss Daisy." Erik laughed, shut the door, and ruffled his hair. "That was fun. Too bad Daisy can't drink right now, she's so funny when she's drunk." Erik grinned broadly as he settled back on the sofa and pulled Asher into his lap. "Having fun, hon?"

"Yeah. It's nice to have discussions that don't revolve around Saturday. It's been a fab day, relaxed and . . . well, relaxed." Asher laughed and took a swig of the red wine he was drinking out of the bottle.

"Be damned if relaxin' ain't one of me favorite hobbies." Connor kissed Angel's hair softly. "It does me eyes good to see such a fine thing, and all mine, *a chroí*. Sure, and I'm the luckiest man in the land." He wrapped his arms around Angel. "Finally home in America, at long last." They smiled at each other and leaned in to kiss.

Erik watched them fondly. "I knew you two were ideal together, the moment I saw ya. Now you're done with school, you can get a job and join the daily grind." He lit up a cigarette. "By the way, your sister seems really nice, but your niece is a handful, isn't she?" He chuckled.

"Aye, she's a bold one, hi. Her daddy, Liam, God rest his soul, died just two years ago. Accident at work, it was. Very tragic."

"Were you two close?" Erik asked.

"Aye, some. He was a fine man. Good to Nora and the babby. Too good to stomach the O'Reilly clan, I'm the only one who bothered with him." He drank down some beer and sighed.

"Do you have to do that in here?" Asher complained, coughing and waving away the smoke of Erik's cigarette. He'd never got used to it and gave Erik grief all the time.

"I was thinking of lighting up myself," Angel interjected. "We can go outside, if you like. It's a lovely night."

"I'm up for that, come on. Con, you wanna join us? The smoker's club's convening our hourly meeting," he joked.

"Sure, an' I'll join ye. Enjoy y'self, Asher, don't tear the place up." With a wink, he joined Erik and Angel outside.

"Are you sure Asher'll be all right in there on his own?" Angel asked anxiously. "I didn't mean for us all to just abandon him."

Erik sucked down a long drag of his cigarette. "He'll be fine, Angel. Quit worrying. Five minutes alone won't be the end of him. Meanwhile, how are you two doing? Obviously pretty well, at least since last time I saw ya."

"Better now we're here. It's been a bit of a struggle. What with Con getting school finished and me getting it started, we haven't been able to be together as much as we'd hoped. These last few weeks in Italy have been pure heaven, especially knowing that when we came here, we'd both be staying. To be honest, I don't think it's really sunk in yet." Angel looked up at Connor and scratched at his beard. "You're stuck with me now, me little Irish shamrock."

"No one better I could be stuck to, me darlin' Angel." They kissed softly, and Connor ran his hand through Angel's thick black hair. "Finally, with me fella for longer than two weeks."

"Oh, yeah. Much, much longer than two weeks. So, how are the wedding plans coming along? I had a quick word with

Daisy earlier. She said Asher's being difficult. I find that hard to believe," Angel added, tongue in cheek.

Erik laughed aloud. "You know him pretty well already, Angel." He swatted his shoe, playfully. "It's . . . just got out of hand. I know the whole planning thing is a pain, but wow. He and Daisy got into it on Sunday night. He's really angry about it not going his way, at all, and said we should elope and be done with it, then Daisy's all *oh no, he won't steal my big spotlight moment*, and so on and on." He sighed. "I just want this to be over, like he does, to be married, happy, and together. I've tried to tell him over and over, but something else is eatin' at him. I don't know what, but I figure we've survived worse, right? I love him to death, I honestly do, but it's difficult on all of us right now. Saturday can't come fast enough." He took a long drag on his cigarette and looked at the couple. "Sorry, I'm stressed about it, as you can tell. Con, you all set with your kilt?"

"Aye. It's all packed up nice like, the whole kit n'kaboodle."

"I've seen him in it" — Angel grinned and waggled his brows — "and I can assure you my man has a beautiful pair of legs for wearing a skirt."

"Kilt, me darlin', no skirts for this Irishman." Connor laughed. "It's a beautiful Kerry green."

"A skirt by any other name will still show a *nice bit o' leg,* as your sister says."

Erik snorted. "Great, I get to see those red furry legs. I'm used to Billy's, though. He's got pencil legs, I swear. But Vince doesn't seem to mind." He smiled.

"Dontcha be pickin' on Billy, now. He's a fine lad. Can't believe he's gonna be a da. He'll be a great one, so he will. Nora was the same age when she had Caitlin. She's such a spitfire, I kid ye not." He drank a swig of beer. "Sure, I don't know where she gets it." He adopted an expression of innocence that all but cracked Erik up

"No, of course not." Angel tried to keep a straight face but couldn't stop the laughter bubbling up. "And if you believe that, you'll believe anything."

Connor snaked his arms further around Angel. "Just for that, ye'll get a surprise when ye come to bed, me love." He kissed Angel's nose. "Speakin' of bed, I think I've got to go soon. Me batteries are runnin' low. I'm drained."

"Darlin', I get a surprise every time I come to bed. It's that you're there in it, just for my pleasure," Angel said sweetly.

Connor leaned in close and gave Angel a long, deep kiss holding him tight, then stretched his back and rolled his neck. "Eh, but I'm fecked. I'm off te bed. Don't be too long, *a chroí*. Good night, Erik." With a final kiss, he went inside and shut the door.

"Well, things have certainly changed in that department, huh?" Erik laughed. "You two are so great together, so much passion with your two personalities." He raised a brow and winked at Angel. "I can tell how in love you are."

"Oh, yes." Angel smiled widely leaning against the wall. "Although, I could say the same about you two. Talk about striking sparks. It's a miracle you've made it this far. I'm really glad you did, though. I can't believe you're getting married on Saturday, three days. Fuck."

Erik coughed. "I know, it's surreal to me sometimes, but here we are, it's almost here. To be honest, I've dreamed about it a lot . . . an awful lot. I see him in his least favorite outfit, a tuxedo, but he wears it for me, and I'm in one, and our parents cheer, our friends cheer and rally around us." He sighed. "It's gonna be so awesome though, it'll be neat with candles everywhere, and at night. I'll be in a tux with a silver vest, but I've no idea what he'll come up with. He's always got a surprise up his sleeve."

"Maybe he'll be in a kilt like Con. I bet he's got better legs for it."

"He's got one helluva set of legs, for sure. I thought you liked yours red and hairy." He winked at Angel and let out a deep sigh. "It upsets me that it's upsetting him so much. He won't even talk about it without an argument and angst and drama. This should be a nervous time, but happy, right? Am I off base? I mean . . . imagine you and Connor getting married. Wouldn't you be thrilled? Even if your father took over all the planning?" He shook his head. "There's gotta be more to this."

"I've been meaning to talk to you about that, actually . . . to ask. Is Asher okay? I mean . . . really? He's . . . I don't know how to say it, but . . . at school . . . His work's been getting very . . . dark. And he doesn't talk like he used to. Is it really all about the wedding? Because I don't think it is."

"I agree. There's something else on his mind right now. I wish I knew what, but he clams up. Last year you guys were acting all strange, even at Christmastime, too. Tension or something. He did something to scare you, didn't he? He yelled at you I bet, didn't he?"

"I'm sorry, Erik, I can't tell you. I promised. But it's been worrying me, gnawing at me all the time. I've tried to talk to him a couple of times, but he gets so angry. I . . . don't know how to handle him when he's like that."

"Not many people do. Look, I understand you promised him, but if it's affecting you, we've got to find out what it is. I won't have him scaring people. I know he's moody and I love him to the end of the moon, but wow, we've got to find out somehow. Gently, and just let him knows it's all right." He shut his eyes and rubbed them. "I thought we'd gone through the worst of this. It was so bad in London . . . I thought he wanted to end it with me forever, but . . . We have to help him. However we can. Stick by him, Angel. I know his temper is scary, but just stick to your guns, all right?"

Angel chewed his nail. "It wasn't like that, Erik, honest it wasn't. It wasn't that he scared me, as such. He wasn't being mean to me or anything like it. It was just . . . the way he reacted, I . . . What happened to him, Erik? I know something bad happened, Connor told me a little, but he can't, or won't tell me anything more than that he was hurt by someone in his past. I know I've got no right to ask, and it's Asher I should be asking, and I will but . . . Please just give me an idea of what happened."

Erik sprawled on the step. "In a nutshell, let's just say he knew a very bad man who did cruel and evil things to him when he was young. In London, a year or so ago, he got hold of him again. Asher's still messed up from what the person did, and I fear he will be for life."

"I . . . know it sounds weird, Erik, but I really need to know, for my own benefit — what did this man look like?"

"A corpse right now, luckily. But he had long dark hair, a goatee, pale, very handsome, but so twisted. Very evil. Why?" He narrowed his eyes at Angel.

"No reason really. I just wanted to picture him, in my head. I think I need to talk to Ash, Erik. Will you leave us alone for a bit? Just a few minutes?"

"No problem at all, Angel. You two need to talk this out. Maybe I'll go sneak an ice cube down Connor's back, especially if he's snoring." He chortled.

Angel followed Erik into the house with a sinking heart. He'd known it. Pretty much from the start he'd known who the sketch was of, but he hadn't *known* it, and he certainly hadn't known how bad it was.

Asher was sitting on the sofa, his knees drawn up and his head resting on them. Angel had come to realize a long time ago it was a defensive stance for him. He did it when he wanted to shut out the world. Tonight, Angel wasn't going to let that happen.

"Is there anything you want, Asher?"

"Huh?" Asher looked up, dazed. He'd obviously been dozing.

"I'm locking up for bed. Is there anything you need?"

"Um . . . no. I-I should go. Where's Erik?"

"Just gone to bed. Ash . . . before you go, can I ask you something?"

"Sure, of course. You can ask me anything." The smile Asher gave him was so much like the old, open, easy smile he used to give that it threw Angel for a moment. But he couldn't let it sidetrack him.

"You know that sketch? The one you got mad over? The—"

"No."

Angel was a little alarmed when all the color drained from Asher's face and he looked as if he was going to faint. "You . . . you promised. You . . ."

"I promised not to tell anyone else about it, and I haven't. I didn't promise I wouldn't ask you about it."

"Well, don't," Asher snapped. He unwound and stood up. "I'm going to bed. Just . . ."

"Just what?" Angel asked quietly. "Just keep my mouth shut? Sorry, we've gone past that. Whatever this is, it's hurting you. I've been worried about you. We all have."

"Oh, so you've been discussing me with everyone have you? I hope you enjoyed yourselves. I—"

"Shut up, Asher. Shut up and sit down. Either you're going to talk to me, or I'm going to call Connor and Erik down and you can talk to them."

"So what? You're gonna tell them everything anyway." There was the damnedest look in Asher's eyes, almost panic, but with a spark of anger too.

"No. The reason I want to talk to you alone is precisely so

you can, I hope, talk to me, just me and no one else."

"Why would I want to talk to you?"

"Because I wasn't here. Because I've no idea what happened in your past, other than it was something bad and it freaks everyone out to talk about it. I'm guessing that's why you're so scared of talking to them, because they'll freak on you. I won't. I don't want to know what happened in the past. All I want to know is what's happening now and what we can do about it."

"Nothing," Asher said flatly, "There's nothing you can do about it."

"Try me. Just talk to me, Ash. It couldn't be clearer that you need to talk to someone."

Their eyes met, and there was a long, tense moment.

Asher was absolutely terrified. He was scared Erik would come down, and he really didn't think he could handle a confrontation. He was scared he'd lose control altogether, and most of all he was scared that maybe this really was an opportunity to talk to someone, to get everything out in the open safely. But would he be safe? Would Angel keep his promise? Would he really keep it to himself, not tell anyone?

Angel was staying very still, waiting. He was a good listener, a good friend. He hadn't told anyone about the sketch, even though Asher had been such a twat about it. He hadn't even asked, not once in all this time.

Suddenly, it was all just too hard. Keeping it inside was unbearable. He couldn't go on like this or he was going to crack or explode, and this really wasn't a good time.

"All right. Not here."

Putting the wine bottle down on the table, he headed for the door, and Angel followed.

They walked in silence for a time, just wandering in the

moonlight. It was chilly, and Angel shivered, but he didn't say anything.

Finally, Asher sat down on a bench in the rose garden and ran his hands through his hair. "James was a monster, an absolute monster. I was fourteen, and the things he did to me sent me to a psychiatric hospital for three months. That's why everyone would freak out if they knew I was thinking about him. Because they'd be afraid it's happening again, that I'm cracking up again."

"Are you?"

Asher's eyes snapped up and met Angel's calm, steady ones. "Yes, a bit," he said. "Not like before . . . I don't think."

"Okay. So, James screwed you up and you had a breakdown?"

Asher nodded.

"Then what?"

"A year ago, he came out of prison and kidnapped Erik. He didn't want Erik, he wanted me so I . . . I went to him and he . . ." Angel shuddered. "He tortured us . . . both of us. Vince's . . . Oh, I guess it was *your* father." He hadn't thought of it before. Strange.

"What was my father?"

"Vince had him send . . . help."

Angel nodded. "Ah, yes, I know."

"You do?" Again, Asher was alarmed, swallowing panic. What did he know? Just exactly what did he know?

"Not everything. I know you were hurt. Oh, that's right . . . someone was killed. Was it James?"

It felt like a slap in the face, but Asher bit back whatever he might have said and nodded. "Yeah."

"So what's happened to bring him back? Why are you drawing him again?"

Asher closed his eyes and bunched his fists. "I think . . . I think I might be . . ." He shook his head. No, he wasn't ready to admit that. He wasn't going to tell Angel, or anyone, that he was afraid he was sliding again, edging toward the chasm he'd fallen into all those years ago. "It was when Erik asked me to marry him."

"It was?" Angel sounded surprised. He sat down on the path and looked up at Asher.

"It made me look back to the only other time in my life when I'd imagined I might get married one day. In the beginning, with James, it was good, it was so good. I was fourteen and he was ten years older. He was beautiful, strong, sexy, and I couldn't believe he'd be interested in someone like me . . . a freak. No." He held up a hand to ward off Angel's complaints. "No, I *was* a freak, Angel. You've no idea how hard it's been to live with these eyes. It's not as if I can hide them. Well, I could wear contacts, but by the time I was old enough to do it, I was too angry and stubborn to want to.

"Anyway, James was good to me, in the beginning. Things weren't going too well in my life. My father was a nightmare. He was down on me all the time, and nothing I did was good enough." *And it was killing me inside.* Thinking back on what his life outside James had been like back then made him lurch a step further toward the chasm, and he physically jerked as he pulled back. "I was fighting every day with someone — my father, kids at school, stupid assholes who thought it was fun to pick on a freak. That's why I worked so hard with the martial arts so I could handle myself.

"The only way I could cope was knowing I had James to go back to. And I really, truly believed that one day, when I was old enough, we'd get a place, get married and spend the rest of our lives together." He paused and sniffed. When had he started crying? Impatiently, he dashed the tears away and straightened his shoulders. "Even when things started to really go downhill, I *still* thought it would all turn out okay in the end, and I'd have my dream of being a real family, of having somewhere I really belonged."

It was hard to take out all these old memories and feelings, brush them off and lay them before someone else. It surprised him how strong they still were.

"It took a lot to take the dream away from me, but he did, he managed it. He took everything, and in the end . . . I think it was more the realization that my dream had been crushed than the abuse that pushed me over the edge and made me want to die. What was the point in going on? No one would want me now, and I'd built my future around that dream. I struggled through every day because I knew it was one day closer to getting what I wanted. When it was taken away, I had nothing to live for anymore."

Angel hadn't moved, hadn't said a word. Asher was grateful for that. It was hard to hold it together, and one word might send him over the edge.

"But all that was after it all fell apart. When Erik proposed I could only think of the good times, the way I felt when I looked at my dream, the golden future and I . . ." He licked his lips, sniffing again. "I missed it," he whispered. "I missed *him*. I know it's crazy. Ha, that's funny, of course it's crazy . . . I'm crazy. But I did. Suddenly I started to miss him really, really badly. It hit me hard that he was dead, and I needed to mourn him. But I couldn't. I couldn't mention his name to anyone, or they'd have me back in the hospital again. So I had to keep it all inside. I had to sneak away to cry and"—he glanced up at Angel then dropped his eyes again—"to talk to him.

"I started to dream about him, and I did the sketch you found. It scared me so badly that for a while I didn't dare do any more. Then the dreams started to get really intense, and I was afraid I'd do something stupid, like wake up calling his name or something. So I started to sketch seriously. I've done probably hundreds of them. I've drawn the way it was, and the way I wished it had been. I drew the future I wanted, and I drew James—in all kinds of ways."

He glanced quickly at Angel, his cheeks heating. Angel had seen one of the ways, and it hadn't even been the worst—or best—of it. Angel continued to maintain an almost holy silence, a silence that demanded words, so Asher was compelled to give them.

"At first, it worked, and everything was fine. Then the stress of this damned wedding started to really heat up. I've been bombarded by it from all sides, but no one will listen to anything I have to say. Every suggestion I make is swept aside. Even the things I begged for have been watered down, and Erik's no help. He's excited about it. You know what he's like, he wants his time in the spotlight, and that's fine. But I feel powerless, completely powerless, as if I'm just a piece of dust caught up in the hoover, battered about all over the place with nowhere to go, and no control. It's unbearable, utterly unbearable, and I've had no one to talk to, no one to turn to. Erik thinks I'm being a spoiled brat, and I guess he's right, but I don't do well when I'm powerless, when I have no control. I had to talk to someone . . . so I talked to James. I talked to him while I drew him, and it made it better."

Asher glanced up at Angel, begging him to understand. He knew he'd done a bad thing. He knew it had been a huge mistake from the beginning, and he'd allowed it to get way out of hand, but he honestly didn't think he'd have been able to get through those last few months without James. He was the only one who'd really listened, who hadn't pushed him aside or accused him of being a prima donna. He was the only one who didn't judge or criticize. Without James, what would he have done? Who would he have turned to?

"You could have come to me," Angel said quietly, "to any of us. If we'd known how you really felt we'd have helped.

You hiss and spit and drive people away, people who would listen if you let us."

He was right. Asher was clear enough to know that. If he'd sat down with Erik and talked it through calmly, Erik would have listened, would have put it right . . . but it was already too late by then. He'd already had James.

"I know," he whispered. "I know what I did was wrong, but it's too late now. It's almost over. If I can just make it through the next few days, it'll be over. We'll spend time in London, have fun, relax and it will all be okay again. I'll make sure it doesn't happen again. If I get stressed like this again, I'll speak to Erik . . . or someone. I'll even see a doctor, a therapist — whatever. Just . . . please, Angel, please don't say anything to anyone, not now, not just before the wedding. Erik would freak. I don't know what he'd do."

"You should talk to Erik. It was wrong of him not to listen to you, to let everyone steamroller you because it's what *he* wanted."

"You know that's what he's like. He doesn't mean anything by it. He thought he *was* listening, doing his best for me. He thought I was acting spoiled and throwing tantrums . . . and I was, because I didn't know what else to do."

"He was selfish, Asher. Don't give him too much credit. He knew you were unhappy. He's not blind, and as he always tells us, no one knows you as well as he does. He did push you aside, and he did make excuses for his selfishness by putting the blame on you for being difficult and moody and all the rest. Don't take all the responsibility for this, or you'll never get it resolved. When you talk to him, don't let him make you feel it was all down to you."

"I-I won't. I won't, I promise. Just please let it be after the wedding."

"I have to talk to Erik about this."

Asher's world came crashing down. He'd trusted Angel.

He'd trusted him with the most personal, most terrifying things he'd ever told anyone outside a hospital . . . and he was going to betray him. He was going to —

"Asher, calm down. Calm down and listen. I'm not going to tell Erik about James, about any of it. But I have to tell him how much the wedding is hurting you. It's not fair. This is supposed to be the happiest day of your life, not an ordeal that destroys you. I won't let it go on, Asher, I can't. I'm going to tell Erik his selfishness is hurting you, and he must listen to you. But you have to do your bit, too. You can't go back behind the screen and hide from him, from all of us. You've got to talk, to tell Erik what you really want. He'll stand by you if you let him."

"I know," Asher whispered. "I know, but it's hard."

"Yes, it's hard, but you have us to help — all of us. No one wants you to feel like this. No one. Your mother, Erik's mother, Daisy . . . they all mean well. They're trying to make this good for everyone, including you. They'd never have behaved like this if they knew it was making you ill. You've got to talk to them."

Asher felt like Angel had plunged a knife into his belly and it was liquidizing his guts. The thought of talking to them — his mother, Erik's mother, Daisy . . . Erik — and telling them . . ."I can't do it."

"Yes, you can. I'll talk to Erik, make sure I get through his stupid thick head that he needs to get down off his high horse and support his man, then you'll have us all to support you. You said it yourself Asher, you need to get the control back, and you can't wait until after the wedding, because by then the steamroller will have flattened you. You have to do it now. Right now."

"I-I'm tired, Angel. I'm really tired. I can't . . ."

"Yes, I know. You look exhausted. And you can rest — after we've spoken to Erik."

"No, please—"

"Get on your feet, Asher. We're going back to the house, and I'm going to talk to Erik, right now. What happens after is up to you."

Asher could barely stand, he was shaking so much. What had he been thinking? Why had he ever trusted Angel? Because he knew Angel cared, and he had half a mind that he'd *do* something. Angel was a *doer*—he *did* things, not just sit around talking about them. Part of him had known he'd do this, take control, speak to people . . . to Erik. And deep inside that was what he wanted. Okay, he could do this. Relief made him weak, and he swayed against Angel, who quickly put his arm around his waist.

"Don't you dare pass out on me. I guess I could carry you back to the house, but you're damn well going to stay conscious until you've spoken to Erik."

"I . . . yes."

CHAPTER FOUR

A ngel's mouth was dry, and his heart pounded as he approached the house. He was positive Connor and Erik would be waiting. As soon as the door had closed behind Asher and him, they'd have been downstairs like a shot and would probably have been pacing the room the whole time.

Sure enough, as soon as their feet began to crunch on the gravel, the door was thrown open and Erik appeared.

"Well, out for a midnight stroll, you two?" he asked as he yawned. "Or hopefully talking, clearing the air?"

"I need to talk to you, Erik. Connor, too." He let go of Asher and squeezed his hand. "Go upstairs and get ready for bed. We'll come up when we're done."

"Angel, I . . . Please . . ."

"It'll be all right, Asher, I promise."

Asher scoured his face, then, with a scared glance at Erik, he brushed past and disappeared. Angel followed him into the house, passing a surprised-looking Erik, who shut the door behind them. Oh shit. Where to begin?

"I'll go get Connor." Angel left for a moment and came back downstairs with the sleepy redhead in tow.

"What's goin' on?" Connor asked, letting out a yawn. "Angel, I thought ye were comin' to bed soon, me love."

"I was but . . . I've been talking to Asher." He sat down on the sofa and looked up at the two men, chewing his lip with a sinking heart. This wasn't going to be fun. "He's in a bad way, Erik, really bad. I'm worried about him."

"I knew there was something else going on with him. Ever

since last year . . . remember? You two fought about something, and at Christmas things were iffy. If he finally told you, I'm relieved. I want to help, you know that. However I can." He tossed a look back at Connor.

"Aye, ye know I'm behind ya. I was gonna be havin' a wee word with him about the way he's been treatin' ya, hi, but if ye've figured it out, all's square." He tightened up his robe. "I'll get us somethin' to be going on with."

Angel's mind was racing. How could he tell them without *telling* them? "We didn't fight, not exactly, and he didn't scare me in the way you think he did. He . . . let something slip, something that scared me, worried me. I knew then things weren't right, but he made me promise not to say anything. I spoke to him again at Christmas and asked him to talk to you but he wouldn't. Do you see? He's never scared me because I thought he'd hurt me, or because I thought he'd do something to me. It scared me because I didn't know what was going on with him."

"What is going on with him?" Erik asked. "I'm grasping at straws here. He's my fiancé, gonna be my husband. I've loved him for over three years, Angel. He should be able to tell me what's up, and the fact he hasn't, worries and scares me a little. I know it's easier to talk to someone else sometimes, but I think I have a right to know what's up . . . I'm the one who lives with him. I want him to be well and happy . . ." He sighed.

Connor squeezed his shoulder. "Don't be takin' on, sham. I'm sure he'd a told ye in the end. He's gotta come te it in his own time."

Erik nodded slowly. "True enough. I wonder . . . if this has anything to do with that." He looked at Angel. "Does it?"

Angel sighed and shook his head. "If you listen, I'll tell you. Erik, don't you see this is part of the problem? I'm sitting here waiting to tell you what Asher told me, and you're both grumbling and making assumptions. You should be listening to me, like you should have been listening to Asher."

They all sat down. "Then tell me, please. Angel, I have to know so I can help him."

"He's in a bad way, Erik. And yes, I think it goes deeper than the wedding, and I've made him promise that once the wedding is over he'll get some proper help, but right now a big part of the problem *is* the wedding. He's out of control, spiraling, and papering over the cracks. He scared the fuck out of me tonight. There's something in him that makes me feel he's holding on by his fingertips, and I've no idea what he's holding on to. He's going nuts. This wedding is making him crazy. He feels totally out of control, that he's being steamrollered, no one's listening to him, and he's being pushed aside."

Erik looked lost, then his expression hardened, and he banged his hand on the table. "Dammit, I should've known, too. I-I should be the one he's hanging on to, and instead . . ." He paused and glanced over at the stairs. "I'll do anything he wants. I'll go to City Hall and elope if it's what he wants. I won't lose him, and I won't let him lose his mind. Not again. Not ever." He stood and ran up the stairs.

Connor watched him and then turned back to Angel. "Well, shite. Who'da thought, hi? Ah, for all his buff and bluster, Erik's a good man, and he loves his fella. They'll get this ironed out."

"I hope so. One of the problems is that Erik assumes things. He assumes he knows what Asher wants, what he's thinking and feeling, because it's what *he* wants. He thinks he's doing what's best for them both but won't listen when Asher tries to tell him it isn't, and Asher's just as bad. He won't . . . or can't talk about it reasonably, tell Erik how he's feeling. I don't think he knows half the time. God, Connor, I'm scared for him. Honest to God, I think he's cracking up."

"Aye, well . . . it wouldn't be the first time. I'm scared, too, *a chroí*. Ah, it was bad, darlin'. I had to lay him out to stop the screamin'. He couldn't get control of himself. He was out of his head. I'm not scared of much, and I've faced down men three times the size o' me with a smile on me face, but . . . It scared the keks off me. I'm a selfish bastard, so I am, and I never want to have to go thro' that again." He pulled Angel close. "God help me, I'd die if ye had te."

Angel laughed. "I'm a big boy now, Con, and Asher's my friend, more than any of the others, I think, even Vince. Vince is my cousin, and I love him, but Asher understands me. He's helped me so much this last year at school, and he *gets* me. The things we talk about . . . He's special. His mind's amazing and his artistic skill . . . I can't bear to think it's all going to be spoiled."

"Dontcha be having any fear of that, me little darlin' Asher's got good friends, so he has, and a strong man at his side. We'll see him thro'."

"He promised he'll get proper help after the wedding."

"Aye, he will fer sure. It's been on his mind, I think. Erik can be a right eejit, but he knows his man, and he knows when somethin's not right. He'll take care of it."

"I hope so."

"Have faith, sweet Angel. Have faith." Connor took him into his arms, and before Angel could say a word, he'd swept him up and carried him giggling up the stairs.

Erik rinsed off his face and walked toward the bedroom he and Asher were sharing for the night. He liked being there. The little house reminded him of their own home a little. It was the same size, although theirs was much nicer. He couldn't wait for their new place to be done, though, so they could move in and have one huge item crossed off their list.

Right now, however, Asher was in pain, and dammit if he hadn't missed it again. No, that wasn't entirely true, he'd known everything was eating at Asher, but every time they tried to talk, Asher would clam up or pull away, or Erik would get frustrated and they'd end up at an impasse. Enough was enough. He knew another episode like London was on the horizon, and he had to brace himself for it. He wished the band wouldn't take him away, but it was their main source of income right now. Asher couldn't make it all.

He sighed and opened the bedroom door. A cool breeze hit his exposed chest, and he silently cursed Asher for insisting they always had a window open. He shivered as he padded over to the bed.

"Asher? Please, can we talk now?" Erik begged as he sat down on the edge of the bed and waited for Asher's response. Asher had his back to him and was curled up in the position he so often adopted when he slept. Erik knew he wasn't asleep though, because his hands were bunched into fists in the bedclothes, and he was tense as a whip. Erik got up onto the bed and sat close to his trembling fiancé, stroking his hair and back. "Come on, baby, talk to me."

"I . . . I'm sorry," Asher said eventually in a tiny voice that sounded as if it had been forced out. "I'm sorry . . . Erik."

He rubbed Asher's back softly. "Ssh, it's all right, love. Just talk to me, I'm here. Tell me anything you want, it's up to you, baby. My beautiful Asher." He lay down behind Asher and took him into his arms.

"I'm sorry," Asher rasped again, his body rigid.

"It's all right. It's all right. Ssh." Erik rocked him gently and kissed his head. "I'm here, baby. I'm here."

Eventually, Asher turned and put his arms around Erik, rubbing his cheek against Erik's chest. "I can't do it, Erik. I can't do it anymore."

Erik stroked his hair softly and then his face. "I wanna take you away from all of this stress, baby. All of it. When you hurt, I hurt. I wanna get you through this again, Ash. I'm here." He held him tighter and sniffed his long hair. "I'm sorry it wasn't me . . . that you had to tell Angel. My failing."

"I-I tried, really I did. I tried but . . . No one would listen." He started to cry, and once the dam broke it flooded and he sobbed, his hands clutching at Erik, raising wheals on his skin.

Feeling Asher sob in his arms again tore at Erik's heart. He had to keep himself strong, to be there for him, though. He couldn't fall apart. If he needed to, maybe he could fall apart later in Billy's presence, but not here, not now. "I'm sorry about before, baby, but now I know, and you can't hide it anymore. I'm not leaving your side until you tell me. I won't let you be in pain like this anymore." The levy nearly broke on his control, but he stopped it. "I love you, Asher. I love you with all my heart and soul."

"But you wouldn't listen." Asher raised his head, and his eyes were wild. "None of you. Not even Daisy. You just . . . You said . . . said I . . . And you . . ." He growled, obviously frustrated he couldn't get out the words he wanted to say. "I'm not here anymore. I'm not anywhere. No one listens to me, and it makes me feel . . . I don't storm off because . . . because I'm angry . . . or . . . or spoiled, or . . . or pissy. I just can't stand . . . and . . . I draw. I draw it all away. I have control of them—my sketches. They're there for me, they listen to me. They don't push me away or tell me to shut up or that I'm being stupid, or silly or just . . . They don't see me anymore, none of them. They don't hear me. They just see . . . I don't know what they see. I can't bear it. I can't bear being near them. It's as if . . . as if . . . I . . . see their mouth move and their eyes . . . they tear me apart with their eyes and I can't . . . Erik, I can't bear it . . . ."

Asher was breathing hard, sounding as if he was edging

toward hysterical, and the words pouring from him made no sense.

Erik struggled to keep hold of him. "Asher . . . Ash. Ssh, I've got you, baby, I've got you, calm down Ssh. Breathe slower, okay? Deep, big breath, okay?" He demonstrated by doing it himself. He was relieved when Asher did one. "There . . . Ssh . . . It'll be okay, love, I'll help you however I can, you know that. I'll listen to you and hold you for as long as you want. We'll shut out the world until we feel better, together. I'm listening, Asher. I want to hear all of what you have to say."

Gradually, Asher calmed down and grew heavy in Erik's arms. After a while, Erik thought he'd fallen asleep, but eventually, he stirred and stared up at Erik. He looked spaced out. "Erik, I-I don't know what to do. Everything's . . . jumbled up inside me. I can't think. Everything feels wrong and . . . I'm so tired. I feel like I'm wading through treacle most of the time. The only time I feel anywhere near normal is when I'm sketching or painting. It's gone so far I really don't know what to do to make it better. I feel like I'm slipping, and I don't know where I'm going to end up. Erik, I-I feel like I'm perched on the edge of a cliff and I-I wanna jump off."

Inwardly Erik panicked. He didn't like the suicide implication at all but had to keep it together. "If you jump, we both do it, together. I'm not living without you. No way, baby. I . . . know what it's like to have your art help, my lyrics help me, they used to a lot more than now." He stroked Asher's face. "As long as they help, I don't see an issue, but you've got to put down the pencils sometimes and step outside of it. Why not . . ." He had a thought. "Why not draw me? Live? I'll be your subject, and you can talk my ears off, baby. I don't get to see you enough, and it kills me. Let's just take time away and be alone for a while?"

"Really?" Asher asked, his eyes widening. "We can just . . .

stop? For a while? Just stop? And . . . and I can . . . sketch you? I can talk to you and be with you and not anyone else?"

Erik smiled at the response. "That'd be perfect to me, Asher. I get to watch you work and see your handsome face and listen to that melodic voice of yours, what could be better than spending time alone with my Asher? Just the two of us?"

"Tomorrow? We can do it tomorrow?" He sounded a little excited, the spark rekindling in his eyes. "Can we go to the house? Our house? It feels good there. There's space and color and light. Can we? Tomorrow?"

"Yes! Let's do it tomorrow. We can set it up however you'd like, you're the artist, baby. I'll pose and do anything you want me to do. At our house, our time together." He kissed his head gently and held him. "I can't wait! What time?"

"Will you take me by the school? Get my things? Can we spend all day there? Watch the sun move past the windows. I can show you the way the light changes. Maybe . . . maybe Angel can come . . . and Con. I could sketch them too."

Erik cupped his face "I'd love it, and I know they would too. They love you so much. They'd do anything. Besides, I'd love to see drawings of them. With you doing them, I know they'll be brilliant. You can capture the sunset and the red in Con's hair and Angel's eyes . . . maybe draw them together. I think Angel's over some of his shyness." He smiled, pleased Asher loved the idea. "We'll spend all day there tomorrow after we get everything from school, I promise. After that, it's all your call, baby."

There was real warmth in Asher's eyes now, and Erik could practically see the thoughts flying inside his head. For once, they seemed to be good ones, because he was smiling.

"I'm tired, Erik, really tired. Can we sleep now?"

"Yes, I'm tired, too. It's been a long day. I'm glad our friends are home for good now." After a long kiss, he snuggled down with Asher in his arms. "I'll hold you all night, baby."

"Thank you. I . . . I'm . . ." Asher's words faded as he relaxed and fell asleep.

As Erik watched his fiancé sleep, his mind wandered. He was looking forward to tomorrow, but knew it was just a band-aid on a bullet wound of an issue. There was something deep inside Asher that was making him unstable again, and Erik hoped he had the strength to handle it like he had before in London.

The moonlight beamed in through the window, lighting up Asher's dark hair. *I love you so much, Asher. I promise you I'll do everything I can to be there for you, every day and night. We've gotten through hard times before, but I swear to you, I'm here.* He remembered what Angel said about Asher promising to get professional help after the wedding. He hoped the pledge stuck. They were sated for now, sleepy, and in each other's arms. He couldn't wait for tomorrow — which had already begun, being after midnight.

Quiet had finally fallen over the room as the couple in the next room fell silent. The walls weren't thin, but they weren't thick, either. Connor had heard raised voices and had been about to check on them when it stopped. After pausing to listen carefully and ensure his friends really had settled, he calmed down and came back to bed.

With a quick glance at Angel, he slipped his body under the sheets and cozied up to his boyfriend and kissed his cheek. "They're quiet now. It's a bad business, and I hope in me heart there's a way out for them both. It's a lonely thing te go through, mental health stuff. I hope they'll get some sleep. They'll need it." He propped himself up on his elbow and softly stroked Angel's chest. He remembered when that would have made Angel jump, just a year ago, in this same room. Now . . . he welcomed it, arched into the touch. Connor smiled and ran his hand over Angel's side. "What're ye thinkin' about right now, *a chroí*?"

"Right now? Right now, I'm thinking—what have I done to deserve this, to be lying here with the sexiest man in the world, looking at me with that expression in his eyes? I'm thinking I'm the luckiest son-of-a-bitch who ever walked the earth."

Connor smiled wide and kissed him deeply. "Me, sexy?" He chuckled, his cheeks heating. "Whisht now, away with ya. Ye'll be having me burning up the bed with me face, so ye will." He sighed, stroking Angel's soft skin. "Aye, I'm some lucky son-of-a-bitch te have an Angel by my side, hi." He laughed and kissed Angel again. "And a damn fine one at that."

"Absolutely." Angel laughed. "I'm a damned god, and you should be worshipping me, so ye should." He stroked Connor's cheek and smiled. "No, wait. Let me worship you."

Angel pushed Connor onto his back and straddled him. Bowing his head, he smiled down. Connor gazed back in wonder. "There now, that's better. Let me worship my hairy Irish god." He kissed Connor gently on the lips, then moved down over his chin, and chest. He had a way of tugging at the hair with his teeth that drove Connor wild.

Jolts of pleasure went through Connor's blood and body as Angel's lips teased his skin and kissed it with a warmth he loved. He shivered with every touch, every look from his lover. "I like yer idea of worshippin', *a chroí*. Yer hairy Irish god commands ye to come closer. As close as ye can get, hi." He grinned, feeling luckier than all the four-leaf clovers in the world to have Angel in his life.

Angel lowered himself to press his body against Connor's, lip to toe. Connor loved the way their bodies molded to each other, and when he slid his arms around Angel, he shivered and felt he was in heaven.

"Oh, Con," Angel whispered, teasing the redhead's beard with his teeth. "I love you so much. You make me crazy, but in the nicest possible way. Make me burn for you, baby."

"I'm already burnin' for ye, *a chroí*, me heart." Connor's voice was hoarse with passion as he squeezed Angel and kissed him deeply, not letting go until they couldn't hold their breath any longer. He touched Angel all over—he was so soft and smooth. God how Conner loved the feel of Angel's warm body on his. It tickled his body hair and made him go wild inside. He couldn't get enough of him, and he prayed it stayed that way, especially now since they'd be living together all the time. "I love you too, Angel."

Angel panted, sweat forming on his shivering skin. Everywhere Connor touched burned and made him tremble with pleasure. He wanted more. He wanted it all. It was hard to believe they'd only been lovers for only a few months.

As Connor's beard tickled his neck, he remembered how it felt the first time—how gentle Connor had been, how sweet and tender. No one could ever have lost their virginity in such a beautiful way. And now . . . now he couldn't get enough. He burned to have his lover's hands and lips touch him everywhere, on every inch of his body. "Oh God, Con, you drive me crazy. I need you . . . Touch me, baby, touch me all over."

Connor smiled. "Ye wish is me command, me darlin'." He rolled Angel onto his back, covering him from head to toe with kisses, smoothing his hands all over Angel's sweaty body.

Angel moaned, shivered, and whimpered when Connor sat up, drawing him into his arms. They sat together, locked in an Indian-style position, their kisses never ceasing.

"I'm . . . so glad we'll be here together . . . all the time." Connor finished his statement by combing his fingers through

Angel's long hair.

"All the time forever and ever and ever and ever." Angel highlighted each *ever* with a kiss, moving down Connor's body until he had his cheek pressed against Connor's belly, his breath stirring the hair and making Connor twitch. Angel laughed and continued with his kisses. "Ever and ever and ever."

Later, when he regained his ability to speak, Connor pulled Angel to him, and they gazed at each other, dazed and sated. Connor had never been so happy. "I promise . . . me love . . . to build ye a proper house . . . with a grand, big bedroom . . ." He smiled. "With a proper lock too, to hide away." He kissed Angel softly as their bodies pressed together again. The wonderful mixture of sweat and cologne tantalized him as he tousled the long locks of his lover before running his fingers down his body again. "Yer me forever man, so ye are. Forever in me heart, *a chroí*."

"Forever man? I like that. Forever man. You're my forever man, too, Connor. As for the house. I couldn't care less about a house. I'd live in a tent if it meant I could be with you. You're my home, not a pile of bricks and tiles. You'll always be my home no matter where we live."

"Well, I'm here now, and I'll make ye a grand home, so I will. I'll give ye everything, *a chroí*. This I swear." He stifled a yawn. "Ah, by God, I'm knackered. The plane ride fair knocked me on me arse, with Caitlin bendin' me ear every five minutes, hi. He held Angel in his arms. "Let's sleep now, just like this." He tipped up Angel's chin for a final kiss. "I love ye forever, *a chroí*."

"Me too, me darlin', my forever man."

CHAPTER FIVE

Asher awoke feeling as if he'd drunk his way across a bar. His head was throbbing and his mouth dry. Everyone had slept in. Then Angel had remembered they were supposed to be meeting his father for breakfast in the main house and had everyone up and out of bed before they were even properly awake.

For a few wonderful minutes, he completely forgot about what had happened the night before. They were followed by a few minutes of hell when he remembered, then back to bliss when he recalled how their discussion had ended — they were going to spend the day at the house. Just the two of them. No weddings, no nagging, no stress. Just him and Erik ... and maybe Connor and Angel. He'd like to draw them. He'd thought about it for a while.

Yawning and stretching, he emerged from the bathroom with teeth and face scrubbed clean and a more positive state of mind than he'd had for weeks. He met Angel at the top of the stairs, and before Angel could even open his mouth, Asher grabbed him around the waist and pulled him close. "You're the best, Angel." He hugged him tightly before releasing him and heading back into his room.

Erik was brushing out his hair and turned toward the door. His smile froze, then widened as Asher threw himself into his arms and kissed him.

"You're the best, too," Asher said. "Make sure you give it a good brush so the light will catch it right later."

"Oh, I will, no worries there. I'm sure my hair'll be my only wardrobe, won't it?" Erik teased and ran a hand over Asher's locks. "You have such gorgeous hair. Maybe Angel can draw you while we're there. I'd love a picture of just you, and maybe one of us, but you especially."

"That'd be nice. I haven't been sketched for a long time and then only at school. It'd be nice at the house, and I trust Angel. He'll do a good job."

He sat on the bed and pulled on his boots. It took a while, but when they were laced and buckled, he grabbed a t-shirt and hurried downstairs.

Angel was already calling anxiously up to them. "Will you two please come on? You're like a pair of girls. I've never known anyone take so long getting ready."

Asher smiled but said nothing

Erik followed behind him as they entered the kitchen, and they all shared the pot of coffee Connor had made.

"Gotta have my fuel in the morning, that's for sure." Erik drank his coffee down fast. "I can't wait for this day, it's gonna be so great." He took Asher's hand and pulled him close. "Thanks for having us here last night, guys. When our place is ready, you've got an open invite."

"I'll make it grand, no sweat. Sure, I've got jobs comin' out me ears right now, hi. Hope it holds." Connor chuckled.

"I've got loads of ideas," Asher said, excitement fluttering in his stomach. "I'm not sure how practical they are. We can take a look later when . . . Oh, I forgot, I haven't asked you yet. We're going to hang at our house today. Just us. No one knows, okay? Keep it secret. I just need a break away from everything. I'm gonna sketch Erik and watch the sun change the colors in the windows and maybe sketch the graveyard." He shook his head, pulling himself back to the present. "It'd be really cool if you two could come by after lunch. I'd like to sketch you, too. And Erik though it might be fun for you to sketch me."

"Really?" Angel looked surprised. "Well yeah, of course, we'll come over. It would be fabulous to get some sketches of me and Con. And . . . wow, yeah I'll sketch you. I'd love to sketch you. It'd be a dream. Can I use it as part of my portfolio, if it's good enough?"

"If it's good enough," Asher said with a wink. "Can't have shoddy work with my ass in it, can I?"

"Who said I was going to sketch your ass?"

"You can sketch what you want, darling." He wound his arms around Angel's neck from behind and kissed his ear, then snatched a grape from the bowl of fruit that always lay on the breakfast bar, and practically danced out the door.

"What the fuck happened last night?" he heard Angel ask Erik and smiled to himself, raising his face to the sun.

Erik's time at the school was blessedly short as he helped Asher with his large stack of sketch pads, brushes, and supplies. He almost felt like a thief taking it all to their car, stowing it in the back, and stealing away into the new morning. The weather was gorgeous, sunny, and not too hot yet. Luckily the air conditioning worked at their new home. It was so large and open they needed good air flow. When they were done at the school, they stopped at their favorite fast food place for coffee and take-out breakfasts.

Teasing and joking, they tumbled inside and over the small crate and boxes they were using for chairs. They sat, ate, and laughed. Erik loved every second of it. It was wonderful to see the glimmer back in Asher's eyes. It was hard to believe in less than two days they'd be married, and he'd be on tour not too long after. The thought of leaving Asher so soon wrenched his gut a bit, especially with everything going on, but he was determined to see it through. At the very least, he'd contact Asher every night, or pass messages or flowers or something daily to remind him of their love and new marriage.

After the last drops of coffee were swallowed, Erik patted his stomach and eyed the room. It needed some tidying up before they could do any drawing. "I'll clear up before we get started, baby. The sun needs to hit me, not a stack of totes."

"Hmm . . ." Asher was staring through the windows with a dreamy expression, lost in thought as he often was.

The stained glass living room windows were one of the main reasons they'd bought the old church in the first place. They were enormous, stretching floor to ceiling in a semicircular wall. They depicted three angels. The middle angel hovered in midair with his hands raised, his head thrown back and his golden hair cascading down his back. Two others faced him, on either side, blowing trumpets. Asher had said from the first moment he set eyes on the windows that the middle angel was Erik, and as long as he was in the house, Erik would always be watching over him, even if he wasn't actually there.

Erik busied himself shoving a few totes out of the way and fashioning a makeshift couch out of some of them combined with pillows and tarps for comfort. He noticed Asher's gaze was still intent on the window, and especially the angel. He smiled to himself. "My twin will keep an eye on you, even when I can't. But the moment hasn't arrived yet. For today, I'm yours. All yours." He kissed Asher softly and hugged him. "So, how would you like your man to pose for you?"

Asher squinted at the window, then his gaze roved across the floor, following the light. His eyes darted around, and ignoring Erik's hard work, he started moving the boxes, then moved them again, and again until, finally, he stood up and nodded. "There. Just sit there, under the Angel."

Erik sat obediently. He knew from experience that once

Asher got into art mode, it was easiest to follow orders without argument. "How should I sit? Pose me, my beautiful fiancé."

Frowning, Asher seemed to glare at him, but Erik knew he was just thinking deeply. "Take your shirt off," he commanded.

"Always happy to oblige on that one." Erik quickly undid the buttons and slipped the shirt from his body and onto the floor. "Anything else?"

"Hmm . . . No. I like those jeans. I've always liked those jeans, they make your legs look longer. Put your arm there." He moved Erik into position, not a very comfortable position at all, and left him there, to perch on a pile of packing cases with his materials scattered around him. Asher looked relaxed and so happy.

Erik's muscles twitched with the pose Asher had put him in, but hey, anything for love, right? He shook out his hair. It fell to just below his shoulders in multiple layers. Sunlight, magnified by the golden glass, hit him on the back of the head and warmed up his body. He hoped he could handle the heat for a long period of sitting. Asher was busy setting up his space. With his tools in place, he looked ready to begin. "Ready when you are, love."

"Ssh." Asher hushed him absently, his pencil already skimming across the paper. It was fascinating to watch.

Occasionally Asher looked up and sometimes swapped his pencil for another, or a piece of charcoal or chalk. Mainly, he either stared at the paper, or scribbled on it, or at least that was how it seemed to Erik.

He was fascinated by how intent Asher was when he drew. He'd never fully realized it before. Maybe that was how the sketches spoke to him. He was so focused on them as he was creating them, perhaps they told him where to put a stroke of red or blue, and how long or how short. He loved seeing his man at work and grew anxious to see the final product. He knew that, even with no one posing, Asher had done gorgeous paintings of them all, and he couldn't wait to see this new work. He wanted to see all of it, Angel's too. Connor raved about his works constantly. Erik had done the same with Asher, especially the band paintings.

A song formed in his head and he started to hum it out loud. He'd have to harmonize with Joey or Billy later on. He dared not approach Daisy right now. Since falling pregnant, she was worse than a stirred-up hornets' nest. He'd keep mum about it. He wanted to talk but wouldn't disturb the artist.

"What are you humming?" Asher asked not missing a beat in his sketching.

"Oh, just a song about this, and us. I'll get with Billy when we come back, or Joey, and get it all out.

"My art takes longer to form in my head."

"I love how you're so into your art. This is going to be dope, just like the rest of your stuff."

"Hardly." Asher laughed. "It's just a sketch." With a final frown and twist of the head, Asher nodded and tossed the piece of paper he'd been working on aside. "Move your head to look into the corner." He motioned with his charcoal-smudged fingers. "And move your arm across the back of the box . . . Right. Stop. Stay still."

Out of the corner of his eye, Erik watched Asher begin to furiously sketch again and sighed. Why had he thought it would be as easy as sitting still for half an hour for Asher to do a picture? It looked as if it was going to be a long day.

After the fourth sketch, Erik's muscles had frozen up, and he knew he was going to be very sore. It was a welcome relief when the doorbell rang and Asher stopped. Erik slumped forward, shaking his arm and leg to get feeling back. "They're

here!" He ran to the door, still buttoning his shirt and welcomed Angel and Connor inside.

"Hi, shams. What's the craic? We've brought enough to
feed an army, so we have. Me darlin' was worried ye'd be fa-
din' away by now, with all the work ye've been doin'." Connor dropped a plastic bag on the breakfast bar. "Asher, come
eat now, ye need yer strength."

"In a minute. I just want to finish this bit."

"Take it through to the kitchen," Angel said. "I'll bring
him. Otherwise, it'll be dinner before you drag him away
from his sketchbook."

"Hey," Angel said as he peeked over Asher's shoulder. "Nice
work."

Asher glanced up and smiled, tucking his hair behind his
ear and smudging charcoal on his cheek.

Angel looked around. "You've brought all your sketchbooks." He was more than surprised.

"Yes."

"Why?"

"What do you mean?" Asher appeared genuinely confused.

"You've brought the pictures of James here?" To say Angel
was surprised was an understatement.

Asher went pale. "I needed . . . I needed to know they're
safe." He looked down and rubbed charcoal into the knee of
his jeans. "I was thinking. I thought we could . . . that you
could help me . . . get rid of them."

"Get rid of them? Why don't you just throw them away?"

Asher shook his head vehemently. "That's not good
enough; they'd still be there. I want to burn them, and I want
you to help me do it."

"Help you? How? Why?"

"Because I . . . I don't think I can do it on my own. Will you?"

Angel nodded and smiled. "Of course I will. When?"

"Tomorrow night. I want it all gone and done with before the wedding. I want to feel free, to leave it behind before I start again with Erik. Will you come here tomorrow night with me, and burn the sketches?"

"I'd be honored to."

Asher beamed and threw down his work. "Come on. I'm starving."

Angel smiled to himself as everyone munched on the sandwiches from a local deli. Connor had heard they had good corned beef and Reubens. By the smile on his face, he was enjoying the heck out of his choice.

"You guys ready for your close-up now? I still can't fully feel my arm from the pose I was in." Erik shook out his arm with an exaggerated pout. "Ah, the things I do for this one." He rolled his eyes playfully and hooked his thumb toward Asher.

Connor laughed. "Aye, but 'tis all out of love, eh? I'm sure this one would have me ravaged by hunger, or bent like an Irish knot if it'd make a good sketch, wouldn't ye?" He winked at Angel.

"I'd have *you* ravaged? Not in front of Erik and Asher, I wouldn't." He smiled and fluttered his eyes at Connor, who clasped his chest and pretended to fall off the chair.

"Come on. I want to get a couple before the light changes." Asher hurried back into the living room and started moving boxes around, then made Connor and Angel strip off their shirts and positioned them in each other's arms.

"Mmm, I could stay here all day," Angel purred up at Connor, who smiled and moved his hand to touch his face.

"Don't move," Asher snapped, and Connor pulled back his hand quickly.

"Begging yer pardon. I forgot how temperamental you artist types get." He chuckled and kissed Angel's hair. "That'll be me last move, Ash. On me word." He winked at Angel. "Sure, 'tis no hardship having me darlin in me arms. Dontcha be missing me hair now, not that ye can when it's bright as a copper penny, hi. Make sure to do it justice."

Erik snorted a laugh and slurped on his soda. Angel tried to keep his face straight, fearing a scolding from Asher, but it was hard. Connor could get lead to lighten up.

Time passed slowly for everyone except, Erik suspected, Asher, who was utterly absorbed in one drawing after another. He flew through them a lot quicker with Connor and Angel, saying he had plenty of time and opportunity to draw Erik. Angel was probably more understanding of the artistic process — at least he never complained — but Conner was squirming, and Erik got more and more bored until they both eventually rebelled.

"Gawd, what're you drawing, each individual hair? You're gonna run out of red." Erik teased and tossed a wink at Connor.

"Aye, this is torture. I've never sat this still in me entire life. What're ye doin' to me?" He stuck out his tongue and pretended to hang himself with his hair.

Angel and Erik both laughed, Asher didn't.

"No. No, don't move . . . not yet . . . I need . . . wait, I just need to get . . . Oh, no." He threw down his book and crossed his arms, glaring at Connor. "You spoiled it." He pouted.

Connor shook out his limbs, and after groaning for a moment, he sauntered over and picked up the drawing. "Get away with ye, ye nutter. It's grand." He held it out for Erik and Angel to see.

"Damn right it is, this is a keepsake item for sure. It's not spoiled or ruined at all, baby." He glanced at Angel. "What's your opinion, Angel?"

Angel took the paper and stared at it hard, chewing his lip. "Well . . ." He paused as he carefully examined the sketch. "The backlighting is superb. He's got the expressions nailed, but he's right." He frowned at Connor. "You've blurred the shading, and the definition of the right side of your face is incomplete." He looked up at Asher, his eyes shining. "How did I do with my crit analysis?"

Asher laughed and grabbed Angel around the neck, hugging him, then let him go. "You're learning, kid," he said. "Right, then. Your turn, Angel. Let's see what you've got."

"Shit, Ash, I don't know." He gazed again at the sketch in his hands. "I couldn't do anything like this."

"Well tough shit. It's been years since I've been sketched, and I'm vain enough to have been looking forward to it. So sharpen your pencil and tell me where to go."

"I don't have—"

"Nuh-uh . . . you've got all my materials and a choice of sketchbooks. No excuses. You're up Picasso."

Connor patted his shoulder. "Awae wid ye now. Don't be so bashful. You've got the eye, eh, and you'd not want for a better model. Beautiful, exotic, colorful, eh . . . Damned if I can find the words te describe ye, but me Angel will make ye . . . magnificent."

Angel snorted and Connor turned him to gaze into his face. "You can do it. Sure, if I'm having' to take yer compliments and not be afraid, so can you. You'll do me proud." He kissed Angel briefly then wandered over to Erik, shrugging his shirt back on

"Amen to that, I've got nothing to add." Erik draped an arm across Connor's shoulders. "You can do it, Angel."

Angel narrowed his eyes at Asher, then laughed. "All right then, but if we do it, we do it right. Take your clothes off while

I think of a good pose for you."

Erik crossed over to Angel and cupped his hand around his ear, whispering, "On his back with one leg up, his head tilted back, his hair hanging down, but his hand over his middle. That'd look damn hot to me, since he's posing nude." He cast a glance back at Connor. "You can do him next . . . but you might not make it past the first sketching," he teased.

Asher shed his clothes without the slightest inhibition. He stood in the middle of the room, stark naked, hands on hips, and grinning. "Where'd you want me?"

"Over there in front of the window. It has to show off your tattoo, although I'm not sure I'm going to draw that yet."

Angel directed Asher to stretch out on the floor in a puddle of light from the angelic windows, then moved his body into the pose Erik had requested — his hips flat and upper body raised on his elbows, with his head tilted back and his face turned toward Angel. His glorious hair flowed over his shoulders and pooled on the floor, the blue streaks catching the light and glowing.

Angel realized, as he sat down and picked up the pad, that however long ago it might have been since Asher had last posed, he had retained what was needed to make a good artist's model, which at this level wasn't as easy as it seemed. Being a model was more than just lying there looking pretty, and Asher was damn good at it. In fact, there wasn't much connected with the art world Asher wasn't damn good at.

Angel worked quickly to capture the drama that was Asher. His black hair, his slender but muscular body, and those eyes. He'd always been fascinated by Asher's eyes.

Erik and Connor looked over his shoulder as he worked. It made him incredibly nervous, and he kept shooing them away, not that it made much difference, because they kept coming back. At least they seemed impressed by all of it. When it was completed, Erik patted Angel's shoulder.

"Looks damn good, Angel." He walked over and kissed Asher. "Of course, you had a lovely subject." He helped him off the boxes. "You feel all right, baby?"

"Not too bad, a little stiff." He ran his hands over Erik's shirt. "Erik . . . would you mind . . . if we got one of the two of us? Together?"

"Not at all, hon. How'd you want to do this?"

Asher bit his lip and kissed him. "But you have to dress like I am."

Erik hesitated for a moment, then shrugged. "Why not? Angel, your hand all right for you to keep drawing?"

"I'm fine here, Erik."

"Then here we go."

Erik stripped off everything and Angel positioned them in each other's arms on the boxes, with Asher almost sitting in Erik's lap. There was nothing sexual in the pose, just the two of them in a lover's embrace, in the last days before their marriage.

When the drawing was done, Angel picked it up and kissed his fingers. "Perfecto." He smiled.

Connor nodded. "Aye, it's grand, so it is. Fair warms the soul of this crusty ole Irishman."

Asher hugged Angel and re-dressed. "Thanks, guys. Now . . . it's your turn. I've had an idea for another one. I promise I won't take as long. All right?"

Grumbling, Angel and Connor agreed and stripped down. Angel shivered and Connor pulled him close. "Come 'ere, darlin', let this bit o' hot stuff warm ye up, hi."

Asher snorted and pushed them into a spotlight. After examining them from different angles, he grabbed a couple of throws and tossed one onto the ground, directing them to lie down. With practiced ease, he moved their bodies into the desired position, using other throws to drape them in such a way it reduced the chill but not the visibility, as far as possible.

"Thanks, Asher." Angel gazed at him and smiled.

Asher paused, breaking his intense concentration, and smiled back.

When he was satisfied, Asher hopped up onto his makeshift workstation and started to sketch furiously.

Erik stood behind him, his head tilted to one side. "Gawd, you guys look happy. Let's call this . . . Euro Passion or something." He snorted.

"Wait, I know." Angel smiled. "*Forever*, 'cause Connor is my forever man." He leaned his head on his boyfriend's chest and Connor kissed it softly.

"Aye. Angel's mine, too. Love of me life, he is."

Asher smiled. "Will you look at the two lovebirds? They're so sweet they're making my teeth ache."

"We figure life's short, embrace it while ye can. Take all the happiness life brings you," Angel remarked.

Erik kissed Asher's head. "I hear you for sure. To happiness." He kissed Asher sweetly.

CHAPTER SIX

"Feeling all right, Daisy? Any sleeplessness or really odd food cravings yet?" Billy asked as he and Vince escorted her into the baby goods store.

"So far, so good. I worry about my guitar, though, but I guess if huge men with beer guts can wear them, so can I." She laughed.

Vince pointed to the baby shower registration kiosk. "Wow, it won't be too long, we'll be doing that."

"Just think . . . we're gonna be parents! My folks are thrilled to death at getting grandchildren. They never thought that'd happen."

Daisy cocked a brow. "Not even when you were young . . . before you knew?"

Billy shook his head. "Nope. Not unless they said it when I was a toddler. I think Mom pretty much always knew I was gay, or I was beating the drums too loud and it drowned her out."

They all chortled.

"How are your parents taking it, Vince?" Daisy asked.

He shrugged a little. "Mom's taking it well. Paulie has no kids, so I guess she was looking to me to give her a grand-child. Dad . . . haven't heard too much. He hasn't spoken to me much since the wedding. Hell, before it even."

"But . . . that was nearly a year ago now. Still?" Daisy seemed shocked.

"What can I say? I'm a disappointment to him, the black sheep. Mom was ostracized until last year, and hell, we never even hear from Paulie. I used to look up to him, but now . . ." He paused. "No. I've got my life, and it's Billy and cooking, and our two precious bundles of joy to be born. That, and our house, our friends. I've no time for grudges."

Billy stopped and hugged him. "It's ridiculous you have to go through that at all, baby. Now Tony and Angel are good, maybe your uncle could help you out with your father. It is his brother after all."

Vince ran a hand through his blond locks. "We'll see how it all plays out. Understanding's all I'm looking for. That's a wish list item at this point, but I'll take what I can get."

Daisy pulled out her cell phone. "Speaking of family, I'm due for a haircut later, and Asher's to join me. I need to speak to him, but he barely returns my calls anymore, so I'm calling Erik."

She stood, and Billy heard it ring once, then go right to voice mail.

Daisy groaned. "Typical . . . Asher probably shut off his phone, too. I'll try Angel and Connor." She tried both with the same result. "I knew it. The four musketeers have struck again."

"What is it, Daisy?" Vince asked.

"No one's answering, which means they're all plotting something together, likely avoiding me. We've got to find them. Do you mind taking me on a search for those bloody grooms?"

Billy chuckled. "Not at all. Come on." They escorted her to the car and took off in search of the wayward men.

Daisy growled as they pulled up to Erik and Asher's new house, after already having checked the student house and Tony's. She got out of the car, not waiting for Billy or Vince, and pounded on the door.

"Asher Berkley, you open this door!"

Billy and Vince joined her and rang the doorbell, too.

"Open up, guys! We know you're in there!" Billy added.

Erik's car was there, the guys were caught.

"Right." Daisy rummaged in her backpack. "If that's the way they want to play it, I can play, too." Fishing out a key, she unlocked the door and stormed in.

"What the fuck," she gasped when she saw the four boys.

Asher was perched on top of a pile of boxes with his sketchbook on his knee, his face black from charcoal smudges. Erik was standing at his side, his eyes wide and horrified at the sight of her. It was Angel and Connor who caught her attention, though. They were on the floor, scrambling over fallen boxes scattered around them and were struggling to get dressed.

"What are you doing? What have you been doing?" she demanded of her brother.

"You've got eyes, Daisy," Asher commented calmly. "I thought that would have been obvious. I've been sketching."

"Easy, easy now, Daisy." Erik held up his hands as if to ward off the impending drama, "We're just having a day of relaxation, all right? Things have been way too whacked, and we're just . . . hanging with our friends."

"Oy, Erik? Ye couldn't have put it another way?" Connor groused as he pulled on his pants.

"Relaxation? Try avoiding me and Mam! There's work to do, Asher! You too, Erik! Connor, Angel . . . you should be ashamed of yourselves, sneaking about like this with them! I'm ashamed of all of you!"

Vince put his arm around her. "Relax, Daisy. It's all right. They'll just have to work harder tomorrow. If they wanna goof off today, so be it. Let them have a day off for once. It's been a helluva busy time. Let's just take a breath . . . and relax—"

"Oh, stuff it, Vince! I'm fucking livid! It's not just today, he's been trying to avoid me for weeks! Well, time's up, my dear brother! You're getting married the day after tomorrow, and I'm gonna make sure you're damn well good and ready! So quit fighting, me and do as you're told!"

"Then I'm sure you have a lot to do . . . so go do it and leave me alone." Asher turned his back and bent over his sketchpad.

"Hey, Daisy . . ." Erik approached cautiously, smiling in what he seemed to think was a conciliatory manner.

She had no time for this. She was tired, her feet ached, and she had a million and one things to do, half of which required Asher's input. Why wouldn't he just do what he was told?

"What do you want?" She practically snarled in Erik's face. "You Nordic mess of a man. I bet he put you up to this, didn't he?"

"As a matter of fact, no." Erik shot back at her. "It was my idea, just so you know. He's been stressed to the fucking hilt, and I'm worried to death about it! Just let us have one damn day off where we do something calming. Tap out for a bit and leave him be. He can do your punch-list tomorrow."

"I think you should go, Daisy. I'm busy, and unless you want to get your tits out and let me sketch them, you don't really have a place here." Asher kept his back to her, his voice dead and cold.

The fact he was ignoring her made Daisy's heat rise, even before she registered the words that had just come out of his mouth. Feeling fit to explode, words momentarily escaped her.

"Asher, that was a bit uncalled for," Angel commented as he buttoned his shirt. "There are ways of saying things, my friend."

Asher shrugged, ignoring him.

"Now, everyone just calm down." Vince tried to mediate,

as usual, joining his cousin's attempt at diffusion. "Daisy, watch your temper, the doctor warns against high blood pressure, but Asher, really? That was a despicable thing to say to your sister! Now, I know wedding planning isn't fun—"

"Oh, stop. Stop!" Daisy put her hands over her ears. "I can't take it anymore!" She stormed over and took the charcoal from Asher's hand. "This stops now! You're coming with us whether you like it or not, and you will do as you're told! Stop behaving like a child!"

Asher looked up at her and narrowed his eyes. "Give it back," he said in a deadly voice.

Erik bent over and successfully plucked the charcoal from her fingers. "Stop it, you two, I mean it!" He handed the stick to Asher and tried to steer Daisy away, but she didn't budge.

"You arse! Don't give it back to him! Get away from me, Erik!" She tried to push him, but he didn't move either.

"Guys?" He looked around at the others, but they were all just standing around like statues with their mouths open.

So much for stepping in to protect their lady. Blind fury struck, and she pushed Erik so hard he stumbled back a few steps, which gave her a tad of satisfaction.

"Get back from me, or I'll punch you! I've wanted to so many times!"

"Back off, Daisy!" Erik growled. "Leave Asher alone!"

"Get your hands off Erik, Daisy. Don't you dare threaten my boyfriend." Asher's voice wasn't quite so calm this time.

There was a heat in his eyes that threatened an explosion, and right there and then, it was exactly what Daisy wanted. How dare he treat her like this! How dare they all treat her like this! She'd worked bloody hard on this wedding, and all Asher had done was toss obstacles in her way and throw hissy fits when things didn't go as he wanted, at least when he wasn't hiding from her. She was sick of it, and she was going to take it out of his arse, right now.

Locking gazes with Asher, she pushed Erik again. Childish, maybe, but she didn't care. Tilting her head in a *so what are you going to do about it* manner she glared at her brother.

Very carefully, Asher put down his art things and stood up, brushing himself down. He climbed down off the boxes and stood next to Erik, facing her sister. "Take your hands off him, Dais. Right now. Then get the hell out of here. Leave me alone. Don't push it."

She pushed Erik again, this time with both hands. "I'm pregnant, Asher, you can't touch me. You shouldn't even yell at me. I'm in a delicate condition," she said in a calm, snide tone. She had an advantage and was going to milk it.

"Guys . . . stop, please? Before someone gets hurts. I don't want our unborn children involved in all of this," Billy pleaded.

Erik backed away from her. "You'd better listen to them, Daisy."

"Oh, go fuck yourself, Erik," she commanded. "I'm tired of being taken advantage of. This is your wedding, Asher!" She tossed a look over her shoulder. "To . . . Erik," she sneered. "You wanted it, so you're damn well going to take responsibility for doing some of the work. God knows I haven't asked much of you. You're never bloody there to ask."

"Back off," Asher snarled at Erik, encompassing the others with his glare. Then he turned the full force of his anger on her. "My wedding? Since when did it have anything to do with me? Since when did I have a say in anything? I'm sick and tired of being pushed aside and talked over. I'm sick of being told what to do and what not to do. You want this wedding, you fix it. Don't expect me to roll over and play dead anymore. I'm sick of it. If you're lucky, I'll turn up Saturday night, and that's all you can expect from me . . . any of you."

Daisy balled her fists, squeezing them tight to prevent leveling a punch at Asher, then grabbed her brother's shirt.

"You'd damn well better show up to the wedding, or I'll send the police after you! You'd disappoint everyone? Including your . . . fiancé?" She wrinkled her nose when she looked at Erik. "You've two days, Asher. Two days to pretend you want this wedding to happen, and dammit, I'm not doing everything!" She pushed him back and wagged her finger at him "You'd better stop hiding and acting like a child, or I'll . . . I'll get Mam on your case, so help me!"

Asher laughed. "You what? For God's sake, Daisy, grow up. This isn't a game. This is my life, and it's supposed to be my wedding. Big joke. Name me one thing . . . just one thing about this whole fucked-up fiasco I've chosen . . . apart from the groom. You picked the venue—not what I wanted. You chose the ceremony—not what I wanted. You chose the officiant—not who I wanted. Okay, I got some concessions in the color scheme, a few hints of black here and there, red roses instead of white . . . oh, and candles, I got candles. I had to fight hard enough to get you to have it in the evening, and even then, it wasn't after dark like I wanted. Congratulations, Daisy, you've achieved your objective. This isn't my wedding . . . it's yours."

Connor hopped in between the two. "In the name of all that's holy, would ya cool your heads? You're not doin' yerself or yer babby and favors. Asher, would it kill ya te—"

"Fuck off!" Daisy and Asher yelled in unison at Connor.

He backed off and into Angel's waiting arms.

Instantly, Asher turned on Daisy. "Don't you speak to my best man like that."

"I'll speak to him however I like! He's involved in your little escape too!" She looked down her nose at Connor. "Typical Irishman . . . so ye are." She scornfully mimicked his accent. "You've all gone too far, and you're going to push me over the edge!"

"Over the edge?" Asher took a step closer, so he was practically nose-to-nose with her. "And what exactly does that mean, Daisy? Tell me about it. What's your *edge*?"

"My edge, dear brother? My *edge* is putting me into this predicament where I'm dealing with both sets of parents, and you and your friends, and this pregnancy all at once! If it weren't for Joey, I'd have gone stark raving mad!"

Asher laughed. "Yeah right. Poor you. You're enjoying every fucking minute of it. And don't try to tell me you're not. I know you. You've been planning weddings since you were five years old, and okay it was yours, but this one might as well be. You're having the time of your life, so don't try to bullshit me how stressed out and overworked you are."

"That's just it." She stamped her foot. "It shouldn't be all me. You're dumping all your responsibilities onto me! This is *your* wedding, Asher! God help you, it'll be the only one . . . ever. I won't ever help you again with another one, that's for bloody sure! As for *my* wedding, when it comes . . . we'll see if you're lucky to even attend!"

"What makes you think I'd want to? What makes you think I'll ever want to attend another wedding ever again? I'm fucking sick of the whole thing. I've dumped on you? I've. Dumped. On. You? Fucking bullshit. No one's dumped anything on you, Dais, you've taken. All you've done is take, take, take from me, and not given a fuck whether or not I have *anything* to give. I'm sick of it. I'm sick of it all . . . everything."

Daisy knew Asher's temper was rising. His hands were clenched at his sides as if he was struggling not to hit her. Not that he ever would.

"I didn't take anything from you, you spoiled, selfish brat! You and Erik . . . you're perfect together. You're both selfish! It's your wedding, and you need to get ready for it! Go get your fucking hair trimmed or I'll do it for you!"

She turned to Billy and Vince. "I've seen enough and definitely heard enough." She rubbed her tummy. "Sorry, my darlings, about your uncle Asher, who wants little to do with you." She shot a last glare at her brother. "You'd just better be there, Asher. That's the end of it."

"No, Daisy, no, it's not the end of it. *This* is the end of it. Get the fuck out of my house. *My* house, not yours. You're not welcome here right now. Just get out. Get. Out."

As he said *get* and *out*, he pushed her shoulder, making her stumble backward.

Vince caught her mid-step. "Don't you dare push her, Asher! Not now, not ever!"

With a glance back at her friend, she patted his hand. "Thanks, Vince." She turned back to her brother. "Fine! I'll stay out of your house, and your life if that's what you want, dear brother! You can remember this as my wedding gift to you!" She pushed him hard, nearly knocking herself over at the same time before Vince caught her again.

"Come on, let's just go, this has gotten insane. We're outta here for now." Vince held her back and escorted her out, with Billy right beside them.

Billy and Vince both sat beside Daisy as she tried to calm down. They were at her beck and call. She carried their future, quite literally, as well as being a good friend.

"Who the fuck does he think he is? He does this all the time. He has to spoil everything with his stupid dramatics. I've been working so hard, and so have Mam and Mrs. Von Nordgren. Doesn't he understand how much work goes into planning a wedding? All I wanted him to do was go for a fucking haircut . . . and go over a couple of things for the rehearsal tomorrow." She gasped. "Oh God, I hope he's not going to mess it all up. We've worked so hard getting everything together. I'm looking forward to tomorrow, and I just know he's going to spoil it."

She let her head fall forward into her hands and started to cry.

Vince held her and rubbed her back. "Ssh . . . I pray he won't, Daisy. He's just pissy right now, but it's their wedding, he knows this is important."

Billy handed her tissues. "It'll be all right, hon. I know it. After what they've gone through, I'm pleased there will still even be a wedding. Remember all the London crap, and afterward? Isn't that why you wanted to become a shrink? To help people like your brother?"

Daisy looked up, feeling the color drain from her face. Suddenly, little things started popping into her head, things Asher had said, things she'd said — and thought — when he'd stormed off. Maybe . . . maybe she'd been expecting too much of him, pushing him too hard. *Shit.*

"Ah hell. Billy . . . I think you're right. Ah fuck, what have I done? He's right. From his point of view, he's right. I have pushed too hard. Shit. Shit. What if I . . . What if I've pushed *too hard*? I mean . . . No, I'd know it. I'd know if Asher were getting ill again. I'd know . . . wouldn't I?" She looked at Billy, pleading.

"Not being as distracted as you've been. We've all been going crazy busy lately, Daisy. It's not just you . . ." Billy smoothed her back.

Vince nodded. "That's right. Between school, houses, all the inspections, the work, the wedding, it's a wonder we're not all nuts right now. Asher's more . . . high-strung than a lot of us. He's been through so much hell in his life. Now don't sock me, but yeah, I think you were a little harsh."

Anger flared again. "He pushed me, the fucker, and not just in the shoulder. God, he'd try the patience of a saint, and . . . and . . ." She slumped again. "And I should know better. Ah hell. Ash can be so frustrating but not . . . Erik's on board with all this wedding stuff, and Connor and Angel aren't stupid. If they brought him here today, there must have been a reason. He's hiding out from it. And I brought it right in the front door. God, I'm an idiot. I should go back. I should —"

"Whoa now . . . not so fast, Daisy. Let things cool off first, all right? If you walk back in there now, he'll pounce on you like a cat. You know he will. He's all torqued up, and it takes a long time to cool him off. Erik's told me over and over." Billy hugged her from the side. "Just let things rest for a bit, and you, too. Getting' our babies all fired up inside there too, lil mama-to-be. You need to be careful."

"Let's go back to the house, okay? Maybe sit on the patio and have some lemonade? Freshly squeezed," Vince tempted.

Daisy managed a small laugh. "You guys are determined to nurse me through this, aren't you?"

"Damn right we are. You're our friend, and we love you. We're gonna be here for you, always, Daisy." Vince dried her face.

"You guys are so sweet. You're wonderful."

"Well, he's sweet, I'm wonderful . . ." Billy joked. "Come on, let's go home and decide on those paint chips for the nursery, okay?"

She sniffed and nodded, let Vince help her into the car, and buckled in, trying not to think about what might be happening inside her brother's house. "Let's go talk babies."

CHAPTER SEVEN

Asher stood stock still. Everything was still and silent. No one moved. No one spoke. It was as if the world had been put on hold. A finger hovered over the fast-forward button, and soon it would all come crashing back like waves in a storm and crush him, but for the moment there was silence, deep, cold, calm silence, on the inside and the outside.

Then he became aware he was shaking. Surprised, he raised his hands and watched the tremors until his sluggish brain kicked in and it hit him. Everything hit him. It hit him so hard and so fast he couldn't process it. He didn't know what to do with it, so he tipped it all into a great big empty pit and closed the lid. It was way too much. He couldn't let himself think, and he damn well wouldn't let himself feel.

Asher glanced around at all his friends. They were all looking at him, seeming almost scared. Was that what he did to people, to his friends? Make them scared? *No, don't think about it. Don't think about anything.* He needed to get away, get out of the house, away from those eyes, those looks, everyone, everything. He needed to get out and walk and walk and walk. When he was walking, away from everything, he could just *be* and not think. He had to keep walking and maybe never stop. It was only when he stopped the trouble started.

Halfway to the door, something stopped him.

"Whoa . . . don't head out there, baby. I can't let you leave, not like this."

"Let me go, Erik." He spoke quietly, focusing on a place over Erik's shoulder. If he didn't look at him, didn't acknowledge him, Erik wouldn't be there. Asher wouldn't have to feel anything for him. He wouldn't have to feel *any-thing*. "Just get out of my way and let me go."

Erik held him by the shoulders. "I'm sorry, baby . . . no. I won't let you go out like this, in your state of mind right now. Talk to me. Tell me anything you want, but just stay inside, all right? Please, Asher . . . I know you want to walk this off, but right now it's best if you stay inside, or I'm afraid you won't come back."

"Don't . . . stop me." The lid over the pit was trembling, cracking. If he didn't get away, it was going to fly off, and he had no idea what would happen. Part of him was already screaming, and all he wanted to do was make it stop. He had to get out of there. He had to walk. He had to . . ."Please, Erik . . . just let me go."

"No. I'm not gonna let you go outside like this. I don't know what you'd do. You need to stay with me. I know you have to let this out, but let's deal with the aftermath together. Scream at me, kick at me, whatever you want." He held Asher tightly. "Just let it out, Ash, with me. Don't leave me."

"Don't do this, Erik." His anger flared. Anger, frustration, fear and . . . *ah, shit*. So much. Too much emotion. He couldn't let it out. He couldn't. Panic flared, and he tried to push Erik away. "Get off me. Get away from me. Fuck you, you're not my keeper. Let go of me." He struggled, but Erik just held tighter, even when he kicked him. "You fucking bastard. What right do you have to hold me like this? Let me go. Let. Me. Go."

"Not on your life. You can kick me all you want, but I'm not moving. I'm not your keeper, I'm the man who loves you and wants to be with you forever, Asher. I'm not letting go."

"Let go, let go, let go . . ." Asher struggled wildly, getting more and more incoherent, beating at Erik with his fists, twisting and turning, fighting to be free. And then it all came crashing down. The lid flew off the pit, flooding him with everything. Anger, fear, pain . . . it all came rushing over him, and if he'd struggled before, there was now an edge of madness to it. Erik could barely hold on. Screaming and sobbing, Asher clawed at Erik's face trying anything he could. He had no plan now, nothing in his head other than getting away, running away, escaping Erik, the house, everything.

Erik was silent now, still as a statue. He gripped Asher tighter, struggling to hold his hands. "Ssh. Stop fighting me, love. Easy. Easy now."

Connor appeared at Asher's shoulder. "Easy, darlin' Ye've gotta stop, or you'll hurt yourself. No one's gonna let that happen, hi. I don't want to have te deck ya, but I will. I've it done it before." He took Asher's hands and stopped them from beating on Erik "That's it . . . give me yer hands, love. It's all right. Erik's not a punchin' bag."

Asher couldn't breathe. Between the two of them, Connor and Erik were holding him so tightly he couldn't get a proper breath and started to feel light-headed and slightly hysterical. He heard the words his friends were saying to him. He even understood them, but they were meaningless, just popping into existence then floating away like bubbles. He watched them almost lazily, realizing that no matter how much he wanted to carry on fighting, his body was giving up on him.

Strangely, as his body slowed down, so did his mind, and when exhaustion and lack of oxygen made him sag against Erik's chest, a strange kind of peace descended. It was okay because Erik was here. Whatever else was going on, whatever had happened or was going to happen, right now, in this moment he was here, and Erik was here, and everything was all right. *Don't think about anything else . . . just Erik . . . Just Erik.*

With a sigh, the last of his strength left him, and he went limp in Erik's arms.

Erik was trembling, his breathing ragged, but his voice was

calm. "Easy, Asher, that's the way." He loosened his grip but still held onto him.

Connor let go of Asher's hands. "Jaysus, darlin', you're gonna have te stop doin' that. Me heart can't take it, hi. Ye all right now?" He ran a hand through Asher's tangled hair, straightening it out.

Asher gazed at him for a moment before his mind caught up and he nodded weakly.

"You need te take it easy. Will ye be wanting your bed?"

Did he? No, he didn't want to be alone. The thought terrified him.

"I want . . . I want to stay here. I don't . . . I want to be here . . . with you."

Connor glanced at Erik and then back at Asher. "Come back te our house. Ye can rest there. I'll not let anyone bother ye."

"I'll carry you upstairs to the bed there, Ash." Erik kissed his hair.

"Leave everything," Connor demanded, pulling Angel to him. "We'll come back for it later."

Asher wondered why Angel looked so scared.

Erik hoisted Asher into his arms. "I'll sit with him in the back. Hey, Red, fish out my keys, you can drive my car. Angel looks like he's gonna jump out of his skin."

Connor gave Asher a final pat. "Come on me little darlin'. Let's be getting ye home."

"Am home," Asher mumbled. He ached to curl up in the light from the windows, or maybe wander through the graveyard. Nevertheless, he allowed Erik to carry him out without a fight.

They all got into the car. Erik held Asher in the back seat while Connor drove, with Angel in the passenger seat. It was a long drive to the house, at least it seemed that way.

When they finally arrived, Erik carried him up to the bedroom and undressed him, then laid him down under the covers and kissed him. "I love you, Asher."

With a final kiss, Asher sank into Erik's arms and was fast asleep.

Erik waited for Asher to be out completely, then slowly eased away. He was exhausted, and his muscles hurt from holding on so tight for so long. Asher was strong, and fighting him was a tough task. He was grateful for Connor's help. It hurt to know Connor had witnessed this type of thing before, but at least Erik wasn't alone.

He was angry with Daisy, but the whole thing had spiraled out of control so fast. He wondered how much longer this would keep happening, if he'd have to get Connor over every time Asher freaked. Better still, how to keep it from happening at all. It made his head spin.

Asher looked so peaceful now, almost angelic. A dark angelic, though. The evil he'd seen and lived made Erik shudder every time he thought about it. He vowed silently to never leave Asher's side, also to get him some real help besides just him. It was all grating on him like metal on metal. It was wearing him down.

He stood and sneaked out the door. With a last glance at Asher, he shut it softly and padded down the stairs. Connor and Angel were huddled on the sofa, each with a shot glass in their hand and a bottle of Irish Whiskey nearby. Poor Angel, this was his first exposure to something like this, and Erik felt bad for him. It was shocking to anyone not used to it. He suddenly felt like a veteran in dealing with panic attacks.

"You all right there, Angel?"

Angel glanced up at him, his crystal blue eyes shining with tears. He looked very young, and it suddenly occurred to Erik that they all were. They were all just kids, really. This was a lot to handle for any of them, but Angel was the baby, only nineteen, and the last to join the group. He was the only one who hadn't had experience of Asher's . . . condition.

"I-I'm sorry, Erik. I should have done something, but I-I was so scared. I didn't know what was happening. I didn't know what to do. Is he all right? Is Asher all right?"

Erik rubbed his face and nodded. "He will be. He gets nasty panic attacks like this. Only a few of them have been this bad, though. Red here was around for one of them. I'm sure he's told you about it. Now you've seen one. It's fuckin' scary as hell. I don't wanna say I'm used to them, but wow, this one was really bad."

"You mean he's been like this before? Like that? Fuck. I-I didn't know. If I'd known maybe I wouldn't have . . . Last night, I should have . . . I should have told you everything."

"Hand me a shot of whiskey, wouldja, Connor?" Erik gulped the contents of the glass Connor handed him and sat on the floor to relax, let his muscles unwind. "What didn't you tell me, Angel? Just so you know, this isn't your fault. A lot of things are to blame right now — Daisy, the wedding, school, house, all of it." He lay on his back and let out a deep breath. "So . . . what'd you leave out?"

"No, I didn't mean I'd left anything out. I meant . . . well I should have known how bad it was. He did tell me. He kind of told me, but I didn't understand. I should have told you everything he said. I didn't . . . I just didn't know."

"Easy now, *a chroí*." Connor pulled Angel into his lap and wrapped his arms around him. "I know how scared ye are. I was for me life. Scared the bejaysus out of me, and no lie. Vince was flapping like an old biddy. I had to put him down. Not Vince, Asher."

Angel gasped. "You had to hit him to get him to stop?"

"Aye. Good thing I'm a scrapper. Got a good right hook on

78

me, hi. I didn't take no pleasure in it, but it got the job done. Sure, it's weighed on me heart ever since though."

"It's all right, Connor." Erik smiled at him. "I'm sure he understands why you had to do it. You were a big help today with this one, thank you."

"Ah, 'twere nothin'. I held him is all. Stopped him scratching yer eyes out. Sure, he's a hellcat at the best of times. Grow yerself some furries, sham." He stroked his beard. "Keeps the claws away, so it does." He shot Erik a smile.

Erik shook his head. "Aw, but that would keep Asher away. He hates facial hair, of any kind. Or most . . . anywhere else for that matter. I give him what he wants. Besides, I like my rockstar look, the hair does just great on its own."

"Aye." Connor glanced at Angel. "Ye feeling any better, *a chroí*?"

"Yeah." Angel wriggled deeper into Connor's lap and rested his head on his shoulder with a sigh. "So . . . Is he all right now? Asher? Is he going to be all right? He's not . . . I mean when he wakes up, he won't freak out again will he?"

"No, he's good for now. He'll sleep it off, and as long as Daisy or the wedding isn't brought up, he should be fine. Just keep things on an even keel for a while."

Connor sighed. "Aye, last time he was down for the day, and not because of me right hook."

Erik nodded and sat up to take another shot of whiskey. "Say, aren't your sister and niece around? Where have they been all day?" He glanced at Angel. "Has your dad been playing host to them all day?"

"No, he took them back to your house. They're settling in. I don't think it would be a good idea to get together with them. Caitlin's a lovely girl, but she's way too much for Asher right now. She'd have him tied up in knots."

"Aye, she's a wild one, hi. Joy of me heart, but in small doses. She's a fine eye for the boyos." He winked at Erik.

"She'll be away with yer man while ye blink." Smothering a smile, he shot a look at Angel.

"I hope you don't think you're being funny, *caro mio*, but that was not fun."

"Oh, so she had her eye on you, did she?" Erik grinned at Angel, who squirmed.

"All the way over, and a plane's not exactly the best place when you're trying to get away from someone."

Erik and Connor both chuckled and Angel glared at them.

"Anyway," Angel continued. "I think Asher's safe from her. He's already established that boundary, but it would probably be best if we keep them apart. In fact," he said wearily, "it would probably be best to keep Asher away from everyone."

Erik nodded. "Agreed, completely. I'm not leaving his side if I don't have to. You and Vince have seen it, Connor. Angel too now. Do you think you could do what we did to calm him down? Hold on as tight as you can and see it through?" He stared intently at Angel, gazing into his blue eyes. He saw fear there, but determination, too.

"I don't know. Honestly, I don't know if I could do that, but I'd try. I'd do my very best. I . . . I think it might be best to keep him away from people though . . . so we don't have to. What about the rehearsal?"

"I know you'd do your best, Angel. You're a good friend." Erik patted his leg. "Oy, shit. The rehearsal. Tomorrow freakin' night. Damn. Family, people, you name it. I'm thinking strong drugs and or alcohol will have to be used for sure. I'll be stressed out enough, and I'm somewhat sane." He chuckled. "We'll have to keep him calm. Which means I have to tell Daisy to cool it or I'll boot her Brit ass outta there. Oh, which reminds me . . ." He took out his cell phone and checked it. "She left with the daddies, right?"

"Aye," Connor affirmed.

"I'll give Billy a call, see what's up with her." He punched up the number and was happy when Billy answered. "Yo, fluffo. How's the mommy-to-be doing? She better? Uh-huh . . . really? Wow. Well, that's good. That's real good. Vince all right? Good. You're doing what? Jesus, you guys are so maternal you need bras and you're all set. All right, you take care. Hugs to you guys, too." He rolled his eyes. "Take care, fuzzball."

"What's going on?" Angel asked. "Has Daisy calmed down? Is Billy okay? Is Vince still mad at Asher?"

"It's all good now, Angel." Erik smiled and tucked his phone away. "Daisy regretted a lot of what she said. The boys took her to their house. Everyone calmed down, had some lemonade, and picked out color swatches for the nursery. It's all hunky dory right now. He said the three of them are getting along just fine and no one's mad at anyone else. You could almost hear cooing, it was so sweet." He laughed.

Connor let out a relieved sigh. "So, do we tell her about Asher, after she left? She should know."

"Should she?" Erik asked. "In her condition? I think Vince would have my head if I upset her, or at least get Angel's father to take it for him. I'm lettin' this one go, man. Let sleeping Asher lie. It's over and done. They just need to chill."

"I don't think you're right," Angel said doubtfully. "She's his sister and deserves to know. Besides, we've got the rehearsal and the wedding to get through, and we need Daisy onside to help protect him. What about his mother? Will Mrs. Berkley help? Do we need to tell her?"

Connor and Erik both laughed and shook their heads.

"Oh, hell no, Angel. Their mother is the biggest . . ." Erik started.

" . . . pain in the arse this side of the Atlantic." Connor finished.

"Amen to that one." Erik grinned at Angel. "You're such a

sweet kid. You want to help and love everybody, but wow, when it comes to Asher, he's an entirely different ball game. Keeping his family away from him is what's gonna help the most. We're his support system, not them. After what Daisy did, I hope she doesn't open her mouth around him tomorrow unless it's to say sorry."

Connor toasted him with a shot glass. "Hear, hear, ye meathead."

"I'm not even going to go into that. I've had enough for one day. What are we going to do for dinner tonight then?"

"Do you want to come up to the big house?" Angel asked. "Oh, I know. What about we take a swim? Bathing suits on this time? Asher enjoyed last time, maybe it will chill him out a bit. Then we can get some carryout and sit in the garden. It looks like it's going to be a nice night again."

"Sounds good to me. Just the four of us, I like it. Though . . ." Erik frowned. "Should we invite Billy and Vince too? They're helpful, and both great guys. I chose my best friend well." He let out a sigh. "He'll be the *best* best man. Now to just get to the wedding, sane."

"Aye, that's as may be, but he won't be after wearing a kilt. I'll be taking all the attention. I've got the legs fer it."

Erik laughed aloud. "That you do, my friend. That you do. I can vouch for that after today. Damn nice sketches of you two. Seems, Angel, you've gotten over your shyness around us, or is it just in your lover's aura?"

"As if I can be shy with Connor around. If I hadn't got over it, I'd have exploded. And . . . Asher's helped a lot. He really has been fabulous to me at school. I don't see him much, but I know he's always there. If I have a problem, I can go to him, and it helps a lot. And there have been so many things, little things, like finding me space in the end of year exhibition and taking my work to the professors when I was too nervous to do it myself. And that's without all the tips and advice he's given me about the work itself. He's amazing. If it hadn't been for you and Con, I'd have fallen head over heels for him myself." Angel laughed nervously and squeezed Connor's hand.

"Aye, but ye couldn't resist this beat up ole Irishman with his hairy legs and a heart as big as the Irish Sea. Sure, and didn't I learn to take compliments just fer ye?" He kissed Angel softly, then more deeply. "You're the love of me life, macushla."

"You too, baby. You're my forever man."

"Gawd, you two make my teeth hurt!" Erik pretended to groan. "Let's go call up the daddies-to-be and find our bathing suits. I need a serious nap first, though."

Connor finally began to feel he was settling into a semi-normal weekend, though they'd dealt with more drama than most people did in a month. He'd lay odds on it. The wedding was stressful enough, but dealing with everything else was exhausting. He'd followed Erik upstairs to lie down—it had been a hell of a long day so far.

Connor couldn't help but pause in the door to Erik's room as Erik snuggled up to Asher and they curled right into each other. It was bittersweet. They were both dear to him. He was excited to be here now to help out whenever they needed him. With a sigh, he padded into the next room and lay down beside his own piece of heaven.

Billy and Vince woke him and Angel when they arrived a short while later, and after long hugs and quick apologies for earlier, all seemed well again. They couldn't stay mad at each other for very long. They sat and chatted quietly while waiting for the other two sleeping beauties to awaken.

"Ye two come up with any names yet? Connor's a fine name in my opinion," he teased.

Billy snorted. "I was thinking William junior myself, but

I'd like something a little more . . . zesty, name-wise. A little punch to it." He leaned back into Vince's arms. "What do you think, handsome?"

"I dunno, I'd like something Italian, but then maybe something Austrian. I'm sure we'll get plenty of British suggestions, too." He thought for a moment. "I dunno . . . what about . . . Adam for a boy? Or Mark? Or . . . Thomas?"

"What about the girl?" Connor probed.

"Oy, girl names are tough. I like older names like my grandma, Ruby, or my great aunt, Eleanore," Billy offered. "Both great ladies."

"If I had a girl," Angel murmured, "I would like to call her Sophia."

"Aww, perfect name, and for Nonna." Vince smiled. "Love it. I . . . know you guys are just getting going, but Billy and I talked about kids even before we got engaged. Do you think . . ." He smiled at Angel.

Angel blushed and turned his head away. "We aren't even thinking that far ahead. We're not getting engaged or anything for a very long time. I-I haven't thought . . ." He flicked a glance at Connor. "Have you?"

Connor smiled. "Well, if ye're asking me do I want te marry ye? Aye. One day, fer sure. I can see ye makin' an honest man o' me yet. As fer babbies . . . I'll not be wanting to bring them into the mess of me life for a while yet. Sure, we're young and after wantin' a bit of life, hi. And there's me family. For the love of all that's holy, I would not put a poor innocent child in their way. Not now. I can see me bein' a daddy though, and sure Angel would be after making the sweetest little Ma you ever did see."

Angel cuffed him on the ear and laughed.

Connor sobered. "I do want te marry ye, though. If you'll have me. Or am I just a lovesick jackass for wantin' it so bad?"

"I . . . no . . . No, you're not a jackass, not at all. It's just . . .

just, I . . ." He looked so sweet but so distressed. Tears welled in his eyes and made the blue even brighter. "I . . . don't . . . It's not that I don't want to marry you Con, I do. It's just . . . There's so much change going on, so much happening in my life. I want to be with you forever, my forever man. I just . . . I don't want to get married . . . not yet. Are you mad?"

"Jesus, darlin', I wasn't after askin' ye. Not yet. Feck, yer a babby, still at school, and I'm just startin' off. But I've got me plan set out, and it's well ye should know—with you being part of it an' all."

"You two have plenty of time yet," Vince intervened. "Though we're the worst culprits—married at twenty, and now twins on the way. But it's the life we chose. Fast track for us. We're lucky. We've got loads of support from Billy's parents, and even mine helped out a time or two." He took their hands. "It should happen when it feels right. No definition, no timetable, just let the moment hit you. I did, and here I am today with my Billy."

Connor nodded. "Aye, and it's agreein' with ye fine."

"It is, Con. It really is. Take your time. Enjoy yourselves. You guys just moved in together. Hell, we lived together, what? Over a year? Then married. You've got time. It's a great daydream, hon, don't stop daydreaming, but remember reality, too. Okay?"

Connor nodded and smiled. "Aye." He got to his feet and stretched. "I'll be off to the jacks, then. Don't be after doing anything exciting while I'm gone, hi."

Connor took care of business and splashed some water on his face. He stared at his reflection, surprised by the emotion threatening to overwhelm him. He loved Angel with all his heart, and he was ready to settle down with him forever. He'd wanted to marry Shaun, too, and start a business, all of it. He'd been emotionally ready then, and he felt ready now, but reality was too much for him. He had to step outside the big picture. After straightening up his hair and drying his face, he stiffened his back and returned quietly to his seat.

"You all right?" Vince asked.

"I'm shagged. All the drama's done me in." He was aware he was running away from the situation, but he was honest about being exhausted and didn't want to get into a deep conversation right then.

"Con?" Angel sat down very close and laid his cheek against Connor's shoulder. "I'm sorry if I upset you. I do love you. You know that, right? I love you with all my heart. I'm just not ready for marriage, not yet. I'm not saying I won't marry you, though. One day."

One day seems like a lifetime right now, Angel. I can't tell you, though. He patted Angel's face and forced a smile. He'd never thought he'd ever have to force a smile in Angel's company. It seemed this was becoming a true test of their relationship. "It's all right, Angel. Maybe one day . . ."

Connor gazed into Angel's blue eyes, and for once, instead of warmth, saw a flash of coldness. Maybe it was just about him getting older, but right now he didn't want to be around anyone. Every little look, comment, or even gesture was grating on him.

He'd loved Asher and Shaun, and even Billy. Now they were all paired up, well, except Shaun, and Connor didn't particularly care where *he* was right now His head was in a right jumble, and his stomach was sour—probably from the whiskey. He was bad at dealing with emotions, and he longed to get into a good punch-up or drown his sorrows in a huge glass of Jameson's.

Billy took his hand. "You all right? You don't look well."

Connor wanted to push him away, but he couldn't. Not Billy. He'd almost wrecked his relationship two years ago, and damned if he'd screw up their friendship now. "Sure, I've got a belly on me like the pits of hell. Ain't nothin' like whiskey fire to put a man out of sorts. I dare say a few laps will help me out." He stood quickly and announced, "I'll be after getting my bathers on, then."

Connor was angry with himself. Angry and hurt. He hated being mad at Angel, and how could he live here, in Tony's house, with all this going on in his head? He was jealous of Erik and Asher, and even Billy and Vince. Their lives were set, but here he was, the oldest of them all, with nothing. He sighed. He wanted their own house and their own money and lives.

With heavy feet, he climbed the stairs to their bedroom and thought about the night before. They'd had such happiness in their homecoming, but he regretted uttering the phrase *forever man*. He wondered if it was even possible anymore. He changed into his suit, then sat down heavily, reluctant to go back.

"Con?" The hesitancy in Angel's voice cut him to the quick, and he tried to compose himself before he looked up. "Con, what's wrong? Is it something I've said, something I've done? I'm sorry, really, I am. Con . . . When I said . . . When I said I didn't want to marry you, I only meant for now. I do want to marry you, Connor, I swear I do . . . just not now."

Hesitantly, as if he were afraid, Angel sat down on the bed and ran his hand through Connor's hair, pausing to stroke his shoulder. "Con?"

Connor shrugged, refusing to look at Angel. "What can I say, *a chroí*? I'm an old man, so I am. Older than the rest of ye, but they've all got their lives squared and they're settled down. I'd never have said it, not a year ago, but . . ." He shrugged. "I was thinking, as the words were coming out of me mouth, that I don't wanna be just Connor O'Reilly anymore. I don't wanna be the man who everyone laughs at, who gets drunk and fights for fun. I want what they have. I wanna settle down, and I wanna do it wid ye." Still unable to meet Angel's eyes, he glanced up, then down, and would have turned away, but Angel caught his chin.

Connor had expected Angel's eyes to be cold, or sad or . . . but his Angel was smiling, his eyes almost dancing with amusement. "What am I going to do with you?" He had the sweetest smile on his face. "You're so silly. Jealous of everyone? Really? Everyone? Okay, Billy and Vince are set, *but* Billy's off with the band in a couple of weeks, leaving Vince all alone. Even when the babies are born, Vince is going to be spending lots of time alone when the band is touring.

"And then Daisy and Joey. Are you sure you're jealous of Joey? Seeing his girlfriend — and they've been together longer than anyone and aren't even engaged yet — having babies for someone else? Can you imagine when they're lying together at night and he's feeling the babies kick and knowing they're not his?

"And Erik and Asher? Really? Settled? Would you want to have to handle what happened this afternoon from me? And what about after they're married? Will Erik really be able to go on tour with the band, leaving Asher behind like this? Will he ever be able to go to sleep at night knowing there won't be any drama the next day, that his life will be calm and peaceful?

"I wouldn't swap with any of them, not one of them, and I wouldn't choose any life other than the one I have here with you, my darling, silly Irishman. You've got a craft now. You're going to start a job soon. You're going to build us our own house, and when it's time for us to think of children, you'll be carving their cribs. You're my forever man, Connor, and I mean it. If . . . if it really means this much to you, then I'll marry you. I'd do anything to make you happy, to not lose you."

As Connor listened to Angel's take on each couple's story, a wave of guilt washed over him. He hadn't considered the others' situations, only his own, and his own feelings. *Selfish as usual.* He sighed deeply and tugged at his hair. "Saints preserve us, Angel. What the feck would I do without ye?"

Connor pulled Angel closer and held him tight on the bed. "Come away here, macushla. I don't want ye to marry me just to make this crazy ole Irishman happy. Sure, I've seen the mess left behind when it happens. Me Ma and Da's relationship was a whole bag o' shite, so it was, and we was the ones who got hit with it. I never want te see us there, hi. I want us both te be ready, coz it's the one marriage I'm fixin' to ever have, to my forever man. I don't care if I sound like a . . . a jackass, or a bollixin' fool, ye make me crazy. I'll promise ye anything. I'll do anything. You got me by the balls."

"Yeah, you kind of sound all those . . . but I don't care. you may be a silly, lovesick jackass, but you're *my* silly, lovesick jackass, and I love you to insanity."

Connor kissed him deeply and held him close. "Aye, there's a lot of it in the air. Careful ye don't get a bad dose." He sighed and settled Angel against him. "Ah, I can wait to build ye our own house. Grand, it'll be. Every bit made with love, hi. And still, it won't be good enough, *a chroí.* God's own home would bare be good enough for my Angel."

"Aw, shush, you. You Irish with the gift of the gab. You could charm the pants of a nun, so you could."

Connor burst out laughing, stroking Angel's soft hair. "Sorry . . . fer bein' a mess right now." He tossed back his hair and cleared the rest of his face. "I'll love ye 'til the day I die, Angel Caliendo."

"You're not a mess, Connor. You're a very emotional man, just like I am. I'm very honored you've let them out with me. I know it doesn't come easy to you. You know what us Italians are like . . . laugh, cry, love, hate, emotions flowing all over the place. It's nice when my man flows all over me for a change."

"Anytime, me love. Anytime. Come on, let's go wake the

sleeping beauties. I feel charged for a swim."

After a deep kiss, they walked to the bedroom next door and knocked softly before entering.

Erik stirred and blinked at them, then yawned. "Hey, guys . . . What time is it?"

"Time for a swim, sham. Te wake us all up, hi. Are ye gonna wake yer man, Erik? Maybe Angel could do it, hi? He won't be wanting to see my ugly mug."

Erik sat up. "Good luck, Angel. He's been out for a long time."

Angel looked very nervous and shot glances at them both, but then he nodded and sat on the bed.

Angel ran his hands through Asher's hair. "Asher? Asher hun, it's Angel. It's time to wake up now." He glanced up at the other two when Asher didn't stir. Connor nodded encouragingly, and he tried again, gently shaking Asher by the shoulder and stroking his face. "Asher. Come on, *caro mio*, it's time to get up. Wake up."

Asher stirred and batted at Angel's hand. Murmuring something they couldn't hear, he turned over and snuggled into Erik.

After a small laugh, Erik shook his fiancé's shoulder again. "Asher . . . time to get out of bed, you've got school in five minutes." The other two men snickered. "The professor's been asking you to draw more pictures of your gorgeous boyfriend. Wake up, Asher. Time to go to school." He shook him some more.

"No . . ." Asher moaned. "No school. All done. No . . ."

"For goodness sake, Asher, are you in hibernation or what?" Angel giggled. "I think we should just carry him to the pool and throw him in."

"Pool?" Asher stretched sleepily, blinking at Angel. "What pool?"

"We're going swimming. Do you want to come? The bad

news is we have to wear swimsuits this time."

At first, Asher looked blank, then a slow smile spread over his face. "Really? Don't know if I want to play, then. Cramps my style."

Erik laughed. "Your style? To play X-rated Marco Polo or do backflips into the water?" he joked. "Come on, get up, baby. Billy and Vince are here, too. It's the six of us tonight."

Connor stretched, his back popping. "I've got some elastics in me bag," he said to Asher. "Keep me wild mop from throttling me in the water. De ye want one?"

"Elastics? Elastic bands?" Asher sat up. "Do you have any idea how much damage it does to your hair? I'm getting married on Saturday, do you really want to be responsible for split ends?"

Erik rolled his eyes. "Oy, you and your hair. Now we've got two of you. Unreal. I'm gonna go get changed. I can't wait to dive into the pool again." He got up and left the room, trunks in hand.

"Angel . . ." Asher's voice was soft and quiet. "I-I know it must have been hard for you this afternoon. I'm really, really sorry. I didn't mean . . . I meant what I said to you last night. After the wedding, I-I'm gonna get this figured out once and for all. Are you still okay to help me tomorrow night?"

Angel hesitated a moment, then nodded. "Yeah."

Asher beamed. "Would you mind if I had a quick chat with Connor . . . on our own?"

Angel glanced quickly at Connor. He nodded to let him know it would be okay. Turning back to Asher, Angel smiled and then disappeared. After he'd gone, silence fell and things got awkward for a time.

"I . . ." Asher licked his lips and dropped his head. "I . . . We keep coming here, don't we? You and me. You've seen the worst of me and you're still here. I . . . I'll never be able to tell you how much you mean to me, Con. I swear you're the best friend any man has a right to hope for."

Connor sat on the bed, a bit awkwardly, and shrugged. "Sure, you're madder than a bucket of frogs, but I'd not change ye for the world. Ye're the best thing that ever happened to me, and without you, I'd never have found me Angel."

Asher smiled and touched his face. "You know . . . if it hadn't been for Erik . . ."

Connor nodded, glancing up to meet his gaze. "I know. We were never meant to be, and now you've got Erik, and I've got Angel, but . . . God help me, but I'll love ye to me last breath. Crazy fucker."

Asher snorted, and they grinned at each other for a moment, then he sobered and chewed on his lip ring. "I was thinking. Now you're here . . . in the US, so close . . . I-I was thinking it isn't fair for me to keep part of you that really should be Angel's. You're my friend, and now I have you close by. I can see your face and feel your arms around me whenever I need to, I . . ." He glanced down at the ring he'd been twirling round and round his thumb. Slipping it off, he handed it to Connor. "I don't need this when I have you, so I thought it might be better if you gave it to Angel. It doesn't mean I didn't and don't appreciate it, Con, it's not that. It's just . . . well . . . I just somehow feel Angel should have this and not me."

Connor took the ring and held it in his fingers. He'd not touched it in nearly two years. Their relationship had changed from one of lust and need to a solid friendship and true understanding. Asher was right. It should go to Angel, the one who had his heart . . . the one whose arms he longed for. "I will . . . as long as you keep holding me in yer heart and I can come cry on your shoulder, too."

"Anytime. We can cry on each other. I promise I'll try not to freak on you if you promise you won't hit me again."

Connor chuckled. "I'm not after promisin' ye. What with ye being so crazy, an' all. Wouldn't be fair of me get your hopes up, hi."

Asher laughed and drew Connor in for a gentle kiss. Then he bounded off the bed and disappeared out the door, leaving Connor feeling strangely melancholy.

CHAPTER EIGHT

Vince glanced up when Erik and Asher came downstairs. He leaped immediately to his feet and hugged them both. "How are you doing? You're looking better, Asher."

"Good to see you, Vince. Sorry about earlier..." Erik started.

"Chill out, Nordgren," Billy teased him as they hugged. "It's all okay now. I wanna go swimming." He turned to Vince. "Remember, I can be your buoy?"

Vince chuckled, remembering the moment this joke had been born. It had been a balmy night in London when a nervous Vince and his boyfriend had sailed up the Thames after a perfect day together. They'd laughed and joked and then it had turned deadly serious when Vince went down on one knee and asked the person around whom his world revolved to marry him.

"Okay, race you to the pool. Last one in's a rotten egg," Asher tore off with everyone racing after him.

"Oy, here we go!" Vince laughed and took off after his friends.

Erik and Asher had the advantage. Erik's super-long legs and athletic build were a natural combo, and Asher's training ensured he was out in front with Erik. Behind them were Angel and Billy. Billy was taller, but not a runner. Angel seemed to be doing fine, given his shorter legs. At least, he outpaced his redheaded companion. Determined not to be last, Vince kept his eye on Connor, who was keeping pace far too easily for such a short man. They were neck-and-neck.

"I'm gonna getcha, Con! This big ol' Italian can hoof it when he needs to!" he teased.

"Ha. I've legged it from too many Garda to be caught by you."

Vince laughed, but he kept pace until the very end. In front of him, they all made their entrances into the massive pool. Erik dove right in, with perfect form, Asher did a forward flip, and Angel jumped. Billy held up at the last minute and jumped in a little more carefully, which made Vince smile — had to be safe! At the last minute, Connor got out ahead of him and jumped cannonball style. Vince slowed, jumped in alongside Billy, and tried to catch his breath.

"Woo! Damn! Nice job, guys! Erik, those legs of yours are an unfair advantage!" he teased. "You're so tall!"

"You did great, Vince, come on. I saw you two come in, nearly tied! You slowed up at the end there."

Billy waded over to him. "Hey, we gotta play it safe. Parents to be! Plus, we're not daredevils like you guys. You know that. I've never been the thrill seeker you are."

"Fuddy-duddies." Connor joked.

Angel playfully slapped Connor. "Behave. Not everyone has to be a cannonball. Some of us prefer to be more leisurely in the way they throw themselves at life. Not that I'm one for dipping my toe in the water first."

"It sure wasn't just yer toe ye dipped last time," Connor recalled. "Feck, the look on yer da's face . . ."

"I'll never forget it," Erik agreed. "I take life full frontal, don't I, baby?" He winked at Asher.

"I don't know. I'm usually too busy staring at your arse," Asher responded with a wink back, then took off swimming furiously.

It was amazing to watch. He was as graceful and powerful in the water as on the land. Usually, he was playful, but today he seemed to be swimming with the intent to drive the stress away, and it made Vince's head spin.

He waded over to Erik. "So, everything better? It appears so. I was worried. I remember that time two years ago . . ."

"It's all over now, Vince. It's fine. He'll be okay if we can keep him calm, or like this, happy doing something he loves."

"I'm all for that." Billy agreed. "Come on, let's float."

Vince relaxed against the side of the pool, watching his friends play, with a smile on his face.

His mind clicked back to earlier that day when things went nuts at Erik and Asher's house and he'd yelled at Asher for pushing his sister. He hated to yell at anyone. He still considered Asher one of his best friends. He waded over to Asher and tapped him on the arm. "Hey, can we chat for a sec?"

Asher shook his head, getting the water out of his ears, then wiped his eyes. "Sure, Vince. Listen . . . I'm sorry about earlier. I . . . wasn't myself. I shouldn't have yelled, and I shouldn't have pushed Daisy. It was absolutely right of you to be pissed with me but . . . I really don't want that to mess up our friendship. We've got too much history to let it go because of . . . because . . . I really don't want to lose you as a friend, Vince."

"I know, and I understand. I feel really protective of her, not just because she's carrying our children, but she's a friend, too." He brushed Asher's arm and looked up into his lilac eyes. "I don't want anything to wreck our friendship, Asher. I'm good with you if you're good with me." He smiled softly.

"I'm good. You were right, I should never have got into an argument with Daisy. I know she's under stress, too, and with her being pregnant . . ." He shrugged sadly, his focus on the water.

Then Asher grinned unexpectedly, and despite his deep and secure love for Billy, Vince's stomach did a little flutter. How could it not? Ash was so beautiful it was almost unreal.

Asher shook his head. "I can't believe she's going to have

twins, and you're going to be their dad. I'm gonna be an uncle. Freaky."

Vince laughed. "You can be Uncle Freaky — or Uncle Ash." Noting a shadow pass across Ash's face, he sighed and quickly changed the subject. "I'm thrilled to death she's doing this for us. To become a father? Wow. It's mind-boggling, but we're so ready for it. I'm literally loving this. I know Billy is too, isn't that right, baby?"

Billy bounced over. "What did you say?"

"Our babies. You're as excited as me."

Billy grinned. "Definitely! Our happy household of four. And all the uncles . . ." He laughed.

"Well, one thing's for sure," Asher said. "Those kids are never gonna be short an ear to bend or a shoulder to cry on. And between the artists, the craftsman, the poets, and the chef, their school projects are gonna rock."

Vince nodded and laughed along with Billy.

"Holy cow, is that ever right? Can you imagine just a birdhouse? Angel designs it, Connor builds it, Asher paints it, and Erik makes up the birdsong." Billy shook his head. "What kind of group have we built here, Vince?"

"The best kind ever." He smiled at his husband and turned to Asher. "Did I tell you? We chose colors already. Now we just need to finish the room off."

"What's this about finishing a room?" Connor asked as he waded over to join the conversation.

Billy laughed and hopped on Connor's back. "Aye! We need a fine Irish builder who can finish 'em off, so we do!" He held onto Connor while they all laughed until Connor finally dunked down and shook him off.

Asher swam away grumbling about them turning into boring old farts, but Vince didn't care. So what if he'd grown up faster than the rest of them. It was his life, and he was more than happy with it. "Seriously, Connor, we're more than grateful for your help."

"It's what I'm here for, sham. Give us a shout when ye know what ye want. I'll even show ye to paint proper. I swear most of ye don't know yer arses from yer elbows when ye've got a brush in yer hand, hi."

"Well, come on over sometime in the next few days, or we'll pick you up and go to the hardware store. We've gotta get this decided before Billy goes away." He pouted.

Billy hugged him. "Aw baby, I won't be gone forever. You can send me photos, but I'll miss working on it, though. I love doing that stuff. Dad taught me a lot. I just can't be physically here. Thank goodness for friends."

Erik joined them. "Hey, guys. What's this about friends?" He put an arm around Asher and the other around Billy. "How's my best man doing?"

"Doing great. Can't wait to see you married off, you juggernaut." Billy stuck his tongue out and dived at Erik, chasing him when he swam away, with loud encouragement from the others.

Vince caught Billy and pulled him close, no longer horsing around. "Well, I won the battle of the rooms; there'll be just one. I wanna get the nursery done asap. I think beadboard with the colors we chose is perfect. Soft shades, lighting, plus the cribs and changing tables, the dresser . . . and two rocking chairs."

"Ahh, taking shifts with everything. Of course, I'll be back by the time they're born, since they're kinda touring with us, inside Daisy of course."

"But you'll be gone again, and I'll have the *uncles* helping out. And my mom will camp out for sure. Yours and mine both." Vince laughed.

Erik jumped in. "You all set for the tour? I need to get with Joey and make sure he's good, too." He kissed Asher. "Sucks leaving, being newlyweds at the time."

Asher gave Erik a strange look but smiled and patted him. "At least I'll be with you for a little while. We'll have ten days in London, just the two of us before everyone else flies out and the craziness begins. I've got so many plans, so many things I want to show you." Looping his arms around Erik's neck, Asher laid his head on Erik's well-muscled chest.

Erik, laughing and embracing his man, couldn't see the look on Asher's face, but Vince could, and it made him frown. Asher glanced up and caught his eye. He smiled, but it was a strained one. Hmm, maybe he should just stay out of it.

"London's so beautiful, I had to see it myself. The Eye of London was the best." Vince elbowed Billy.

"Ha! The best? I was scared shitless! You harangued me into the cage! You knew I was petrified of heights," Billy teased.

"Was, being the operative word, my love. You calmed down and enjoyed the view after a few minutes."

"Well, I had you to hang on to." He looped his arms around Vince's neck and laid his head on Vince's chest. "It was exciting."

"What's going on over here?" Angel asked, jumping on Connor's back from behind and dunking him. "A guy could get a complex, being left out in the cold."

"Sorry, cous. We weren't excluding you, I guess we all kinda gravitated together. You're the new kid in the group. We have to build your orbit around Connor here." He winked at them. "You guys all right . . . from . . . ya know?"

"Aye. 'Twas a bit o' nothin'." He patted Vince's shoulder and held Angel closer. "That right, *a chroí*?"

"He's an old fool, Vince. He'll fit into our family just fine." Angel hugged Connor tighter. "He's my forever man, so don't ever forget it."

Vince wasn't sure if he was talking to him or Connor. Either way, it made him smile.

"Who ye callin' old?" Connor teased Angel. "Yer naught but a babby, ye are. With the face of an angel and eyes that tied me head in a knot and shot me straight in the balls."

Angel snorted. "I was aiming for your heart."

"Aye, ye got that with yer second shot, but I've always been one for leading with me dick, hi."

Angel almost choked and threw his arms around his lover, kissing him hard.

Billy prodded Vince and waggled his eyebrows.

"Oh! Yes, thanks, hon. Always good to get a prod from you." Vince joked and everyone laughed. "Guys, we wanted to ask you something."

"Which us?" Erik asked.

"Connor and Angel, actually." Vince took Billy's hand. "We've been talking about the future, and the kids, and we'd love it if you two would agree to be godfathers to them."

"What?" Angel gaped and exchanged a look with Connor. "Godfathers? Us? Well, I . . . I-I don't know about Connor, but I'd love to. Thank you so much." He threw his arms around Vince and hugged him so tightly he almost drowned him.

Billy shook his head at their antics and looked at Connor. "How about it, Con? Ye're a good man, with a heart of gold. You'd be perfect for it, if you'd say yes?"

"We'd love it, Connor," Vince added.

"Aye. If yer sure ye want a bit o' baggage like me te be a bad influence on them, I'd be honored to stand for them."

"Awesome choices," Asher said, popping up again. He ruffled Angel's hair, showering everyone with droplets of water that flew from the sodden locks. "They'll get both a sexy godfather and a useful one."

Vince laughed. "Okay, I'm afraid to ask who the useful one is. They're both sexy, ya know, for one of them being my cousin and all." he laughed.

"Aye, good point. We're both the sexy ones, I think. Which

one were ye thinkin', Asher?"

"Ah, but I'd hate to make either of you feel inadequate, so I'll leave it to your imagination. In our relationship, of course" — Asher glanced up and grinned at Erik, who immediately swam over — "I am both the sexy and the useful one."

"Are you talking about me? Telling everyone how sexy I am?"

"Nah, educating them on the fact that I am both the sexy and useful one in our relationship," Asher said, adding a cheeky grin.

"Oh, is that so?" Erik grinned and held Asher closer.

"Yeah," Billy chimed in, "although you're not too far behind. What?" He grinned at Asher. "We can't risk damaging his ego too much, he might bleed out."

Asher snorted.

"You're both perfect for the role, I think," Vince said to Connor and Angel. He dismissed the other couple's antics with a shake of his head.

Connor held Angel close and grinned at Vince. "Now that's all straight, what ye gonna call the wee ones? Any ideas from the British duo?"

Asher shrugged. "If you want. Hmm . . . Poppy and Paul. Or Lulu and Luke. Or Ditzy and Mitzy?" He laughed. "I'm crap at choosing names. Daisy's already had me trying and laughed at them all. So I'm keeping out of it." The smile dropped off his face. "I'm keeping out of everything."

Vince scowled. "Asher? You all right?" He put a hand on his arm. "What does that mean, you're staying out of everything? We want you involved in their lives, you're the only uncle who's actually around. Paulie sure as hell wants nothing to do with me. We want you around, Ash." He gazed into Asher's lilac eyes, but wasn't sure about what he saw anymore.

"Hey, is anybody else starving?" Erik broke in, putting an

arm around Asher. "It's all right, Vince. Maybe we'll talk more when we get back. We've got time yet, okay?" He widened his eyes at Vince and backed away.

"Um, yeah. It's fine. I'm sorry, I seem to be the instigator of uncomfortable conversations today." Vince tried to smile but bowed his head and stepped back.

Billy took his hand. "Come on, baby, let's go to dinner. You didn't do anything wrong, there's just a high level of stress. If anything, you're helping get it out in the open. You're sweet and helpful, my handsome hubby." He kissed him softly. "Let's go eat, okay? Guys? You coming?"

Asher shook his head. "I didn't mean that. I'll be there for your kids Vince . . . I hope. It's this freaking wedding and Daisy's obsession with it I'm having nothing more to do with." He sighed. "I'm freaking everyone out today. Maybe I should just go home. Get out of your way so you can enjoy the rest of your day."

"Not a chance." Erik hooked an arm around Asher's neck. "You're going back to the little house, getting dressed, and taking your man to dinner."

Asher stared at Erik for a moment, then grinned. "If you say so . . . *man*."

After a quick shower, Angel dressed carefully and stretched out on the bed watching Connor brushing out his hair. He loved the way it shined when he stood underneath the light. After playing around in the pool, he felt heavy and sleepy and relaxed.

"I can't believe Vince and Billy asked us to be godparents. See . . . they have faith. They have faith in us, and that we're going to be together forever. I told you . . . my forever man."

"Aye, that, or they saw the other choices and ran scared. Could ye just imagine Asher as a godfather? Saints preserve us!" He flailed, making Angel laugh. He finished brushing out his hair and faced Angel. "I have faith in us, Angel, I do. I know it in me heart. But I'm scared to me bones ye'll wake up and see what a feckin' mess I am. I'm a hard man, Angel. I've been around, hi. I'm no angel, nowhere close. That, and I'm an old man beside ye."

Angel almost choked. "Old? Connor, you're not twenty-two yet, and I'm not twenty. Two years is fuck all."

"Aye, it's true enough, but I'm not gonna lie, I mostly feel much older, hi. I've done more in me life than ye've dreamed of, and most of it was hard and brutal. I'm a hard man and all of this is new. I'm a joker and a fighter, a fucker, not a lover. All this . . ." He swept his hand around the room, but Angel knew he meant more. "It puts the fear of God in me. I'm waiting fer ye, or someone else, to yank me back by the collar and say *this isn't fer ye, Connor O'Reilly. Get back in the gutter where ye belong.*"

"Do you think it's not scary to me too? Things have changed so fast for me recently. It's been less than a year, and already my whole life's been turned on its head, and then some. Sometimes I feel like . . . I get really insecure sometimes, Con. I think, here I am, this kid with no life experience, no experience at all, playing at being a grownup in a real relationship with a real man. I wonder when you're going to wake up and realize you're babysitting, not in an equal relationship. You're so . . . strong and brave and wise and . . . worldly. I feel like a pathetic baby next to you, and it's got nothing to do with age."

Connor sat beside him. His long hair tumbled over his shoulder. "Ah, yer no babby, my love. I remember my first love. I was fifteen and out o' me head with it, hi. He was a gutter rat, like me. Steal the fillings from yer teeth while ye were yawning, but he had a body on him, so he did. And eyes deep enough to make an angel cry." Connor smiled sadly and sighed. "Scared the shit out o' me, it did. Sneakin' around. Quick gropes in the back alley. Fucking in some bastard's garden shed knowing if we were caught, we'd get the hammering of our lives. This ain't nothin' like that, you and me. This is special. It's pure." He laughed. "Besides, yer getting a great education now between the lot o' us."

"An education? That's for sure. Better than any boarding school I've ever been to by a mile, and it's a school I really enjoy attending." He wound his arms around Connor's neck, pulling his head down, and kissed him. "You're beautiful, Connor. I love every bit of you."

"Are you two ever going to be ready?" Asher's impatient voice demanded from the other side of the door. "I'm hungry."

"Why don't you and Erik go ahead," Angel waggled his brows and licked his lips at Connor. "We'll follow in a couple of minutes."

"See, Erik," Asher yelled. "I told you there were shagging again."

Angel looked at Connor and they both collapsed in fits of laughter as Asher's footsteps retreated down the stairs.

Connor strolled beside Angel on the path leading back to the main house. It was dusk, not quite dark, but the fairy light twinkling in the trees guided their way. The evening seemed to have a unique quality to it, the sound of their feet on the gravel crisp and clear. The voices of their friends on the terrace ahead carried to them clearly through the still air. The lights of the house were on and bright, spilling in great pools onto the patio and beyond to the lawns.

Connor was grateful the warm day had cooled considerably. He'd never quite grown accustomed to the heat in Italy when he was there. Ireland was cool and damp, but it held so many bad memories he didn't want to live there anymore, only visit at most.

His life had straightened out, to an extent. At least school was done now, and he could work, and be with his fella and his friends. Ah, his fella. Beautiful Angel, the blue-eyed beauty who'd taken his heart by storm. He'd fought it and fought it until he was forced to surrender. Now he was fully engulfed in the fire of love. *Aye, and getting a sentimental old fool with it.*

He looked down at their joined hands as they walked slowly to the house along the lit path. The wind caught their hair and momentarily intertwined it, red and black together. He loved long hair and was happy Angel did, too.

He kissed his boyfriend's hand. "Are ye hungry, *a chroí*? I'm starved after swimming and actin' like a babby with their rattle up their arse."

"You weren't a baby, Connor. You were honest. Emotional honesty is the hardest of all, and I totally respect you for it."

Just his words alone made Connor's heart warm, and he smiled. "Thank ye, darlin'. I'm nowt but a tool that hides away from anything honest or hard, hi. Talk about sticking me head up me arse. I was eatin' shit for so long it's all that ever came out of me mouth."

"Charming image to take to dinner. Thanks for that."

"Proves me point though, eh? The likes of me don't belong with the likes of ye. Not that there's a damn thing I can do about it. You're stuck wid me, so ye are. Stuck like glue. Yer even teaching this old fool that a few tears here an' there are not such a terrible thing after all."

"That's because it's not a terrible thing. I thought you'd have realized from the number of times you've seen me — and my cousins — cry. Did you see the way Gianni blubbed when we said goodbye? Who would have thought I'd be sorry to say goodbye to those two meatheads?"

Connor laughed aloud. "I sure didn't. Aye, I guess it's not

so bad if I have ye and our friends to turn to." He glanced at his ring, thinking of how he and Asher had pledged to be there for each other . . . shoulders to cry on forever. "Angel . . . if I gave ye somethin', would ye take it?"

Angel smiled. "I love you, Con. If there's something you want to give me, how could I refuse it?"

"I love ye too, Angel. With all me heart and soul. I . . ." He took off the Claddagh ring and held it up. "Do ye know what this ring symbolizes? A Claddagh ring?"

Angel narrowed his eyes. "It's kind of a friendship ring, isn't it? Asher explained it once. Hang on, Is that Asher's ring?"

"Aye. I gave it to him a long time ago, when things were bad. Worse than they are now. We'd . . . um . . . got close. I was there fer him, but he had to go away, so I gave him the ring, a piece of me to keep close, to keep him safe."

"And he did. He did keep it close. All this time. Why did you take it back?"

"I didn't . . . he gave it back to me, today, said he doesn't need remindin' of me when he can see me ugly mug whenever he wants."

"I see." Angel was blushing a little and gave Connor such a hot little look from under his eyelashes it sent a flush through Connor's body. "So, what did you have in mind to do with it?"

Connor loved the look. So cute yet so seductive. Angel wasn't a minor anymore, he was a young man, a very sexy one at that. The longer hair made him look even more incredible. "It's a piece of me, me darlin', of me heart, and I want to give it to ye, as a sign of my love, hi." He gazed hopefully into Angel's mesmerizing blue eyes.

"Oh, Connor, I . . ." Angel's smile blinded him. "It's so . . . Wait. Just wait there, Connor. Don't move."

Connor watched in shock and Angel took off, running back

toward the little house. A bolt of insecurity shot through him, as he was left holding the ring, but he had faith in their year-old relationship which had already weathered a lot of storms, with travel, schooling and so many separations. He twirled a long lock of his hair and even chewed on it as his nerves grew. His emotions were in a jumble, until . . . He heard running footsteps and saw Angel heading back to him. His heart soared and he smiled.

"I couldn't . . . I couldn't let you give me a piece of your heart without having something to give back. Hold your hand out."

Slightly hesitant, Connor held out his hand and Angel slipped a ring onto his finger. It was . . . gold, with a brilliant blue gem in the center. On one side of the stone was a Pisces symbol, on the other side was a symbol representing his art. Connor stifled a gasp.

"My class ring." Angel beamed with a bright smile. "I never had one before. It's not a thing in the schools I went to in Europe. They're far too posh. It was the first thing I got when I started college and found out about them. It means a lot to me. It made me feel like I belong."

"A-Angel . . . it's fecking fierce! Are ye . . . are ye sure?"

"It's only fair, my darling Irish leprechaun. You give me a piece of you, and I give you a piece of me. We'll *live in each other's hearts,* as that cheesy song says, and as long as you're with me, I'll always belong."

Connor turned his hand so the light caught the stone, making it sparkle. "Sure, and that's some pretty stone, what is it?"

"It's Aquamarine, a gemstone. It's supposed to give you courage and fortitude. Maybe now you'll stop being so scared of losing me. You have a piece of me I can't live without, so you know I'm not going anywhere."

He was terrified of losing Angel, but if he was too scared, he'd make it happen somehow. He couldn't allow that. He gave Angel the Claddagh ring. "Aye, I will, or I'll drive meself mental, hi." He laughed. "I'll take what comes and focus on me deadly fella and his fine arse."

Angel yelped when Connor smacked his ass, then laughed and put the ring on his finger, holding it up to the light as Connor had with his. "I love it, Connor, really love it. Thank you." He threw his arms around Connor and hugged him close. "I really, really love you. You're the best boyfriend ever." He kissed Connor sweetly, then grinned at him. "For God's sake, don't go mental. One crazy person in the group is quite enough."

Connor laughed. "Aye, you're right there, me love." He cupped Angel's face. "I love ye to the ends of the earth, me angel." He tipped Angel's head back and kissed him deeply as their arms wrapped around each other. "Shall we go show the others . . . and eat of course."

"That's the best idea I've heard for ages. I'm starving."

Linking his arm with Connor's, Angel practically bounced along the path. His excitement was contagious. By the time they got to the terrace, they were both laughing and more relaxed than they'd been for days.

As they drew close, Caitlin ran out to meet them. "Uncle Con!"

She wore a huge smile when Connor bent to greet her, though she was almost his height. He picked her up and swung her around.

"Me darlin' Caitlin! What've you been up to today, me love?" He kissed her cheek, and she twirled his long hair.

"I've been playing with Mam and Uncle Tony. He's not me real uncle, not like you, but he said I could call him that. He's got a fierce house. There's a feckin' massive pool, and he said I could swim whenever I want. Will ye bring me . . . will ye? Go on, Uncle Connor, go on."

"Whoa, whoa there, me darlin'. Right now, it's time to eat."

He tapped her on her freckled nose. "I promise I'll take ye. Do ye mind if Angel comes too?" He figured he'd give her the option if she was comfy with Angel yet. They had only just met, after all.

"Sure, an' I won't be minding if yer fella dives in, Uncle Con. I'll see if his body's as pretty as his face, so I will." She batted her eyelashes at Angel and skipped off back to the table.

"Has she always been like that?" Angel asked a laughing Connor. "I mean . . . er . . . so forward?"

"Only since she was ten. She's a sweetheart, just a flirt. Dunno where she gets it."

He whistled sarcastically and walked to the table.

CHAPTER NINE

Billy couldn't help but breathe in the wonderful scents of the veritable feast laid before them. Marisol was an excellent cook, almost comparable to his own Vince, who was getting better every day. He looked around the table and was so happy to see nearly all his friends in one spot, plus two new ones, Nora and Caitlin. That girl was a pip for sure, inquisitive, charming, and funny, with a mouth that'd stop you cold. She was a chip off the ol' block of her uncle for sure.

He started on his bread and noticed something glinting on Connor's finger. "Hey ... what's that?" He looked closer. "Aww, you guys exchanged rings? That's so cool."

Angel and Connor exchanged startled glances. "Umm yeah," Angel said. "Thanks."

"Engagement rings?" Tony asked sharply, from the head of the table, narrowing his eyes at Connor.

"No, Papa," Angel said, coloring at Tony's sharp tone. "Friendship rings, that's all. Or ... maybe a little more ... but not engagement rings. Not that we haven't talked about it." He rallied, jutting his chin. "I just don't feel ready yet."

"Humph," Tony grunted. "Take your time. I've had enough wedding planning for a while."

"Amen to that," Asher commented, raising his glass and emptying it in a single draught.

Erik cut in. "It'll all be over soon, no worries. Then we can relax in the grip of the London fog." He draped his arm over the back of his chair.

"Maybe this time you can enjoy it," Vince added. "Not be

in a hospital half the time." He smiled at Asher. "It has so many great sights. You've got to send loads of photos back."

"I second that." Billy agreed. He glanced at Nora and Caitlin. "Have either of you ever been far out of Ireland?"

"Not as far as this," Caitlin piped up. "I've been to London, t'ree times, so I have. I've been on de London Eye, and to the Tower of London and Madame Tussauds. Me da used to say if I kept on bein' so precious I'd have me own model there one day. I intend fer that, I do. I'm gon'ter be a famous actress or a model."

"I believe you." Angel gave Caitlin a broad smile. "You've certainly got the looks and personality."

"I don't know," Asher said dryly. "Don't you have to actually shut your mouth when you're having your photo taken? Oh, and when you're on stage, I thought you had to take direction and shut up when it's not your turn to speak."

Caitlin glared at him. "Well, ye can keep yer mouth shut when ye like, ye gobshite. I know all about you, so I do. Ye're a freakin' head job, and as if I give a toss about what ye think."

Silence fell for a moment, then Nora gasped. "Caitlin! That's enough. How dare you! For one thing, since when did you think it was acceptable to use that kind of language at the table. And second, you apologize to Asher, right now."

Asher shook his head and laughed. "Don't worry, I asked for it, and it isn't as if she's wrong." He lifted his glass to her. "You go, girl. Never lose the spark. Don't let the bastards grind you down . . . and all that."

Caitlin went purple and lowered her head, her curls covering her face. After a moment's silence, everyone started talking again, although, Billy noticed Caitlin was stealing glances at Asher from under her hair.

Billy savored the salad that came next, Caesar, of course. He addressed Nora again. "So, Nora, what do you do for a living? Have you been looking for a job around here? I hope the old student house is working out for you."

"I work freelance, so my work is wherever the computer is. I'm a journalist and regular correspondent and article writer for a couple of cookery websites. I'm in the middle of writing my own cookery book actually — traditional foods from around the world. I was hoping I might pick your brains for some Italian recipes."

Vince's face practically lit up when he heard that. "I'm a student chef, Nora. I'd love to share some of the recipes I've made up. I got my grandmama's old-world ones too, straight from Italy." He grinned widely, and Billy patted his shoulder.

"There ya go, hon. Perfect for you. Vince's Vittles or something, huh?"

"I love it. You're so creative, Billy." Vince pulled him close. "You're gonna rock our kids' worlds. Think of how creative they'll be with you!" He looked at Nora. "I'd love to talk with you anytime, Nora. I've got free evenings for the most part . . . if you don't mind me doing some homework too."

"Homework of the cookery kind? Sure, would be my pleasure. I'm always lookin' for something to write about. Maybe I can do an article on what it's like to be a student chef. I've already spoken to Daisy about some of her family recipes. She's a lovely girl, so excited about the babies."

Before Vince could respond, Caitlin, bouncing back once more, piped up. "Sure, an' that's a quare thing, if it isn't. Why is Daisy having babbies fer ye? She's yer friend, and" — she tossed her curls in Asher's direction — "his sister. Ain't that weird?"

Everyone chortled or stifled a laugh, at least. Billy took Vince's hand.

"Aye, she's a marvelous friend, and that's why we asked her if she'd do us the honor of carrying our children for us. Not like we could do it ourselves." He winked at the girl.

Erik laughed. "Hardly, unless one of you has something

you need to tell us."

Vince's hazel eyes glittered with amusement. "No, no. Nothing like that. But they will be our children. They'll carry our DNA, and Daisy's. As Asher and Daisy are twins, they'll have a splash of Asher, too." He made a scary motion and laughed. "He's not so bad, Caitlin. You two are more alike than you think."

"I dunno." Billy laughed. "I think she's worse. I think she's just like her uncle." He nudged Connor.

"What're ye draggin' me in for?" Connor pretended to be angry. "I love me sister's child, so I do. Since her Da died, I've tried me best for her."

Caitlin snorted. "Sure, ye tried." She patted his hand. "I'm sure ye tried hard, Uncle Connor, but ye're not exactly a good role model, are ye?"

Connor laughed. "Awae wid yer cheek. Sure, I'm a damn fine role model, hi. I'm set up, so I am. I've got a trade and a job, and a damn fine fella." He winked. "And the love of me family, even the cheeky little scrap like ye." He glanced at his sister. "Where the feck did she get the mouth on 'er?"

"You have to ask? Ye're not her only uncle, remember. And her Gran and Granda, too. Sure, she's a grand kid, but sometimes it's like I'm sharing my home with a particularly frustrating housemate."

"Mama," Caitlin gasped, her big green eyes flashing. "Sure, an' that was a savage thing to say about yer baby girl. An' me the sweetest colleen ye ever had the luck to be blessed with."

"I'm thankin' the saints every day, sweetheart," Nora said with a smile.

"Well in the least, I'm not sellin' me body te make babies for a pair o—"

"That," Nora snapped, her eyes blazing at her daughter, "will be *quite* enough, thank you. If you want to stay for the rest of the meal, you will sit quietly and behave yourself. Any more nonsense and I'll be takin' ye home."

"Sad. Am I not to speak me mind now? Weren't ye the one te say—"

"I never said be rude, Caitlin and that's exactly what you're being. Tony was kind enough to invite us into his home, and I won't have his hospitality abused. You will sit quietly, and you will behave, and if you're very lucky and I forget you're here, you might make it to the end of the evening. *And* you will apologize for your behavior."

"Sure, and I did nothin' wrong."

"Apologize, Caitlin."

"I'm sorry," she said to her plate, not sounding the least bit contrite

Vince stood, his chair scraping as he pushed it back. "I know you're a little girl, Caitlin, so I'll let it go, but in future I suggest you think before you say such awful things about something so beautiful."

Without another glance at anyone, Vince took off at a fast pace down the garden. Billy followed.

"Wait up, Vince! Wait!" Billy was short of breath by the time he reached his angry blond. "What the hell was that all about?" He put his hands on his knees and breathed deeply, then straightened. "Talk to me. You can still talk to me, you know that, right?"

"I know, I know." Vince shook his head. "Gawd, this has just not been a good day overall. The incident with Asher and Daisy, now this . . ." He paused. "Is this what we're gonna face all the time? You'll get it worse. You'll be with her when she's growing." He paused and gave a deep sigh. "You get to be with her and feel them moving, I won't! I'll miss a lot of that stuff. Then there's lil miss mouthy at the table there. It makes me scared of what our daughter will be like!" He huffed and turned around.

114

Billy pensively put a hand on his hubby's shoulder. "Ssh . . . Hey. She's thirteen, and if I recall, not even I was a saint at that age, baby. She's mouthy, yes, but she doesn't understand. We do." He massaged Vince's shoulders. "Hey, look at me."

Vince turned around slowly. "What?"

"This is our deal, not hers or anyone else's. End of story. Ignore everyone else. Only we matter, and Daisy and our children. We're a family, baby. Just us. Don't worry about Asher. They're twins, and you know what they're like. They're always getting into it. He's not doing so well right now, but he'll get back to normal after the wedding. Well, as normal as he ever is."

Billy tried to garner a smile out of Vince but didn't get much of one. "Look, yeah I'll be with her when the babies are growing, but I won't be with them after. Besides, I'll be Daisy's little manservant on tour, I know it. Even Joey is second place right now. Imagine how he feels. You'll be here for all the important things, like first words and steps. I'll probably miss most of it." He brushed back Vince's hair. "It's not just that, though, is it? Something else is bothering you. What is it, baby? Tell me, please?"

Vince sighed and dried his eyes. "I just . . . I heard from Paulie."

"Oh shit! Really? What'd he want?"

"Not much, just to tell me I'm sick and evil for doing what we're doing. He's such an ass, Billy. I hope you never meet him, but I know you could stand up to him. He used to be a decent brother, 'til I came out, then he became the jackass extraordinaire."

"I could think of a lot or worse words to describe him. Don't take it to heart, love. He's nothing. His opinions don't matter. You're not evil, you're perfect just as you are to all our friends, the friends who love you, and of course to me. You're not just my hubby, you know. You're my best friend, even over Erik. I love you 'til death, baby, hell, even after that."

Vince pulled him in for a sweet kiss and a long hug. "You're right, you're right. I'm so sorry about today . . ."

"Hey, no problem! None at all. We all have shitty days, it was your draw today. Tomorrow will be better. Though . . . I could make tonight all right . . . bubble bath sound good? Some wine?"

Vince sighed and smiled. "I love you, Billy Caliendo."

"And I adore you, Vince Caliendo . . . my own forever man." He gave Vince another sweet kiss.

"Come on, let's go back. I'll give Uncle our regrets, and we can bolt."

"Sounds good to me."

Nora met them at the door. "Vince, Billy, I'm so sorry Caitlin upset you. Sure, she'll be grounded for the rest of her life if she doesn't learn to keep her tongue quiet in her head."

"Good luck with that." Asher sneered. Erik glared at him, but he shrugged and poured himself more wine.

Vince and Billy approached Tony. "I'm sorry, Uncle, but we're going to call it an early evening. It's been a difficult day, and we just want to relax. Tomorrow will be busy too, so we need to — "

"He knows, hon. He knows." Billy stopped him, putting his arm around his shoulders. He looked at the rest of the table. "Guys, we're sorry, but we're gonna go. We'll see you tomorrow, okay? Oh, Connor, if you want to go to the hardware store, that'd be great. I've got some ideas."

"Aye, sounds good to me, sham. You two take care, hi. Sure, it's been a hard day for us all." He stood and hugged them both. "Take the weight off, have some wine and some . . . relaxation."

"We will. Thanks, Con."

Erik stood and put one arm around each of his friends.

"Hey, everything all right?"

"I'll text you later," Billy whispered.

"Gotcha, well, enjoy your night, guys. See you about four tomorrow."

"I'm sorry." Asher got to his feet and draped his arms around Vince's neck. "I screwed up your day, and I'm so sorry. I'm such a fuck up. I'll make it up to you. I promise I'll make it up to you." He frowned and turned his eyes away. "If I can."

"I know, Ash, I know. Can I tell you a stupid lil secret of mine? I was . . ." Vince sighed. "I was actually a little hurt you asked Con to be your best man, instead of me. It kinda nagged at me, and I dismissed it. I thought I'd let it go. If you don't want me, it's fine. I get it but . . . I've got a lot of things running in my head right now. It's not just you, this day sucked all around."

"Jesus." Asher pulled back to look Vince in the eye. "I didn't know. I . . . If I'd known . . . I asked Con because he . . . he's like me. Crazy like me. I knew . . . I know . . . Tomorrow isn't going to be easy for me, and Saturday even worse. I needed . . . I need someone who can . . . handle me. Doesn't today prove me right? Erik won't be there with me on Saturday . . . just before . . . when I'm . . . scared. I need Con. Do you understand? Please understand, Vince. I don't want to hurt you. I'd never want to hurt you. You've been so . . . so special to me. Please . . . Please understand."

Asher gripped Vince's arms so hard Billy saw Vince wince as the fingers dug in. He was pretty sure Asher had no idea he was hurting Vince, so he didn't jump in.

"Let go of me, Asher, you're givin' me a death grip." Vince didn't struggle. "Like you? No one's like you, not on earth. I think we're pretty much over, aren't we? Just let go of me, I want to go home and be with my husband . . . my real best friend." He tried to shove Asher away, without success.

"Let him go!" Billy commanded. "You freakin' ninja."

Asher stared at Vince, then down at his hands and back again. Letting go as if he'd been burned, he took a step back, shaking his head. "Vince?" he said. "Vince, I . . ."

Billy started to pull Vince away but stopped when Vince turned around. He returned to Asher, threw his arms around him and sobbed. "I'm sorry. I'm so sorry. This . . . shitty day, very shitty day. I'm such a jerk, Asher. I know Con means a lot to you, too. I'm losing my mind, I think. Must be going around." He tried unsuccessfully to lighten the conversation but immediately sobered again. "It's not you, it's my brother."

"Your brother?" Angel cut in. "Paulie?"

"What is it with Paulie?" Tony rumbled, getting to his feet. "Has he been in touch with you? Has he hurt you?"

Asher looked shocked, but he just put his arms around Vince and held him while he wept.

"As he has since I was twelve, Uncle." Vince snuffled. "I made the mistake of telling him he'll be an uncle himself. He said it wrong and evil, that I'm sick, Billy's sick. He's such a . . . jackass."

Billy put his hand on Vince's shoulder. "He's the evil one in my mind. I hate that guy, and I've never even met him. Even your cousins were nicer than he is. What the fuck is his problem?"

"Paulie's an embarrassment to the family. It was . . . suggested to him, he might not want to talk to you anymore. If he has overstepped the line, Vincenzio, I will have him reminded of that."

"Papa," Angel cut in, looking alarmed. "It wasn't Paulie who contacted Vince. It was the other way around."

"Be that as it may. He has clearly upset your cousin and . . ."

"I've blocked him on social media, and I'm trying to in my own head, that's for sure." Vince scowled. "I've got a lot of stress right now too, and it doesn't help when he's like this."

Connor joined the group. "Now don't ye be worryin' about it, sham. I'll be bouncin' around like a bad penny, so I will. I'll not leave ye on yer own, and I'm wantin' te give me godbabbies the finest nursery ye ever saw. It'll be banging, see if it won't."

Billy smiled. "See? You're in great hands." He kissed Vince's cheek. "You'll be okay, honey, I promise."

"You hear one more word from Paulie, and you come to me, capisce?" Tony glowered.

Even though Billy knew the scowl wasn't for him, he shivered.

Vince nodded and drew away from Asher.

"I'm truly sorry, Vince," Asher whispered, tears pouring down his cheeks. "I . . . didn't know your brother was . . . like that. I . . ." He shook his head and stumbled backward. "I think . . . I think I need . . ." Holding his hand over his mouth, he ran for the door.

"Uncle, we're going to go home for the night. I'll relax, I promise."

Billy nodded. "I'll look after you, you know that."

"Yes, I do. Thank God for you." They kissed softly. They hugged everyone good night and left.

"Are you sure you're all right?" Angel worried as Asher stumbled and Erik had to steady him against his side, yet again.

"I'm . . . fine. Absolutely . . . fine." Asher said carefully, smiling a blurred smile.

"I told you it was a bad idea to finish the wine after being sick. You're going to be sick again," Erik grumbled.

"Fear not." Asher pushed away from Erik and threw his arms around Angel's neck, causing him to stagger back until steadied by Connor. "I promise you . . . I will not . . . be sick . . . on you."

"Ye'd better not be, or ye'll be cleaning his clothes yerself," Connor warned. "Come on wid ye, little darlin', let's be getting ye back te yer bed, hi."

Erik propped Asher up against his side. "I'm all for that. Come on, my betrothed. No more puking out here. You're going to bed."

"I am not going to bed. I don't want to go to bed. I wanna dance." Asher turned in Erik's arms, grabbed his hand and waltzed him around the path.

"Asher, be careful. You're going to . . ." Angel winced and turned his face away as Asher caught his foot in one of the path lights and went crashing to the ground, pulling Erik after him. "Oh, my God . . . are you all right?"

Connor hauled a cursing Erik to his feet while Angel tried to help Asher. It was impossible, because Asher just lay on his back on the ground, laughing helplessly.

"You are such a mess, Asher." Erik shook his head but couldn't help laughing at the scene. "My future husband, the falling down drunken klutz. Where's my ninja?" He leaned over and tickled Asher's sides.

"Fer feck sake stop actin' the maggot or ye'll have him dumpin' his guts again. Jaysus alive but ye're a right pair o' tools, are they not, *a chroí*.?" He put his arm around Angel.

"Who'd believe they're getting married in a couple of days?" Angel shook his head watching Asher writhe under Erik's tickles as he continued to laugh hysterically. "Let him up, Erik, He's gonna blow chunks."

"I so am not," Asher gasped as Erik yanked him to his feet. "I'm perfectly fine." He giggled and stumbled again, falling against Erik, who grabbed him around the waist and steadied him.

"I think we should get you two back to the house before

you break something . . . or someone." Angel grabbed Connor's hand and headed for the house.

"Come on, my beloved dark angel . . . Asher Washer . . . my dearest. Let's go follow these two back to the house before you hurt yourself, or me again." Erik held Asher up and they made it into the little house. He bypassed the living room and walked Asher upstairs to the bathroom. "Just in case," he called out to Angel and Connor. "I'll be back in a minute."

Angel kicked off his shoes and collapsed onto the sofa. "God, that was some night." He sighed as Connor settled down next to him.

"No shittin'." Connor gathered his hair forward and let it rest over his shoulder. "Sure, that Paulie sounds like a right fecking gobshite, and I've made me own trouble for Vince, hi." He sighed. "I should give him a bell, eh?"

"Nonsense. What trouble have you caused him? None. And I'm sure he won't be thinking it any trouble at all when you're working hard on their nursery."

Connor nodded and sighed again, pulling Angel into his arms. "I suppose. Sure an' I think we've got past the pain of what I did before. Don't I still feel bad though . . . with the best man thing. Since Asher was Vince's, it's right it should him, not me."

"It's Asher's choice who he wants for best man, and it wasn't fair of Vince to call him out on it. Maybe he *has* known Vince longer, but there was obviously something about you, even if it was only the strength of your arms and the way your legs look in a skirt, that made him want you for the job. I may be biased, but from my point of view for sure, he made the right choice."

"Awae wid ye. Ye're biased, so ye are, te say so over yer own kin." Connor playfully batted Angel with a cushion, then sobered. "I think your man Vince is feelin' the stress. With the babbies, and Billy goin' away. He'll be all alone in that big house, sittin' on his thumbs. He's a doll, and that feckin' little menace didn't help none. Pisht, I love her, but she tries me patience."

"She's a kid. It's what kids do. Hell, it's what I was doing a few years ago. I was petty as hell, especially with the cousins. They'll be okay. We'll make sure Vince isn't lonely. There'll be enough of us still here. You, me, Asher . . . we can take care of Vince fine, and once the babies are born, he'll be too busy to be lonely."

"Amen to that one," Erik commented as he came down the stairs to join them. "He's a good guy, just stressed. I wouldn't worry too much. Just hang out with him." He wiped his hands on his pants and sat on the floor in front of the couple.

"How's Asher?"

"He's all right. I got him some antacid. I told him to stay up there until he didn't look green anymore." Erik chortled.

"At least he's smiling. He seemed to enjoy himself tonight. Maybe it'll help him relax a bit about the dinner tomorrow night."

Erik looked at his friends. "Angel, from your lips to God's ears. I seriously hope everything goes all right. We just need to keep him calm and happy, and hopefully without emptying a liquor store to do it."

"Give 'im a few belts o' whiskey, and an' if all else fails I'll wrap him another knuckle sandwich, hi." Connor joked.

"Hah! I hope it won't come to that." Erik lay back on the floor. "Gawd, I'm sick of this, so much."

"Sick of it? Sick of what?" Angel asked, distracted by Connor's hair, which he was twirling 'round his fingers.

Erik shot him a look. "You're kidding, right? The stress, Angel. All this damn stress from Daisy and the wedding and just all of it. Me leaving doesn't help either. God, ever since the first tour, they've all been total fucking disasters. Because of me, basically. He says he's okay with it, but I know he doesn't trust me, and I don't blame him. It didn't exactly get off to a good start. Couldn't keep my hands off a couple of guys. I was such an ass." He sighed and shut his eyes.

"Aye, ye were, but ye pulled yerself up off yer arse and now ye're getting' hitched. God help ye both." He glanced down in amusement at the braid Angel had formed in his hair. He smiled. "Well wouldja look at that?" He waved the braid around. "Whaddya think about givin' me a tail fer the wedding, hi?"

"Really?" Angel sat back and admired his work. He laid the braid against the side of Connor's face. "Hmm . . . yeah, yeah it'd look good. Shall I? Shall I do that for the wedding? What do you think, Erik?"

Erik shrugged "I didn't think you'd look good with long hair. I don't want to sound too gay, but you look cute. It suits you." He grinned. "Do it up nice, Angel. Hey, Con, you should wear it like this when you work, so you don't get crap in your hair."

Connor kissed Angel's cheek. "Thank ye, darlin'." He turned to Erik. "Aye, right ye are. I'll not be wanting this sawed off. Took me two years to get to this."

"What are you getting sawed off, Con?" Asher asked, appearing in the doorway. He definitely looked less green, but he was still clearly very drunk. He winked at Connor and flopped down next to Erik on the floor, pulling Erik's head onto his lap. "It had better not be anything too crucial, or Angel will kill you. And did I also hear you, my darling" — he tickled Erik's face, with a lock of hair — "say you didn't want to sound too gay? Don't you think it's a tiny little bit too late for that now? I mean, on Saturday you're going to be saying *I do* to a man . . . how gay is that?"

Erik held Asher closer to him and ran his fingers through the curtain of black hair. "I just see it as marrying the man I'm in love with, that's all. Being gay's got nothing to do with it, it's love, it's a life we're gonna build together, hell, we are building together. Forever." He glanced at his class ring on Asher's finger. "I love you, Asher, you're mine, and I'm yours." He smiled softly.

Asher bent over and kissed Erik, covering them both with his hair.

"Now *there's* hair that should be braided." Angel laughed. "You could lose someone in there and they'd never be found."

Asher looked up and grinned. "There's all sorts of things hiding in here," he said, running his fingers through his long, silky locks. "I think I sent a battalion of paratroopers in there last week . . . had to hide them quick when Erik came home unexpectedly. I'm gonna have to find them, because I'd only worked my way 'round half."

Connor laughed, as did the other two. "Aye, ye're a header, *a stór*. Wouldja be after lettin' me darling plait yer hair? It'd be grand." He held up the braid, its three perfect plaits together in a mix of brilliant red strands, held in place with a small hair band. "Do ye like it?"

"Oooh, you look like Braveheart. Don't go running down the aisle shouting about freedom on Saturday, or I might be lured into running after you." Asher grinned and kissed Erik again. Then he sobered and stroked Erik's cheek. "I take it back. When this man's around, there's only one direction I'm gonna be running . . . right into his arms, and I don't give a fuck who or what else is around."

The look he gave Erik was so intense and deeply personal, Angel had to turn his face away. He busied himself smoothing Connor's plait.

Connor stroked Angel's arms and smiled. "Once you're done, put those fingers to work on somethin' else maybe." He waggled his brows and kissed him softly. "Almost time for bed, and checkin' up on the family that had to leave."

124

Asher looked up. "Have you heard from Vince? Is everything okay?"

"Not yet. I was gonna call 'im. Sure, an' I feel awful for how badly he felt, about everything. Me, the babbies, and his bastard brother. He's been through a lot, so he has. He's piling on more with the house and still in school . . . maybe too much."

"I . . . I didn't think I'd hurt him by not asking him to be my best man. I keep on doing that . . . hurting Vince, and he doesn't deserve it. Maybe I should have asked him, too."

Erik perked up. "Hey, now there's a great idea. Why not? Have two best men. I can have another too, then, right? Billy and . . . maybe Joey? Why not? It'd make him feel better, I'm sure. You know how he feels about ya, Ash. Why not ask him?"

"What? But I . . . I was only joking. Erik. It's two days before the wedding. The women would flip. There'd be so much to organize. There's clothes and places and where to sit and . . ." He shrugged, a small grin tugging at his lips. "Why not. Maybe it will keep them off my back. They can hassle Vince instead. Give me a phone."

Erik handed him his cell phone. "Here."

"Dial it," Asher commanded, thrusting it back at Erik. "I can't see the screen."

"Maybe you should wait until tomorrow. You're both drunk tonight and—"

"Shush, Angel," Asher said, flapping a hand at him. He took the phone off Erik and held it to his ear. "Ssh . . . No, not you," he said into the phone. "Is Vince there? Yes. No. No, I'm not going to upset him again. Just put him on, Billy. Oh, for fuck sake." He thrust the phone at Erik. "Tell him. He won't let me talk to Vince."

Erik sighed and sat up slightly. "Billy? It's me. Hey, he's not gonna upset him, I promise. I'll talk to him first, all right?

Just put him on, fluffo." He waited a moment and spoke again. "Hey, Vince, how you doing, buddy? Good. I'm so sorry about tonight, you've put too much on your plate, bud. Hey . . . if it's all right, Asher wants to talk to you, too. Uh-huh, all right, here ya go." He handed it back to Asher. "You're on, baby."

"I didn't know I could do it, but I can, and now I know I can I want to. What? Have two best men, of course. Well, no, of course I didn't. If I'd known I wouldn't have had to go through the torture of choosing . . . Ha, no, actually I tossed a coin." He held the phone away from his ear and giggled. "No, of course not. So, will you? Will you be my best man with Connor? . . . And you really think I care? The women can freak out all they like. Ha, ha, yeah well, what can I say, I like to spread around the misery. Woo-hoo. You can tell Daisy. No, no, no, no, no, I can't hear you . . . lalalalala." He handed the phone to Erik. "You can tell Billy now about him having to share you and don't you listen to anything Vince has to say about me telling Daisy what we're doing. He's the best man, it's down to him to do all that stuff now . . . yours too, Connor," he emphasized with a pointed finger.

"It'd be a pleasure, Asher. I think ye just made his whole night, and mine too."

Erik was still on the phone. "That's right, Billyboy, we're shaking things up at ye ole wedding ceremony. Poor old Joey feels so left out of everything. Do you mind sharing the great Erik Von Nordgren with him? Stop laughing, fuzzball," he teased. "I'm asking him tonight. No worries on the tux, we've got monkey suits. So you okay with it? Good. You had me worried for a sec. You take care. We all send one big group hug. Night, guys." He hung up and started dialing Joey. "One big happy party."

"Joey? Hey, it's Erik. Listen, we've been yappin' here, and I was wondering if you wanted to be my best man. Nope, not kidding. We're throwing the women a loop, Asher has two, now I can have two. Whaddya say? You will? Thanks, Joey, appreciate it. You'll do great, bud. Say *hi* to Daisy for me, you can give her the grand news. We'll talk to you tomorrow. Night, Joey." He hung up and laughed. "All set. Four best men, which means four speeches. Oy, can't wait for this."

"Erik you'd better . . ." Connor started.

"Wait . . ." Erik held up his hand and turned off his phone. "There, now I won't hear the inevitable rebuttal." He laughed.

"Inevitabubble what?" Asher mumbled, making everyone chuckle.

"Ah, my hubby-to-be." Erik kissed him.

Chapter Ten

A buzzing alongside Erik's ear broke his dream of something involving elevators and a pit. He slapped at the noise, making it stop for the moment and tried to go back to sleep. A minute later, the sound was back. He thought it was a bee or some big bug . . . and opened his eyes slightly to look. Nope. It was his phone and the caller . . . Oh shit. It was Daisy. The inevitable rebuttal had arrived, and she wasn't one to give up. Ah, could he have asked for a better sister-in-law?

He shook his head, found his voice, and answered the phone. "What? Whoa, simmer down there, wouldja? Geez, I just woke up. You woke me, thanks. What? Nope, he's still sleeping. No, I'm not gonna wake him." He sat up, got out of bed, and went into the hallway. "No, no. A million nos, missy, I'm not waking him. Deal with me, your brother-in-law-to-be, sweetheart. What? That's right, I asked Joey, and Asher asked Vince. Yup, two more best men, so what? So you add two more names to the program and we have two more tuxes, big fuckin' deal, Daisy. No, I'm not gonna stop and wake him. After what you did yesterday? You're nuts to think I'm gonna do that, Hell no, girlie. This is how it is and I'm taking care of it. You leave Asher alone, and if you upset him tonight . . . I hope you've learned to not do that again."

"You wanna know what happened? He completely freaked out and it took me and Connor to calm him down, that's what happened. He about clawed us both to bits, but we finally got him to chill. That's exactly what I don't want to happen again. This wedding shit has been way too much for him, and all the other crap going on in our lives, so just keep a lid on it, missy, all right? Unless you like watching your twin brother freak out of his head and start hyperventilating."

There was a long pause, and Erik wondered if they'd been cut off.

Then Daisy started to sob.

"I know, I know. Ssh. It's all right. I know you love him. So do I. I want what's best for him, you know that. Just keep things low-key all right? I've got your boy and Vince taken care of for today, all right? You keep those babies healthy and your mom under control, all right? I'll tell him you say hi. Bye, Daisy, see you later."

Erik tucked his phone back into his pocket and rubbed his face. "Oy . . . Please let these next forty-eight hours go smoothly." He shook his head and tousled his hair. "I need a shower. Wonder if the other two are up yet?" He waved his hand. "Meh, I'll find out in a bit." He showered and donned the robe hanging behind the door, then went downstairs.

Connor and Angel were at the table, enjoying English muffins and jelly along with some scrambled eggs. "Mmm, that smells good and looks great." There was a large pot of fresh coffee, too, which he went for first, grabbing a mug and filling it. "So, how are you guys? Is Asher our only casualty?" he joked.

"I'm fine," Angel responded with a laugh. "Some of us showed a little restraint last night. Was it Asher I heard you talking to earlier? How's his head today? I'm surprised I didn't hear him crossing the hall last night."

Erik shook his head and took another swig of coffee. He reached for a small plate and a muffin. "Me too. I'd be worshipping the porcelain myself, but he's okay. Oh. As for who I was talking to?" He smiled to himself and made a face. "That was our lovely miss Daisy. She was a little peeved." He chortled as he spread jam on the muffin.

"Yer the wizard of downplay, Erik, so ye are." Connor joked. "I bet she wants to skin ye alive. Did she talk to her brother?"

"Nope, I didn't let her. Kept her in my ear, not his. He doesn't need her right now."

"Too bloody right, not if we want to make it to the wedding." Angel nodded thoughtfully. "I was thinking. I don't really have any part in the wedding. It might be an idea to have me babysit today. Keep him away from the preparations. I'd be lying if I said the idea didn't scare me, I mean I have no idea what I'd do if he freaked out again, but I thought maybe if I keep him away from wedding-y things and his mind on something arty, we might avoid that happening. I thought to take him out sketching somewhere."

"It's an awesome idea, Angel. Thanks so much, I really appreciate it. Anything to keep things on an even keel. If he freaks out, call us, we'll be there before you know it. But sketching seems to be his cure-all for most things. Too bad we don't have a flower girl and ring bearer, you'd just fit," he joked. "Such a cutie pie you are."

Angel lowered his eyes, his usual blush coloring his cheeks.

"Aye, I second that one. I'll have to get yer help with me ensemble tomorrow, makin' sure I'm legal." He winked at his boyfriend and smiled.

"Aww, do you have to?" Angel pouted. "Mind you, I have first call to check up your kilt to see if you're authentic."

"Who's checking up whose skirt?" A sleepy voice said from the direction of the stairs. "I really hope you're talking about Connor, or I might be sick. Come to think of it . . . someone get me some dry toast, or I might not have to think about women bits to be running for the toilet."

"Oh, trust you," Angel said, rolling his eyes. "You always turn up when there's sex in the air. No . . ." He held up his hand. "That was a mistake. Don't you *dare* say a word."

Erik snorted and nearly spit out his coffee. "Angel, there will be very few times when there won't be sex in the air with him, or us. 'Tis the language we speak, isn't it?" He handed some toast to Asher. "Here, eat slowly." He poured some water for him too. "Easy now, m'dear."

"I might have to play down the kilt, me dear, don't want to scare the parents. Especially with all the high-steppin' later on with dancin'. I miss doin' the jig, so I do. 'Twas a tradition. I mimicked it as best I could."

"Spoilsport," Asher said, chewing toast. "I'll hold you to the jig, though." He frowned. "What's on the agenda for today?"

Erik couldn't help but notice his hands were shaking. Could be the alcohol, of course—damn, the boy was most probably still half drunk.

Angel preempted his response. "We're going to go out sketching while the big boys go play with the ladies."

"We are?" Asher's eyes widened. He looked excited but anxious. "Will they let me?"

Erik nodded. "It doesn't matter what they'll *let* you do, baby. I'm taking all the heat for us from the estrogen pond. I'm taking Vince and Joey to get their tuxes and take care of any last little details. They won't bug you at all, or they'll answer to me." He ran his hand through Asher's hair. "You've dealt with too much shit lately, let me help."

Asher turned to Erik, his eyes wide. "You'll do that? You'll do it for me? But you won't... Hang on a minute." He squinted. "Did I... Did I ask Vince to be another best man?"

Erik nodded and kissed his love. "Of course. Anything for you, baby." He took a drink of coffee and another bite of muffin. "By the way, yes, you did ask Vince to be your best man. A move which I thought was very sweet... and kinda my idea."

"Aye, it was. He was elated, I'm sure of it," Connor added.

"Wow, was I really that drunk last night? No, don't answer, I think my mouth and stomach can tell the tale better than you can."

"You were really drunk. Things got out of hand last night, too. Vince was upset, and with you being so drunk . . . I think you, being what you are to him, made his day, though. He loves you like fuck." Erik kissed his cheek.

"Yeah, yeah, everyone loves me. I'm so lovable after all."

There was a definite edge to his voice that had the others exchanging glances.

"I kind of remember Vince running off. Was it because of me? Did I hurt him? Is that why I made him best man? Because I upset him? Shit. Was I really that drunk?"

Connor cocked his head. "True, it was part that, and all the other crap in his own life. He'll miss Billy somethin' fierce, and feelin' the babbies grow. I vow to help him with their house, and yours, too." He turned to Angel. "I told ye about them, didn't I? Asher was Vince's first love, before Billy."

"Thank you so much for discussing my past love life over the breakfast table, on the day before my wedding. How many other lovers are we going to be talking about today? You, maybe?"

Connor chuckled. "None others, dear Asher." He turned to Angel. "I didn't think to tell ye about that. He's yer cousin, I thought he might've told ye himself. So just be sweet to him, he's goin' through an awful lot, too. Sure, an' it was fair. He had Asher as his best man." He tapped Angel on the nose.

Angel scowled. "Don't you do that to me, you philanderer. I think Asher was talking about you and not Vince." As much as he tried to maintain his scowl, he couldn't help but laugh. "Did you realize, Asher, that out of all of us, Daisy and Joey are the only couple you haven't slept with half of? Maybe you are particularly lovable after all."

"Yeah, right. Nah, I'm just a slut. Just like Erik. We make a good pair, don't we? Neither of us can keep our dick in our trousers. What can I say?" He shrugged. "I started early."

"You started before I did, that's for sure." Erik laughed. "I was sixteen when I lost my virginity . . . kind of. It's not like I didn't try." He winked at Asher. "Just too into the band yet to date."

"How long has the band been around?" Connor asked.

"Shit . . . since then, so five years now? It was just me and Billy, then we met Joey and then his new gal, Daisy, two years later, and we all hit it off and got along great." He rubbed his arms. "Damn, that's a long time ago now."

"Yeah," Asher said, staring at the wall, "A long time ago. Isn't history interesting?"

Erik swallowed some more coffee. "Oy, is history ever interesting, especially with this crowd." He smiled at them all. "You feeling any better, or you need some hair of the dog?" he teased.

"You mean the dog that crawled into my mouth and died? I think not." Asher sighed deeply. "Ah well. I think tonight will mark the end of an era . . . and the beginning of a new one. History in the making."

Erik was sure he caught a look passing between Asher and Angel, but it was the last thing he was worried about right then, so he ignored it.

"Well, speaking of ends of eras, I need to corral the boys together. I'm taking us to get those tuxes taken care of, then just hang out."

"Need some company along, Erik?" Connor offered. "I'd love to talk shop with Vince and yerself, too."

"Sounds good to me, man. Join the party. These two will be drawing 'til their hands fall off I'm sure."

"After that conversation, I'm surprised you trust me with him," Asher grumbled.

"Okay, what's wrong?" Angel asked the moment the door closed behind the other two.

Asher looked up. "Wrong?"

"You've been sniping since the moment you got up. And don't think I don't know what you were talking about when you were talking about *history* and *the end of an era*. You're thinking about that man again, aren't you?"

Asher glared, then nodded. "Yes . . . He was the start, my first. He was the one who fucked me and fucked me up, and Erik is the one who's going to save me. I need to close the chapter, get rid of James from my life once and for all before I start a new life with Erik."

"You know Erik can't save you, don't you?"

"What?" Asher scowled at him. "What do you know? You know nothing about—"

"Asher, only you can save you. You can't put the responsibility on Erik."

"Didn't I just tell you I am? I'm getting rid of James for good . . . tonight. And haven't I told you I'm going to help myself? I'm going to go see someone in London. I'm going to get my head sorted, Angel. I'm going to make this marriage work."

He sounded so ferocious it made Angel smile.

"What are you smiling at," Asher demanded.

"Do you know you're a nightmare when you have a hangover?"

Asher tilted his head to one side with a thoughtful expression. "Yes. But then I'm a nightmare without a hangover, too. I've no idea how Erik puts up with me." He grinned and got up, waving a piece of toast at Angel. "I'm going to take a shower. We'll need to call at the house for my art stuff." He stopped and turned, eyeing Angel thoughtfully. "How do you feel about posing for a painting? Not just a couple of sketches, but a full-blown study in multiple mediums. I have a project to do for my course, and some spaces to fill at the gallery."

"Me? In the gallery? Umm . . ."

"Not ashamed of your sexy little body, are you?" Asher asked with a twinkle in his eyes

"Don't start. Don't think you're going to work your way any further 'round our group."

Asher grinned. "Perish the thought. So, are you?"

"Am I what?"

"Up to posing for me?"

"When you put it like that, how can I say no?"

Erik watched Vince check out his tuxedo in the mirrors. "I gotta say, Vince, you're looking damn good. How much weight have you lost?"

Vince blushed. "Thanks, Erik. Over thirty pounds, actually — amazing, being a student chef with all the sampling and cooking. But I was determined to make it happen. A new dad has to have energy and vigor to deal with two babies at once."

Connor laughed. "Don't ye mean three, with Billy, too?"

Joey chimed in. "Billy's no baby, he's the glue. He's a goofball, but he's mature enough to do this. I still find it kinda odd, to be brutally honest, but I couldn't think of better parents."

Vince smiled at Joey. "Thanks, buddy. You're the most stand-up guy, having your lady preggers with our babies."

Joey patted Vince's shoulders. "I'm not going to lie, it's weird, and yeah I've had my moments, but I trust Daisy and I trust you. You guys will be fantastic parents, and I know one day I'll be the lucky one. For now, I'll be content to be their uncle." He smiled warmly, then brushed down Vince's suit. "You look great."

Vince beamed. "Thanks. You do too. You did last year, as the usher."

Erik cleared his throat. "Don't mean to interrupt the mutual admiration society here." He laughed. "Connor, you've got the easiest, you have your own ensemble already. You don't have to even wear pants!"

The Irishman laughed. "'Tis true there. I love it. I haven't been in a weddin' since Nora's, an' I was a wee boy back then. 'Tis nice to dress up as an adult now."

"I bet. Your sister seems really nice," Vince commented.

"Just duct tape your niece's mouth." Joey chortled. "Wow, are all your nieces and nephews like that?"

"To be honest, I've not kept up with too many since I left home, when I was fifteen. Had no call to go back, y'know. Nora's the only one who made the effort." He shifted his weight, Vince noticed.

"You all right? Hey, you can tell me all about sibling woes, I've got the worst on earth. I would've loved to have my brother be my best man at my wedding, but no way in hell."

Erik scowled. "Is that why you chose Asher?"

Vince nodded. "Partially. We had a weird history. You know it all, Erik, I don't need to rehash it. I will love Asher till the day I die, even though he doesn't always make it easy, but my best man ever is gonna be Billy, always."

"Where is El Fluffo, anyway?" Erik asked.

"Oh, I think he was hanging with his parents, looking at house stuff. We wanna do some landscaping, so his dad took him to the store. I'd love to meet up with them, Connor, maybe look at some stuff ourselves."

"To be sure, Vince, it would be my pleasure. We're about done here, I think. Everyone loves the hardware store?"

Erik nodded. "I'm good. Joey?"

"Of course. I loved shop class to death."

Vince took out his phone and dialed Billy. "Hey, adorable.

You guys still at the store? Don't leave yet, we're all gonna join you for a little bit. Yeah, those stones we were thinking about? Perfect. See you soon. Love you more!"

Erik was wearing a groove in the summerhouse floor as he paced back and forth, and even around it, over and over, wondering where Asher and Angel were.

The area was such a gorgeous setup. The trees were lit up with white lights. Bright lights lit the path of weathered stones that formed a graceful curve between the gardens and the main house. The grass was more manicured than a pro golf course and smelled sweeter than a spring meadow.

The summerhouse itself was made from artificially aged and weathered stone and was circular in shape. It had two benches, one on either side, perfect for a wedding in the center. It was similar in size to a gazebo, so the seven of them wouldn't be crowded.

It was the perfect place for a wedding, yet here he was, alone. He was getting half-pissed and half-worried about their whereabouts. They were running late, and it was irritating him that Asher was late to his own wedding rehearsal.

He tried the cell phone again, same result, right to voice mail. He wanted to find them, throw them both in the car, and wring their necks, but it wouldn't help.

"Dammit, Angel. You promised you'd get him here. Now you're both in hot water with me," he groused to himself.

"Hey, where's the gothic bride to be?" Billy asked as he broke away from the small knot of people grouped around the officiant, who wasn't looking too pleased about the delay. "Running late as usual?" He laughed.

Erik shook his head and tried to smile but couldn't. "Yeah, dammit. Pisses me off he's late to his own damn rehearsal.

Angel promised me they'd be here. They got caught up drawing or some shit." He let out a huffy breath.

"Chill man, easy, easy there, big fella. They'll be here. If anything, we'll put one of Angel's shirts under Connor's nose and he can go sniff him out."

Just the image that conjured made Erik laugh out loud and hug Billy warmly. "Gawd, what would I do without you to keep me sane, Billyboy?"

"You'd just have to lose your marbles, Von Nordgren," he teased. "Well, while you wait, I offer my charming company, as does the better half of me, the lovely and talented Vincenzo Caliendo." He held out his hand and waved his hubby over. "Come on over, baby."

Vince jogged over, took Billy's hands and kissed him. "I'm here, as requested. Always." He looked up at Erik. "Running late again, huh?"

Erik shuffled his feet. "Yep, and it's pissing me off big time. I know they get into it, but shit. This is ridic—" He was cut off by his parents coming down the path. A pig-tailed redhead girl followed, and he groaned.

"Erik? What's wrong, sweetie?" his mom asked, her voice always so melodic. She put her arms around him. "Is he running late?"

"Molly, he's fifteen minutes late at least," his dad chimed in. "I know time means nothing to you, my love," he teased.

"Sure, my mother says it's rude to keep people waitin', so it is. But I know he's always rude. He's a tool, so he is. I knew right off de bat." Caitlin skipped up to Erik and took his hand. "Darlin', ye'd be a lot better off wid a nice girl, and ye're not so very much older than I am. And such pretty hair ye have, hi." Smiling wickedly, Caitlin reached up and tugged at Erik's hair where it had come free from the band he'd wrapped loosely around it.

"I'd thank you to keep your hands off my man, if you

please," Asher's voice said from between the trees.

Caitlin tossed her head. "Sure, an' do ye have radar now? Every time I open me mouth, ye're there wid yer cocky answers."

Asher laughed, strode across the clearing and ruffled her hair. "Do me a favor, munchkin, go let the others know we're ready down."

She practically growled at him. "I ain't no munchkin, ye geek, an don't ye be sayin' no different."

Asher laughed again as she took off down the path. Then he turned and put his arms around Erik. "I'm so, so sorry I'm late. I was sketching Angel. I'm going to do a series of paintings of him. We turned our phones off so we wouldn't be disturbed, and the time just disappeared. When I realized the time, I got Angel dressed and we rushed straight here. I'm really, really sorry. Don't hate me."

Erik shook his head and put his hands into Asher's hair. "I don't hate you, Asher. I'm a little peeved. I know how it is with your art, and I get that, but today's important, too." He gazed into Asher's lilac eyes, shining with sincerity, and calmed down. "It's all right now, you're here, and we're ready to rehearse our wedding. I admit, I'm excited about it, are you, even just a little?"

"About the rehearsal? No. About the wedding? Oh yeah . . . you just wait." His eyes glittered with mischief. "So . . . *I do, you do, we do,* let's go eat." He grabbed Erik's hand and would have dragged him out of the summerhouse if he hadn't resisted.

"If only it were that simple." Erik mused as they assembled the rest of the wedding party participants. It was seamless, and all were pleased with their roles.

After the rehearsal was finished, Erik pulled Asher aside. "Hey, did you remember the gifts for after we eat?"

"Fuck. I left them at the house. I'm sorry Erik, it was full-on panic when we realized the time and Angel was naked and we couldn't find his shoes and . . ." He winced at the look in Erik's eyes. "I'm sorry. I'm really sorry. I'll go get them. Give me the keys. I won't be . . ."

"Oh, no you don't, mister head in the clouds. I'll go and get them. You stay here and have a lovely chat with Caitlin." He kissed his cheek and laughed. "Don't worry about a thing, I'll be right back. Love you."

"I love you, too, but don't expect Caitlin to still be alive when you get back. Look for her under the patio."

Erik chortled. "She's a spitfire, that one. I know the type." He winked at Asher and kissed him again. "I won't be long."

He made his way to his car and sped off into the early evening toward their house.

CHAPTER ELEVEN

Erik pulled up in the driveway and shut off the blaring music he'd played the entire drive over. He laughed to himself at Asher's antics, especially his art — how absorbed he got into all of it. He entered the house and ran to the closet where they'd stowed the gifts, then propped them up on the table in the living room. The place was still a mess, both from moving in, construction, and the drawing from earlier. He caught a glimpse of one of Asher's works, just peeking out from the folder.

"Oh, what the hell? He won't mind."

The first few were of Angel, naked. Wow the boy was beautiful. Connor was a lucky man. Erik loved the kids' eyes and his longer hair . . . so hot, but none compared to his Asher. He flipped through a few more, and saw drawings of himself, in very sexy poses, all nude of course, and smiled. "Damn, baby. Caught my good side, which is all of me."

He got involved in the drawings of himself and sat down on the table. The presents spilled over and pushed one of the folders onto the floor. A wave of drawings splashed across the floor.

"Shit! Nice work, Von Nordgren." He tried to pick them all up, and got the ones furthest away, almost under the chair they'd set up. Then he stopped cold. "What the — "

He had to turn on the lamp to see more clearly and picked up the drawing. It wasn't of him, or Angel . . . Who the hell? His eyes widened, and his fists clenched tight. He felt like he was going to be sick right there and then — the drawing was of James! Worse, it was of James and Asher, in a very, very sexy pose . . . together?

He stumbled backward, the drawing in his hands. "What the fuck? What the fuck! Why are you drawing that bastard, Asher? Why?" He flipped through the other drawings on the floor and found over a dozen more, and that was just this folder. Were there more?

He couldn't catch his breath. It was all too surreal. Why the fuck would Asher draw them like that? Why at all? He wanted to crumple them all up and burn them right there, but he had to know. This was one question Asher wasn't going to evade, not again. James was dead, let him be dead and gone, and buried. Why was he still in Asher's head? Was he missing him? Or sick of Erik and longing for a psycho?

"What the fuck?" he kept repeating. He swiped at his face and was pissed it was wet. He couldn't let Asher see he was hurt. He was angry, most of all. Very, very angry. "How could you? How could you hide these from me?"

Erik composed himself, gathered up the drawings of James, and the gifts, and headed out the door so fast he nearly forgot to lock the door. Once in his car, he peeled rubber to get back to the rehearsal.

Once he was back at Tony's house, he flew out of the car, folder in hand and ran to the tent where dinner was to be served. He passed right by his parents, who gave him a look.

"Honey, what . . ."

"Just a second, Mom." He held up his hand and threw the folder on the table, right over Angel's shoulder.

"You ass! You owe me a huge explanation, Asher Berkley! I want one right now!"

Asher stared at the folder and frowned. He looked genuinely shocked and surprised. Sliding the sketches out of the folder, he froze and stared at them, then up at Erik. "E . . . Erik . . ." he whispered.

Erik leaned in as close as he could. Their noses nearly touched, but he was in no mood for an Eskimo kiss. "You want me to tell them what kind of sick sketches you've been doing? Sketches you've been hiding from me for God knows how long? Or shall I just play show-and-tell, huh? You tell me!" he finished with a yell.

"Erik, what the hell?" Billy asked.

"Shut up, Billy. This is between us. Asher's gonna show what, or shall I say who, he's been drawing, aren't you? Aren't you?"

"No, no I . . ."

"Asher? What's the meaning of this?" Mr. Berkley, sitting a seat away from Asher, reached out and snatched the sketches from his hand. "Asher! What in God's name were you thinking?" He thrust them back into the folder, trying to stop his wife from seeing them. Unfortunately, he wasn't quite fast enough.

"Asher?" Mrs. Berkley stammered, her face draining of color. "Asher why? Why . . . him? Why . . . why . . . *him*?"

"I . . . I don't know. I . . . I wasn't . . ." Asher's eyes were darting around, like a cornered animal looking for an escape route.

"Chill out, Erik," Angel said. "He only brought them to the house so we could get rid of them. He didn't want to just throw them away. We were going to burn them."

Erik leaned back and shot Angel a cold look, the iciest Nordic glare he could muster. "Are you telling me you *knew* about these and didn't say a damn word to me? You don't think I had a right to know about this? You kept it from me on purpose?" Angel was quiet for a second, and Erik banged his fist on the table. "Answer me! Why didn't you tell me?"

"Don't shout at me, Erik," Angel said, appearing indignant. "Yes, I knew about the pictures. I saw one accidentally the day we went to the meeting at the school. Asher was upset about it and I promised I wouldn't tell anyone. I have to say, I didn't understand why, not then, but art's personal. No one has a right to see what the artist doesn't want them to. When Asher was . . . upset the other day, I spoke to him about them, and he explained some things to me. Again, he asked me not to tell anyone and I respected that."

"That was the day ye got shook up, wasn't it, Angel?" Connor asked as he looked up at Erik. "I remember that day, too."

"I wish you would've said something to me, Angel," Erik said in a calmer voice, his breathing steadier. "Connor, I take it you didn't know Angel knew about these? With it being James? Knowing everything you know about this?"

Connor shot Angel a look, too. "No, and I sore wish I had. We could have dealt with before now." He glanced at Asher. "What the feck are ye drawing him for? Why? I thought he was dead to ye!"

"Hang on a minute." Angel's voice was slightly less calm than before. "I'm beginning to feel I'm on trial here. I have no idea what you're going on about or why this is such a big deal. Okay, I know the guy's an ex, and he gave Asher a bad time, but for God's sake, Erik, he's dead. He's hardly a threat, is he? What's the big deal?"

Erik pinched his nose to stave off a headache. "Angel . . . Asher obviously told you very, very little about the monster James was. He's a threat to Asher on every level, mentally, even dead! Christ, this proves it." He turned to Asher, his eyes blazing. "Shall I tell them what he did to you? Maybe describe how you reacted? Show them the scars? Show them the pictures so we can clearly see the sick images of that . . . that evil devil and you together! Why were you thinking about him? When did it start again? I thought you were doing better!" Erik knew he was getting hysterical. He felt out of control, then he became aware of hands on him—his parents', and Billy's, too. He took a breath and willed himself to calm.

144

"Calm down, honey. Asher, he deserves an answer, young man. If you're dreaming about another man, you're not ready to get married to our son."

Asher was white as a ghost and shaking. He hadn't taken his eyes off Erik. Standing up, he pushed his plate away and gripped the table. "How could you?" he whispered, his voice shivering and broken, locked in by the tightness of his throat. "How could you do this to me . . . here . . . now . . . with all our family and friends? How could you say those things . . . *show* . . . my mother . . ." He bit his lip and tears began to pour down his face. "What did I do that made you hate me so much you'd do this to me?"

Erik fought tears. "I don't hate you, Asher. Let's get that clear, right now. I just want to know why the hell you've been drawing James! He's still haunting you, isn't he? He's in your mind forever, and you alone own him, for all time. Are you still . . ." His voice broke. "Are you still in love with the monster who did all those horrible things to you? Some of them I witnessed myself! Asher . . . please . . ." Tears dripped down his face. "Why did you start doing this, and why did you hide it from me? I've been helping you this whole time, and I thought you weren't hiding anything from me anymore. Why did you start?"

Asher was shaking so much he could barely stand. "Why did I hide it?" He spread his hands. "I think this makes it obvious. Why did I do it? I . . . I told you why I did it, Erik. I told you the only way I could handle things is to get it all out on paper. I was losing control . . . of everything, and I couldn't handle it. You were helping me? Bollocks you were. You were as caught up in this whole wedding crap as everyone else, and you didn't give a damn how I was feeling." His voice rose, his eyes flashing with anger.

"I was suffocating, sinking under the never-ending questions and demands. No one listened to me . . . no one, and you were as ready as anyone else to smirk and call me temperamental. *Oh, Asher's having a tantrum again.* You didn't *see.* None of you saw. None of you cared. I don't know how many times I tried to talk to you, and no one *listened.* I had no control." He dropped his head and rubbed his face with his sleeve. "I . . . have no control."

"Excuse me? I didn't help you? I didn't listen? I didn't care? I've been there for you every step of the way on this recovery, which apparently wasn't enough, was it? You refused professional help and wanted just me to do it. Well baby, I did, and I guess I suck at it, don't I? Don't we all? Not even your accomplice Angel could help you out. You swore him to silence and secrecy! Dammit, Asher! What is it going to take? Is it going to take me losing my marbles just so you can find yours again? Is drawing James even helping you at all? It doesn't look like it to me! You don't want me to help, do you? You want to collapse in on yourself again, and want me to pick up the pieces, over and over, like I've been doing for over three years!"

"Erik . . ." Billy tried to interrupt, but Erik brushed him off.

"Asher . . . I know I wasn't a good boyfriend at first, but things got better. I thought they'd got better, especially since London I've been helping you! Now we're at square one again, aren't we? I can't . . ." He put his hands to his face for a moment. "I . . . I dunno what to do anymore. I love you and all I've ever wanted is the best for you, for you to be healthy, for you to be functioning. Hell, I suggested the outing yesterday! I'm here . . . but . . ." He shook his head and pointed to the sketches.

"It's not me you want. It's him. You want James. You can have him, baby. I'm not the one you need or want . . ." He stood quietly in his parent's arms and wept.

"No, Erik, no. It's not James I want. It's not and it never

was. That's why I was going to burn them. Me and Angel, after the dinner. We were going to burn them. We . . . were . . . It was . . ." He looked around at the faces, some of which were looking at him and some at Erik. Some were shocked, some were sympathetic and some, like his father, were downright hostile.

"All right . . . okay . . . You want the truth . . . all the truth? Here it is. James was a huge part of my life. Okay, not a good part, but a huge part nevertheless. Even when he was in prison. Even when he was in the UK and I was here—he was still part of my life. I worked hard to get rid of him, and I was doing it. It wasn't my fault he came back. It wasn't my fault he did those things in London. But it's felt like it. He died, Erik. He died right there at my side, and okay, part of me is glad, gladder than you could ever know, but part of me wants . . . needs to mourn him, and no one would let me talk about it. To all of you, James was nothing but a monster, but to me . . . to me he was the man I used to love, the first man I ever thought I'd marry. Can't you understand? Can't any of you understand?" He glanced around, but no one said a word.

"I had no choice but to lock him up inside. What else could I do? What else would you let me do? But he wouldn't stay there, and when all the shit with the wedding started and I was going crazy, I couldn't keep a lid on it all. Something had to give. So I let him out. I . . . sketched him to get him out. I needed to mourn him, to get over him, to move on from him and I couldn't do it. So I sketched him, and it made things better. When I was having a hard time coping, I did a hard sketch and I spoke to him. I told him what I thought of him, how much I hated him for what he'd done to me, how glad I am he's dead, how sorry I didn't kill him myself. And it helped. It *helped* me. Why can't you understand? Why can't anyone understand?"

"It's all right, Asher," Angel said, putting a hand on his arm. "I understand." Asher didn't look as if he even knew Angel was there. His focus was still locked on Erik.

Erik walked away from his parents and took Asher's hands. "I know your drawing helps, I do know. I do understand. I get it, I do. I do it with my own art — my music. What I don't understand is why you didn't tell me. Do you know what it was like for me, finding them? Thinking you were fantasizing about him and not me? Your fiancé?"

He gulped and looked into the sparkling, lilac eyes. Asher looked so wild, so hurt.

"I love you more than life, Asher. I wish you would've come to me, to Connor, to anyone who knew the story, and made us listen, to just get it out. Or called someone . . ." He meant Rita, the only therapist who seemed to have been able to get through to Asher, and whom he hadn't seen since London. "I feel like I've failed you again, haven't I? We all have."

"You just don't get it," Asher croaked, shaking his head and licking tears off his lips. "I tried to tell you. I tried my best but . . . I just . . . it didn't . . . You couldn't even hear his name without freaking out. You got angry. You told me I should forget him. I talked to Angel in the end because I couldn't . . . I couldn't . . . and he . . . he listened to me. We were going to . . . to burn them and . . . and it would . . . it would all . . . all be over and . . . and now . . ." He glanced over at his parents — his mother in tears and his father looking as if he wanted to tear out his throat. "How could you do this to me? Here. Now. How . . . how could you? I-I can't . . . I can't do this. I just can't . . . I can't marry you." Pushing Erik hard in the chest, unbalancing him, Asher leaped lightly over the table and fled.

After catching his breath, Erik glanced around the room. The expressions were mostly shocked. He glared at Angel. "You should've burned them today, or months ago when you knew about this and didn't say a word to me, or Connor." He snarled. "If you knew what the bastard did to him, your lips wouldn't be so damn tight or so quick to keep a secret about something so serious." He glanced at Connor.

"I'm sorry you didn't know, Con. You know how bad this is as well as I do, Vince, you too, buddy." He shook his head and handed the folder to Angel.

"Erik . . ." Connor began in a tone that drew Erik's attention. "I wish Angel had told me, but only coz I thought he trusted me more. Don't be mistaken, I wouldn't have made him tell ye."

"I get it, Con, I do."

He looked at Angel again. "You do whatever the hell you have to do, Angel. Hang onto them." He wiped his face. "I'm getting the hell outta here."

"Wait up, bud!" Billy followed him, as did Vince. "You're not leaving without us. Not after something like this. Come on." They put their arms around him.

Erik turned and glanced over his shoulder. "I'm sorry, everyone. Looks like we rehearsed for nothing." Just saying the words brought a pain to Erik's heart that cut him to the core. He gripped his friends' hands tighter and corralled his parents. "Let's get outta here, please?"

His mother gave him a weak smile. "Let's go, baby. We'll sit with you for a while."

Angel was stunned, to the core. He felt shaky and sick. How could a day that had been so good end so badly? The wedding was off, Asher was goodness knew where, and Erik was a mess. Was it really all his fault?

"I . . . I'm sorry, Con, I didn't know. I swear I didn't know it was such a big deal. If I'd known I would have told someone. Asher told me . . . He promised me that when they went to London on honeymoon, he'd get help and he'd stay there until he got things sorted. I thought . . . I thought it would be . . ." He sighed and rubbed tired eyes. "I should have told you. I know I should have told you, but it was all so new and . . . I've really bolloxed things up, haven't I?"

Connor rubbed his shoulders. "Feck, Angel. I wish ye'd told me, I do. All of it. Asher's me best friend and now . . . all of it's fallen to the ocean, I think. It wasn't just yer doing, darlin', it's been everything else, but he didn't help his case by hidin' it. I wish he'd a told me. I thought he knew me better. I guess he doesn't."

"Would you have told Erik, Con," Angel asked, his voice tight with intent. "If Asher had told you in confidence, would you have told Erik?"

"Aye, well, that's a pickle, isn't it?" He rubbed his beard. "Since it was regardin' James, I'd have had to say somethin', would I not? But I wouldn't have landed it on him all at once. Not like those drawin's did. I can understand why Erik was upset, fer sure. It's like finding out yer lover has a secret lover they've loved longer than ye. Sure, I'd be gutted te the core, just like him."

"No, it isn't, Con. James is dead. He died a long time ago and was never a threat to Erik . . . not as far as Asher is concerned. I may not know all the facts, but I know enough to understand *that*. I totally understand Erik's upset. Goddamn it, he has every right to be, given what seems to be the history, but really, Con? Would you have done that to me? In front of all our family and friends? Drawings like that? Knowing how fragile Asher is right now? Would you have done it?"

"Playin' devil's advocate for a second, darlin', he didn't show 'em to everyone, he put 'em in Asher's lap. His parents were the ones who saw 'em. Second, if ye knew the whole story and what he did to Asher, and to Erik, I think ye'd change yer mind quicker than a jig."

"No, Con, I don't think I would change my mind. In fact, I

think it'd make it up even more. If Asher went through such a terrible time, and we've all seen the way he's been these last few days, I wouldn't dream of doing something as horrible as that, and neither would you, at least I hope not, because I'm telling you now, Con, I don't think I'd ever forgive you. He didn't *put them in Asher's lap*, he threw them on the table. Anyone could have picked it up. It could have been Caitlin. Erik's such a hotheaded idiot sometimes, and he just doesn't think. I'm sure — I hope — when he calms down, he'll realize what he's done and put it right." He sighed. "I hope so."

"Aye, but don't ye be knockin' Erik so quickly, *a chroí*. Asher doesn't respond to subtlety, and ye know that, hi. Erik knows it. Sure, he's impulsive and a hothead, but he had to get an answer, and dammit he deserved one. Ye may not agree wid what he did, or how or where, but his mind wasn't exactly workin' proper, now was it?"

Angel stood and gazed down at Connor. He stroked Connor's beard and tucked his hair behind his ear. "God knows, I love you Con, and I love Erik too, in my own way, but for me, what he did tonight, with Asher as fragile as he is, was unforgivable. So maybe we won't talk about it anymore, darlin', because I'd hate it to hell if we fell out over it. Now, Billy and Vince are taking care of Erik, so I suggest we both keep our views to ourselves and we say and do whatever it takes to calm Asher down and take care of him tonight . . . okay?"

Connor sighed. "Right you are, *a chroí*. It's a bad business all 'round. But how to find where Asher ran off to? It's late and dark, I dunno where he'd go. You're his confidant lately, would ye know?"

Angel glanced around. "I'm guessing he'll be back at the house. Where else would he go?"

Connor rose and hugged Angel, then pulled away to gaze into his eyes. "Ah, but I hate fightin' with ye, hi. Our first fight and all, well, officially. Just make me one promise? Dontcha keep a secret from me? Even if ye're asked. Sure, an' it does more harm than good, as we've seen tonight." He tipped Angel's chin to meet his eyes. "I love ye, Angel. We'll find him."

Angel sighed hugely and dropped his eyes. "I'm sorry, Con, I really am, but I can't promise. You know what my family's like with honor, and it's a matter of honor that we don't betray confidences. If I'm asked to keep a confidence again, I promise I'll do my best to get the full facts and to push the person to confide in others, but I can't . . . I can't promise to break a confidence for you. It would be dishonorable, because I wouldn't be able to keep it."

"Aye, I understand. We Irish have our honor, too. Irish honor and pride saved Vince and Billy's relationship, or else we might never have met. Can ye credit it? I didn't mean yer family secrets anyway. I meant involving our friends, and us. Not the family business. I really don't care to know what goes on. All I know is they saved Erik's life," he clarified. "Can ye at least agree to that?"

"No. Honor's honor, and it means a lot to me. I can only promise I'll be as honest with you as I possibly can, and I'll guard your secrets and your honor with my life. Is that enough?"

After a long pause, Connor nodded. "Aye, it must be. I don't want to fight with ye anymore, ye stubborn Italian." He took Angel's hand. "Let's go find Asher."

Angel smiled at him and kissed the fingers laced in his own. They hurried to the house to find it deserted and in darkness.

"Shit," Angel said, his heart sinking. "What do we do now?"

"We start callin' people. See if they've heard a word."

Angel collapsed into a chair and made some calls. Daisy, Joey, Billy . . . none of them had heard a thing. None of them had a clue where Asher might be. After checking Erik and

Asher's new house, they were completely in the dark and starting to get seriously worried.

Erik had never felt so lost and so angry at the same time. Billy and Vince were doing their best to calm him, but he had smoked at least three cigarettes already, almost in a row. His mind was a maze of thoughts, feelings, and what-if scenarios. He sat with his knees up under his chin, tilting the chair so far back it nearly hit the concrete steps behind him. Billy sat as close as he could without being on the chair with him. Vince had gone in to get them some beer.

Billy shoved a plate of crackers and cheese in front of him. "Here. You didn't have dinner. You need to eat. Here, I'll help." He popped a cracker in Erik's mouth.

"Where would he go, Billy? Where the fuck would he run off to? I can't even call the police, not until it's been twenty-four hours, and he's hardly a child." He snorted. "Though you wouldn't know it sometimes by how he acts. Maybe we should ask Caitlin where she'd run off to, I think they're on the same mental level right about now."

"Here's some more beer." Vince re-entered the scene. "I've been trying to think of spots where someone like him would go. All I can think of are dark alleys and shadows." He sat down, popping open a fresh one using his thumb.

Erik raised his bottle. "Here's to the wedding that almost was. Asher . . . wherever you are . . . you . . ." He drank before he could speak what was on his mind. New resolve filled him. "We have to find him, no matter what."

"What will you do when you find him?" Vince asked.

"Nothing, Not right off. I can't help him, it's obvious. Two years of working solely with me after the London shit, and he's still incurable. He's fucked in the head, man. I think I dodged a bullet, honestly. Right now, I just want to know if he's alive and safe. Then it's up to him what he wants to do with me."

"Baby, I think you might have a good idea there, with the dark alleys and such. Have we checked the hospitals? Or . . . shit. Down by the river? He was a nightmare when he left. We don't know what he'll do."

Erik shut his eyes. "Maybe he went to draw another picture of James." He shoved another cigarette between his lips.

"Now, that's not fair, Erik—"

"The hell it ain't, Vince. I'll tell you what, that twinkie cousin of yours is not on my good side right now. He knew all this shit, and I betcha he could have told me way more when he should've. That kid had better steer clear of me."

"I wonder how Connor took it." Billy wondered. "It doesn't matter right now. We have to find Asher. I know Daisy's worried, as are his folks. I say we check the hospitals. I'll go do it." He went indoors and shut the sliding door.

Erik let out a slow sigh. "Vince, do you think I was wrong for doing what I did? For how I did it?"

Vince lit up a cigarette himself. "Nope. I think you had to do it like that. I'm on board with it a hundred percent, Erik. He fuckin' lied to you and held info back on that jackass, and my stupid cousin took his family *honor* too damned far. I'm sick of family honor. Sick of being Italian at all, any drop of my blood."

"Dude." Erik leaned forward and rubbed Vince's shoulder. "Wanna talk about it?"

"Nah . . . not right now. I wanna find Asher and slap him about first."

"I hear you. I wanna just shake him and burn those damn drawings myself. Then I wanna shake Angel-boy and ask him what the hell else he knows."

The door opened. "He's not registered at the hospitals, but it's early yet. If he wasn't an emergency, he wouldn't even have been admitted yet." He sat on Vince's lap. "Maybe . . . oy, and this is gonna sound terrible. Maybe we should just let him get it out of his system and he'll come home when he wants to. He's a big boy."

Vince nodded. "True enough, there. He's twenty-two, he can make decisions, obviously, he's made enough of them lately. He's bound to calm down eventually and seek help somewhere, then we can track him down."

Erik's eyes widened. "Track him? Track. Hmmm." He pulled out his smartphone and punched in Asher's number. "I can pull his GPS coordinates up if the phone's on. Now, to wonder if he took the damn thing with him."

After a few minutes of frantic tapping, Erik threw his phone onto the table. "Damn. Of course he doesn't have it with him. Naturally. Why does he even have one at all?" He picked at some cheese. "I'm at a loss, guys. I truly am."

"I think he'll come back, I really do," Billy offered. "I think he'll get worn out and wander into a hospital or a store or even a fire station, and we can pick him up. I did call the police. My dad knows some cops, and they promised to put out an APB. They can identify him pretty quick, he . . . kinda stands out."

"Amen to that one. So, we wait now — in angst and anger, yet again." Vince replied.

"Yup . . . fun shit, huh? Boy, do I know how to pick the guys or what?" He shot a look at Billy.

"Don't look at me, you made your choice. I had a better offer and I jumped on him." He kissed Vince. "Besides, I couldn't take some of your traits. Somehow, Asher has, for over three years. How, I don't know, but he has. You're not the easiest guy to get along with sometimes."

"I know, but at least I don't flip out on people like this and run off without a word. I did once, and I came back in an hour. It was dinnertime." He laughed.

"True rebel you are, Von Nordgren." Billy shook his head. "I say we eat up, since we missed dinner, and wait for some news."

Vince's phone rang. He picked it up and groaned. "Shit. It's Angel." He hesitated but finally took the call. "What? Nope, not a word, you? No idea. Uh-huh. Well, not like we knew or anything, did we? Yes, I'm pissed at you. Oh, stop it, you brat. Angel, stop it. We have an APB out on him. If he does anything, we'll know it. What? Nope, don't want to talk about it. We're giving it a couple hours, then we'll search, cool? We'll talk after this shit's over with." He hung up.

"Damn. Who are you?" Erik said half-joking.

"Someone who's sick of being in that family. Billy, I should've taken your name instead, maybe we can once we're done with all this."

Erik stood and stretched. "Now, you guys are the ones who are meant to be married. Not me, apparently. Fucker . . . Damn Asher!" He pitched his cigarettes across the expansive yard and collapsed back down into his chair, flanked by his friends as he sobbed.

CHAPTER TWELVE

A sher was lost, in more ways than one. When he ran from the dining room, he had no idea where he was going. All he cared about was getting away from those eyes. All of them. They looked at him as if they hated him. Dammit . . . they did hate him. He'd always known his father despised him, although, for a little while, he'd thought maybe things were getting better. Now . . .

All his friends were there. *All* his friends. His only friends. They hated him now, too. And Erik. Erik was supposed to have loved him. Fool. He should have known. He wasn't meant to be loved. He'd never been meant to be loved. He was meant to be fucked . . . and he had been. Tonight he'd been royally fucked, and he couldn't handle it.

To stop himself thinking, he ran. He ran as hard and as fast as he could, his thundering heart and panting breath drowning the screaming in his head. But they couldn't drown it forever. Eventually, he had to stop.

First, he ran through countryside and woods, leaping over roots and obstructions, falling, getting up, pushing on, always pushing on. For hours he ran, and ran, and ran. But he couldn't outrun the pain. It stayed with him, lodged in his heart, roaring through the chasm that was open and bleeding. Every thud of his foot on the floor screamed *gone, gone, gone.* It was all gone. Erik was gone. His friends were gone. His home was gone. His life was gone. He had nothing.

Over and over and over, it echoed in his head, punching into his gut. It was all gone, all gone, all gone.

How could he have done it? How could Erik have done that? He knew the way it was, the way his father was, the way his head was. Why? It was all so close to being good. For a while, he'd let himself believe he was going to have his happy ending, that everything was going to be all right after all. Tonight, it was supposed to have ended — the pain, the torment, the bad times. Tonight, he and Angel would have burned James, got closure once and for all and tomorrow — today? — he'd have started new. He wouldn't have been Asher the fuck-up anymore, the Asher who couldn't do anything right, who was a freak and a nutjob and a worthless son and . . . He was going to have a fresh start. When he went to London, he'd have got help, proper help to get his head sorted out once and for all. With Erik at his side, he'd have been able to do anything . . . and now it was gone.

Why had Erik done it? Why? What had Asher done that was so wrong? He'd tried to tell Erik. He'd tried to tell him so many times. He'd tried to tell them all. Maybe he wasn't good at talking about how he felt. No, he *knew* he wasn't good at it. His words got jumbled and choked and when it got too hard, he ran away. But he'd tried, he really had, but . . . Every time he'd mentioned James, tried to ask about what had happened to him, how he'd died, where his body was, they'd yelled, or shut him down, and looked at him as if he needed to be locked up. They didn't understand. They couldn't understand. James had always been there, in his life, in his head. How could he just . . . get over it? He needed closure. He was desperate for it. He'd needed to talk about it, to work through it. He'd needed to assimilate, to mourn and move on. And no one had listened . . . no one understood.

Maybe he should have gone to Rita after all. She'd have understood. She always understood. You can't go through those things with someone, have them invade every part of you and just shrug them off as if it had never happened. You just can't do that. He couldn't do that. But no one had understood. No one ever understood.

He'd done the first drawing because he needed to say goodbye, to get James out of his head. Then he'd started thinking back to the good times, the way James had made him feel, to wish it had never got so bad, that James had never screwed him up. He wanted to be innocent and untouched like he'd been with James. He wanted to be like that for Erik. So he'd started to draw James again, every bad thing he could remember him doing, being, saying . . . He drew it all out. It was his way of dealing with it.

And then with the wedding. He'd tried so hard to tell everyone how bad he was feeling, how stressed, how pushed aside, how out of control. He'd tried so, so hard, but no one *listened.* So he'd told the pictures he was drawing. He'd told James. All the negatives in his life, all the things he'd had no control over. He drew them out and put them down. He'd had it all planned. All the negatives would be out of him by tonight, and he'd burn them and start again. It had all seemed so simple, so easy, so within his control. And even when it had started to go wrong, he'd still thought he could control it, that he'd go to London and get help and . . . and . . .

And now it was gone. It was all gone. Why did Erik do that? Why? Why? In front of all those people. It was enough he'd looked at him like that, had spoken to him like that. It was enough he didn't trust him, didn't understand him, hated him so much. It was enough . . . but it wasn't.

He fell to his knees and didn't bother to get up. Sagging against the side of a building he wept, and wept, and wept, until he was empty. Then he lay there, just a puddle of shadow at the foot of a wall, not thinking.

It was all gone. There was no going back now. There was nothing there for him. Nothing behind, nothing ahead. Nothing. And then it was all so clear. He was nothing. A nutjob, a freak, an unstable liability. He hurt everyone around him, and he spoiled everything he touched. Erik would be better off without him. Everyone would be better off without him.

Staggering, he got to his feet and looked around. It was the early hours of the morning, but the part of town he'd staggered into was still busy. Cars were zipping past, heading to or from the night clubs, and half the drivers would be drunk or high. Their reflexes would be dulled, and they wouldn't be watching the road. It would be easy, so easy. If he made sure the car was big enough . . . and traveling fast enough . . .

Standing on the curb, Asher felt calm, calmer than he'd felt in a long time. The pit was open and empty, his fears and pain had disappeared along with his hopes and dreams. He was an empty vessel, a vessel that would be easy to smash, to shatter.

A screech of breaks from way down the street caught his attention. A silver sports car was skidding where the driver must have lost control for a moment. It straightened and sped up, hurtling toward him at an ever-increasing speed. Perfect. Taking a deep breath, Asher closed his eyes and stepped off the curb.

"I've rung the local hospitals and the police." Angel knew he was shaking as he sat at the kitchen table taking the coffee Connor held out to him. "One of the others must have rung, too, because they knew about it. They've got an APB out on him so maybe . . . I-I've spoken to my father, too. He's got people looking who will probably have more luck than the police. I guess all we can do is wait. Erik must be off his head."

"Aye, I'll bet he is. If ye were missin' I'd be beside meself, so I would, hi." Connor grabbed hold of Angel's shaking hand. "Stupid question, but are ye all right? They'll find him, ye know it, have faith. What else is it, Angel?"

"It . . . It's Vince. He sounded . . . He sounded as if he hates me, really hates me. I . . . Connor, maybe I should have told someone something, maybe I should have told you. If I'd known how big a deal it was, I might have. At least I'd have done my best to talk Asher into getting help. But I didn't know. All I knew was it was a picture of an ex he was afraid Erik would be angry about. It seemed innocent enough. I didn't know about what happened in the past. I didn't know about anything. I still don't. I don't know what all the fuss is about. And . . . then . . . It was only two days ago I saw the other pictures, and he promised me he was going to get rid of them and he was going to get some help with his panic attacks. I thought . . . I thought it was the best. I didn't *know*. And now . . . now everyone hates me."

The coffee cup fell from his fingers as he buried his head in his hands and sobbed.

Connor held him tight. "Ssh, easy, easy now, *a chroí*. I don't hate ye. I don't. I disagree with ye on some of it, but I don't hate ye. Angel, look at me . . ." He tipped up Angel's face. "It's out there now. Done and dusted. What's important is findin' Asher. Makin' sure he's okay. Right? Yeah?"

Angel nodded quietly against Connor's chest.

"As fer Vince." He shrugged. "He's been havin' it bad, so he 'as. It's not you. He doesn't hate ya. He's after bein' angry with the world, so he is, hi. You're family, and as much as I think me brothers and sisters — Nora besides — are a bunch of scummy bastards, they're still family and I love them." He rocked Angel gently. "Sure, this is just one grand mess, but we'll get it sorted. I promise ya."

"I love you, Con," Angel sobbed. "I don't know what I'd do without you. I can't imagine how Asher's feeling. He must be so lost and alone." Calming down a little, Angel looked up at Connor. "Con? You know all the shit that happened, with Asher . . . in the past? I mean, it's really screwed him up, hasn't it? And now all this . . . You don't think . . . I mean, he wouldn't . . . he wouldn't do anything stupid . . . would he?"

Connor shrugged. "I've not told ye this, *a chroí*, but it wouldn't be the first time he's tried. Back in the beginnin' when all the shit with James was goin' down . . . I think he tried twice, and it was pure luck that saved him. Truth is, I'm scared to death he'll end himself before Erik finds him."

Angel felt sick, the bile rising to his throat. "Seriously? I . . . I didn't know. I had no idea. Oh, God. Why did I let this happen? Why didn't I do something? Why didn't I go after him? Why didn't Erik? Does anyone else know?"

Taking a lock of Angel's hair, Connor twirled it between his fingers. "I don't know. Probably I shoulda told ya. I thought Asher would be after tellin' it himself. It's not a pretty story. As fer Erik, I'll bet he's out lookin' like everyone else. Trouble is . . . Asher's damn good at hidin' when he doesn't want te be found, hi."

"Oh, my God, Con, his father was there. Asher's father was there, and he didn't say a word. His parents know . . . they know what happened in the past. They know how he is, what he's done. Why? Why did he just look at him like that, as if he was disgusted, as if . . . No one, Con. No one said anything. No one tried to help him, to support him. And Daisy. Oh, shit Daisy . . . why didn't Daisy? Why? Why? Why?" He crumpled again and sobbed. "If anything happens . . . If anything happens to Asher, I'll never forgive myself . . . and I'll never forgive them, either."

"Why didn't they speak up for him? I don't know. Maybe they were as shocked as Erik. They all know the story, hi. I'll tell ye a bit of, so ye know. James got his claws into Asher when he was fourteen. He tortured him, cut him, drugged him, and messed with his head. He had Asher convinced he'd die without James. That the darkness would get him. He was after convincing the boy Erik was the darkness, and Asher

162

woulda killed him if your da hadn't saved them. But Erik's been takin' care o' him, so he has, tryin' to sort his head out."

"Con, babe, you're doing my head in. Do any of you actually listen to yourselves when you talk? The more I hear, the more it feels I'm in a psychological horror and *my* head's getting screwed up. Either that, or none of you give a fuck about Asher and can't wait to push him out of your lives. You can't see, can you? You just can't see. It sounds like Asher's spent his life being abused . . . in one way or another. Fucking hell, Con! No one said a word to him. No one supported him. No one cared. Maybe he was wrong. Maybe he was as wrong as it was possible to be. Maybe what he did was unforgivable. I don't think it was, but that's not the point. Even if . . . even if what he did earned him a place in hell . . . He's already been there." Angel's voice shook and he couldn't look at Connor.

"He's been to hell over and over. He's been abused, and scarred, and screwed up . . . and tonight we did it all over again. Can't you see? Can't you see what we did to him? And no one went after him. No one gave a shit. If I'd known. If I'd known what you just told me, I'd never have sat there and let him go through that, and I'm damn sure I'd have gone after him. I'd have run until my lungs burst and my legs gave way."

"Then that's what we'll do. I can't sit around here any longer. You're after bein' as right as ye can be. We fecked the boy, and now we're goin' te put things right. Come on. Asher might be tricky, but I'm trickier. I can find him. I'm sure of it."

Erik shot up out of his chair. "I can't do this anymore! Dammit all to hell. I can't . . . I can't sit here while he's missing, and other people are doing the work. I-I should've gone after him, shouldn't I? Yes, I should've, stupid question."

Billy took his hand. "We're ready to go when you are, boss.

We've been thinking the same thoughts. I feel guilty as sin, too."

"Same here. And for yelling at Angel like I did. He didn't know the whole story, apparently."

Erik put his arms around them. "Then we should have them along." He pulled out his cell phone and called Connor. "Con? It's Erik. Yes, really, you leprechaun. We're forming a search party, wanted to know if you wanted to join us. Yeah, Angel too. So whaddya say?"

Erik corralled the posse at the small house. He held up his cell phone. "Okay, we all have each other's numbers, right?"

Everyone nodded.

"Okay then, I say we start from the tent. He took off out from there. On foot, he couldn't have gotten too far. It's been, not very long, not even an hour. But he's tricky, so search the woods, creeks, roads, whatever you can find. Phone Joey for info, all right? If we see anything, call immediately."

"Do ye think we'll find him in the dark like this?"

"Yes, it's not too dark out yet, the sun just set. We've all got flashlights and phones. Let's hit it, gentlemen. Bring him back."

"Let's hit it!" Billy repeated with enthusiasm.

They fanned out in all directions, each hoping to find Asher.

Asher was flying backward, completely unable to comprehend what happened. "What the fuck?"

"Easy there. Don't struggle, and you won't get hurt."

"What?" Unable to stop himself, he did struggle, and the arm that had appeared around his waist and yanked him back from the curb tightened until it almost squeezed the life out of him, along with his breath. Colored sparks exploded in front of his eyes and he went limp.

"Calm now?" The voice said again as the arm released a little.

"Yes," he whispered. "Please let me go."

"If I let you go, do you promise not to run? I really don't want to hurt you this time."

"This time?" Things began to slot into place . . . Italian accent, dark suit . . ."You? You're one of Tony's . . . associates." *Damn nearly said goon. That wouldn't have been wise.*

The man set Asher on his feet and let him go, keeping a firm hold on his arm. Asher squinted. He didn't recognize the man, but there was something about the voice . . .

"It's a pleasure to see you again . . . with your clothes on," the man said, giving him a blindingly white smile.

Asher's eyes widened and he blushed furiously. "You were there. In London. You were one of the men who rescued us."

The man winced slightly, his smile slipping a little. "Rescue is such a relative word. To be precise, I'm the man who shot you. Whether you consider it to be a rescue or not is up to you."

"You? It was you? I . . ."

"If it helps, it was a mistake."

"No, no, I understand. Erik explained and I completely understand. It . . . it looked . . . I'm very grateful to you. If you hadn't . . . I would have . . ." He stammered to a halt.

The man's smile brightened again. "Glad that's ironed out. Now, if you'd like to step over here, your chariot awaits."

"What?"

The man indicated a large black car that had slid silently into the curb in front of them. "Someone would like to have a word with you."

"I don't want to go back," Asher said. He was so tired. "Please. Don't make me go back."

"My . . . instructions were to take to see Tony, and that's exactly what I'm going to do. I kinda like you, kid, so I'm hoping you'll be sensible about it. I really don't want to hurt you."

"I . . ." Asher panicked for a moment. All kinds of things flashed through his mind, one of them was *Get free, run, and maybe he'll shoot you,* but in the end, he nodded and got into the car. The man got in beside him, sandwiching him between two of them. They were taking no chances, it seemed.

He didn't want to go back. He didn't want to face it all again but . . . Maybe . . . He sighed and leaned his head against the back of the seat.

He woke with a start, his head resting on a black-clad shoulder. "What . . ."

"We've arrived," the man said with surprising gentleness. "You need to get out now."

"Where are we?"

"Where do you think we are?"

"It's dark."

"We're in a garage."

"At Tony's?"

"There you go. Mind's back online. Come on. This way." The man led Asher out of the garage and through a part of the house he hadn't been in before. They stopped outside a door marked *Office* and the man knocked. Without waiting for an invitation, he opened the door and ushered Asher inside, closing the door behind them.

"Thank you, Vittorio. You may leave us." Tony was sitting behind a huge desk looking at Asher in a way that made him really not want Vittorio to leave them.

Vittorio squeezed his shoulder, and when Asher turned, he was treated to another of the man's blinding smiles before the door closed. Asher turned back and sat, head down and hands between his knees. He had no idea what was coming, but whatever it was, he was too tired to fight anymore.

"Vittorio tells me you were about to make a very unwise move."

Asher jumped and looked up. "I . . ."

Tony raised a hand. "No need to explain. I have a clear enough picture. I am not happy, not happy at all that my son has been dragged into this unpleasant business."

"Angel? But I . . . Oh. I see. I-I'm sorry. I didn't mean . . ."

"If I thought for one moment you had deliberately got my son involved in this mess, I would have had my associates handle you far more roughly. *Far* more."

"Y-yes, sir. Angel has never been anything but a good friend to me, a really good friend."

"And you repay his friendship by walking in front of a car?"

"No. No, I . . ." He closed his eyes. "I wasn't thinking of that."

"I can't imagine you were thinking of anything very much."

"No, I wasn't. I was thinking of nothing." Asher lowered his head again and sighed as tears beginning to slide down his cheeks. He was so tired and so . . . hopeless.

Tony got up and walked around the desk and put a hand on Asher's shoulder. "What do you want, Asher?"

Asher looked up into eyes that were kinder than he would ever have imagined. "Want? I . . . I have nothing, I . . ."

"I didn't ask what you have, I asked what you want. I can help you. I can help you more than you could imagine. If I had known the way things are, I would have offered before. First, I have arranged for you to see a doctor I know well. He will help you get your head together. He's based in London, but we can work it out when we know what's going to happen."

"I-I can't . . ."

"Yes, you can. It is already arranged. Only the details need to be worked out."

"Th-thanks. I . . . don't know how to thank you."

"Then don't. Now, what else do you want?"

"I don't know what you mean. I don't know what I want. I don't know . . ." He was already overwhelmed, and his brain wasn't working. He was so tired and so confused.

"I can give you somewhere to go, somewhere to rest and get back on track. I can give you somewhere to live, a way to continue your art studies and your career in London. Is that what you want?"

"I . . ." Asher's mind was racing. A fresh start. A new chance to make his life work. Proper help, a new home, a new school, a new life . . . But . . ."No," he whispered. "No, it's not what I want but . . ."

"What do you want?"

Asher couldn't speak. His throat had closed with the tears pouring down his face and choking him. Images flashed through his head . . . memories, thoughts, hopes, fears, dreams, visions . . . And through it all . . ."Erik," he whispered.

The woods were so thick around Tony's house, denser than the ones around Erik's, for sure. Erik stumbled through the dark. His flashlight was running out of power. "Asher?" His voice had faded to a whisper as the enormity of what had happened rang through him. He stopped and knelt at the creek to be sick.

A pair of headlights appeared, and a car pulled up on the road next to him, not too far away. "What the . . ." He figured it might be a property owner wondering who this kid was getting sick in their creek, but no. The car stayed put. Erik stumbled to his feet, wiping his mouth off on his sleeve.

"Who . . ." As he got closer to the car, a very large man climbed out. He froze, but the man seemed familiar. "Holy shit. You're the guy . . . the guy who . . . had a gun to my head in London!" His legs started to freeze up, but he kept moving.

"Mr. Von Nordgren? Come with me."

A hand took his arm and escorted him into the car. Erik was relieved someone on board had an antacid, which he took prompt advantage of.

"You look really pale."

"I feel pale and drained to death. Taking me back to the big house? The scene of the crime I committed?" he partially joked.

"Yup. Tony wants to speak with you."

Erik shut his eyes. "Well isn't this my lucky night? The big guy wants to see me for once."

The car stopped, thankfully, and they escorted him to a large office, where the first face he saw was Tony's. Almost immediately, however, Tony's face became unimportant, when he saw Asher. His heart almost leaped from his chest. "Asher! You're okay! Thank God!"

"Sit down Erik." Tony indicated a chair in front of the desk on which he was sitting. "Thank you, Vittorio, you may leave us. Stay close in case I need you." Vittorio inclined his head, winked at Asher, and disappeared. "Vittorio seems to like you, Asher," Tony said with humor in his voice. "There may be a previously unconsidered third option on the table."

Asher turned his head away quickly and stared at his hands. He was deathly pale and looked scared to death.

What the hell was going on here?

"I've put some offers on the table for Asher, and before we decide which ones to take forward, we need your opinion. I will tell you one of the offers, which has already been approved, is that an appointment will be made as soon as possible with a psychiatrist I know who will help Asher resolve his mental issues. Asher has promised me he will cooperate in every way and work hard to get himself back on track."

Erik smiled wide. "Really? Oh, Ash, that's great! I'm so glad you said yes. I hope they can help you out, heal you, and get the closure you need." He dropped his head and chewed on a thumb. "I did what I could, but this is beyond me, beyond all of us . . ." He reached out toward Asher but let his hand drop at Asher's bleak expression.

"In order to consider the other two options, I . . . and more importantly, Asher, need to know one thing. Do you want this relationship to continue, to work?"

Erik nodded without hesitation. "I want it to . . . yes. I know we've had all kinds of issues, but Asher, I *know* we can do this. We've worked through things before. Maybe with the right kind of help, I can learn to be a better guy, because you need the best, Asher. Hell, you deserve it after everything. But yes, to answer, I want this relationship to continue." He rubbed his stomach and his arms. "Sorry, I was sick before they picked me up, not used to running."

"I believe you have your answer, Asher. I'm guessing I'm taking the other offer off the table?"

Erik turned to Asher, who simply nodded. Tears were pouring down his cheeks, and he seemed so lost, so helpless.

Erik knew he'd hurt him, and his heart almost broke with how awful Asher looked. He glanced over at Tony.

"Do you mind . . . if we talk alone for a while? Maybe not here, but . . . we have some things to work out, as you know."

"I've said what I had to say and done what I had to do. My part is over. Oh . . ." He paused with one hand on Erik's shoulder. "I believe you have something to say to my son." The fingers tightened, not quite to the point of pain, but with a promise of violence restrained. "As you know, Angel and I have not always been close, but he is my son. He is a man of honor, and men of honor do not betray their friends."

"I understand, sir. I'm sorry. When this is over, I'll speak with him."

"You will indeed, and you will speak to him with more respect than you did tonight. If I *ever* hear you speak to my son like that again, things will not go well for you." With one last squeeze, Tony patted his shoulder, then strode out without a backward glance.

Erik turned immediately to Asher. "You look so tired, baby, are you hungry at all? I'm sure there's leftovers from our rehearsal dinner. Let me look after you? I promise I won't fuck it up this time. Just looking at you and knowing . . . It breaks my heart." Tears streamed down his face. "My Asher." He held out his arms, and after a moment's hesitation, Asher threw himself into them.

Asher clung to him and sobbed. "I'm sorry, Erik. I'm so sorry. I never meant . . . I didn't want you to get hurt, not for a moment, not . . . I couldn't help it. I needed . . . He was still there . . . still in my head. I needed to get him out, I had to . . . I tried to. I . . . No one would talk to me. No one would let me talk, and I needed to. I *needed* to. I couldn't even say goodbye. I couldn't . . . I was just there and then . . . then with the wedding . . . and . . . I couldn't . . . and no one . . . and I . . . I had to get it *out*. I had to get it all *out* and I didn't know what else to do. I wasn't thinking. I wasn't thinking of you, or James or anyone . . . I just *did* it. I . . . The last thing I wanted was to hurt you.

"You're right. You weren't enough. You're not enough, but it's my fault. No one could have done it—no one. I needed proper help. I should have . . . I should have taken it when it was offered. It was all my fault. It was never you, never. I . . . I don't blame you if you hate me . . ."

"Ssh, no, God no, I don't hate you, Asher. I've never hated you, not ever. I'm sorry I didn't listen and was wrapped up in everything but you and wasn't the one you could pour your guts out to about needing closure with James. That was my failing, my fault, all of it. I'm glad you could talk to Angel. He listened. He was a kindred spirit for you, and he didn't know the whole story." He rocked Asher gently as he held him tight and kissed his hair.

"I know, I know. I had the same regret about you not getting help before. I thought I was good enough, but I'm not. I'm not trained to help you properly, but you'll get it now, baby. You'll be healthy in all aspects. Ssh. I . . . have to say I'm shocked you wanted to keep going with me. You were free. You could've had anyone, anyone at all. Why did you want me back?"

Asher laughed, a strange hiccupping sound. "Tony offered me a new start. The doctor I'm gonna see is in London, and he offered me a place to stay, a place in art school, a career. A whole new life."

Erik's hands started to sweat. "So what made you stay? What made you want to not take the offer?" He gazed into Asher's lilac eyes hopefully. "I guess you'd have to leave everyone behind then . . . But you aren't . . ."

"I love you," Asher said with a half-shrug. "I can't have a new life without you. You are my life. There *is* no life without you."

Erik couldn't help the smile that crept across his face. "I love you, too, Asher, so much. I . . . wouldn't have a life either. It's all meaningless without you, baby." He held him close for a long moment and kissed him sweetly, then had a mischievous thought. "I think I know another reason you stayed. I can read your mind, baby."

"Another reason?" Asher looked up at him, puzzled.

Erik nodded and smiled wide. "Of course! Caitlin." He snorted and laughed aloud.

Asher blinked at him. "Caitlin?" A tiny smile tugged at the corner of his mouth. "Wouldn't want to break her heart."

"Not at all. Or anyone else's, either." They snickered together for a fun moment, a welcome relief to the drama of the past couple of days. "Hey . . . I have another question, more of a request. Maybe, instead of Angel . . . I want to help you . . . help you to burn those drawings. If you want him to be there too, that's fine, but I want to help."

"Really?" Asher smiled, then frowned. "I . . . don't know where they are. My father . . . Oh, God. Oh, God, my father. My mother. They saw. They . . . Oh, God. He hated me enough before and I . . . I . . ." Asher gripped Erik's arm, squeezed his eyes closed, and started to rock. "No, no, no, no, no."

"Ssh, it's okay. It's okay, Ash. I can pilfer anything out a parent's house. Are you kidding? I'll get them back that way if need be. Or I'll talk to them, or we can, together. Maybe tomorrow? We should burn them as soon as possible." He smoothed down Asher's hair. "I was idiotic enough to bring them there. I'll get them back."

"But . . . but my father. He hates me now. He really hates me. They all do. I saw . . ."

"They don't hate you. I don't know how your father feels, but I don't think he hates you, Asher. He was surprised for sure, but I know for a fact no one else hates you. They were shocked and stunned maybe, and some may hate me, and I don't care if they do, but no one hates you. If they do, they're beyond stupid."

"Really?" he whispered. "You really think so?"

Erik nodded. "I know so. No one's pissed off at you. They were at me, but you know me, I go for the shock factor." He grinned. "Though you rival me sometimes, dontcha?" He kissed Asher, and his nerves started to rise again. "So . . . uhh . . . what're your plans for tomorrow night?" His heart pounded, and he couldn't take his eyes off Asher.

Asher frowned, causing Erik's heart to skip a beat. "To-to-morrow night?" He shook his head, and Erik very nearly threw up again. "I . . . don't understand . . . what you mean?"

With a soft kiss to Asher's hands, he answered. "Will you still do me the honor of marrying me tomorrow night?" He paused. "Unless you've made other plans."

"What? You . . . You mean you still . . . I . . ." Asher swallowed hard and then seemed to light up from within, like a candle in a lantern. The glass was frosted, but it was bright nevertheless, bright enough to light Erik's life. "Yes. Yes, I'll still marry you. Yes, yes, yes, yes." Asher threw his arms around Erik's neck and kissed him furiously.

"My Asher. My sweet Asher." Erik murmured. "Oh! I need to tell the others. We were out looking for you, Daisy was monitoring the police radio. Lemme text her."

He pulled out his phone and sent a quick message off to both Billy and Daisy.

All's kewl, getting hitched!

"There, now it'll spread like wildfire. Are you hungry? Tired? Let's go relax, shall we? At the little house with some Irish Whiskey?"

"Wh-whiskey?" Asher seemed dazed, as if he couldn't quite believe what was happening. "I think . . . I think that would . . . be good."

"Come on, let's go to our temporary home." He stood and took Asher's hand. "My fiancé." He smiled, and they were on their way.

CHAPTER THIRTEEN

Connor was dispirited, and by the look of him, Angel was too. They'd searched for what seemed like hours and got nowhere. At just after midnight, they collapsed on the sofa in the little house, having just met up.

"Have you heard from anyone?" Angel asked. "I'm exhausted. I've no idea where else to look."

Connor shook his head. "Oy, I hear ye, love. Me feet are killin' me." He took off his shoes and rubbed his feet. "Maybe try callin' your da. He knows everything and then some. I'm sure he knows somethin' *for your eyes only*."

"My father isn't God, Connor. He doesn't know everything." With a smile, Angel took out his phone and walked to the other side of the room to make the call. A few minutes later, he disconnected the call and turned, his face a mask of shock. He collapsed on the sofa next to Connor. "I don't believe it."

"What? What is it?" He sat up and leaned over Angel. "What don't ye believe? Don't' keep me in suspense, darlin'."

"They um . . . They're there, at the house with my father." He shook his head in disbelief. "The wedding's back on and they're on their way here."

Connor smiled wide. "It is? They are? Well saints preserve us, I knew they'd work it out, so I did! I knew Erik wasn't such a big a meathead after all. Sure, I can't believe it. They've been next door this whole time? While we've been out walkin' our arses off?" He scowled. "It's a lousy trick, so it is, but at least it's solved now. I wonder . . ."

There was a knock at the door, and before Connor could even get it open all the way, Erik and Asher burst inside, Asher being carried by Erik.

"Hello? Anybody got room for two grooms-to-be?" Erik was positively glowing.

"What the fuck? Asher, are you okay?" Angel leaped to his feet. "Over here, Erik. Put him down. Is he okay? What happened?"

"As far as . . . where he went or how the wedding's back on?" Erik asked as he set Asher on the sofa and sat beside him.

"Well, first things first, Erik." Connor turned to Asher, his expression still dominated by a worried frown. "Where'd ye go, darlin'? We were huntin' all over for ye, so we were."

Asher yawned and snuggled into Erik. He looked exhausted, his makeup smudged to hell and his hair in a complete mess, but he was smiling, and there was a light in his eyes that hadn't been there for a long time.

"I don't know," he said. "I just ran. I couldn't tell you where. I wasn't thinking, wasn't looking where I was going. I ended up . . . somewhere, on a street near the clubs. I-I was in a right state and I was going to . . ." He paused and licked his lips, his eyes getting intensely introspective. He shook his head slightly. "Tony's guys—would you believe, the one who shot me, Vittorio. He found me and took me to Tony's . . . um . . . your father's house." He glanced up at Angel, and the light came on again. "He made me an offer I couldn't refuse."

Erik laughed. "Wow, that's not too different than what they did with me. I guess they all operate the same way. I never got the name of my guy, you're lucky. Did he apologize for shooting you?" He rubbed Asher's shoulder where it had taken a bullet almost two years ago.

"Kind of. Actually . . ." He looked up at Erik with his old flirtatious smile. "He may have been one of the offers on the table. He seemed to like me."

Connor shook his head and sighed. "What are we gonna do wid ye, hi? Can't help yerself. Thank the Good Lord it's Erik takin' ye on. I think I'd a killed ye by now."

"Nah, I'm too good in bed for that."

Connor laughed and bent to hug Asher. When he pulled away, he gripped Asher's shoulders and gazed into his eyes. "Dontcha ever do nothing like that te me again, ye hear? I was out o' me mind, so I was. If I'd lost ye . . ." Connor gave him a quick, hard hug then stood. "Ye had us all running in circles, ye fecker, and all the time ye were flirtin' with some good looking Italian. Not that I fault ye fer it." He grinned at Angel, who smiled back

"I'm okay. I'm okay, now." Asher gazed up at Angel, and a completely different expression crossed his face. "I'm sorry, Angel. I'm so sorry for getting you involved in this mess. If I'd known . . ."

"Don't you dare say that." Angel glared at Erik and at Connor. "You needed someone, and I was there. I guess I was in the right place, at the right time and in the right frame of mind. Sometimes you need someone with a bit of distance, who's not entangled in the history. If it turned into a mess for me, it was my fault. I didn't ask enough questions, or at least I didn't ask the right ones. I had absolutely no idea what happened to you. If I had . . . I'd have put a lot more pressure on you to talk to Erik."

Asher dropped his head. "I wouldn't have. It doesn't matter what you said, I wouldn't have, and I'd have backed away from you, too. Without you I'd have been alone. I think I would have cracked long before now, and there might not have been anyone there to . . . to bring me back."

"It's all right, *a chroí*." Connor put his arms around Angel. "It's over. I'm after being sorry I was harsh with ye. Ye're a good man, and ye did what ye had te do, hi. I proud of ye, so I am." He kissed his boyfriend's hair. "And wouldja look at me forgetting me friend, Erik! Are ye all right? Ye're right pasty lookin' there. Did ye see a ghost?" He put a hand on his arm.

"It's all right, Con. I'm good. I just got a bit sick. I'd run so fast and my stomach was all churned up anyway, it happened. That's when they picked me up and took me up to the house. I'm feeling better now, thanks." He smiled at the Connor

"You're not going back to Vince and Billy's tonight," Angel stated with a firm nod. "The two of you can get showered and into bed as soon as you like. We can talk in the morning. Tomorrow's going to be a big day for you."

"I think we're being shuttled off to bed, my love. Come on, up you go, I've gotcha." He picked up Asher off the sofa and kissed him. "Practice for carrying you over the threshold, my future Mr. Berkley-Von Nordgren or whatever you decided on," he teased.

"I don't want to be Berkley anymore. I want to be someone else, someone new." Asher sighed and closed his eyes, snuggling into Erik's arms. "I want to start all over again."

Erik kissed him. "Then, my future Mr. Asher Von Nordgren, let's get to bed. Tomorrow is our day." He looked over his shoulder as he started up the stairs. "Be sure everyone else knows the news. We're heading to bed. See you in the morning!"

"Aye, we will, guys!" Connor put an arm around Angel and held him close. "Sleep well!"

"I . . ." Angel sat down and laughed. "I don't know what to say. The only thing that comes to mind is *What the fuck just happened?*"

Connor laughed. "Aye, it's been a rough day. But the weddin's back on, and dat's the main thing, hi. I thought fer sure it was done and gone." He kissed Angel gently. "I'm ready for bed meself, how 'bout you?"

"Yes, yes I am, but I don't think I'm going to be able to sleep, I'm too wired. I'm going to need to wind down. Think you could help me relax?"

"I think I could do that for ye." Connor kissed him again. "What would ye be havin'? A glass of Ireland's best, or a long, slow, and completely naked massage?"

"Is there any reason I can't have both?"

"None at all. Shall we start with a drink then?" He winked. "I'll get the glasses."

Connor grabbed a bottle and glasses and headed upstairs, leaving Angel to take care of the texts.

Angel stretched to ease the kinks in his back. He'd slept awkwardly draped over Connor, not that he was complaining. He smiled to himself as he put the coffee pot on. Two arms slid around his waist ,and he let his head fall back onto a shoulder still damp from the shower. It belonged to a furry ginger Irishman. Angel smiled and wriggled his bottom against his lover, earning a playful slap on the backside. They'd already made love twice, and Connor was clearly not up to round three right now.

"Aww . . . Come on, Con. I was only trying to help get rid of your wedding day nerves. Being best man is a heavy job, so much responsibility, so much pressure . . . and you're not getting any younger."

Connor tickled him, and they laughed together. "Using me age against me now, are ye? And yerself just a wee babby. This old man can show ye a thing or two." He kissed Angel's neck. "Sure, I knew ye'd be a right cracker. Ye wear me out, so ye do. Hand me some o' dat coffee before I lose me awesome sexual prowess and leave ye to please yerself."

"Oh no, no. It cannot be." Angel pressed the back of his hand to his forehead dramatically. "But what shall I do, for the coffee is not hot. Ah, but I am hot, so I will distract you with my cure for all libido difficulties." He turned in Connor's arms and kissed him, pressing himself against Connor in the most suggestive way he could, making his meaning very clear.

"Hey, hey . . . guys! Hump like rabbits upstairs, wouldja? I'm getting married tonight, and my eyes are still pure," Erik joked as he walked in on the suggestive scene. "Damn, I knew you two were cute as hell together. Called that one." He reached for the coffee and poured himself a cup.

"It's not hot yet," Angel said with a smirk. "And we've already humped like rabbits upstairs. Now we were trying to move it downstairs. Unfortunately, someone let the fox out."

Erik laughed. "Well, this fox is hungry and raring to get going on this all-important day. The future Mr. Von Nordgren is still sleeping off last night. I had to talk him into some pre-marital sex." He laughed as he flopped down on the sofa.

"You had to talk Asher into sex? God, he must have been worse than I thought," Angel teased, although even he could hear the note of concern in Erik's voice.

"Gawd no, I was joking. We'd both been sick and were exhausted, but we got through it just fine. From what little I could hear, I think you two had no problems at all." Erik waggled his brows. "Just kidding, didn't hear a thing, too busy . . . getting busy." He wiped his hands on his robe. "So, besides getting married, what's on the agenda today?"

"As little as possible," Angel implored. "After last night, staying in bed all day was an attractive option. Unfortunately, this one" — he ruffled Connor's hair — "was a dreadful spoilsport and made us get up. Well, no, that's not entirely true. I did manage to get him up earlier, but that was very different." He kissed Connor, who gave him another slap on the backside.

"Whoa . . . Angel! What has he done to you? You used to be this shy kid. Oy, those Irishmen will rock your world, eh? I've never had one, so you'll just have to tell me about it sometime, but not while I'm eating." Erik chuckled and took another bite of toast.

"It was me distinct pleasure corruptin' this one, so it was. I think a daily dose is needed." Connor kissed Angel's hair. "Now, as for today, I'm all set. I'll check in with me sister and mouthy niece."

"Tell Caitlin I'm sorry, but I'm off the market now." Erik grinned.

Angel groaned. "I think I've changed my mind about ever wanting to marry you, Con. Can you imagine being related to that little bag of fireworks? Actually, it might be safer to be related than to be available. Ah hell, can you imagine her as a flower girl?"

Connor snorted. "Sure, she'd never make it all the way down the aisle, and no man between would be safe. Better be stickin' with our friends. When you're ready, *a chroí*. I'll not be rushin' ya."

Angel hugged him. "We will. One day, we will, I promise."

A sharp rap on the door startled them all. "I'll get it," Erik said, getting to his feet. He opened the door to find a perturbed Daisy, hauling a suit bag over her shoulder. "Well, mornin', Miss Daisy, how are you today?" He grinned widely.

"How do you think I'm feeling?" she snapped. "Get out of the way and take this bloody thing off me. It's heavy. Do you have any coffee?" Sitting down at the table, she fanned herself with her hand as Erik draped the bag over the back of the chair.

Connor poured her a cup quickly. "Here ye are, darlin'." He handed her a cup of freshly brewed coffee. "Dontcha be getting yerself in a tizz now. Ye've got the babbies to think about."

"He's right. Let us big strong men handle things," Erik agreed. "What's in the bag?"

"Asher's suit. Yours is at Vince and Billy's, because that's where you're supposed to be. We have to pick up Vince and Joey's later. When is Vince coming here, and when are you going there?"

"I'm not sure, I just got up. I'll call him and find out. We can all just get together and be in the same spot . . . maybe Billy and Vince's house, it's the biggest besides Tony's." He paused, and his face contorted. "Wait, did you say a suit? Asher's going to wear a suit? Have you thought this through? I don't think it would be a good idea to bring that up again."

"Sure, an' there I was thinkin' he'd be in a kilt like me," Connor added with a cheeky grin.

Daisy frowned. "Erik . . . I don't want to get into this too much right now but . . . Is he up to this? Is Asher really up to getting married today?"

Erik nodded. "Yes, we talked about it a lot last night and he was absolutely sure. I asked him again, just to be sure, and he said yes about ten times! I know this isn't over. I know he's not in a good place, but it's what he wants, and God knows it's what I want, so I don't see any reason why not to. I'd like to keep things low-key, but yes, he's far better than yesterday. I'm sorry for upsetting him, and you, and everyone else . . . we're gonna work on it, together. But he's raring to go. Once he wakes up that is." He smiled. "Maybe you should rethink the suit, though."

"I . . . Erik . . ." She shook her head. "I should trust you. You were there but . . . I was scared last night. More scared than you could imagine, and much more than I'd ever admit to Billy and Vince. I was so sure he'd . . . I thought he would . . ." She shook her head again. "Did you know Tony's had a word with my parents?"

"Papa?" Angel snapped, staring at her wide-eyed.

"Yes. He *suggested* they might not want to discuss what happened yesterday with Asher."

Angel's jaw dropped. "He warned your parents off from Asher?"

"In a manner of speaking."

"I'm sorry. I'm so . . ."

"Don't be sorry, Angel," Daisy said, waving one hand at him, as the other raised a piece of toast to her mouth. "They needed it. You don't know what they — especially Dad — are like with Asher. They wouldn't have left him alone. Dad would have nagged at him for causing a scene and Mam would have been fussing around him. I can't see her holding off all day, I have to admit. He's going to get fussed, Tony or no Tony, but they needed to be reined in, or Ash will never make it to the wedding." She sighed. "All right, you'd better get that brother of mine down here so he can try on his suit and I can get out of here. This place stinks of men — stale beer, smelly feet, and sweat."

Connor took in a deep breath. "Aye, that's me aftershave, darlin'. The real funky smells are in the bedroom, hi."

Erik put his arm around Connor. "Not all of them, stud. Can't you smell the wonderful scent of cigarettes and un-washed clothes, still draped over the couch." He walked over and patted Daisy's arm. "I'll go get him up."

"So, how are you feeling, mother-to-be?" Angel asked, handing her another piece of toast, this one dripping with butter.

"Tired. I could do without the drama in my life, that's for sure."

"You're Asher's sister. I'd have thought you'd be used to it."

She gave him a hard stare, then unexpectedly grinned. "You never get used to Asher. I hope Erik knows what he's getting himself into. Just when you think you understand him a tiny little bit, he throws something new in your face and everything goes spinning off again. Sometimes I think he does it on purpose." She paused and sighed, shaking her head. "Sometimes I know he does. But sometimes . . ."

"Aye, sometimes he takes the whole world and shakes it, then drops it on its head." Connor laughed. "An' isn't that just what he did to me. Came into me life like a whirlwind and stole me heart before I knew what hit me." He sobered. "And he still holds a piece of it now, even though most of it belongs to me darlin' Angel. Eh, *a chroí*?"

Angel smiled softly at Connor. He was changing, his hard edges rubbing off. Even his accent was softer. Angel wouldn't have changed Connor for the world, but he liked him this way. "It had better," he only half-joked. "As for Asher . . . He's been a very good friend to me, and I'm going to be a good friend to him. If anyone so much as looks at him wrong today they're going to have me to deal with." Angel surprised himself with the vehemence in his voice and, by the look on their faces, it surprised Connor and Daisy, too.

"Sure, ye're a grand friend for any man, *a chroí*. Don't worry Daisy, we'll keep a weather eye out fer yer boy."

"I hope my brother realizes how lucky he is."

"I'm sure he does." Angel poured a coffee and sat down at the breakfast table, yawning and rubbing his eyes. "God, it's crazy. In . . ." He checked his watch. "In less than ten hours, Erik and Asher will be married. Can you believe it? Did you always know? From the start? I know they had a difficult time when they first got together . . . all the way through really, but was it always obvious they were going to end up being to-gether or was it really as crazy as it seems? I mean the thought they'd actually get married and settle down?"

"Don't look at me, I don't know their whole story," Connor replied.

Daisy laughed. "From the very first moment they met. I was fuming mad with Ash. He taunted Erik when he was on-stage, an activity akin to poking a lion with a sharpened stick. And it got worse from there. Within the first couple of weeks, they'd split up so many times I felt like I was playing ping pong . . . and Erik put Ash in the hospital and . . ."

"Hospital?" Connor nearly choked. "Sure he wasn't tellin' the truth when he said Erik tried to kill him, eh?"

"No. They were fighting, and Erik accidentally knocked him into the swimming pool at school. He hit his head and ended up in hospital with a concussion. He was going out with Vince at the time."

Connor snorted. "Now that was an unlikely couple if ever. Vince a mouse and Asher a lion."

"More like a panther," Angel said, thinking of how sleek and graceful Asher was.

"Aye." Connor nodded. "A big, black cat, that's yer man Asher. And Vince the mouse, the prey, hi."

Daisy nodded. "He was when he was with Asher but . . . Asher hurt him. He hurt him badly, and he turned to Billy. They'd always been friends and it just . . . grew."

Connor turned to Angel. "Did ye know any of this about yer cousin?"

"I knew he was shy and unhappy when we were younger. He was always kind to me, though. I was the baby, and he stood up to Gianni and Lorenzo when they were teasing me."

"He's after bein' a wee dote, so he is. I remember Joey's party. Asher and Erik had a barney and Asher hightailed outta there. I think Vince went after him, though I weren't there, hi. Had me hands full with my man Billy."

"Ladies, ladies, what terrible gossips you are." Asher slid into one of the chairs and grabbed a piece of toast that Angel had just taken out of the toaster. "Don't let me stop you. I'm breathless with anticipation as to what Joey told you I did to

Vince . . . with Vince." He considered. "To Vince."

Connor shook his head. "Go on wid ye. I was thinking that with yer likin' for the Viking types, it was weird that ye be bagging a dote like Vince."

"I didn't. He bagged me—seduced me with a spliff and shoulder to cry on. Speaking of bags, what's that one?" he asked, nodding toward the suit bag. "Erik told me you'd brought me a suit, but I know he can't be right, because not even you're stupid enough to think I'd wear one."

"Oh, I see you're feeling better today," Daisy said, her voice dripping with sarcasm. "If you remember, you promised to wear a suit. In fact, you've promised more than once."

"*If* I liked it. I promised I'd wear it if I liked it. And I don't like it."

"But you haven't seen it," she protested. "How do you know you don't like it if you haven't even seen it?"

"It's a *suit*, Daisy," he said as if explaining something obvious to a small child. "It's a suit."

"Just look at it. Please. Just take a look, at least."

Asher gave an exaggerated sigh and got up. Helpfully, Erik, his face one broad grin, lifted the hanger so Asher could unzip and have a good look at the suit inside.

"Wow." Angel gave a low whistle and Erik craned his neck to see.

Daisy swatted him. "You're not supposed to see it before the wedding. Well. What do you think?"

Asher looked at the suit with his head tilted to one side. He fingered the silky material. It was night black, shot silk, with a long tailored jacket and straight fitted trousers. The shirt was wine colored and the vest a black brocade with deep red roses.

"It's all right." Asher shrugged and sat down.

"That's it? All right? Do you have any idea how much trouble I went through to get you something I thought you'd like to wear?"

"It would've been better if you'd troubled to listen to me when I told you I wasn't going to wear a suit."

"It's your wedding. You have to wear a suit."

"It's *my* wedding. I'll wear what I want."

"Children! Now, now, you two, break it up." Erik laughed. "Daisy, it's a fine suit. Asher . . . couldn't you wear it, just for a while? It's so nice." He looked at it again. "You don't have to wear it the whole time, people do change outfits during a wedding you know . . . for the reception, even at the end." Erik offered.

Asher glared at him. "I won't . . ." Then he sighed deeply. "All right, I'll wear the suit."

A strange look came over Asher's face. Angel noticed, but apparently, neither Erik nor Daisy did, because they were beaming, relieved, believing him.

Yeah right. He's not going to wear the suit. I wonder what he's planning.

"Ye'll look grand, Ash, but there was me thinkin' ye'd be wearing a dress." Connor sported a cheeky grin. "Can't tell ye how glad I am these little hairy legs won't be competing wid ye."

Erik laughed. "A dress?" He stood back. "Well hell, why not? You can pull it off, baby. You've got the hottest damn figure for it, that's for sure." He ran his hands down Asher's sides and kissed him.

"Don't tempt me." Asher laughed.

Angel groaned inwardly. He was pretty sure Erik and Connor were joking, and he was pretty sure Asher wasn't. He prayed they'd drop the subject before the idea was lodged too firmly in Asher's mind.

"Would I dream of tempting you, my future husband? The love and driving force of my world?" Erik smiled. "You look best in anything you wear, and I do mean anything, especially . . ."

Connor cleared his throat. "Ladies present, sham." He grinned. "Ye can't be soiling her virgin ears with your dirty talk. And won't someone be thinkin' of the children."

"That's it. I'm out of here." Grabbing the toast, Asher headed for the stairs.

Erik laughed. "Well, think I'll go shower up, pack up, and head to Billy's. I'll call Vince on the way and he should be here soon." He sighed and smiled. "Married . . . to Asher! Who'd have thought it, eh, Daisy?"

After a brisk shower and a farewell to Asher and the others, Erik stepped out to the car and called Vince.

"Hey, bud! How are you? Yeah, on my way over now. You ready to come over here? Ha, yeah, two ships passing in the night, aren't we? You doing better today? Good. Good! Awww. I'll see you later. Be nice to Angel and Asher. I know you will, it's all good now. Take care, bud."

With a final look at the massive house, he thought about Asher and the night to come, and couldn't help but be a little giddy. He began to hum the Bridal March on his drive to Billy and Vince's house.

"Billy!"

"Hey, loggerhead! How are you today?"

Erik picked him up and spun him around, which was easy enough. When he set Billy down, he patted his hair. "I'm thrilled to death to be getting married! I . . . didn't think I could feel this way, but I do."

"Aww, that's great! That's just how I felt last year when Vince and I took the vows. It's an amazing feeling." Billy put a hand on Joey's shoulder. "You gonna make Daisy feel that awesome soon?" he joked.

"Soon enough, Billy. Soon enough." Joey hugged Erik hello. "You look awake and alive, always a good thing! Was worried to death, with what happened."

Erik put his arms around both of his friends. "Water under the bridge now, thank God. Like it's been an easy journey, come on, you both know that's the truth."

Billy punched him lightly. "Amen, bro. So, you guys wanna check out our newest toy? We just got it installed a couple days ago, but things have been insane.

"Toy?" Joey asked. "Guys, your sex life is your own—"

"Joey! Holy shit!" Erik laughed so hard he nearly choked. "Billy, please tell me it's something not meant for that!"

"Argh! You guys are so gross. Totally. Follow me!" He led them down to the basement, where Erik heard water running, no . . . rushing.

"What the . . . I think I know that sound. Is that . . . What is it?"

Billy smiled and turned on the light. "It's a new . . . hot tub! Woo-hoo! Awesome for relaxing, chilling out, and maybe some of what Joey was thinking about. But don't worry, it's brand new. Vince hasn't even been in it yet. Neither of us have! We can christen it with locker room talk about sex, drugs, and rock 'n' roll."

Erik smiled along with his friends. "Awesome! Except . . . whoa. We don't have suits!"

"Ah, never fear. After the last pool incident . . . I bought everyone a pair of trunks. I'm holding off on Daisy's until she's not pregnant anymore, she can't use it anyway right now, don't wanna cook the babies!"

Erik hugged him from the side. "Billy, you're awesome! This is just what I needed."

Billy kissed his cheek. "Anytime, bud, my bestest bud ever. Come on, let's suit up and boil our cares away."

Asher twirled in front of the mirror. It amused him to see the expressions on the faces of his friends and it would amuse him even more to see the expressions on everyone's face at the wedding. A suit huh? Well, no one could say he hadn't warned them.

"You're not serious, Asher? Please tell me you're not serious." Vince looked horrified.

Asher found Vince's reaction strangely satisfying. Vince was almost as bad as the women about all the wedding nonsense. You'd swear he was the one getting married — again.

Asher grinned. "Deadly. What do you think of the boots?"

"Killer, of course. But really? Asher . . . this is a wedding, not a gothic party or some weird vampire festival." Vince teased.

"Exactly," Asher said with a sly smile and slung the boots over his arm. "What about underwear?"

"Will you have room for any?"

Asher looked at Angel and they both burst out laughing. Vince shook his head, rolling his eyes, although he was grinning.

"Like you'll wear it for long anyway," Vince said quietly, shaking his head. His lips were twitching though. "Asher . . . you are definitely one of a kind. I never, ever . . . it's you. That's all I can say. You took my breath away the first night and you do today . . . Erik will keel over."

CHAPTER FOURTEEN

Erik paced around and about the summerhouse, taking deep breaths and enjoying the warm summertime air. He was really starting to love being at Tony's house. It felt like his second home, with how much he'd been staying over there — all the dinners, the pool.

Angel crossed his mind, and how everything had blown up. He felt awful he'd had to have Angel tell him Asher was doing badly again, but he got distracted easily. Maybe too easily at times, but his devotion was straight to his core. He loved Asher and wanted to marry him, very much.

Everything was coming into place, and the time drew nearer. Dusk was falling, and the fireflies appeared, adding their own twinkling bodies to the lights in the trees and the summerhouse itself. Red roses surrounded the area, their intoxicating scent filling the air. Chairs were set up on either side on the lawn, with a red runner down the center. He smiled at his best men. Billy and Joey both looked so handsome in their tuxedos. It looked like Billy's hair was gonna behave after Erik had applied a generous amount of gel.

It was almost time! He didn't feel nervous, just antsy to see Asher and to make them a family as husbands. He smiled at the thought and looked at his friends again.

"You good, man?" Billy asked.

"I'm great, actually. Not nervous, just happy."

Joey clapped him on the shoulder. "That's terrific, man. You two are gonna have a great life, I know it."

"Thanks, guys."

He looked across the lawn, past the guests, and he squinted to see Asher, Vince, and Connor arrive . . . waiting. He turned his attention to the crowd and saw his parents. They seemed so happy for him. He'd been so relieved when they finally found out he was gay. He thought how great they'd been about Asher, and how they'd helped him. His father nodded at him and his mother smiled through her happy tears. She blew him a kiss and he blew one back. Wow, what a difference it made to him, to have support and love, and help.

Asher's folks . . . well, folk. His mother was there, seated next to Daisy, who held her hand. Mrs. Berkley was in tears too, but hers looked both happy and sad . . . if that was possible. Not having her husband there was not good, and Daisy looked to be calming her as best she knew how. She smiled at Erik and gave him a thumbs-up gesture. He smiled back and gave his mother-in-law-to-be a sympathetic look. Mr. Berkley was a grown man, but wow, he acted like such a jerk.

Behind them were Angel and Tony, then other guests from his neighborhood, his parent's friends, and even some people he didn't even know. He was happy to see support for their marriage, considering it was two men.

"Let's get this show on the road, folks," Billy said with an eye roll. "Geez, ours didn't take this long. Your guy has to look just perfect, so he'll hold up the show I betcha."

Erik laughed. "I think you've pegged it, Billyboy." He looked back at the officiant, who looked at his watch.

"The sun is nearly down now, it should be any minute."

"Hope so. My feet are already killin' me." Joey teased.

"Are you sure, really sure about this, Asher?" Vince asked.

Asher beamed at him. "I'm as sure as I have been about anything lately. Not as sure as I want to marry Erik, but sure enough that nothing you say is going to make me change my mind." Asher smoothed the soft leather over his hips and shook out his hair. He gave a last tweak at the long leather gloves that laced up to his elbows, then reached out a hand to each of his friends, who took them. "You ready to do this?" He grinned at his two best men.

Connor nodded and made sure his braid was tied tightly and his knee socks up. "Yer gonna stir the shite up, an' that's fer fecking sure. I'm betting on a heart attack or two in the front row." He chuckled. "Sure, an' I'm glad Daisy's not further along, or she'd be dropping in the aisle, hi."

Vince scowled. "That's not a nice thing to say, Connor."

"Lighten up, darlin', it's nothing but a joke, hi. Yer babbies will be here when they're ready, and they'll be finding two of the best daddies they could hope for."

"Thanks, Connor," Vince replied with a blush.

"Sure, ye blush like an Irishman. Sure ye don't have Irish blood?"

"Actually, I do. So we're brothers o' the Emerald Isle, Connor." He smiled and kissed Asher's hand. "Come on, let's go."

Taking a deep breath, Asher let go of Vince and Connor's hands and stepped out onto the patio, the ridiculously high heels of his boots clacking against the stone. Suddenly he found he was, in fact, nervous after all. He smoothed the soft fabric over his stomach and hips, raising a calming scent. He loved the smell of leather, and it was the fabric he felt most comfortable in. If they'd bought him a leather suit, he might have thought about wearing it. He grinned. But then he'd have missed all the fun.

As he walked, the boots kicked out the skirt and showed just how high the boots went. He grinned to himself, a feral grin. Think they'd get him into a suit, did they? Think they'd taken all the power away, backed him into a corner, forced him to conform? They'd think again in a minute.

When they reached the edge of the orchard, a signal was

passed, and music began to play as they stepped onto the red carpet. Asher was a little disappointed, because not only did his heels sink through but the lack of clicking detracted from the overall effect.

Chewing on his lip ring, which Daisy had tried to bully him into removing for the day, he held his head high, ignoring the gasps and whispers, and fixed his eyes on the only face he cared about right then. Erik's eyes were wide and shocked, but his sexy little smile made it very clear he was shocked in a good way and would be showing him just how good later on. Once he'd seen that, nothing else mattered.

Erik's eyes widened the moment he saw this tall, dark, gorgeous man walking his way, with legs to die for. His feet and legs were encased in boots, which had heels so high they made Asher taller than him. He looked beyond amazing to Erik, beyond description. The black leather dress was perfect for him, as odd as it might have seemed. It was him. It was Asher. His love, his life — the one he'd fought for, fought with, had lost, and won back, and finally . . . Finally, they were here. Together. Getting married.

The thoughts spun through his head and he felt dizzy just looking at his Asher. It was hard to take in everything — his black hair brushed out and straightened to his slim waist, the gloves hiding some of his long arms, his fingernails painted jet black, the makeup, all of it. He was a sight to behold, and Erik was so happy he was the one beholding it.

When they reached the end of the carpet, at the lip of the summerhouse, Erik took his hand. "You look wonderful, Asher — sexy, daring, hot. It's perfect on you. Sure beats a suit!" He gazed into Asher's face, into those eyes. His magnificent, alluring, hypnotic lilac eyes. With black shadow around them, they seemed to glow in the low lighting of the darkened gardens. "You are . . . Oy, I can't find the words. You've made me speechless."

Billy leaned in. "You look amazing, Asher, next to my Vince of course." He smiled and took Vince's hand as they stepped off to the side.

"Great leather, man. It suits you completely, it's awesome," Joey added. "Even over this kilt-wearer," he teased as he pulled Connor to his side.

"Sure, be pickin' on the other one not wearin' pants, will ye?" he joked.

The officiant cleared his throat. "Are we ready to begin?"

Asher was floating on air. For a moment, no one and nothing existed in the darkened garden, or anywhere else in the world, except his Erik. He'd never seen him look so handsome. Even the tuxedo he'd worn to the prom had nothing on this. His glowing blond hair had been pulled back into a ponytail and tied with a velvet ribbon, but it was already escaping, leaving long strands framing his beautiful face. Asher reached up and tucked one behind his ear, lost in the glorious blue of his eyes. Erik trapped his hand and laid it over his heart. The silk of his silver-gray vest felt cool through the thin leather of his gloves, and he drifted closer.

"Enough of that," Vince commented sotto voce. "You kiss the bride *after* the ceremony."

Asher giggled and kissed Erik quickly on the nose.

Turning to Vince, he winked and slipped off his gloves, handing one to each of his best men.

"Ahem. If we're quite ready?" the officiant began, then his eyes glazed slightly as both Asher and Erik turned to him at the same moment.

Asher barely listened to the ceremony. He was so happy he could explode, and the great big hole inside was hardly there at all. All his friends and family were here, and most importantly, his Erik was here. There were no thoughts in his head other than how much he loved this man who'd been at his side through so much. All right, sometimes he'd tried to push him away, but he was so glad he hadn't succeeded. Every few moments he sneaked a peek at Erik, and more often than not, Erik was peeking back. They were both smiling.

"If anyone here can show just cause as to why these two men should not get married, speak now or forever hold your peace."

Connor cracked a smile and spoke up. "Ye sure ye know what yer doin', sham?" He grinned at Erik "This one's a handful, so he is. Are ye up te it? I consider it me duty as best man to ensure you'll be doin' the right thing by me darlin'."

Erik shook his head. "You goofball Irishman! I'll do more than the right thing, I'll do everything, give him everything — my heart, my life — everything."

There was a smattering of applause and then everything went quiet.

Asher started, glancing up at the officiant, who was looking at him expectantly. "What?" he whispered.

"Ahem . . . the vows."

"What vows?"

Erik laughed. "We're not the traditional vow-taking people. But we have vows, um . . . From the top?" He fumbled, used to being on stage and having everything scripted for him. "You wanna go first?"

Asher grinned. "Ah, those vows." His smile faded as he half turned and took Erik's hand, gazing into his eyes. "I know I'm not the easiest person to love. Certainly not the easiest person to be with. Can't think why, but people seem to have trouble *getting* me. But you . . . you never have. Even when we're fighting, when I'm trying to push you away, or running away . . . Through it all I knew . . . I've always known, from the beginning, that next to my sister, there's no one in the world who *gets* me as well as you do, and it means the world to me.

"For anyone to be able to get under my skin like that is a miracle but someone like you . . ." Asher searched Erik's eyes, his own growing bigger and brighter with the tears he held in check. "You're strong and powerful, but so gentle and loving. You're a meathead, but you have capacity to think and understand. If you'd stop running headlong at things you'd . . . well . . . you wouldn't be you so . . ." He shrugged. "You're the most beautiful man I've ever laid eyes on, a Nordic God. A Viking come to steal me away and never let me go. I feel safe with you like I've never felt safe, ever before. You're everything to me.

"There's not much I can vow to give you. My heart and soul, everything I have, everything I am, everything I could ever be. I'm nothing without you, Erik Von Nordgren, and I'm yours in every way imaginable for as long as you want me."

"Holy cow, how can I possibly do better than that?" Erik teased as he tilted his head up slightly to look into Asher's eyes. "Asher Berkley . . . we've had the most insane journey, but I wouldn't change a thing, well, maybe the pool thing, although that's what got us to talk again, and for me to see you as someone I wanted to really get to know well.

"I thought only Billy could stomach my antics and my mouth that overflows like a waterfall in a fjord, but you did. Once we got through to each other, we found understanding. You'd already taken my heart — almost right away in fact. You put a spell on me the first time I looked at you, and dammit, you weren't going to get away, I couldn't allow it.

"You're smart, incredibly talented, sweet, thoughtful, and wow are you everything I've ever dreamed of in a man. You had my attention right off, and you always will. I vow to you,

Asher. I vow to be the best husband I can be, even being a meathead, and to give you my love and understanding, and listen and talk with you forever. You have enriched my life so much, it's unlivable without you. I'm yours, Asher. Forever."

Asher was mesmerized, lost in the sapphire blue eyes and swept away by the beautiful words. He was too happy even to smile. Thinking of nothing but Erik, he raised his hand and pulled the ribbon free to run his hands through the golden tumble that was now well below Erik's shoulders and seemed to glow in the flickering light of the candles filling the summerhouse.

Erik took the hand and kissed the palm, holding on tight to Asher's fingers curling around his own.

"I love you, Erik," Asher whispered.

"I love you, too."

"Ahem. If we may continue. Do you have rings?"

Again, the officiant took on the expression of a startled rabbit as Asher and Erik stared at him. He licked his lips nervously. He obviously wasn't used to his couples being so . . . intense.

Billy took the ring from his jacket and gave it to Joey to hand to Erik. Asher's eyes widened. It was beautiful. Chunky, as he liked them, but with a certain delicacy. A band of white gold was sandwiched between two bands of bright yellow and was set with four lozenge-shaped stones of a deep wine color, interspersed with pear-shaped diamonds. It was so beautiful he couldn't take his eyes off it. Erik had to reach out and take his hand to raise it so he could slip the ring onto his finger. He took the class ring off and put the new ring on and their eyes met again, as they both fingered the beautiful bauble.

"It's perfect on you," Erik murmured.

"Repeat after me . . . I, Erik Von Nordgren . . ." the officiant started.

Erik smiled. "I, Erik Von Nordgren . . . take you, Asher Berkley . . . to be my husband . . . to have and to hold . . . for richer, for poorer . . . in sickness and in health . . . forsaking all others until death do us part."

Asher stared at the ring sitting perfectly on his finger and shook his head, aware that if he wasn't careful, he was going to get lost in it again. Squeezing Erik's hand, he turned toward Connor, who'd already stepped forward. He quickly slipped the class ring onto his other finger and took the new ring from Connor, who winked at him, making him smile. It was a work of art unto itself, a white gold band with a single, large, twinkling blue diamond as the center stone. It was embedded into the gold, surrounded by its shimmering setting. Erik smiled widely at it and looked almost afraid to touch it. He slipped off the dragon ring and watched the lovely wedding band take its place.

Taking Erik's hand, Asher repeated the same words, barely listening to the officiant, staring into Erik's eyes. There were other words and other things to do, but he didn't really register them, going through the motions until he heard the words *you may now kiss* . . . and then almost knocked Erik off his feet, throwing himself into his arms.

Turning to face the guests as Mr. Von Nordgren, Asher beamed . . . right up to the point where he spotted the empty chair next to his mother. For a moment, it felt as though a dagger had pierced his heart. Then he tossed his head. *Fuck him. His loss.* Holding Erik's hand tightly he strode along the carpet and onto the path toward the marquee.

"Hey Erik," he said as they approached the entrance, "guess what?"

"What?" Erik smiled as they walked in perfect cadence together.

"I just got freakin' married. How nuts is that?"

Erik gasped and looked down at his left hand, at the sparkling ring. "Well go figure! So did I! We must both be nuts!"

Asher grinned at him as they reached the end of the tunnel. "I'm gonna take a look. I *know* I'm not supposed to. Do I look like I care what I'm supposed to do today?"

Hurrying away, the skirt of his dress swaying and almost brushing the carpet, he drew aside the curtains and peeked into the reception room. He hadn't been expecting much, but was pleasantly surprised. Okay, there was a lot of white. Boring round tables, white tablecloths, white chair covers, white balloons. But there were accents of black on the chair bows, runners, place settings, and especially on the top table. And there were red roses everywhere, dark red ones that made the room smell heavenly and reached out for him through the parted curtain, inviting him in.

"Hmm . . ." he said, resuming his place at Erik's side. "Actually, it's not bad."

"Wow, if you say it's not bad, it must be great," Erik said with a snort. He ducked his head inside too and surfaced a minute later. "Wow, that's really nice. I love the dark red roses this time, and all the black. Very cool, very goth. Just like you. Of course . . . your outfit upstages it all." He took Asher's hands and twirled him around. "One in a billion you are."

"Yes, thank God." Daisy's voice had them rooted back in the real world in no time. "Asher Berkley, what the hell do you think you're playing at? You look . . ."

"Who the hell is Asher Berkley?"

"What?"

"Asher Berkley. Don't know anyone by that name. Do you, Erik?"

"I'm sorry, what was the name again? I think I knew someone by that handle in high school, but . . . nope. Not ringing a bell." Erik grinned at the face Daisy made.

"I know an Asher Von Nordgren, Will he do?"

"Asher, just shut up with your stupid sarcasm and face-tiousness. You're making yourself a laughingstock, after all our hard work—"

"Will you listen to yourself? It's not your wedding Daisy, it's mine . . . and Erik's. You've not listened to a word I've said throughout this whole process. How many times did I tell you I wasn't going to wear a suit? If you hadn't tried to force me, I'd probably have been wearing leather trousers but, no . . . despite everything, you still had to have the last bit of control over me. And I'm sorry you searched hard for a suit and I'm sorry you spent what was probably a lot of money on it, and yes, actually, I *do* love it and I *will* wear it . . . but not for my wedding, for *my* day. On *my* day I'll be me, just me all the way through—the freak, the nutjob, the crazy one. Because that's who I am, and I'm sick of running from it and excusing it and denying it. This is me. Live with it."

Asher put his hands on his hips and sized up the situation. Daisy's outraged face, his mother's shocked one, his friends grinning, and his father . . .

"Know what? No. This isn't me. Not quite."

Vince and Connor winced as he tugged at the zip of his dress. It split like a banana skin, revealing what he was wearing underneath. Daisy's eyes widened and everyone gasped. Tossing his head, Asher whirled and the unzipped dress swirled around him showing off the tight fitting leather basque, laced up the front, over a leather mini skirt, which was laced up the sides and short enough to show that underneath the high boots he was wearing stockings held up with black lacy suspenders. A black and red garter nestled around his thigh, just visible under the hem of the skirt.

"*This* is me. Love me or hate me, this is what I am."

Ending up in Erik's grasp, he threw his arms around his neck and kissed him.

"And what you are is the man I love, Asher Von Nordgren." Erik ran his fingers along the laced sides of the skirt and fingered the stockings. "This outfit outdoes them all, by far. If we're not careful you'll get arrested, for being too damn sexy," he teased as they kissed again. "My incredible husband."

"Ok, you've made your point. Do the bloody dress back up."

"Do it up? Asher looked at her in confusion. "I was going to take it off."

"Don't you bloody dare." Daisy physically dragged the edges of the dress together.

Asher batted her hands away, but caught his mother's face over her shoulder, then relented and quickly rezipped.

"It's coming off again later," he grumbled.

He took his place in line beside Erik with Joey and Billy on one side of them, and Connor and Vince on the other. Fortunately, Daisy and his mother were forced to move away from him, for which he was very grateful.

When Erik's parents appeared in the front of the line, he hugged them both. "Thank you both so much . . . I can't tell you how much it meant to me, and to Asher. I feel very lucky to have you guys as my parents."

Mrs. Von Nordgren kissed Erik's cheek. "You're the best son we could've asked for, Erik. We love you so much, and we love Asher, too, and all your friends. It was a wonderful ceremony." She looked Asher up and down. "You made all the women jealous, Asher. You definitely have the physique to pull off wearing that dress," she said with a sweetness to her voice. "I'm proud to have you as my son-in-law."

The effect of Mrs. Von Nordgren's words had Asher floored. They completely threw him into a loop, and for a moment, he had to close his eyes to stop himself staggering. The look in her eyes was so open, so caring. She meant what she said. She accepted him totally in a way his own family never had and never would. Glancing at Mr. Von Nordgren, he saw the same expression in his eyes, along with another that told him his new father-in-law also understood what he was feeling right now.

Chewing his lip, Asher threw his arms around both his in-laws and dragged them into an awkward but heartfelt hug.

Next in line were Nora and Caitlin. Erik smiled at them both. "Ah, two of my favorite Irish people." He bent down to hug Caitlin. "You look great, Caitlin, very grown up." He winked at her and turned back to Nora. "You both do. I appreciate ya both being here."

"Sure, and I wouldn't have missed it for the world." Nora smiled.

"I was always after takin' ye fer a princess, Asher, but I didn't realize ye were the bride of Frankenstein."

"I think it's very rude of you to talk about Erik like that," Asher said with mock severity. "Did you hear, Erik? She said you look like Frankenstein."

Caitlin's face turned instantly red.

Erik rubbed his jaw. "Frankenstein, eh? Hmmm." He jutted his arms out and began to wander toward her, his knees locked. "Must . . . get . . . Caitlin!" He staggered, doing a spot-on Frankenstein impression.

"Sure, an' he knows I didn't mean it like that," Caitlin said with a stamp of her foot. "Why does he always have to twist whatever I say?"

"Because everything you say is so rude to him, Caitlin," Nora said, stifling a grin.

"Look, it's my wedding day. Let's make a deal. I won't rag on you if you don't call me a freak and give me a dance later on."

"You're gonna have te take yer shoes off, so ye are, or I'll be after getting a nosebleed."

"Deal." Asher held out his hand and Caitlin took it, shaking solemnly before moving on to Erik.

Reaching up, she took his face between her two small hands and kissed his cheek. "Ye're a nice man Erik, so ye are. Ye have te be, to be taking on a charity case as dat one." She tossed her curls at Asher and skipped on toward the curtains, having little interest in Billy and Joey.

"I'm sorry about her," Nora said with a long-suffering sigh.

"It's okay." Asher grinned. "She keeps us on our toes."

"I'd be happy if she just stopped being so rude."

Connor cut in after giving Caitlin a hug. "Nora . . . remember how Ma and Da would be after us? We were ruder than her, so we were! You told me they were on ye all the time, and I was even worse!" He smiled at his sister. "Ye were me role model."

Erik chuckled. "Apple doesn't fall far from the tree sometimes, eh?" He made a face at Asher. "She's a spirited girl who's a rude teenager. I wasn't quite so nice myself. It should pass."

"And if not," Asher said, making sure Caitlin was listening. "Send her to us and we can use her head as a toilet brush. At least then someone will be getting some use out of her."

Erik laughed softly as the girl skipped out of sight. "You certainly have your hands full. Maybe Uncle Connor can be a help, teach her the jig or something. Keep her mouth occupied by stuffing her with food," he teased.

Asher's mam reached the front of the line and Erik took her hand gently. "Mrs. Berkley . . . thank you . . ." He paused, clearly not knowing what else to say. She patted his hand.

"It's all right, Erik. I'm very happy for you both, you've proven you love my son, and that's all a mother could ask for. I'm proud to have you in our little family." She smiled up at him. "I'm . . . sorry . . . about Mr. Berkley too. I thought . . . I'd hoped . . . he'd be here. But I guess he made his choice."

"I know it's complicated, and there's a lot involved. Maybe there's hope for him. Give him time, Mrs. Berkley."

She nodded. "I hope so, Erik. I hope so. Now then, you must stop one thing."

"What's that?"

"Calling me Mrs. Berkley. My proper name is Lily, or Mam to you." She grinned and hugged him. "I'm sorry for being such a pill at times. Mothers do these things . . ."

"I know, I know. Well, Lily . . . thank you again."

She turned to Asher and had to tip her head back to look into his eyes. "Asher, my darling son, you left me absolutely speechless."

Asher smiled ruefully. "I'm sorry but . . ." He closed his eyes and lowered his head, shaking it. What could he say? He wasn't going to apologize, but he didn't want to hurt his mam. She'd been hurt enough. If he'd known his father was going to be such a twat maybe he'd have worn the suit.

"It's all right, Asher. It is. Yes, a suit is proper, but it's not you. You've always gone your own way and done your own thing. You look beautiful, and I'll defend you. Just don't wear it to any other weddings. Promise?"

Slowly, he raised his head and gave her a small smile. "It depends who's wedding it is," he said softly. "I'm going to get a flowered one for Daisy's."

Erik laughed, but his mam didn't . . . not at first. "Oh, Asher . . . I declare. You are one for the books, my son. At least you got my legs. You were always into my dress shoes as a boy." She touched his hair and put it behind his shoulder. "Your best man here has good legs, too, if he can be a gentleman, you Irishmen . . . hmpf!"

Connor stifled a laugh. "Sure, and I think we're after bein' on the same side this time." He sobered. "Asher's a grand man and a good friend. I've got his back—against everyone."

Despite his loaded comment, she seemed to mellow.

"Well . . . I appreciate that. Not always the way you speak to me, but I suppose I understand." She held out her hand for him to shake, which he turned up and kissed softly.

"I'm a gentleman at heart, but fierce when it comes to me friends. Thank ye for sayin' I have nice legs."

"Right. Well, you're welcome, Mr. O'Reilly." After a hug to Joey, she looked over her shoulder. "Come along, Daisy, be civil now."

"That's rich. Me be civil? I . . ." Daisy sighed, shook her head, and rolled her eyes. Standing on tiptoe, she kissed Asher and hugged him warmly. "Keep those outfits. When I'm back to my super slim self, I'll wear them on stage. Not the boots, though, I'd kill myself."

Asher hugged her back. "You can borrow my clothes whenever you want."

Erik gave her a peck on the cheek and a long hug, making sure not to squeeze her. "Hey, sister-in-law! Not to mention a great guitarist and singer to boot."

"Don't forget mother-to-be." She laughed.

"How could I forget? I had to hold my breath in so I don't squish those little darlings inside of there. Are you feeling all right? I'm sure Billy and Vince will tend to anything you need, and their Uncle Erik, too." He smiled proudly.

"I'm fine. No thanks to *that* one." She flicked her head at Asher. He sighed and turned away to talk to Angel, but Daisy caught his arm. "I'm teasing, Asher. I know I get mad at you sometimes. Hell, I get mad at you all the time, but you're my brother, my twin brother, and I love you so much I sometimes think I'll go crazy with how much I worry about you. Nothing you ever say or do will ever make me love you any less. I'm your big sister."

"Only by five minutes," he murmured and hugged her close, holding on tight.

Just behind Daisy, Asher noticed Angel grin at Erik and

hold out his hand for a shake. "I don't know whether to say congratulations or deepest sympathy. Hell, you've got your hands full."

Erik laughed and took the young man into a hug. "I know I do, but I couldn't be happier about it, Angel." He held Angel at arm's length. "Hey, just wanted to thank you for being there and setting me straight again on things. I get so tied up in my own head I just don't pay attention . . . I'm grateful for what you did."

"I didn't do anything, Erik. I was there for a friend. It's what anyone would have done."

"No, Angel." Still holding on to Daisy, Asher smiled at him. "You did a lot more than most people would have done. Most people would have run for the hills after the first stupid incident and kept on running at every stupid thing I did. You were a true friend, and not everyone is lucky enough to have one of those. You've no idea how much I've appreciated everything you've done for me these last few days. I'll never forget it."

"For us both," Erik added. "You're a great friend and we're really glad we met you."

"I'm glad I met you too, for so many reasons." His eyes flicked to Connor. "I don't know where I'd have been without you all . . . especially you, Asher. Oh, don't look like that Connor, you know you're excepted, in a completely different category. But Asher's been my rock. You've changed my life . . . everything. You took me under your wing, opened up my eyes to so many things. I'll never forget you. You're my guardian angel."

"Aww." Asher let go of Daisy with one arm and dragged Angel into an embrace.

"I guess angels do have their own guardians, huh, Con?" Erik nudged Connor. "Two artists, and I swear you two look like brothers . . . although, right now . . . maybe brother and sister." He snorted, ducking a *look* from his new husband.

Asher chuckled. "What do you think, Daisy? Should we adopt Angel as a triplet? Then we'd have one of each. On boy, one girl, and one me."

Daisy snorted and almost choked.

Erik laughed too and had to pound his chest to clear it. "Are you calling yourself a hermaphrodite? No way . . . I've checked, you're all male. You've just got a killer bod."

Connor nodded. "Aye, ye're a married man now, so ye are."

Asher grinned. "I am what I am. I don't like boxes and labels. I'm not *an* or *a* anything. I'm me. Unique. Special."

"Special?" Mrs. Berkley laughed, patting her son on the arm. "Special you are, and that's for sure. Both my children are. I'm proud as can be of both of you."

Vince nudged Billy, and they tapped on their wine glasses to get the crowd's attention. Billy smiled and stood to do his bit first.

"Good evening, everyone. If you don't know me, I'm Billy Caliendo, Erik's best friend since about the first grade. As one of his best men, I'd like to propose a toast to the happy couple and their new life together. Erik, you were always my protector, my friend, and the one I was bailing out when your mouth got out of control." He laughed. "Asher, I liked you from the moment we met, and I knew once you guys started listening, you'd be just fine. Well, I was right. Chalk one up for Billy," he teased. "You're both terrific guys and I love you both." He raised his glass. "To the happy couple!"

The crowd followed suit, adding their own cheers.

Vince stood beside Billy and took the microphone. "Hi, I'm Vince Caliendo, Billy's husband. I'm one of Asher's best men but feel close to them both. They've been there for me and I hope I've been for them too. I'm happy it all worked out, you two. It's about time." He raised his glass. "Saluté!"

Next was Joey. "Hi, I'm Joey Miller, also known as the quiet one, besides Vince," he joked. "I've known Erik just a few years, and Asher about as long. I've seen them evolve from squabbling to sexting, and I've enjoyed every second of it. Thanks, guys!"

Finally, it was Connor's turn. He straightened his kilt and brought his braid forward. "Me name is Connor O'Reilly . . . and I'm an Irishman. Oh, sorry, thought this was AA." The crowd chuckled. "What can I say? Sure, dis one 'ere" — he nodded at Asher — "is the light of me life . . . next to me Angel. One thing I can say is true, since the moment I laid eyes on him, me life has never been the same. Sure he has a way of picking up yer life, shakin' it like a dog with a rat, and droppin' it on its head. I think that's what he did with Erik here, who may be after suffering brain damage from it." A smatter of laughter forced him to pause. He cast a glance at Erik, who was grinning. "I think, brain damage or not, they were made for each other, and I wish them nothing but the best." He drank down his beer in salute.

After the applause died down and the music began for dinner, Vince spotted Angel at the table just next to the head table. He tapped Billy on the knee. "Hey, I'm gonna go talk to my cousin. We've got some things to iron out."

"I know you do. I hope it goes well, hon. Love you, good luck!"

"Love you, too. See you soon." He stepped a few feet away and put a hand on Angel's shoulder. "Hey, um . . . can we talk for a few minutes? I . . . wanna set things right with us." He had a lump in his throat the size of a boulder. He was almost sure Angel would say no and turn away, but he was surprised.

"Vince, there's nothing to set right. Nothing at all. I understand you were upset. We all were. I even quarreled with Connor. It was a crazy night, a crazy situation, and I'm just glad it's all over and has ended so well."

The lump moved a little, but not too far. He forged a smile. "Y-You understand? I was such an ass to you, though. I've been really snippy lately. I'm glad you're still speaking to me." He glanced back at the grooms. "They do look very happy."

"They will be happy. Papa is sending Asher to a doctor in London. He'll stay there after the honeymoon and get himself together. He'll be okay. As for Erik . . ." He shrugged. "He's Erik."

"That's great! That's so great to hear . . . he should've done it two years ago, but it's fine, as long as he's doing it now. As for Erik, yeah, you're right, he is who he is. He learns, eventually." He laughed out loud. The lump went away at last and he took a deep sigh of relief. "Hey, listen, I might be able to sneak away from Billy for a dance or two, if you'd do me the honor? That is if yer man is all right with it, too. You are my cousin. We didn't get to dance last year at my wedding."

"It would be my pleasure, Vince. You're my favorite cousin, after all."

Vince put his arms around him and hugged him tight. "Thanks, Angel. I'm so glad . . . very relieved." He straightened up and patted Angel's shoulder again. "See you in a bit. Gotta go soak up as much of my hubby as I can while I still have the chance."

CHAPTER FIFTEEN

Billy sat quietly off to the side as the music began for Erik and Asher's first dance together as husbands. The lights dimmed, the crowd quieted, and the spotlight was put on the happy couple, with the band playing a song about being a keeper for life, a guardian. It was perfect for them, as Erik had vowed to protect Asher, and for the most part, had done a damn good job. He was proud of Erik, after watching the entire relationship evolve from sniping classmates, to injuries, drama after drama, breakups, and finally to this moment, being married and having their first dance together.

Watching the two together warmed Billy's heart, but also tugged at his own. He'd been so in love with Erik and for just a brief flash, could picture himself in Erik's arms, as his husband, or just as his lover. He'd wanted just one more chance, one more try, but it'd all been snuffed out when Asher came along. To be honest with himself, no matter what he'd said, he hadn't liked Asher at first. But after a time, he'd tamed his feelings and wanted only the best for them. He'd always love Erik and would never forget the time they'd shared, even as unromantic as it had been. It was still his first time, and his first love, and it was still special to him. He sighed to himself and ran a hand over his hair, which had become a bit unruly again in the humid air.

He caught a glimpse of something shining on his left hand—his wedding band. He paused and looked at it carefully, thinking back to a year ago and his own wedding day, how wonderful it had been, and the past year since. He was grateful. Most couples struggled in their first year, but theirs had gone well. He shut his eyes and focused on the here and now, then felt a pair of arms go around him.

"Hey, honey. You awake? Or just mediating?"

Billy looked over his shoulder but knew already it was his dear, wonderful, sweet, loving husband's arms around him. He held him tight and kissed him.

"Just thinking about last year. In case I haven't said it a ton, I'm the luckiest man alive, and I love you forever, Vince. Always."

Just the warm smile he received was enough to punt thoughts of Erik and Asher out of his head. This was the man he belonged with, the one who fit him perfectly. They'd be fathers by the end of the year, or early into January, and they couldn't wait. It's just as they'd wanted, hoped and dreamed.

"I love you, too, Billy, you're the love of my life." Vince leaned in and they kissed again. He took a seat and pulled Billy into his lap as they sat to watch the dance, encased in each other's arms.

Erik and Asher's dance finally ended, and with happy tears in his eyes, Billy applauded his friends.

The band leader came on. "Okay, now I need the wedding party up here."

Billy patted Vince's hands. "Come on, hon, we're up. Let's show 'em how we do it, again."

"Works for me, baby."

They hugged tightly for a minute before Billy got off his lap and they walked to the dance floor.

Connor was quite the handsome sight in his full Irish regalia. His tartan was green, almost matching his beautiful eyes, and complementing his long, red hair. The black jacket and fly plaid looked wonderful on him, as did the knee socks with fringe. He looked so different from them in just their tuxes — more special, more unique. The kilt was the clincher, showing off those fuzzy red legs of his.

Billy smiled at him. "You look great, buddy! You definitely have the legs for the kilt." He chuckled as Connor did a little twirl.

"Cheers, sham. Dontcha think me hairy pins give Asher's a run for his money? Sure I'm graceful as a panther, me."

Vince laughed. "A panther with a broken leg. Just be careful with doing those twirls, we've got enough fainting women here with Asher's ensembles."

Connor laughed. "I wouldn't do that to 'em, Vince. I'm not goin' regimental, shall we say. I'm savin' it fer later, hi. For Angel only." He winked. "We gonna do this, Joey?"

Joey nodded. "Absolutely, cous! You're a great dancer, and I'm thrilled to be your partner. I can't hold Daisy close anymore, not for a while anyway." He winked at Daisy, who sat, rubbing her stomach and smiling.

The music began and the two pairings began to dance and were soon joined by Erik and Asher.

About halfway through, Billy felt a tap on his shoulder.

"Mind if I borrow you? Wanna dance with your juggernaut buddy?"

Billy laughed and nodded. "Of course. Vince, if you don't mind?"

Vince shook his head. "Not at all, have fun you two."

"You're a great best man, both of you are." Erik smiled.

"Thanks! Well, had to make sure you were married off properly, and me and Joey are the best around." He glanced over at Joey and Connor and had to laugh. Connor was just about throwing his poor cousin around like a ragdoll. He moved so energetically. "I think someone needs to rescue Joey."

As soon as the words were spoken, Billy saw Asher almost float over to Connor. He couldn't hear them, but he saw them pair up and start to dance, a little slower this time.

"Aww, such good friends, like we are." He glanced up at Erik and caught his ice blue gaze. "For life."

Erik clasped him tighter and nodded, seeming speechless for once. Billy smiled to himself, he had always been able to get to Erik on a deeper level than most anyone else, even Asher at times. They'd share a bond forever, as Connor and Asher would.

Connor gazed into Asher's lilac eyes, surprisingly visible in the dim light, and the distance he stood from the towering Asher. "Sure yer lookin' grand, *a stór*, but how ye can dance in those heels, I'll never know. Sure, I'd be on me arse, so I would."

Asher leaned close. "Ssh, don't tell anyone, but I've been wearing my mother's shoes since not long after I started to walk. I've had plenty of practice."

Connor sniggered. "Sure ye wear them well, hi." He sobered. "Erik's a lucky man to have a cracker like you in his life. Me darlin' Angel is beautiful, so he is, but you . . . Damn me if ye're not a fine cracker, love."

Asher's eyes twinkled wickedly. "You're not bad yourself, especially in that outfit. Hey, do you think it's getting rather hot in here?" Asher momentarily stepped back from Connor, unzipped his overdress again and tossed it carelessly off the dance floor. "Care to turn up the temperature? I'll have a word with the band. You up for some serious jigging?"

Connor felt his temperature rise and unbuttoned his jacket a little. "If ye can keep up in those shoes," he joked, removing his jacket and handing it to Joey. "I'm ready when ye are, love."

Quickly, Asher went to speak to the band, and as soon as the song was over, they started on a much faster one with a heavy beat.

Billy and Vince stood off to the side with Joey and Erik to watch as he and Asher danced.

Connor twirled about, his braid whipping around, almost throttling him at times. Asher's hair flew — no, floated around him as he moved elegantly to the pulse-pounding rhythm. He spun Asher around, and the man moved perfectly in the stiletto-heeled boots he was wearing. There were a few catcalls and whistles, which spurred them on even more.

Connor's smiled wickedly as a layer of sweat bloomed on his face. Asher looked cool as ever, and Connor marveled at how he managed it. They got up close and gyrated together, Connor's butt into Asher's body. Asher held him close and then bumped him and sent him out, twirling, and laughing. It was funny, and more than a little risqué. Connor wondered once or twice whether they were going too far, but he was having too much fun to give it more than a passing thought.

After the dance was over. Asher kissed Connor lightly and they hugged. "Thank you, *a stór*, ye made me night, so ye did. Next time, me an' Nora will show you a real Irish jig."

Joey hugged Connor from behind. "You guys stole the show!"

Asher waggled his eyebrows and winked. "It is my show after all."

Vince looked up just as Asher and Connor finished dancing and tensed.

Billy leaned in. "Hey . . . what is it, baby?"

"I . . . still feel like an idiot around him."

Billy ruffled his hair and kissed him. "You have nothing to be sorry about, baby. He means a lot to you. He was your first. Trust me, okay? I know. *I know*." They hugged for a long moment. "Go ask him to dance."

"Are you sure?"

"It's all right, you're my hubby, baby, and he's Erik's. No more drama, not tonight, okay? It's okay."

Vince nodded and kissed Billy again. "You're the only one in my heart, Billy. Always. I'll keep it short." He walked over to Asher. "Hey . . . um. I'm sorry about the other day, and for being such a pain sometimes . . . but if you've got the stomach for it, would you dance with me?"

Asher looked at him, unsmiling. "Vince, I thought . . . Last night I thought everyone hated me and I believed they were justified. I-I know I've been . . . difficult and I wouldn't blame you if you . . . especially you, never wanted to speak to me again." He smiled a small smile. "If you add up who's been a pain to whom, my list is a lot longer than yours. It started earlier, too. Actually . . . I'm surprised you can even bear to be in the same room as me. If you want to dance with me, it would be my honor."

He held out his hand and drew Vince gently into his arms.

"I'll always be your friend, Asher, for as long as you want me to be. Part of me will always love you and thank you . . . for being so kind to me that night, and other nights, too. Besides, I've gotta see you move in those heels." He laughed lightly.

"Well, seeing as you're so much less of a man than you used to be . . ." Asher grinned, and as the music was still quite lively, he shocked everyone, yet again, by physically lifting Vince right off his feet and swinging him onto the dance floor.

Vince gasped at the amazing feat of being lifted off the floor. He wrapped his arms around Asher's neck and let out a happy sigh.

After the dance with Asher, Vince was winded. He snuck up behind his hubby and caught him in a bear hug.

Billy turned in his arms and smiled while he curled a lock of Vince's hair around his fingers. "There you are, beautiful. Just in time. I hear they're about to cut the cake."

"Mmm cake," Vince said with a dreamy expression and had to stop from drooling. "I miss cake. Come on, let's get some."

Angel's head was spinning. Everyone was enjoying themselves, and he was happy enough just watching, although he was a little melancholy. For one thing, he realized he was still the outsider in the group. They were all such good friends with so much history together. He had none. True he was making it, but still . . .

And . . . He didn't want to admit it. He'd fought really hard against it, but the fact was undeniable. When he watched Connor with Asher, he was jealous, pure and simple. He didn't like the feeling at all, but there it was, and there wasn't really very much he could do about it other than making sure he didn't show Connor, or anyone else. His thoughts were so consumed with not showing his jealousy that he startled when Connor flung himself into the next seat.

"Penny for yer thoughts, *a chroí*."

"Nothing there worth paying for. Just watching everyone and thinking. Everyone's having a great time, aren't they?"

"Aye, that they are." Connor wiped his face with his sleeve and took a drink. "But ye're not, are ye me sweet? What's the matter?"

Angel squirmed under Connors far-too-shrewd gaze.

"Nothing's the matter." Angel forced a smile. "Not really. I just . . ." He shrugged, losing a little edge on the smile. "It's just that you're all so close and you have so much history . . ."

"Aye, and history's a grand thing, but it doesn't just jump into being, does it? History's made of memories and we're makin' 'em right now, eh? Trust me, *a chroí*, I was the new boy once, but it doesn't take long to feel like you're all patches on the same quilt, and always have been. Come awae and dance with me. Make some memories."

Angel allowed Connor to draw him out of his seat and onto the dance floor. He was welcomed enthusiastically and relaxed again, although he couldn't quite stop himself looking out for Asher all the time. He began to wonder whether he should talk to Connor about it. Or whether there was more to it than he'd even admitted to himself.

The music slowed and Connor tightened his embrace. He laid his cheek on Connor's shoulder, feeling peaceful and happy. A tap on the shoulder startled him.

"Mind if I cut in?"

Angel's heart thudded in his chest, even before he looked up and saw Asher grinning down, his hand on both their shoulders.

Connor chuckled. "Dontcha wear him out too much now, sham, eh?"

Asher laughed and clapped Connor on the back. "I'm making no promises. So, Angel, are you up for it?"

"I . . . Why not?"

"You're the only one I haven't danced with so far," Asher said, nudging a grinning Connor out of the way. "Connor's being selfish keeping you all to himself."

"What can I say?" Connor said with a shrug. "He's me heart, and I like to keep me heart close, but let no one say an Irishman won't share his good fortune." He kissed Angel, then walked away, leaving him with Asher.

Angel watched Connor disappear into the crowd and a sudden case of nervousness flutter in his stomach.

"You've been very quiet tonight," Asher said, gazing down at him. "Shit, I never realized how short you are."

"I'm not short," Angel snapped. "You're wearing those ridiculous shoes. I *told* you it would . . ."

"Would what? Be a bad idea? I don't see anyone else complaining."

"I'm not complaining, I . . ."

Asher, still dancing and holding Angel close, cupped his chin and peered into his eyes. "Something's wrong. What is it?"

"Nothing. Nothing's wrong. I wish people would stop asking me what's wrong."

"Temper, temper." Asher let go of his chin and ran a hand through his hair, frowning thoughtfully. "Have we been neglecting you? That's unforgivable. I owe you too much to let you feel excluded anywhere, especially not here."

"I wasn't feeling excluded . . . exactly."

"Hmm . . . well, no more. You're special to me, Angel. You've always been special because of your art, but after last night . . . Erik told me you'd quarreled with Connor and Vince over keeping my secret."

"No, not quarreled, not exactly, not . . ."

"Whatever. You stood up for me, you stayed true to me, and you were there for me. It's important. I've got history with just about everyone." He laughed. "Ha, I'm such a slut . . . But it's different with you. A different kind of history. I dunno, maybe a better one, purer, and one I really want to carry on into the future. I consider you to be one of my best friends and I'll always be here for you, no matter what."

Angel was totally speechless. He ducked his head, his cheeks blazing, and gasped as Asher's hand on the back of his head pressed his face gently against his chest. He inhaled the scent of leather as Asher's fingers toyed idly with the curls at the back of his neck, twirling them around his finger. Part of him really, really wanted to ask him to stop, but it felt so good, especially when Asher rested his cheek on the top of his head.

Eventually, the touch of Asher's hand and the movement of his body against his own simply got too much. Blushing furiously, Angel pulled away and smiled up at Asher. "We'd better get back before our men storm the dance floor." *What a fucking stupid thing to say. Damn. Damn. Idiot.*

Asher gave him a shrewd look and laughed, hugging him tightly before letting him go. "You're right. Those Irishmen can get very possessive."

Still holding his hand, Asher led him across the dance floor to where Erik, Connor, Vince, and Billy were having a break and sipping their drinks. Joey was dancing with Daisy, and after a quick gulp of cider, Asher disappeared to cut in for a dance with his sister.

"And here's the man himself," Connor said, throwing his arm possessively around Angel's shoulders. "Me own angel from heaven. What's yer poison, *a chroí?*"

"Wine, please. You know us Italians and our wine."

Connor kissed him and disappeared into the crowd. Angel found himself smiling as he watched him go. Asher was something else, for sure, and what the hell, he might as well admit he had a crush on him—a big crush—but Connor was . . . Connor was softer and sweeter and sexier . . . in his own way, and . . . Connor loved him. Connor was his. Angel sighed, a shiver going through him. He loved Connor with all his heart . . . well, with enough of it for it not to matter if he gave one tiny corner to someone else.

Connor bounced back cradling a large glass of red wine.

"Did I mention, ye're lookin' like an angel tonight, *a chroí?* Sure I'm a lucky man te have a true angel as me fella."

"Yes," Angel purred, "I am yer fella. And yer mine, so ye are. My feisty, funny, furry Irishman." He playfully tugged on Connor's beard. He leaned closer and whispered into Connor's ear. "I'm partial to a bit of furry Irishman, especially one wearing a skirt."

Connor's rich chuckle rolled over him. "Ye like me kilt, *a chroí?*" He smoothed down the vivid tartan. "It's one of me favorite outfits, so it is, especially when worn . . . correctly." He raised his red brows suggestively.

"I'm on a promise later, right?" Angel laughed. "Proper attire" — he winked — "is to be saved for the bedroom when it's my man wearing it . . . or not." He kissed Connor. "You look amazing. To my eyes, you're the sexiest man in a skirt in the room."

"Thank ye . . . though Asher's givin' me some stiff competition, so he is." He grinned across the floor at the tall brunette. "He and Caitlin ought to dance. That'd be a grand t'ing to watch, to be sure."

Joey chuckled. "Damn, would it ever. I have such a crazy family." He adjusted the fly plaid on Connor's jacket and tickled his nose with the fringe, getting a laugh from Connor.

"Easy, easy now, I'll toss me drink and then you'll be in big trouble. I'm wearin' less than Asher underneath."

"Erik, quick," Angel said, "pass me your pint, there's not enough in this wine glass."

Connor hid behind Joey as Angel hefted his glass.

"Hey, hey, none of that now, you crazy people. I've got my hands full with Asher in that scandalous outfit of his, don't need a lot of red fuzz appearing, if you get my drift." He took a sip of his drink. "You two were awful close out there. You'd better keep your eyes on your Irishman, not my crazy Brit, boy." Erik winked with his teasing, but it stopped Angel cold.

"Sure, an' I'm after havin' more than yer eyes on me, later." Connor joked as he drank down his beer and started another.

"I . . ." Angel panicked like a frightened rabbit. "I didn't mean . . . I-I'm sorry." Angel's heart thudded. Did he know? Did Erik know he had a crush on his new husband? Was he mad? Was he warning him off? Was he —

"Hey, hey, take it easy now. I'm messin' with ya." Erik nudged him. "I know he's hot and you two are close. It's cool, bud. Relax. Have a drink of wine. Cake's next." He rubbed his stomach. "Damn. Can't wait. It looks too damn good to eat."

"Sure there's no cake too good for this Irishman te eat. Ye

up fer it. Billy?"

Billy laughed. "Of course! My baby's lost thirty pounds, so I think he deserves some cake."

"Amen to that one, I've been dying for a piece of it since we got here." Vince chuckled. "How about you, cous? Hey, you still owe me a dance, too, don't forget."

Angel accompanied Connor as they all wove through the crowd to the buffet table where the cake was displayed in all its glory, gathering the rest of the gang as they went.

The cake was something to behold. Four tiers of offset circular cakes, covered with white chocolate. From the top of each layer, dark chocolate dribbled down, giving the impression the cake was *bleeding*. Red and black roses nestled into the base of each tier and spilled over the table on which it sat, trailing to the floor. The cake topper was astonishing. Somehow, Daisy had commissioned the creation of two figures made entirely of chocolate to represent Asher and Erik, although the little chocolate Asher was wearing a black suit. Asher had laughed when he saw it and tried to steal it, but Daisy had hidden it until right before the cake was put on display.

"Damn . . . now that is one gorgeous cake!" Erik commented, drawing Asher to his side. "Love the little you in a suit! Can you imagine the chocolatier making you in this dress? Now that'd have been a feat!" He ran his fingers down the sides of Asher's outfit. "And this would quite literally take the cake." He kissed Asher deeply. "Ready?"

"Can't wait," Asher said. "If you don't cut it soon, I'm going to start grabbing handfuls. Oh, hang on. There's something I've been wanting to do all night."

Even to Angel, standing further back, the wicked glint in Asher's eyes was obvious and made him nervous. Whenever Asher looked like, that something outrageous happened.

With a wink at his new husband, he plucked the little chocolate Erik off the cake and nibbled him from the feet up. When he was done, with everyone in fits of laughter, he licked his lips and said. "I never thought I'd get to eat you in front of all our friends. Was that good for you, darling?"

Erik shook his head and plucked the chocolate Asher from the cake, devouring the entire figure in two bites. "Mmm, good head, baby! Damn!" He kissed Asher again and held up the knife. "Now . . . let's show 'em how we cut a cake together."

Choking on his wine, Angel cheered with vigor as his friends cut the cake and fed each other a piece. Of course, it wasn't that easy with Erik and Asher, and it was only Daisy who stopped a full-on food fight.

The wedding night hadn't been exactly what Asher might have expected. They'd both been so exhausted after the drama leading up to it and the excitement of the wedding, that after a brief shower, they'd fallen asleep almost immediately, entwined in each other's arms.

They'd slept late the next morning, too, and were late getting to Tony's house for the present opening. Everyone was already there, looking tired and a little worse for wear. Their expressions were generally sour and grumpy. Except for Angel, who was hardly ever bad-tempered.

"Don't start," Asher said as soon as they walked through the door. "I have a hangover, and I'm going to kill someone if they so much as mention the fact we're late."

He threw himself down on the floor and leaned back against the leg of the chair Erik had just occupied. Erik dropped his hand and toyed with his hair.

"My precious husband, as sweet as a pie that's been in the sun too long when he has a hangover." he joked. "Okay, who wants to take notes this time? Joey again?"

"Yeah, I'll do it." Joey hopped up and took the notepad and pen. Billy handed him the first gift.

"This one's from . . . Billy and Vince." He handed it to Asher.

"What's this?" Asher asked, shaking the box and listening to the clinking from inside.

"You'll find out when you open it, won't you?" Angel said.

Asher glanced up and stuck out his tongue.

"Oh, very mature."

"Shut up, Pollyanna."

"Polly what?"

"You don't know Pollyanna?" Asher asked, and laughed as he carefully tore the paper off the box.

Erik grinned and shook his head. "Angel is not a Pollyanna, you goofball."

Asher shrugged and continued to open the box. "Aww, cool! Thanks, guys!" It was a set of barware for their new house, when they got around to installing one. "These'll be great!" He grinned warmly at his friends.

"Up next . . . Connor, Nora, and Caitlin."

"Sure, he is a Pollyanna, I think," Connor interjected, kissing Angel's head, "But he's my Pollyanna, so he is. I hope ye like it. Made it meself, so I did, hi. With a bit of help from me friends." He nodded toward Nora and Caitlin.

Erik held up the wooden sign. He gasped and handed it to Asher. It was a hand-carved wooden sign, saying *Beware of the viper.* A jewel-bright snake reared, its tongue flicking out to lick the hand that held it loosely.

"Holy cow! Connor, this is fantastic! It's awesome! Thank you so much!" Erik gushed as he hugged them all.

Asher, as always, was more reserved. "It's a bit big isn't it?" He frowned at it thoughtfully. "It's meant to hang around Caitlin's neck, right?" Asher grinned.

Caitlin bristled and stood with hands on hips, her green eyes blazing. Asher tilted his head to one side, crossed his eyes and stuck out his tongue, making Caitlin laugh and shake her head. Asher held out his hand and she bounced over and sank onto his lap.

"Could I be after helpin' ye with yer presents now?"

"If you behave yourself . . . and you have to pay for each one with a kiss."

"Kiss *you*?" she asked with mock horror. "Sure, I can't think of anything worse."

"Not even kissing Connor. He's an ugly little bugger."

"Don't ye be after saying those things about me uncle Connor, or I'll be beating ye 'round the head wid yer own gift, so I will." However, this time she was smiling and ended with giving Asher a chaste little kiss on the cheek.

"Why thank ye, Caitlin," Connor said with a snort. "It's nice to know ye'd stick up fer ye old uncle, so it is." He grinned at her.

Erik jumped in. "Besides, you're not ugly, Connor. Who else could pull off wearing a kilt like you do and be an excellent craftsman to boot?"

Connor answered with a grin. "Sure, an' we'll drink a fair few drafts under the sign when I'm done buildin' the bar."

"You tell him how it is, Caitlin. Connor's beautiful, so he is." Angel kissed Connor, whose smile lit up his face.

"Bless ye, *a chroí*." He wrapped his arm around Angel and held him close.

"All right over there, let's move on." Joey interrupted. "This is from Angel."

Erik laughed as Asher and Caitlin open the gift together.

"Oh, wow. Angel, it's beautiful!" Asher held up the painting for everyone to see. "This is amazing!"

It was a painting of Erik and Asher at Vince and Billy's wedding.

Angel blushed and lowered his gaze. "I didn't think it was good enough, but Connor made me."

Asher examined the painting carefully with Angel looking as if he wanted to crawl away and die. Yes, there were flaws, there were things Asher would have done differently, and there were things he was sure Angel himself would be doing differently in a year or so, but even he had to admit it was a damn good piece of art.

"From one artist to another, Angel, you're never going to think a painting is good enough to sell or give as a gift. It must have been scary to put yourself out there like this, but this is wonderful. Even if it was two stick men on a gray wash, we'd have loved it, because it came from you. But this . . . It's a work of art, and it's getting pride of place. I know. It's going behind the bar."

"See, *a chroí*? Was I not after telling ye they'd love it?" Connor sighed. "He comes down harder on himself than a bucket of stones, so he does."

"I love it, and it's gonna be the showpiece for sure," Erik agreed. "You do fantastic work, Angel. Have some faith in yourself."

"I do. Honestly, I do . . . sometimes."

Asher laughed. "I know the feeling. Don't worry, it gets better . . . sometimes."

"Here's an odd one . . . um . . . from the old record company." Joey arched a brow. "What the?" He handed it to Erik.

"Well, let's see. Odd they'd send something now." Erik opened the box. "Holy crap . . . Asher!" He pulled out the bracelet Asher had given him to wear on tour, the one that'd gotten *lost* and caused a wave of problems. "Omigod . . . where . . . what?"

"Is there a note?" Billy asked.

"Yes. It's from Jeffrey. He stole it, but apparently had an attack of conscience and returned it." He strapped it on his wrist and put his hand on Asher's shoulder. "I'll never take it off, I promise. No little urchins stealing it from me again."

"Not even this one?" Asher asked, ruffling Caitlin's hair, and earning a glare.

"She'd be in major trouble if she did," Erik answered. "Turn her over to the Irish police there, Mom and Uncle."

"Sure, an' the Garda'd just hand her straight back," Nora said, earning a frown from her daughter.

Joey grinned and pressed on. "This is from Daisy and me."

"Thanks, man!" Erik replied. He kept hold of the parcel and opened it himself. It was a set of cushion covers and curtains, a deep blood red decorated with black beads and tassels. "Wow, Joey, you have such a flair for this stuff, huh? Or did Daisy make you turn in your man card for a sewing machine?" He laughed.

"Very funny, Von Nordgren, very funny. I helped her pick out something gothic you'd both love. What the hell, huh? I like 'em, too, actually, although when we get out own house, we'll have something cheerful."

"Hey," Daisy cut in. "I'm not all lace and flowers, you know. I like to walk on the dark side now and again. It's the only time I get to see my brother — when I walk in the shadows."

Asher stuck his tongue out at her. "You? In the shadows? I think not. There's no shadow out there dark enough to stop you shining through, Miss Glitter."

"Wow, was that a compliment, Asher? To Daisy? Aww, how sweet? Even with a hangover." Erik patted his hubby's head. "Go give her a big smooch."

"I can't, I've got a munchkin on my lap."

"And it wasn't a compliment, Erik," Daisy groused. "Not if you know my brother." She stuck her tongue out at him.

Asher grinned. "Ah, you do understand me still. Okay, maybe you could wrap yourself in some really, really thick shadows *if* you don't wear your necklace and those sparkly earrings."

"I know him well enough, dear sister-in-law. One thing's for damn sure—you two are never, ever dull."

Joey nodded. "Omigod, you're not kidding there." He chuckled and handed Erik an envelope. "This is from Mr. Caliendo." He looked decidedly nervous.

Asher chuckled to himself at the way Joey said *Mr. Caliendo* as if he was talking about the Godfather. Asher pondered for a moment. Ha. Maybe he was. He had wondered, to be honest, exactly what the *family business* might entail, and why Tony seemed to have so much power. It was a road best not walked down, he decided.

"It's cool dude . . . chill," Erik commented. "It's just a plain envelope with the family crest on it. Nothing sinister." He flipped up the flap and reached inside. It was a check, and Erik covered his mouth. "Holy cow . . . really?"

"What is it?" Connor prodded.

"It's a note . . . saying the house will be done by the time we get back!"

Connor chortled "Sure, it's no surprise te me, shams. I've had me orders from the boss-man, so I have."

"You knew?" Asher gasped, picking up a cushion and throwing it at him. "Something as huge as this, and you knew and didn't say anything. You evil Irish leprechaun."

"When Mr. Caliendo politely requests you keep yer lips buttoned, this Irishman ain't gonna be the one to flap them about, especially not when his boy is the shining light of me life." He gazed fondly at Angel, who blushed but smiled back.

"Well thank you, Connor, and Mr. Caliendo . . ." Erik stood. "Breaktime. Come on, Asher, I need your ear."

"What?" Asher glanced up at him, confused. Erik motioned with his head and strode out of the room. With a shrug, Asher shooed Caitlin off his lap and followed. "What's wrong?" he asked, suddenly nervous at the expression on his new husband's face.

"It's all right." Erik whispered in Asher's ear, "Tony wants to talk to us." He showed him the note. "Come on, don't keep him waiting."

"Wait," Asher grabbed Erik's arm. "What do you mean he wants to talk to us? What—"

"Just come on. Something about London, I'm sure . . ." He took Asher's hand and practically dragged him to Tony's office.

"Ah, boys," Tony said as they stepped through the door after being granted entrance. "I won't keep you long. I have some information I'm inclined to give you. Before I do, there's something I would like to ask Erik. If you wouldn't mind stepping outside for a few minutes, Asher?"

"What? Outside?"

"Just for a few minutes."

Bemused, Asher went back out into the hall and closed the door. He was sorely tempted to listen but figured that, under the circumstances, it wouldn't be a good idea.

It seemed to be a long, long time before the door opened and Erik appeared, ashen-faced and looking as if he'd been crying. Asher was alarmed when Erik strode across the corridor to where he was lounging against the wall, threw his arms around him and held him tightly.

"What? What the hell's going on? What's wrong, Erik? Erik?"

"It's all right, Asher," Tony said, appearing in the doorway. "I've been explaining a few things to Erik he hadn't previously appreciated. The need for closure being one of them."

"Closure? What do you mean? Closure from what?" Asher's mind was racing, running through possibilities, and none of them were pleasant. "Please . . . Don't . . ."

"This is my wedding present to you, Asher." Tony held out

an envelope, and Asher eyed it suspiciously.

"What is it?"

"Take it. It isn't going to burn your fingers. You don't even have to open it if you don't want to."

"What's in it?" Curiously, Asher took the envelope, which was large and fat.

"It's directions to a particular place and the means to get there . . . if you want to go."

Erik sniffed and squeezed Asher's hand and that, more than anything, scared him. He looked at Erik, but Erik wouldn't meet his eyes. "What the hell's going on? Less of the cryptic crap. What is this?"

Tony smiled. "Direct and to the point as always. I like you, Asher. I've liked you from the moment we met, and after everything you've done for Angel, and the antics you've got up to in this house, you feel like part of the family. I wanted to do something more personal for you. Yes, I know the house is personal, but this, I think you'll agree, is different. In the envelope, you'll find directions to James' grave. There's also a receipt for a car and driver who have been arranged to take you there. It's entirely in your hands. Whether you go or not is up to you."

Asher felt sick. He stared at the envelope as if it was about to burst into flames. His head was a complete mess. It was what he'd wanted. It was what he'd wanted ever since it happened. He wanted it and he needed it, but the thought terrified him. It was a few moments before he realized Tony was speaking again.

"This wasn't done lightly. I spoke to Dr, Carey first, to make sure I wouldn't be doing more harm than good, and he agrees it would be good for you to get closure this way. He also said he would be more than happy to work you through it if you wanted to wait until you started therapy. It may be you never want to go there. That's fine. It's in your hands."

"But . . . Erik?" He looked at Erik, even more scared of his reaction than of the prospect of actually doing it. Since the ill-fated rehearsal dinner, the main emotion dominating him had been fear, pure blind terror, and the thing he was most afraid of was Erik's reaction. The last thing he wanted was to hurt Erik, especially not now. Would he understand how big this was, how important? Would he be angry with him for wanting to? "Erik?"

"I understand, Asher. I do. If it were me, I'd want to go, but it's up to you." He hugged Asher hard. "I'll support you in whatever decision you make, baby. I'm by your side, always. I-I'm sorry I didn't listen to you, that I wasn't sympathetic before . . . but I'm ready, and we're together, we're married now. I want to help you. Just like I've been trying to."

Asher could barely believe what he was hearing. It was overwhelming. Too much to hope for. "Really? You understand? You're okay with it?" He half expected to see Erik's face change when he realized it really was what he wanted to do. Was he just pretending in front of Tony? Was he just saying it but not meaning it? Asher closed his eyes, his head aching. There was too much spinning through his brain, too many what-if's.

"Yes, I'm okay with it. Asher . . . gawd, after all we've been through and the other night especially . . . I want you . . . no, I need you to be okay and healthy and happy and I fully support any efforts toward that. If you want me to go to therapy with you, I'll go. Anytime. I've got lots of downtime with no rehearsals. We'll see the sights and get our heads straightened out, together." He held Asher tight. "I love you so much, Asher. Always."

A huge weight lifted off Asher's shoulders and he felt, possibly for the first time, that things were going to work out. Things were really going to be all right now.

CHAPTER SIXTEEN

"Are you sure you want to do this? *Really* sure?"

"I'm sure." Asher's voice was shaking, as was his hand tightly gripping Erik's. It was still only the first day of their honeymoon, but he'd been very insistent he couldn't wait to take up Tony's offer of visiting James' grave. Initially, he'd wanted to go alone, but had relented and allowed Erik to accompany him, at least to the cemetery.

"At least let me—"

"No. I need to do this alone, Erik. James is my past and you are my future, and I need to do this on my own."

Erik nodded, clearly nervous, and squeezed his hand. Holding his head high, Asher picked his way between the graves, clutching the folder of sketches Daisy had retrieved from their father. The real shocker was that his father had turned up at the airport to say goodbye. Not a word was spoken, but the hug had said it all. A tiny smile tugged Asher's lips thinking about it.

It didn't last long. As he got closer and closer, he felt sicker and sicker, barely able to keep walking. Then he saw it. It was a simple grave, not even a mound of earth, just a rounded stone block, in the middle of a whole load of other stone blocks laid out, like rows of dominoes on a lawn. It was identical to all the others, except for the name engraved on it. *James William Kash Born 13th February 1975 died 15th May 2011.*

Asher's hand shook like crazy when he reached out to touch the stone. He was feeling so detached it hardly seemed to be part of him, a white ghost hand touching but not feeling the cold surface, tracing the letters. And then it hit him. James was there. Somewhere under the sweet green grass, James was *there*.

He sat down suddenly as the strength seeped out of his legs and he couldn't stay on his feet. Crawling over the grass, he sat with his back against the stone, hugging his knees. Somewhere underneath him was a box full of bones, all that was left of the man who had meant so much to him. The man he had loved with all his heart and who had abused and betrayed him as profoundly as anyone ever could. Yet still . . . still, he couldn't hate the man, and there was a tiny part of him that still loved James. Asher *needed* to let go of *all* the parts.

Completely unaware of the passing of time, he sat quietly, his mind roving over the times he'd spent with James, good and bad, deliberately forcing himself to face the best and the worst. Eventually, the cold of the stone seeped into his bones and forced him to acknowledge it. It wasn't until then he noticed it was raining, a fine mist drawing a curtain around him, shutting him off inside a cocoon of gray silence. Alone . . . almost.

Taking out one of the sketches, he stared at it, letting the rainfall smudge the charcoal. He licked the droplets off his lip.

"Do you remember this time, James? Do you remember me? Do you remember the things you said to me . . . the things you did to me? You thought I wasn't strong, that I couldn't live without you but hey . . . here I am." His voice sounded strange to him — distant, cold, harsh, not him at all. He touched the paper, smudging the sketch even more.

Shivering so much he could barely move, Asher dragged himself to his knees and took out his pocketknife. Carefully, he cut a hole in the grass at the base of the stone, hollowing it out as deeply as his numb fingers would allow. Then he tore up the picture as small as he could and dropped the pieces into the hole.

"Do you remember this time?" he asked, taking out the next picture. Again, he ran his finger over the damp paper, touching the beautiful face that had looked at him with such love in his eyes as he tightened the ropes around Asher's wrists. "It was about three months after I turned fourteen. It was the first time you tied me up. I was scared, but I trusted you. What an idiot. It was a good night, though, except you made me bleed and bruised my wrists so bad I had to wrap them in leather for a week to hide them." The picture joined its predecessor in the hole.

"And this one was the first time you drugged me. Wow, what a night. I let you do whatever you wanted to me, and God, you did." The picture was torn to shreds. "Now this one was the time you first told me I'm worthless, that I'll never make anything of myself, I'll always be a punk. Well, you were wrong there. I have paintings exhibiting in galleries all over the world as we speak and my own exhibition coming out next month, which is going to set me up for a long time. You should see my house. My art paid for that . . . and Erik's money from the album. It's a converted church, which is ironic, considering you told me I belong in hell.

"And remember when you told me no one would ever love me like you did, that no one *could* love me like you did. In fact, you told me no one else would ever love me at all. You were wrong again. I got married, you know, two days ago. You remember Erik? Of course you do. You screwed him, too. Not literally, of course. You know, I think it was the truth when you told me you loved me, that I was the only one you loved. In your own twisted way, I really think you did . . . and God knows I loved you." He stopped because his voice ran out.

Sitting back on his heels, Asher was shocked. All of the pictures had gone, each one torn into tiny pieces and dropped neatly into the hole. It was pretty full. He closed his eyes and shivered. For a moment, it almost seemed as if James was there. Not just his bones, in a box, deep underground, but there, right there with him in person.

"Are you there, James?" he whispered, his voice quavering. The deep, misty silence stole the sound almost as soon as it left his lips. He glanced around nervously. The rain had brought a mist that billowed over the grass, creeping around the gravestones.

Trying to shake the feeling that if he looked up, he'd see James leaning on the stone with his familiar sardonic smile and nonchalant pose, Asher busied himself replacing the earth and the grass. No matter how he tamped it down, there was a lump there. Ah, well.

When everything was said and done, there was nothing left—nothing at all. Asher placed his hands flat against the turf, closed his eyes, and hung his head. "I'm sorry, James," he whispered. "I'm sorry you're dead, because I never wanted to hurt you, but I'm sorrier I ever met you at all. No, actually that's not true. If I hadn't met you, I don't know where I'd be now. Probably not here, not married to Erik, with all my friends around me, an amazing career ahead of me and the monumental rise to fame of the band to document with my art. So no, I'm not sorry I met you. I'm not sorry for any of it, but if I let you live inside my head anymore, I *would* be sorry, so you have to go now, James. You have to leave me alone now. You have to leave me alone, just leave me alone."

Somehow, he'd fallen and was lying with his cheek pressed to the earth, his fingers digging into the soft grass, tears pouring down his face. James was gone, but he was still here. He was gone but he was still . . ."No," he croaked. "No more. No more. It's over James. You're dead. You're not here. You can't be here. You can't touch me anymore. I won't let you." But he didn't really mean it. It felt as if there was a battle going on inside him he had no control over, no part in. An absurd image of Erik and James fighting for his soul came into his head, and once there, he couldn't get it out. He squeezed his eyes shut and prayed for Erik to win.

"Asher? Ash?"

Asher startled as Erik dropped to the ground beside him, took him into his arms and held him. "Are you all right? Is there anything I can do, baby?" He brushed the long hair from Asher's face and held him tight.

"No, you've already done it, Erik. You made me safe. I'm safe now. I was scared. I felt . . . It felt like James was actually here, lurking in the mists, looking for me. I think . . . I think I was hallucinating for a minute, because it felt like you and James were fighting over me . . . for my soul. Crazy isn't it? Crazy like me."

"Not after what we've both been through, baby. It's not crazy at all. You're safe with me, Ash, for life. I promise you. Come on, it's cold down here." Still holding him tightly, Erik helped him up. "Do you want to go soon?"

Asher felt weak and cold and shaky and . . . light and safe and . . . happy. He turned his head and looked at the grave again. "Bye, James. See you in hell." Then he looked into Erik's eyes and grinned. "Er . . . actually, no, I won't."

Apart from the miserable cold Asher caught from getting wet and lying on the ground, the following week was filled with fun and laughter. He delighted in showing Erik all the things he'd loved and missed about being in London. They did all the *touristy* stuff — rode the Eye, visited the Houses of Parliament, Madame Tussauds, and of course the Tower and London Dungeon. Erik insisted that one of the actors in the dungeon was, at one point, more scared by Asher than they were by him.

For Asher, the long walks beside the Thames at night and

through the parks in the warm sunshine were more than heaven after the dark days he'd lived through. However, by far his favorite times were the long afternoons spent in Covent Garden — essentially an enormous and utterly unique indoor market, where everything from magic tricks, to jewelry, to sex toys, to fine art was sold. Surrounded by quaint and eccentric shops, restaurants, and cafés, it was the perfect location for Asher's quirky side to be fully indulged, especially when there was live entertainment, which was pretty much every day in the summer.

They were sitting in a pavement café, laden with bags full of everything from band t-shirts to ornaments made from bent forks, eating chocolate cake and watching a pair of jugglers, one of which was on a six-foot-high unicycle. Gradually Asher became aware of someone watching them and glanced over at a group of young people who seemed to be pointing at them and whispering and jostling each other. Eventually, they pushed forward one of their number, a boy of about fifteen with a definite grungy look. When he saw the t-shirt the boy was wearing, Asher grinned and elbowed Erik, almost making him drop his fork and causing him to smear chocolate over his cheek.

"What? You made me drop my cake. Do I have chocolate on my face? Wanna lick it off, baby?" He followed Asher's line of sight and saw the boy had on a *The Von* t-shirt, and lots of leather bracelets and necklaces, complete with baggy pants and a chain wallet. The kid was definitely a fan. He smiled at the boy. "Hey, kid! Love the outfit."

The boy froze like a rabbit in headlights, and half turned back to his friends, who energetically waved him forward. Unable to turn back without losing face, he walked haltingly to their table.

"Err . . ." he said, then tugged at the hem of his shirt. "Are you . . . um . . ."

Asher nudged Erik again. "I think your fan wants something." He turned away and hid a snigger in a cough.

Erik looked mystified.

"Um . . . Autograph?"

Asher chewed frantically on his lip ring to keep from laughing.

Erik patted down his pockets for a pen but had none handy. "Hey kid, you have a pen?"

"P-pen?" The boy swallowed and shook his head, looking stricken.

Rolling his eyes, Asher called over the waitress and borrowed her pen and pad. He wrote something and handed it over to Erik. "Sign it," he commanded.

Erik glanced at the paper and almost choked. *To my dear fan – Erik Von Nordgren – meathead and superstar.* Erik waved the kid over closer and picked up the pen. "What's your name, kid? I'll make it out to you especially." He smiled at the young man and held out his hand. "Erik Von Nordgren. Great to meet you."

"J . . . Jake, I . . . Um . . . Thank you."

While Erik signed his name, with a particularly elaborate flourish, Asher waved over Jake's friends. After initial shyness, the group of fifteen-year-olds quickly thawed and in minutes they were all talking at once and thrusting bits of paper in front of Erik's face. Some of the girls, however, couldn't take their eyes off Asher. One, in particular, sidled closer, shooting him looks out of the corner of her eye.

He put his arm around her and hugged her. "I appreciate the attention and all, but if I were you, I'd find someone else to look at. Like Jake, for instance. He's been gazing at you the whole time, and he really is a great kid, I can tell. You know, if I wasn't a respectable married man, I might be winking at him myself."

The girl looked shocked for a moment, although not as

startled as Jake, but they both descended quickly into laughter, and when they left, clutching their autographs, the girl and Jake were walking very close together.

"So?" Asher chuckled. "How was your first taste of fame?"

Erik picked up the cake he'd been eating and put a large piece into his mouth. "Mmm, sweet! It's awesome. A little nerve-wracking, but man, it was great!" He finished chewing the cake. "Of course, you're a draw as well, looking all hot and sexy." He winked at Asher.

Asher rolled his eyes. "What have I told you about that winking habit. Let's go, superstar, I have a hankerin' for something sparkly."

Erik couldn't stop smiling. Everything was going so well. So far, married life was incredible, and he loved it. They'd lived together for a long time, and he hadn't expected being married to make a difference, but it did. A lot. His level of commitment and devotion to Asher felt like it had at least doubled. He would do absolutely anything for him. He'd hung back at the graveyard because he knew it was something Asher needed to do on his own, but he'd never taken his eyes off Asher once, and as soon as he'd felt Asher had had enough, he'd been there for him. He'd always be there. It killed him to think they'd soon be parted when the band went on tour, but he'd be in contact as much as humanly possible. No more wild parties for him. Hell no.

Gradually, little things started to edge into his awareness. He could tell Asher was aware of them too. "What'd going on?"

"I think your little foray with the fans has attracted some attention." He nodded to a guy just across the street who had a camera glued to his face. "Smile for the camera. I'm pretty sure he's a reporter, and I think there'll be more on the way."

"Oh shit. What should we do?"

"Hide?"

Erik steered them into a movie theatre to take in a flick. "Let's hide in there. Maybe they won't follow."

After buying the tickets, they were ushered inside and sat back in their seats. Erik put his arm around Asher and kissed his cheek. "I never even took you the movies at home, like a normal couple. Now we can make up for it and make out during the movie." He grinned and waggled his eyebrows.

"Damn, if I'd known we'd have gone to see a film I didn't want to see," Asher said, making it clear, even in the darkness, he was teasing. With a sigh, he snuggled into Erik's side. "It's been a busy day. It's exhausting being married to a superstar."

The previews started, and Erik tugged Asher closer, lowering his head to kiss his husband gently on the lips. "I love you . . . my wonderful, sexy, husband . . ."

A voice broke through their loving haze. "Hey! Get a room!"

Erik looked around and located the source of the voice—a group of kids, maybe seventeen or eighteen-year-olds, a couple of rows in front and over on the right-hand side. One of them, a boy with a mean-looking face and buzz cut, was leaning over the back of his seat and glaring at them.

"No thanks," Asher said, "I'm happy where I am. I'd ask you to join us, but my husband's not up for sharing me."

"Filthy faggot freak," the boy spat out. "Get the fuck out of here, you sickos."

"If I were you," Asher said in a voice that made Erik decidedly nervous, "I'd turn around, watch the film and mind my own business. What goes on between my husband and me has absolutely nothing to do with you, so go back to your little friends, have a laugh and watch the film."

"Or what, fag?"

"Or I'll get the management to throw your skanky arses out on the pavement."

"I'm not afraid of you, freak."

"Do I look as if I care? Do everyone a favor and just turn around. I don't want trouble, and my husband doesn't want trouble, but I ain't gonna run away from it either, so if you really, really want a fight, then let's take it outside."

The girls sitting either side of the boy were tugging on his sleeves, urging him to turn around, but his gaze was locked with Asher's, and it appeared neither of them was budging.

Erik sighed and looked at the kid. "Look, just back off, all right? Watch the damn movie. We're not here to get in a fight unless you have an overwhelming desire to have your face on the pavement outside." He held Asher tighter. "Just leave us alone, kiddo. We're not bugging anybody, so bugger off."

Breaking eye contact with Asher, the boy glared at Erik, then was finally persuaded to turn around by his girlfriend.

"Dick," Asher growled just loud enough for the boy to hear. The kid glanced over his shoulder but didn't turn again. "Wanna chuck popcorn at him?" Asher whispered. "Fiver says I can get one down the back of his neck without him even realizing it."

Erik chortled and shook his head. "Down boy, down. Come on. He shut up, let it go and let me get back to those lips of yours."

Apart from the occasional jibe from a few rows ahead, the film passed uneventfully. Erik and Asher held back at the end to allow the rowdy crowd to leave and get away from the cinema before they exited.

"You know, I thought I really wanted to see this film," Asher said, "but as it turns out I really didn't give a shit about watching it. Much more fun to engage in alternative activities."

The night outside was much cooler than it had been when

they entered the cinema, and Asher shivered. Erik put an arm around him, and they turned to walk back to the hotel.

"Hey, you! Faggots!" a voice shouted from behind.

Erik and Asher both tensed.

Erik groaned and held Asher closer. "Shit. Those asses wanna start something? They're picking on the wrong people." He rolled up his sleeves and turned around. "You wanna try a better word than that, you moron? Eh?" His fists clenched as he glared at the troublemaker.

"Erik," Asher warned, in a soft voice, "There's press around. Don't do anything stupid. Let's just walk away and ignore them. I know, I know, it's not like me, but you've got an image to think of now. If they start anything, get out of the way and let me take care of it. Can't have you with a black eye."

"You're telling me to back down? Wow, that *is* a first." Erik paused. "Well, okay. I guess you're right." He glanced around and noticed cameras and phones ready to record his every move. "Fuck. This is what sucks about being famous. I can't even have a good fist fight." He pouted.

Asher looped his arm through Erik's, and they turned to walk away. Something hit him on the back, and he whirled to find the asshole kid grinning at him. A half-eaten burger lay on the ground near his feet, and the boy was holding out his hand to a friend for another one. The friend didn't seem too pleased to be handing over his lunch.

"Don't like the way I speak, cocksucker? Then do something about it. Or are you a pair of pussies, too? You! Freaky goth boy! Are you a pussy? Or are you a chicken?" He started to make clucking noises with his friends following suit.

Asher laughed. "Sorry kids, I'm a grown up and don't have time for silly games. Come on, Erik, let's go somewhere that doesn't smell so bad of bullshit."

The second time something hit his back, he ignored it.

"Don't walk away from me, you fucking freak. Stand up for yourself. Fucking queer."

The kid was playing to the audience now, and Asher knew they had to get away from there as soon as possible, because he could feel Erik's muscles bunch under his fingers. The problem was a crowd had gathered, and it wasn't easy to get through.

"Come on, let just get—"

The third time something hit him in the back, he couldn't ignore it because it was the kid, and the weight sent him staggering forward. He would have fallen on his hands and knees, but he was holding onto Erik's arm, so he twisted and came down hard on his side. He cursed and tried to get up, but before he could get to his feet, the boy was on him, and a fist in his face made him see stars and took the fight out of him for a moment.

Erik lunged at the boy and grabbed his collar. "You touch him again, and you'll be eating your own teeth!" He shoved him away, hard, but it didn't deter him. He came back and met Erik's large fist face first, with a sickening thud! The boy backed away, nursing a bloody nose.

"Erik," Asher hissed, back on his feet and pulling him back. "Calm down. Come on, let's go. I'm fine, he didn't hurt me. Come on."

"That's the way, pussy," the boy taunted, nursing his nose. "Just walk away. Take your thug with you."

Asher ground his teeth. "Just walk away, Erik. Walk away."

"Pussy. Poor little gay boy got scared and is running away. Run away, freak, run away."

Asher growled under his breath. "Don't let me do it. Walking away's the right thing. I know walking away's the right thing."

The clucking noises didn't bother him as much as the taunts about being a freak. He'd heard way too many of them to let them go by without a struggle.

"You'd better knock it off, boy!" Erik yelled as he tried to move them away from the situation. "Come on, baby, let get away. Let's go, let's go." He picked up their pace, but it was pointless. They were becoming surrounded.

"Move aside! Nothing to see here!" Erik tried to clear the crowd, but like mindless zombies, they didn't budge. "Move! Or I'm calling the cops!"

"Shit!" Asher was starting to panic. There were just so many people. He was suddenly acutely aware of how many there were, how they were surrounded, with nowhere to go, and all he wanted to do was run. "Erik, I don't like this. Please . . . please let's just get out of here."

Erik searched for an escape, and he grabbed Asher's hand firmly. "Come on, we'll plow through this mess. Duck."

They stooped over, and Erik put his shoulder to the crowd, breaking through as fast as he could, pushing everyone aside. As soon as they were clear, they took off running around the corner and ducked into a public building with security on the door.

Erik looked around. "I think . . . I think we lost 'em. We just need to watch our backs." He struggled to catch his breath. "Shit. I think we need to hire some security after this."

"I don't know about security, but we maybe need to be a bit more careful, babe." Asher clenched his teeth, angry his voice was shaking. He closed his eyes to steady himself and took a deep breath, rubbing his hands together to try to stop the trembling.

Erik wrapped his arms around him in a bear hug. "It's all right now, hon. It's all right. Come on, let's call for a ride, I don't think we should walk outside right now. Let's just sit over there and calm down for a bit." They sat together on a thick-cushioned chair, so close Asher was almost in Erik's lap. Erik dialed the record company and arranged for some safe transportation. He tucked the phone away. "They'll be here soon, hon. We'll go back to the hotel and just relax. Try out the hot tub in the pool area maybe? Or just go to our room and get naked and bombed."

"Whatever." Damn. He was still shaking. *Goddamn it.* "I'm sorry, Erik," he said, struggling to keep his hands and voice steady. "It's not . . . not the fight. I've been in enough of those. It . . . it's the people. I-I just panicked. There were so many and . . . and no way out." He took a deep breath and blew it out. "I don't know why it's affecting me like this. It's not as if they're here now, but I just can't . . . I just can't stop sh-shaking."

"Ssh. Hey. I've gotcha, I've gotcha, Ash. I'm not going anywhere. I'm right here." He stroked Asher's hair and held him tight. "I'm right here."

Erik rocked them back and forth until the car arrived, which seemed to take an eternity. Finally, a man slipped through the security guards and looked around.

Erik nudged Asher to his feet. "I think our ride's here. Come on, let's walk out with our heads up, baby. Don't let them see anything but confidence. You're Asher Von Nordgren now, my husband, my love, my life. Come on, baby."

Nodding, Asher tossed his hair and straightened his spine. He was okay all the way to the door, right up to the point where the doorman had his hand on the door handle. Then suddenly panic hit him and he skittered backward.

"I can't. I can't do it. They're all out there and I can't . . . Please . . . Can't we stay here a bit longer . . . just a bit longer. I-I'll be all right and . . . and I'll . . ." If Erik hadn't been holding his hand so tightly, he would have bolted and run. He had no idea where he would have run but . . .

"Is everything all right, Sir?" The doorman asked.

"I-I'm . . . People . . . There were so many people and . . . I-I'm sorry, I . . ." No matter how hard he tried, Asher couldn't get out a coherent sentence. The thought of walking out into all those stares, those people staring at him and calling him a freak, even if it was silently.

"Do you have a car, collecting you, Sir."

"That would be me," the driver confirmed.

"If you'd like to pull in through the gate, I'll alert the box to let you through." The driver nodded and left. The doorman turned back to Erik and Asher. "You can take the door over there, through to the corridor and turn left. At the end, go through the double doors, and you'll find an outside exit to your right. It will take you out to the courtyard where you can wait for the car. There won't be anyone there."

"I . . . really? Thank you, I-I don't know why I'm acting like this I-I just can't . . ."

"My pleasure, Sir. You're not the first and you won't be the last." The man smiled and tipped his cap. The fellow was already speaking into a walkie-talkie.

Erik smiled. "See? I told you we'll be all right. Thank you very much, Sir."

They made their way through the corridor the man had spoken of, and Erik let out a huge sigh of relief as they opened the door and there was a black car waiting, shaded windows and everything. He kissed Asher's head. "Come on, baby. Our chariot awaits. Let's go chill out. We'll be fine now."

Once they got inside, Erik chatted with the driver for a moment, and they were on their way.

Asher curled up on the back seat, in Erik's arms, his face pressed against Erik's chest. He fought to control his racing heart and shaking body until the driver alerted them they were free and clear, then he opened the windows and breathed great lungfuls of fresh air, letting the wind whip his hair and blow away the horrible fear that had gripped him like a fist around his heart. By the time he sat back, he was calm.

"I guess I have another thing to talk to the doctor about, huh?" he said with an unsteady laugh.

Erik kissed him gently. "Yes, I'd say so." He kept Asher tucked to his side. "It'll be all right. The doctor will help you out and show me how to help you better." His gaze was gentle and sincere. "Anything for you, dear husband. Anything."

Asher smiled and relaxed. The look in Erik's eyes melted him, and if his hand trembled as he tucked a thick lock of yellow hair behind his husband's ear, it had nothing to do with being frightened of anything at all.

CHAPTER SEVENTEEN

Vince laid his head back and let out a deep sigh. His arm, still wrapped around Billy's shoulders, felt numb, but he had to hang on for dear life, or he swore his man would disappear. He'd been dreading this flight from the very beginning—not the flight itself, but that the dearest part of him would be gone for three months. Again.

He closed his eyes, trying to block out the coming pain and focus on the present. He was going to enjoy himself in London and have a terrific time at the concert, watching his husband in action on the drums. Yet he couldn't get past it. It overwhelmed his thoughts and even his actions, going everywhere Billy did, even to shower, just for those extra few minutes together.

Tears welled in his eyes again, for the third time that day. It was too much right now, and secretly he prayed the tour would be canceled and they could all go home together. He could provide for Billy and him. He sighed, knowing it couldn't happen, not yet anyway, and he refused to take any more help from Tony. He wanted them to make it on their own. He wiped his eyes quickly when Billy stirred. He didn't want Billy to know how badly this was affecting him, how worried he was that he simply wouldn't be able to cope without his redhead at his side.

Luckily, Billy just shifted his head, and he was still out cold. Vince let out a relieved sigh. The flight had been uneventful for the most part, and most of them had managed a few quick naps. Joey had tried his best to keep everyone amused until Daisy stopped his one-liner fest. Vince cracked a smile thinking of some of the others. He'd miss Joey, too, and Daisy. Especially her right now. He'd loved her before, but now she was carrying his children. Not being able to see her or touch her growing belly, to feel a connection with the babies, was going to be pure torture. He was grateful for one thing—they'd be back in time for him to at least feel a kick or two, maybe hear the heartbeats, and he'd be there for the birth.

A voice broke his train of thought. It had a distinct Irish tone to it. He opened his eyes and turned to Nora, who sat across from them.

"Ye all right there? You're looking very contemplative. I thought you'd have fallen asleep with the rest of them," she asked.

"I'm not asleep," Caitlin chimed in impatiently. "I just put me music on, so I did. Was nothin' else worth listenin' to. They're after being lightweights, all o' dem." She snorted and adjusted her iPod. The buzzing grew louder, but it wasn't possible to work out what song was making it.

Vince felt suddenly embarrassed and made sure his face was dry. "I can't seem to sleep much anymore. Not for a long, anyway." He smiled weakly.

Nora was so pretty, with her short red hair and emerald eyes, like her brother and daughter. They were one lovely family. He'd always found Connor cute, and Caitlin was adorable, despite her mouth.

"I'm sorry. I'm just out of it, completely. How are you? We'll have to get together when we get home, work on our cookbook." He finally found something to smile about at the thought. Projects might keep his mind busy. He hoped.

"Sure, it would be just lovely. The cookbook has been a favored project of mine for years. It will be good to work with someone, and your Italian recipes will be a wonderful addition. Maybe you could help me make some of them up . . . a test run, so to speak."

The idea made him brighten somewhat. "I'd really like that. I've made some of them lower in calories, to keep this new figure of mine," he joked. He glanced down at Billy, then back to Nora. "Though I think in the coming months I'll be eating like a crazy man just to keep myself sane while he's gone." He had to look away. He didn't want to see pity in her eyes. When he forced himself to look back, he was surprised to find nothing but understanding.

"It's hard, I know, to be parting from someone you love." Her gaze became distant for a moment, then she moistened her lips. "At least you know he's coming back. You'll speak to him every day, you'll reach out to him, and he'll reach back. You have a beautiful new home, two babies to prepare for, and friends around you. The time will fly."

He put his hand to his mouth, feeling the cold of his wedding ring on his lips. "I hope so, Nora. I hope with all my heart. Last time we were apart—I dunno if your brother told you, maybe not." He let out a huff. "Let's just say it didn't go so well. We broke up." His voice cracked and he took a breath, fortifying himself. "But we weren't even engaged then, now we're married."

"If that's what you're worried about, I think you can stop right now. Yon man of yours is clearly madly in love with you. People who are that much in love don't cheat. Besides, if I remember correctly, it was my incorrigible brother who turned his head last time, and he's going to be right where you can keep an eye on him. Besides, he's got his hands full with Angel. He's such a little sweetheart, but he's got a mind of his own, no doubt."

"He's a hottie, so he is," Caitlin announced. "Not as hot as the other one, but uncle Connor's been after doin' well fer himself."

"By *the other one*, I assume you mean Asher. It would be less rude if you actually used his name."

Caitlin huffed and turned up the music.

She's got a huge crush on Asher, Nora mouthed with a grin on her face.

That made Vince smile. Billy sighed and adjusted his head again, but he was still out cold. "I wish I could sleep like he does." He kissed Billy's hair. "Thanks, Nora. I feel better. I'll miss Daisy a ton though, too, and those babies. I can't wait to be a parent." He tapped her hand. "Is it . . . Is it scary and awesome or just overwhelming?"

For a moment, Nora tilted her head slightly. "It's all those things and more. The responsibility is terrifying. The first time you look into the tiny little face and they stare at you with the most absolute trust anyone will ever have in you, you just fall hopelessly in love. You know the baby will rely on you totally, for everything. Without you, it will wither and die. You are everything, the center of the world . . . and then they grow up into that." She cocked her head at Caitlin and grinned.

Connor poked his head from around the corner. "Aye, and that's when ye wonder what the feck were ye thinkin'?" he joked.

Vince laughed at the look Nora gave him. "Now, now, Uncle Con, she's your niece."

"Aye that she is, and I love her to death, so I do, but she'd test the patience of a saint." He paused and looked Vince up and down. "Ye don't look up to a jig, sham. Sure, ye've got a powerful lot weighin' on yer mind, but it'll be grand, ye'll see."

Vince nodded slowly. "I hope so. I know I'm being needy and a worrier, but I . . . I've just got a lot on my plate. Our plate is too full, I think. I wonder if we can handle any of it anymore." He looked between the two.

"You'll be fine, Vince," Nora said kindly. "It's not as if you're on your own. If I can manage Caitlin alone, you'll manage fine with Billy, your family, and all your friends around you. You have so many babysitters you barely need to see the little angels if you don't want to."

The three of them laughed at that one.

"Just don't ye be after lookin' my way fer no babysittin'," Caitlin commented.

Vince made a mental note never to assume Caitlin couldn't hear or wasn't listening to anything.

"I know, I know. I appreciate all of it, very much. Thank you . . . and I know I'll be busy before they come. Con, we've gotta finish the house, Nora, we've got our cookbook. Angel . . . Angel?"

Connor tapped him. "Vince is pagin' ye."

Vince laughed lightly. "Were you lost in dreamland too? I'm sorry, were you asleep, cous?"

"Huh? No, no, I wasn't asleep. I was just . . . daydreaming. It's not exactly the most exciting thing to do is it, sitting on a plane for a year." He laughed. "Well, it feels like a year. Sorry, what were you saying?"

Vince laughed. "I was saying you and I are gonna have to hang out, do some sketches and painting. You are my cousin, after all, and I hardly see you. Connor has your time tied up, for sure."

"Oh. Yeah, for sure. I've never really spent time with any of our family. I've not spent much time in the county. I . . . If you still want to after what . . . happened, then I'd love to spend time with you. Maybe I can paint some murals in the nursery."

Vince made a face at him and would've kicked his chair if he weren't still holding Billy. "Of course I do, you little goofball! Connor, I can't kick his chair, so would you please slap that cousin of mine upside the head for me? Trust me, it's an Italian way to give affection." He chuckled. "We're fine, Angel. I overreacted, trust me, I've been on some weird fine-line lately, I swear I'm pregnant, too, sometimes."

"It's possible, actually, you know," Daisy broke in. "It's an actual medical condition called phantom pregnancy, where the husbands of pregnant women experience the same symptoms or even worse ones. Maybe you've got that, Vince. Tell me, how are your breasts? Are your periods regular? Do have swollen ankles in the mornings?"

Vince laughed so hard it nearly woke Billy. "Well, I think my cycles are regular, but I've got some breast tenderness right about now." He nodded to Billy's head on his chest. "As far as swollen ankles, I don't have that, but I was a lot bigger than you are now, just from being fat. I think I'll be eating for two though while you guys are gone."

"I'll keep ye on the fit 'n' trim, Vince," Connor said, his eyes twinkling. "Dontcha worry. I'm a scrapper, I'll teach ye how to box and ye can teach me how to cook somethin' decent for me man here." He put an arm around Angel, who startled.

"Huh, what?"

"Geez, calm down there. Where the heck is your head? Ooh. I bet I know. I should've guessed it all along, cous."

"What? I-I'm sorry I got a bit lost. I'm tired and can't concentrate. What were you saying?"

"You're a million miles away there, Angel. Anxious to land? I know I am."

As Connor glanced away, he gave Angel a quick scowl.

You little minx you. I know what you're hiding. You've got the hots for Asher, and Connor doesn't have a clue, as usual. Maybe because he's still got feelings left over himself. I knew it. And what about that whole scene when Connor mentioned marriage and Angel didn't seem on board with it? Damn, What to do?

"I can't wait to get to London, see the sights, go to the concert . . . and of course, see Erik and Asher again." He narrowed his eyes at Angel.

"What? Why are you looking at me like that? What have I done?"

"Nothing, Angel. I'm just freaking tired. Billy here can sleep through the apocalypse, but I barely sleep a wink anymore. Maybe I can get some sedatives or something while I'm here."

"Sedatives aren't the answer, dear," Nora said in a concerned voice. "You need to relax. Have you tried a hot bath before going to bed?"

Billy stirred again. He didn't lift his head, but he spoke. "If you guys are gonna hold a rousing conversation, do you mind if I sleep through it in peace?"

Vince glanced down at his husband. "Sorry, baby. Didn't mean to wake you. I wish I could be out like that."

After a quick tickle to Vince's arm, Billy sat up and stretched, finally freeing Vince's arm. "I thought you were out, baby," Billy joked.

"You're seem really stressed, Vince," Angel said, sounding concerned. "Maybe you should take up tai chi or something, help you wind down. I'm sure Asher would show you some moves."

"Oh, I'm sure he could, Angel." Vince smiled, then sobered and frowned. *I wonder what he's shown you?* "I like the hot bath idea, but I'll lose my partner soon. Maybe Connor can knock me out with a quick jab?" He snickered.

Billy shook his head. "No way! No one's touching that perfect face. I'll be home soon enough, and we'll relax every night."

The sensation started to return to Vince's arm, and he yelped. "Goddammit, that hurts. It's coming back to life."

"Hon? I'm so sorry!" Billy rubbed the arm to quicken the process. "Here, let's get up, swing the arm around a little.

Wanna go upstairs and get a snack? I've gotta use the john big time." Billy offered.

Vince nodded. "Yes. Come on."

Angel watched Vince and Billy walk away and felt weird. Vince turned and gave him such an odd look over his shoulder. He'd said they were cool. Had he lied? Was he trying to screw with his head? If so, he was doing a pretty good job of it, and his head was screwed enough as it was.

Sighing, he sat back and laid his head on Connor's shoulder. He was tired. Tired of the flight, tired of the stress, of the feeling of having to walk on tiptoe all of a sudden, and tired, tired, tired of wondering every time he had a quiet moment if Asher would be meeting them at the airport, and feeling a stab of excitement whenever he thought he might. Dammit. It was just so screwed up. He loved Connor. Connor, not Asher. Connor.

"Don't ye be taking on so, *a chroí*. He's good wid ye, hi. Sure, he's just goin' through the fire right now. He don't mean nothin'."

"I don't know what I'm supposed to have done. One minute he's saying he wants to spend time with me, the next, he's looking at me as if . . . Well, I don't know what. What have I done?"

"Dontcha pay it no mind, darlin'. Wasn't he after saying things were good wid ye? He's not himself. Didn't he just say he's stressed out."

"Yeah, I suppose. It's just . . ." He shook his head. Of course, it didn't have anything to do with what he'd been thinking. No one knew about that, no one — and no one ever would. He loved Connor with every . . . almost every particle of his being and he wouldn't hurt him for the world. Asher was a friend, a bloody good friend, but that was all it would ever be. Hell, he'd never be able to cope with Asher even if they were both free. He smiled to himself. No, Asher was a good person to have a crush on but a terrible person, for Angel at least, to have a relationship with. Asher was his casual dream . . . Connor was his forever man.

It was quite blustery when they got off the plane. It felt strange, being on solid ground again. There were people everywhere, milling around. Even though he knew it was impossible, Angel found himself searching the crowds for a sign of Erik or Asher. There was none, of course.

Vince and Billy stepped up behind Angel and Connor, and Vince leaned in and whispered in Angel's ear. "My goodness, look at all the cameras. They capture everything. Hey, do you see him . . . oops, I mean them?" He straightened again and nudged Billy. "Get a load of all the press. Smile pretty for the camera, baby!"

"What? Vince, what . . ." Before Angel could say anything more, the doors into the terminal opened, letting in a cacophony of sound and the flash of many cameras. "What the . . ."

Above the general babble of voices, one name was being shouted over and over.

"Erik."

"Over here, Erik . . ."

"No over here, Erik . . ."

"Would you like to comment, Erik . . ."

"Erik."

"Oh shit," Angel groaned. "What's he done now? What?" Angel frowned again as Vince threw him a look.

There was no chance for Vince to answer Angel because suddenly there was a roar, and like the tide crashing against the sand, a wave of people washed over them, and suddenly they were surrounded. People were talking over each other and through each other, thrusting microphones in their faces, flashing cameras in their eyes.

Erik's name was yelled more than once together with *The Von,* and surprisingly Asher's name, too. Suddenly, Angel was scared. Had something happened? Had something happened to Asher?"

Billy put his hand on Angel's shoulder. "Holy crap! What the hell is all this?"

A reporter shoved a paper into Billy's face. It was the Enquirer. No sooner had he taken it than the reporter thrust a microphone into his face. "Any comment, Billy?"

Billy looked irritated. Angel, Connor, and Vince all craned their necks to see the photo. It was a little blurry, but it was clearly Erik and Asher. Erik was in front, fists balled, as a young man hung suspended in the process of falling backward, holding his nose.

"Aw, shit," Billy whispered.

"What did you say? Can I quote you on that, Billy?"

Connor bristled. "Why don't ye back the hell off, ye eejit?"

Billy pulled Connor back. "Don't! You'll only encourage them!" He turned back to the man. "I have no comment! Where the hell did this come from anyway?"

At the back of the crowd, head and shoulders above the rest, Angel spotted Erik, accompanied by some rather large men wearing dark suits, wading into the crowd and creating a path.

"Hi, guys! We have to go . . . now!"

He waved them on, bouncing with nerves until they got the hint to race along the barely cleared path. The dark-suited men were able to hold off the boisterous crowd long enough for them to make it out of the airport to a waiting car.

"What the hell was all that about?" Billy yelled over the noise.

"I'll tell you later! Come on, into the car!"

Everyone handed their luggage to one of the men, and once

they were loaded inside the vehicle, the door was shut, and everyone let out a sigh of relief, especially Erik.

"Holy crap, that was insane!" Erik reached for a bottle of water. "Anyone else want one?" They all held out their hands, and he passed them out.

Billy sat back in Vince's arms. "What was it all about? Did you see the newspaper photo? What did you do now? Where's Asher, anyway?"

Erik drank down a third of his water before answering. "Relax, it's okay. Some punks were giving us trouble, calling us names. We had to put them down, man! I punched the biggest asshole, and then we took off, ran down some alleyway and ended up having to call for secured transportation. I don't go anywhere without them now. This is nuts. You know me, I love being a celeb, but holy shit, this side of it I could do without!"

"So it's true? It's not a doctored photo? What're you thinking, Erik? He could sue you!" Billy pressed.

"Hey, they came at us first! Never mind, it's all been *taken care of*." He used air quotes. "Likely some payoff to the kids. Now then, I didn't get to say a proper hello to any of you . . . but it'll have to wait until we can stand again. In the meantime . . ." He sat forward and raised his bottle. "Welcome to London!"

"Where did it all come from? Last time I was here no one had heard of you." Angel shook his head, dazed by it all. Then he grinned. "Wow . . . you guys really are famous."

"Oh, fuck yeah. Big time. Famous and infamous, it seems. Sure does have a downside, though. They went after the whole band this time too—Billy, Daisy, Joey. I wish we could have warned you. What a sucky entrance for you guys to come into there."

"Eh . . . forget it for now, you loggerhead," Billy quipped, his smile big. "Looks like they were more interested in showing us what you two got up to on your honeymoon. Outside the bedroom, that is."

"Very funny, Caliendo the Red. I only punched him once. I've been a perfect gentleman the rest of the time." Erik grinned and drank more of his water. "We're almost to the hotel. You can ask the other Mr. Von Nordgren yourself how sweet I've been." He peered out the window and sat up. "Umm . . . yup. We're here. This is the celeb way in, so get ready to walk. It's not as glamorous as it sounds."

"So, how come Asher didn't come to the airport?" Angel asked. "Is everything okay?"

"He's fine, Angel. He hates crowds." Erik corralled them all, and the suited men took their luggage. "This way."

Angel walked with Connor as Erik led everyone through the corridors and finally to the freight elevator and then their rooms. After dumping their bags, Angel and Connor joined the others as they all congregated in Erik and Asher's room, eager to know more about the fight.

Erik got everyone a fresh drink and sat down again. "I've gathered you here today . . . to announce the name of the murderer," he joked. He grinned when everyone chuckled, then rubbed his face and started again. "Asher will be here in a sec, just making himself beautiful. So, besides the horrific circus, how was the flight?"

"As long as I remember from the first two trips," Billy stated as he played with Vince's hair. "Ugh . . . I slept a lot of it, though."

"That you did, putting my arm to sleep with you. I didn't sleep a wink. Did you, Nora? Caitlin?" Vince asked.

"Nobody slept but you, Billy," Caitlin piped up, "on account of all the snoring. I was after puttin' me music on so loud me poor head was near blown off, just to drown out the noise. Sure, an' those other poor passengers must have bin going out of their minds."

"Enough, Caitlin. Billy was only snoring a little . . . and drooling . . . and making those cute little noises . . . and snoring." Nora put a hand over her mouth to hide a huge grin.

Billy blushed. "I did? I was? Vince! Why didn't you tell me?" He slapped his husband playfully.

"I'll get you a bib for our next trip," Vince assured him in mock seriousness.

Connor laughed. "Sure, an' we'll get ye a drool cup for the ride home, hi. It'll be after bein' yer goin' away present."

"Am I mistaken, Erik?" Joey cut in, as Erik checked his phone. "Did Asher text you from the bathroom?"

"Yup. You know how he is. He'll be here in just a sec . . . Ah. Here he is." Erik's face lit up as Asher appeared from the bathroom and looped his arms around his neck.

"Heya," Daisy said with a bright smile for her brother. "That ridiculous trip is over with. We're all safe and sound."

"Did you get hassled?" Asher scowled. "You wouldn't believe what happened last night. It was fucking awful. Goddamn crazy people. Speaking of which, how you doing, munchkin?" He ruffled Caitlin's hair affectionately and threw himself onto the bed, curling up with his head on Erik's thigh.

Caitlin rolled her eyes and huffed, but she couldn't hide the grin. "Sure yer like a big kid, so ye are," she said loftily. "Me ma'd have a mare if I went an' did like ye, bouncing on the bed like tha'."

"Go right ahead," Asher said. "Bounce all you like. Just try not to go through the floor."

Huffing, again, and shaking her head in a *what can you do with them* way, she sat down demurely on the other side of the bed. Quick as lightning, before she knew what was happening, Asher twisted, and she was laughing helplessly as he held her down and tickled her.

"Help . . . help . . . he . . . he . . . he's attacking me . . . Help,

Con . . . help me," she gasped between giggles.

"Fear not, me darlin' I'm on the case, hi!" He lunged for Asher and grabbed his waist, but before he could dislodge him from Caitlin, Erik knocked him aside.

"Hey, that's my job now!" He laughed and went for Asher's ribs and then Connor's as well.

"Help me, Caitlin! The big one has me, so he does. I'm done for!" Connor pretended to struggle and flail, which had the room in stitches. "Angel! Billy! Anyone! Would ye sit an' watch me die like this."

"Augh!" Erik cried out as Billy got him from behind. He *would* know right where to go.

"Gotcha, loggerhead!" Billy cried out in victory. "Ah! Vince!"

No sooner had Billy thrown Erik down than Vince had him 'round the waist, tickling him mercilessly. Squirming, Billy twisted and pulled Vince down on top of him on the bed. Instantly Angel pounced on both Vince and Billy, while Connor tackled Erik, then Nora attempted to rescue her daughter from Asher, only to be pulled into the melee. Joey and Daisy stayed on the sidelines, laughing hysterically at the antic.

For a few minutes, the bed was a seething mass of bodies. Angel giggled helplessly, tickling whoever he could find and being tickled by hands that could have belonged to anyone, except when he was being tickled by Asher. He always knew when it was Asher, because he knew how to use his long nails to devastating effect. From what Angel could see and hear, Caitlin was proving remarkably adept at finding those nails even though she made a big show of seeming to struggle to get away.

The mass of bodies began to fall apart, literally, when Connor burst out, falling to the floor and taking Nora, Erik, and Billy with him. Angel struggled to sit up, to watch Connor and Billy hold Erik down on the floor while Nora tickled the heck out of him, raising curses and giggles and language Nora kept threatening to wash out his mouth for.

"Will you hush now. Such language is not for me daughter to be hearin'."

Erik giggled louder when Nora followed the threat with even more energetic tickling and threats about his language. Angel noted that her accent was getting thicker as she laughed harder.

Back on the bed, Caitlin was screaming with laughter as Asher poked her with his nails. Vince and Angel rushed to the rescue. They *captured* Asher and held him down for Caitlin to tickle. Unlike Erik, Asher didn't swear but threatened dire retribution.

"Stop, you evil witch, or I'll shave off those curls while you're sleeping. I . . . I'll paint your face with permanent ink. Get her off me you pair of turncoats. You . . . you . . . Aagh no. Angel, you traitor, I thought you loved me, and as for you Vince . . . Ow. Shit, Cait, that hurts. You've got sharp claws, you demon."

"And ye can talk. Sure, an' you can't hurt me, no way. Angel and Vince are on my side now, so they are. Yer after being in serious trouble now ye are, me lad. They're in my gang and . . . Oy." She kicked and squealed as Erik lifted her bodily off the bed and held her as her mother tickled her a lot more gently than the boys had been.

Angel came up for air, gasping. Everyone was still laughing in intermittent bouts as one set off everyone else again. They wiped tears from their eyes as they began to calm down.

"Asher, you all right, buddy?" Vince asked as he reached for Billy's hand. "Did she scratch you up too much? Omigod . . . that was so much fun. I can't remember when I last laughed so hard."

"Aw come on now. Bein' married to Billy's got to be a fun house, right?" Erik wiped his face, still chuckling. "The kid kept me in stitches all the time. Well, in between the advice and lectures. But I can't imagine you need much lecturing, Vince."

Vince chuckled, then shot Angel the coldest look he'd had in a while. Angel froze, staring back in confusion. Asher, clearly oblivious to the byplay, threw his arms around Angel and pulled him closer.

"At least my buddy Angel stood by me." Asher laughed and squeezed him. "The rest of you just abandoned me to my fate. A fate worse than death. Oh, my God, death by munchkin." He giggled, and releasing Angel, leaped off the bed and threw himself on Erik, who caught him in a hug that turned into a tender kiss.

"Eew, enough already." Caitlin wrinkled her nose.

"Leave them alone, they're on their honeymoon," Nora said, pulling Caitlin away.

"Ain't no more," she mumbled.

"Ha! Angel held you down for *death by tickling* too, Asher." Vince pointed out. "You called us both turncoats." He gasped for air between laughing spurts. "Your mini-me there isn't perfect, Ash." He shook his head and bowed over his knees, wheezing.

"Mini-me?" Asher giggled. "Ooh, I'm an evil super villain. Angel, you're my minion, come help me plot my world domination." Asher tried to sound commanding, but his giggles spoiled the effect.

"I think Caitlin would make a better minion." Angel smiled, although he couldn't help shooting Vince a questioning look, more certain than ever that he knew.

It was ridiculous, just a stupid crush. Asher could never mean to him what Connor did. Any relationship other than friendship between them would be disastrous. But would Connor believe that, if Vince told him his suspicions? For sure he could never pretend he didn't feel anything—he wasn't good enough at lying.

"Cop out," Asher accused. "So what do you think, Cait? You up for world domination?"

"Sure, an' that I am, but it ain't as no tool's minion. If anyone's after being an evil genius, that would be me."

"You're looking at me to be your minion, girl?" Asher put his hands on his hips and struck a sassy pose. "Look in the other direction . . . right now. "

"Aw, go on wid ye. Ye'd make a fine minion, so ye would."

"All right, come on, everyone off my husband except for me. He's mine, and only mine, so he is, Cait. You can't have him as your minion. He's my minion." Erik drew Asher back down onto his lap and kissed him.

Angel glanced at Vince, who had gone still, bowed over and leaning against Billy. Billy caught his glance and followed it. Seeming alarmed, he put a hand on Vince's shoulder. "Baby? You all right? Vince?"

"Ssh." Joey put a finger to his lips. "He didn't sleep at all on the plane."

Nora glanced at Vince with a soft expression on her face. "It's worse than that. I-I don't mean to be out o' place, but he said he doesn't sleep at all anymore. I think the poor thing's just about at the end of his tether. He's exhausted."

Billy knelt beside his husband and moved his hair slowly. "Vince? You sleeping?"

A sob emerged from the huddled man at the foot of the bed, and Vince whispered, "No . . . no, I'm not."

"Hey, Vince." Asher crouched next to Billy and put his hand on Vince's shoulder. "What's going on? What's wrong, babe?"

"Vince?" Angel, too, scooted off the bed and knelt next to his cousin. Was this because of him? Had he upset Vince?

"Give the boy some space," Nora warned, and Angel moved backward.

Vince's voice was a whisper, barely audible. "I'm so tired, Billy. Gawd, I can't sleep anymore, and things just suck right now. I'm sorry, baby. I'm sorry . . ."

"Ssh. Hey, you just relax, okay? We're all here for you, honey." Billy drew Vince closer, and Vince rested his head on Billy's shoulder, his eyes closed, and tears leaking from under the lids. "You've got to stop practicing for sleep deprivation, sweetheart. I told ya." He rocked Vince back and forth slowly. "Ssh. Come on, let's go to our room and take a nap. Would you like that?"

Vince nodded. "I'd love it. But I won't be able to sleep. I told you. I can't . . . I can't sleep anymore at all."

Erik tapped Asher. "Hey, you have anything that could help him out? One of your sedatives?"

"I . . . I don't know. They're not . . ." Asher frowned, then shrugged and headed for the bathroom. When he came back, he handed two pills to Billy. "I need two, but you'd be better off just giving him one first and see what happens."

Billy nodded at Asher. "Thank you. Come on, babe. Let's go to our room. Hopefully, these will work, and I don't want you falling asleep on the floor. It's a tad uncomfy."

Vince hiccupped and raised his head. He hadn't stopped crying for a moment. "I'm so sorry, everyone. I'm just . . ." He sighed and glanced up, meeting Angel's gaze, tears streaming from his dark eyes.

"What are you sorry for?" Billy said. "Hell, Vince, you look exhausted. Let's just go to bed and sleep it off. You'll be fine."

"Hush now, would ya, sweetheart," Nora murmured. "I've been worried about you all the way. Off to bed with ye. Connor, help Billy."

Erik and Connor helped Billy haul Vince to his feet and made sure Vince was relatively stable, leaning on Billy. Erik handed Vince his water bottle. "Take the pills, bud. I hope they help out."

Vince nodded. "So do I, but I doubt they'll last . . ."

"Well," Billy said, "we'll keep our fingers crossed. Come on, down the hatch, baby."

He handed a pill to Vince, who took it in one swallow.

Vince wiped his face and glanced back at Angel and then Asher. "I'll see you guys later."

"Come awae wid ye now," Connor said. "Give yer man a break an' lean on me. We'll get ya there."

"Thanks, bud. Appreciate it."

"Feel better, Vince!" Joey and Daisy said in near unison.

"Let us know if you need a doctor or anything. We can get one here, you know." Erik told Billy. "Get some rest, okay. I'm exhausted too, bud." He collapsed backward onto the bed, which groaned. "Let us know about dinner later, okay? This is room three-five-nine."

"I will. Thanks, everyone." Billy sounded rattled but kept it tempered. "Come on, Connor."

Together they helped Vince out of the room and left a heavy silence behind.

CHAPTER EIGHTEEN

Connor jogged down the corridor, out the door, and into the waiting car. Security seemed to be having a hard time keeping up with the wild crew and were a few steps back as they tumbled, laughing, into the back of the limo.

Billy and Vince were absent. Erik had told him that Billy had texted about an hour after they left and said that Vince was asleep, but things had got pretty harrowing before he passed out and Billy had been scared out of his wits.

Still, he'd insisted they go out to dinner and raise a toast for them to London, and to the start of their tour in a few days. Connor wasn't sure about going, but Erik had insisted Vince would want him to. So, with his hesitation on hold, he took Angel's arm and they went off with the rest to a pub.

The atmosphere was perfect to Connor, who loved pubs of all sorts. It was similar to the sports bars he'd been in with Angel back in the States, with long tables, big enough for all of them at once. Erik took one end, with Asher next to him, and Connor took the other with Angel beside him. The others ranged on either side — Joey and Daisy on one, Nora and Caitlin on the other.

After they'd ordered, Connor took a breath and raised his beer. "A toast! To Friendship! May ye always have a clean shirt, a clear conscience, and enough coins in yer pocket te buy a pint." He took a large sip of beer and smiled when everyone else raised their glasses and sipped too. He sobered and raised his glass again. "Te The Von an' all who sail with her. May the wind fill her sails and bring us all te gentler ports.

Especially Vince."

They all seemed to appreciate Connor's metaphor, because no one laughed when they toasted that one.

"I knew he was tired," Nora said quietly when Connor sat down, "but he seemed so . . . forlorn. I watched him from time to time. He looked lost, like a puppy."

Erik almost snorted on his beer. "Omigod, Nora. You just hit the nail on the head. That's what some of us" — he threw a glance at Asher — "used to call Vince. It became kind of his nickname after a time. He's like a puppy for sure, but now he's a little more grown up, about to have pups of his own . . . well, kinda anyway." He laughed. "He'll be a daddy soon. Maybe that's getting to him, along with school, and everything else. He'll be all right. He's in the best possible hands."

"Yes, he did mention about worrying about being a parent soon. Asked me about raising this one. I had help for a long time, but since my Liam died, it's been a bit rougher. If not for Connor's help, I'd be lost."

"Sure, our Connor's bin a good 'un, Ma, but we don't need him. We're fine on our own, so we are. Yer after doin' a fine job as me ma." Uncharacteristically Caitlin smiled a warm, sincere smile and hugged her mother tight. There was a glitter in Nora's eyes when she pulled away and went right back to being the old Caitlin again. "So why are ye after givin' up yer babies, Daisy? Do ye not love them? Do ye not want Joey te be their Da? Why —"

"That's quite enough, Caitlin. We've been over this. It's none of your business and just plain rude."

"But, Ma . . ."

"Enough, Caitlin."

"It's all right, Nora, I don't mind trying to explain to Caitlin," Daisy said with a smile. "Yes, I love my babies, Caitlin, and I'm not giving them up. They'll still be my babies and I'll still be their mother, but they'll live with Billy and Vince and be their children, too. And yes, I do want Joey to be a daddy to my children one day . . . just not these children. He's gonna be a wonderful uncle to the twins . . . just like Connor is to you."

"But then, who is their Da? I thought Vince and Billy were . . . er . . . gay. How did they —"

"Caitlin," Nora warned, and Caitlin huffed and tossed her head.

"Old enough to ask; old enough to hear," Asher said. "Both Billy and Vince are the daddies, Cait. They both —"

"Asher, no." Nora cut him off. "Please. She's thirteen years old. Too much information is not a good idea, even if she does want to know."

"It's all right, Ma. Sure, an' I know what they did. See you —"

"No. That's enough. It is not a subject I want to be talking about in company, especially not in public. Behave yourself, Caitlin, or I'll be taking you right back to the hotel."

The girl fell silent, and Connor exchanged an amused look with his sister. "Ye sure are a curious one, aren't ye, hi? Ye remind me of me, only I was curious about makin' things, takin' them apart, seein' how they work and putting 'em back together again — mostly." He laughed. "Ye can ask yer ma te tell ye some of the times it didn't go so well." He flashed a grin at Caitlin, who scowled for a moment, then reluctantly smiled.

"Aye, he had a way with him, that he did, and it wasn't always the right way, but it was always *his* way."

"And what's that supposed to mean, now?" Caitlin demanded.

"It means I'm a stubborn little bugger who don't listen to no one and does exactly what the feck I want as long as I don't get caught." He laughed, again, and flicked the end of his braid at her. Then he paused to examine it. "What the feck de ye do to yer hair te keep it so fine. Fecked if I can tame mine. Sure it's like a chewed rope."

"Well, tell Angel to stop chewing it and find him a bone." Erik offered.

"I can find my own bone, thank you, Erik." Angel laughed. "I've nothing to complain about in that department."

"I'm sure you don't," Asher said flicking a look at Connor from under his eyelashes. "In fact, I know you don't."

Connor chuckled, remembering their single night together. Even though they'd only just met, they'd bonded over alcohol, and their time together was far more than just about the sex. Still, it was a pleasant memory. He still remembered how his body ached after Asher's exceptional skill and warmed recalling the compliments he'd received from the sexy Brit. He blushed and took a drink of beer to hide his embarrassment.

Nora groaned. "Can we get off this general topic, gentlemen? There is a young lady present, and I'm sure there are others."

"Sorry, Nora," Erik responded. "This one has a mind of his own and an uncontrollable mouth. I do my best to keep it occupied, though." He winked at his husband.

"Who me?" Asher said innocently. "Uncontrollable? Nonsense. Meek as a lamb, I am. Although, I will admit that sometimes my mouth fails to engage my brain before it leaps into gear." He turned to Erik and smiled sweetly. "Maybe you should keep it occupied more often and with bigger ... um ..." He faltered at the warning expression in Erik's eyes and glanced over at Caitlin. "Kisses."

"Aye, right ... kisses. I'm sure that's what was on yer mind." Connor put an arm around Angel. "I'll have te watch meself, coz this one here looks up te ye, he does. God knows why. Don't ye be putting ideas into his head now."

"I'm sure he's got plenty of those on his own," Asher said, winking at Angel.

"Oh, aye, fer sure, but with all the art stuff, and the hair, here's me thinkin' he's turning into another version of you."

"Nah, impossible. There's only one of me, so there is." Asher gave Connor a wink. "Although . . ." He squinted his eyes at Angel, who squirmed uncomfortably, "I'd pay money to see him wear the dress I wore at the wedding. I bet he's got a lovely pair of legs."

"Well, spend your money on something else," Angel said, his cheeks flushed as he looked away from Asher. "The only way you're going to see me in a skirt is if Connor persuades me to wear a kilt at our wedding."

Nora smiled, as did the others. "Wedding? What wedding?"

Connor shook his head. "No, no, not right now." He groaned as the old pain hit him. He took a drink to cover his discomfort. Dammit, he'd thought he was over the nonsense. It was ridiculous. Of course, it wasn't now. Angel wasn't ready, and he had so much on his plate. It was a bad time to think of marriage, and yet . . . To be here, surrounded by the people he loved, with Erik and Asher newly wed . . . To have to shut down the thought, the longing . . . hurt. "In time," he added, setting down his glass. "When it's right." He glanced at his boyfriend. "Right?"

Angel rested his head against Connor's shoulder. "Absolutely. When it's right," he purred, looking relaxed and happy.

"Are you all right with that, Con?" Asher asked, a shrewd expression on his face. For all his flippancy he was perceptive, and it made Connor squirm uncomfortably.

He picked up his beer and took a long drink, then finally answered with a small nod. "Aye. Sure. I mean . . . Erik, it took three years te propose, right? It takes time. Sure, an' we've only had a year."

"Well hold on now, Con. We were in high school and I was

nothing. Now the band is huge, and Asher's nearly done with college and a huge success in the art world. It wasn't easy . . . but I wanted to wait." He took Asher's hand. "Well, to be honest, I wasn't sure about marriage, or if you'd say yes."

"I didn't think I would until the moment you asked me. I didn't think I'd ever marry anyone. But then you asked me, and I couldn't imagine *not* doing it. The thing is, though, it was the right time. It has to be the right time. If it isn't, then it won't work. To . . . to be honest . . ." Asher took a long drink before continuing. "I have wondered whether it was the right time for me. Not" —he looked up quickly and squeezed Erik's hand—"that I don't love you, or that I'm sorry we got married, but looking back I don't think I was really up to all the things that went with it."

"Amen to that one." Erik nodded and glanced at Daisy. "Oh, yes, that was a nightmare unto itself. I tell you, Con, when you two decide the time's right, elope." He sent Daisy a pointed glance and winked. "Or your sister will never, ever let you have control of any of it, like that one." He pointed a finger at Daisy and smiled.

"Don't you start, Erik Von Nordgren. You have *no* idea what it takes to plan a wedding. Do you think everything just appeared by magic? Do you believe in the wedding pixies who just turn up the night before and lay everything out perfectly? Do you—"

"Oh, shut up, Daisy," Asher teased. "I'll arrange for the medal to be delivered later."

"Don't you dare . . ."

"Um . . . maybe we should order dinner," Angel cut in.

Connor grinned at him, hoping the interruption would defuse the situation and deflect an Asher-Daisy argument, which, in his experience, tended not to end well.

"I second that one, Angel." Erik agreed.

The waitress came over and took their food orders and

drink orders. A short while later two waitresses arrived with laden trays of drink.

Connor grabbed his whiskey and dove into it, despite a warning look from his sister. "I'm not mopping you up if you get drunk again, Connor O'Reilly. You get like that, it's your man's task to look after you."

He rolled his eyes. "Thank ye, sister dear. Damned if ye don't sound like Ma sometimes. I forget you're so much older than me." He winked playfully at her. "But I love ye te death, so I do." He leaned forward and kissed her cheek.

She whacked him on the arm. "Don't you be reminding me of me age, dear little brother. You're not the youngest yerself, but you are the most . . . unique of us all." She put her arm around him. "And, by far, my favorite."

"Why thank ye, darlin. Sure, an' ye wouldn't be plannin' to dive in like the sergeant major would ye? I know ye, macushla. Ye're already planning the color scheme, aren't ye?" He grinned at her silent confirmation.

"Well . . . I'd love to help. I'm sure your cousin would, too, Angel." She sipped her beer and sighed. "Oh dear, I hope he's all right. Has anyone heard anything more on him?"

Erik glanced at his phone. "Nope, nothing here. Hopefully, he's still asleep."

Connor checked his phone and was surprised to find a text from Billy. Fortunately, before he said anything, he read it.

I'm freaking out. Vince is sleep-talking. He keeps mumbling things about you and Angel and Asher and Paulie. Keeps saying things like He's just like him, and He'll hurt you too. Any ideas Text me plz

Connor frowned. He had no idea what it meant, but it didn't sound good.

"Is everything okay?" Angel whispered, trying to look at the screen over Connor's shoulder.

He quickly turned the display off.

"Aye. Seems like sleepin' and dreamin'. Good sign. I'll

drink te that." He toasted the whiskey and knocked it back, trying to figure out what the hell the message could mean.

"Well, thank goodness," Joey said. "He had me freakin' worried back there. Billy looked petrified. Any of you guys catch that too?"

Erik nodded. "Oh yeah. I've known him forever, and nothing gets past me. It's been a long time since he looked so scared . . . although . . . there was that time when he poured glue into the kid's shoe at school." He laughed and drank some more beer. "Dang, I'm starving to death, should we have gotten some appetizers?" He rubbed his stomach.

Nora shook her head. "We don't have hot wings or whatever you're used to, Erik. You won't die. You'll just have to wait it out. Shouldn't be long, the kitchen looks busier than an ant farm."

"Sure, an' here's me dying of starvation," Caitlin said with a dramatic flare. "I've got the hunger pains somethin' savage, so I have. I'll be fainting on the floor if I don't get feedin' soon. Would ya pick me up, Asher?"

"Nope. I'd step over you and eat your chips."

"An' you would not. I'd be biting yer fingers off ye if ye did."

"I don't think you'll be needing to do that, Caitlin," Nora said, hiding a grin. "Our food's here."

They waited impatiently as the plates were shared out, their mouths watering at the smells.

"Can I get anyone a refill," the waitress asked.

Connor held up his glass. "Aye. Another whiskey, if ye please. Make it a double."

"Yessir. Anyone else?"

"Can we just get some water for her?" Nora asked, nodding at Caitlin.

"Of course. I'll be right back." The waitress walked off and returned shortly with the water and whiskey.

"Can I have some of your wedges, Erik? Are they spicy?"

Smiling indulgently, Erik fed his new husband a plump and spicy potato wedge. Asher closed his eyes and sighed, licking Erik's fingers.

"Would ya just stop now?" Caitlin grumbled. "Ye'll be makin' me sick in me burger over here."

Asher grinned. "What kind of burger? It smells good. Gimme a bite."

"In yer dreams. Dis is after bein' all mine."

"Selfish cow."

"Greedy pig."

Asher laughed. "What you got Angel?"

"Lasagna. Not as good as Sophia makes, but it's okay and the garlic bread's nice and crisp, dripping with butter, too."

Asher's eyes lit up. "I love garlic bread, can I try some?"

Breaking off a piece of garlic bread, Angel held it out over the table. Instead of taking it with his hands, Asher did the same as he had with the wedge he'd taken from Erik. Closing his eyes, he sighed as he accepted the morsel, crunching bread and dripping butter on his chin. He sucked Angel's fingers clean, before licking the sweet butter from his own lips and wiping it from his chin.

"Mmm, it *is* good. Maybe I'll get some."

Angel, open-mouthed, stared back and forth between Asher and his fingers. Asher, as usual, was oblivious, but Connor wasn't.

His hands shook as he picked up a piece of fish and bit into it, keeping his focus on Asher and Angel the entire time. The message from Billy kept running through his mind, especially the part—*he's just like him*. Connor thought about it over and over, until it finally clicked that he meant Angel was just like Asher. Well, he couldn't argue with that, at least to some degree. It was the second part of the message that disturbed him most, though. *He'll hurt you too.* What did it mean? Was it a warning? Was Vince clairvoyant? Or was he keeping a secret? He shook his head and rubbed his eyes with oily fingers.

"Augh, damn! Got oil in me eye."

Nora handed him a napkin quickly. "Here, dab it. Dab it, Connor."

With a sigh, she snatched the napkin away from him to stop him rubbing it into his eye, then dabbed at his eye, holding his chin in her soft hands. She'd been a second mother to him, and a terrific sister. None better existed, he was sure of it.

Once she was done, she kissed his forehead. "Better?"

He nodded slowly and glanced away for a second. There was more than just oily residue in his eyes now as he put the pieces together, but he wiped it away quickly and sipped his whiskey, relishing the burn at the back of his throat.

"I'm fine, Nora," he said a bit sharper than he intended.

She grinned at him and shook her head.

"Are you okay, Con?" Angel asked, sounding concerned, covering Connor's hand with his own. "Your eyes look sore. You look as if you're crying," he said in a light tone, with a smile.

"Well I'm not, and don't ye be accusin' me of it, neither," he snapped, surprising everyone at the table.

"Dude. Cous. Chill out. It's just a question . . ."

Connor wanted to toss his drink at Joey but thought better of it. He needed the whiskey. He wanted to drown away the signs and everything he'd missed. How had he not seen? How could he not have known? It took an exhausted man's dreams to tell him the truth now? He shut his eyes and reached for another napkin. "It's oil, ye . . . It's just damned oil. Nothin' else."

"Is there something in the air here," Asher asked no one in particular, "making everyone crazy today?"

Connor pulled away when Angel tried to put his arm

around him.

He looked confused. "Connor? What's wrong? Please, baby. I know something's wrong. Is it something Billy said? Is Vince really okay? What are you not telling me?"

Connor shook his head, not trusting his voice. What could he say? He could pretend it was all in his head, but how could it be? It wasn't all in his head. There was very definitely something not being said, but it wasn't on him. He'd let his heart run wild again, and it'd made him blind . . . again. He hated love so much sometimes. He felt stupid, like the whole world was laughing at him.

Abruptly he got to his feet and made a dash for the men's room. At first, he thought he might toss his whiskey right there, but a few deep breaths made him feel better. He had two options now — he could hide and maybe slip out the back door, or face the question head on. Well, there was a tempting third. To brush it aside, to move on and just ignore it, but he couldn't. He couldn't . . . not anymore. He pulled out his phone and texted back to Billy.

we'll talk l8tr..plz keep calm

After a few splashes of cold water on his face, he returned to the dining area, ordering another drink on the way, which he waited for. After shooting it down, he wiped his lips with his arm and looked intently at the table of friends and family. He could face them down, right? Or could he?

"Sorry. I'm back." He laughed at the double meaning and took a bite of fish.

"Connor? What's going on," Angel begged. "I know something's wrong. Is it something Billy said? Something I've done? Please, Con, don't shut me out. What's gone wrong? Is it the marriage thing again only I . . . ."

Connor badly wanted to cover his boyfriend's mouth, but chose a safer route and put two fingers on his lips. "Angel, me darlin', it's not that. Not at all. Somethin' different. We'll talk about it later. Right now, I'm starvin'. Don't worry, Angel.

Don't worry." He was sure his wild green eyes didn't calm Angel in the slightest, but he didn't care right now. He was too drunk to care or think or feel. He didn't want to, so he didn't. "Good fish."

All the way back to the hotel, Connor remained quiet and watched. His gaze roamed between Angel and Asher and even Erik, then back to the window, where he could see his reflection. He put some of the pieces together as he sat quietly.

Angel curled up beside him playing with his braid. He'd often said how much he loved it, probably because he loved long hair, just like Asher had. Connor had a sudden, irrational urge to take a knife and cut the bloody thing off.

Once they got to the rooms, his mission was clear — he had to talk to Vince. He had to hear it all. After a bathroom break, he headed out, meeting Angel at the door.

"Please, Con, please tell me what's going on now? We're alone, baby. You're scaring me."

Connor almost lost himself in Angel's brilliant eyes and soft voice. There was nothing he wanted more than to stay behind and just be with him, to talk, to hear it all, but he couldn't. Not yet. It cut him to the quick, but he had to leave.

"I'm sorry, but I've got to go out for a while. I'll be back as quick as I can, though. I promise. I need to talk to Billy. I'll be back, love. I will." Without waiting for a reply, he kissed Angel on the forehead and left.

The few steps between rooms felt like miles. His feet seemed numb, as did the rest of him. He hadn't had too much to drink, not for him. Five drinks were his usual, but now he felt like hitting the pub, hard.

He knocked lightly on the door. "Billy? Vince?"

The door opened and Billy pulled him inside. "Thank goodness. Everyone's checked on us, but I keep stalling them, saying he's fine. He's not. There's something wrong, I know it."

"Ssh, it's all right now. Come on, let's go talk." They stepped further into the bedroom, where Vince was sitting up in bed, looking worse than before, if that were possible. "Vince? Saints preserve us, man, what's wrong?".

"It's a lot of things, Connor . . . an awful lot. It's my brother, it's the house, school, babies, the tour, our friends. It's everything right now."

Connor sat on the bed and patted Vince awkwardly. "Aye, ye've a lot or yer plate, so ye have, but ye have friends, Vince, people ye can talk to. Don't hold it in. We'll all help ye, so we will. Ye'll be grand." He glanced away. "Yer man sent me a text. Says ye've been talking in yer sleep . . . about Angel."

Vince took Billy's hand. "I figured you'd ask. We've already had our chat about this while we were waiting, so we just need to fill you in."

Connor tensed. "Fill me in on what?" *As if I don't already know.* "Tell me, please. Angel's sick with worry so he is, and I'm puzzling it out in me head."

"Connor . . . we know Asher and Angel are best friends, right? They're both artists, they spend a lot of time together . . . and it's all good. Asher's like a mentor to him in a way, someone he can look up to and he kind of idolizes. But . . . Gawd, I hate to even think it, but . . . Everything I've seen just reminds me of how I was a long time ago . . . after I hooked up with Asher. It haunts me to this day, Connor."

"I don't understand."

Billy moved closer to Vince. "Go on . . . it's all right, baby."

After a quick nod, Vince spoke again. "When Asher and I got together . . . couple of days later . . . I told him I loved him. I thought I did. It felt real enough. I'd given him my virginity, and he'd told me I was special. When I told him . . . he pushed me down into the gravel on the front walkway and stormed inside! I pounded at the door, but he wouldn't let me in, so I left. I was so hurt. The next day he'd gone cold and mute. He wouldn't speak to me at all. I ran to the men's room and cried my eyes out, I was so hurt. I was so in love with him, or I thought I was, at least." He took a quick breath and cleared his face. "When he was in the hospital, for his concussion, I brought him roses, and he told me I was beautiful, but he didn't love me. He said he couldn't love anybody."

Billy held him tight. "Ssh. It was a long time ago, Vince. He loves ye now, I know it."

"I thought he did too . . . until you came along. I was so angry with you, just for Billy and what happened. I finally thought I got over it, but it stayed in the back of my mind. Especially here and now." He took a quick breath. "I know you're wondering what all this has to do with Angel. Maybe it's my imagination, or my mood, or whatever, but I swear sometimes they act more like they're dating than just friends. I know people get close, I thought I was to Asher too . . . but this is different. All Angel talks about is Asher, all he mentions is his art, or his hair, or martial arts. It's like he's obsessed. Like I was back then. I've wondered . . . if I ever really got over him. Billy asked me before we got married." He shrugged. "Asher's like a drug. You never completely kick the habit. Part of me will always love him, but I'm committed to Billy."

"Aye, I know what yer sayin'. I fell deep for Asher, too. I love the bones of the man. But me Angel . . ." Connor sighed and shook his head. "Sure there's no one like him in the world. Asher's like a . . . firework. He lights up the sky and dazzles ye, but Angel . . ." Connor sighed again, fiddling with his braid.

"Jaysus, I feel like a fool. After yer text, I got te watchin', and yer right. Sure, an' I don't think for a minute me Angel's cheatin', but I'm not so sure he wouldn't if he had the chance. Feck, it's like Asher's some kind o' friggin witch who's got us all under a spell."

"Yeah, I've thought that more than once," Billy said. "I'm not entirely immune myself."

"I changed meself for him," Connor murmured, feeling dazed. "Maybe not out of knowin' why, but I did. I grew me hair out because it's what he likes. Was it to be more like Asher? Did I start sketchin' me house designs to keep his attention on me, not him?" A few tears escaped. "Jaysus, I feel like such a feckin' fool!" He covered his face.

Vince gripped his shoulder. "I prayed I was wrong, Con. All the time. But I'm not. I know it. He loves Asher, too, just like we do. I guess we always will. I love my cousin, too, Connor, and you, but I've been worried since the day we mentioned getting married and Angel bobbled the topic. I know you were upset about it. You want to make it more serious, don't you? And he's not open to it, is he?"

Connor shook his head. "No. See, he says it's too soon, and I get it. Shite, he's hardly more than a babby. I'd not fer the life of me push him into somethin' he's not ready for, hi. And I know he loves me. I'm sure of that. It's just . . . He won't talk about it. Just says he's not ready. Which is fair enough, but that doesn't mean we can't talk about it, plan a bit. Sure, an' he spends half his time daydreaming, and I'm wondering if I'm even in there anymore."

"I'm so sorry, Connor." Vince offered. "But only he can answer that question. You can just pray he'll be honest."

"Sure that's all I ever asked for." Connor rubbed his temples. His head was reeling from all of it. "I got to go. Try te get some more sleep, and don't ye be worryin' about me. I can take care of meself."

"I'd hoped I was wrong . . ."

"Hush. It's all right. I'll be off now. You two take care now."

After a quick visit to Billy and Vince's bathroom to splash

water on his face, he headed back to his room. He was surprised to find it darkened. Hushed voices came to a sudden stop. He hated it—like he was being talked about. It didn't help his already paranoid mind. No. It wasn't paranoid if it was true, which he knew it was.

Taking a breath, he stepped forward to find Angel clinging to Asher. Erik was there too. Connor had no idea what to say, so he simply stood there.

"Connor." Angel leaped up and threw his arms around Connor's neck. "Where have you been? What's going on? I'm scared, Con, please tell me what's wrong."

Feeling Angel pressed against him was wonderful and painful at the same time. He laced his fingers through Angel's hair and held on for a moment, then dropped a kiss to Angel's head and moved back. "I need te talk te ye, darlin', alone." He glanced over at Asher and Erik, unable to keep the hostility from his stare. "If ye don't mind. Could ye both please leave? This is between us."

Asher narrowed his eyes at him, a look he knew too well. The boy was too shrewd by half. "What's going on?" Asher asked. "I get the feeling it's not just between you and Angel at all."

Connor shot him a look back. "Aye, well, I'll not be controlling yer feeling fer ye, hi. Just take them next door wid ye when ye leave." He couldn't look Asher in the eye for very long, nor Angel. Not after knowing what he now knew.

Erik put a hand on Asher's shoulder. "Come on, this is between them. Besides, it's damn late and I'm tired, aren't you? Come on . . . let's just go."

For a moment, Asher didn't move, gazing at Connor with a suspicious look on his face. Then he shook his head and shrugged. "I've no idea what's going on here. What the hell are you so angry about, Con? All right, all right." He held his hand up to Erik, who was tugging him toward the door. He hugged Angel briefly. "If you need me, you know where I am," he said and allowed Erik to lead him out of the room.

Connor rubbed his face and let out a long sigh. He glanced at the ring on his finger and thought about the night they'd exchanged. He noticed the Claddagh ring on Angel's finger and wondered if it even meant much anymore. It was only a scrap of metal, bent into a shape. He started to untie his hair.

"Feck me, I'm shagged." He rubbed his eyes and took Angel's hand. "Ah, Jaysus, I'm sorry, *a chroí*. I didn't mean te scare ye. It . . . I've got a lot banging around in me head, so I do. Don't know if I'm on me ear or me arse sometimes." He sat on the bed and tugged at the hairband. It'd gotten tangled, and the more he fussed with it, the more tangled it got. Connor gritted his teeth. "Fer the love of God, I hate this fecking hair."

Angel knelt on the floor and gently took the braid out of Connor's hand. "Here, let me." His deft fingers easily untangled the hair and slipped out the band. Unwinding the braid, he avoided Connor's eyes until it was free and he could run his hands through it. "If you hate it so much," Angel murmured, "why don't you cut it? You're not Samson, that you'll lose your strength if you lose your hair."

The words cut through Connor like a sharp knife through butter. He cupped Angel's face and gazed intently into his eyes. "No, but I might lose you."

Letting go of Angel, he fell back on the bed, covering his eyes with his arm, blocking out the world.

"Lose me? By cutting your hair? What the hell's going on with you, Connor? That's the most ridiculous thing I've ever heard. I love you, not your hair. *You*, you ridiculous Irishman. You could be bald for all I care."

Connor's thoughts slowed for a moment and he shut his eyes. "God knows, Angel, I love ye so much, but . . ." He took a deep breath and sat up, his long hair trailing. "Sure, an' if I cut me hair, how would I look like your ideal man then, hi?" There was the first grain of the real conversation. Let it come. He was sick of hiding it.

"My ideal man? What's that supposed to mean? Connor, I don't know what this is all about, and I'm lost. What the hell's going on in your head that you'd think I'd leave you if you cut your hair because you wouldn't look like some *ideal man* that doesn't even exist? What's happened? Tell me."

Connor shook his head, crossed his arms, and mumbled, half to himself, half to Angel. "Eh, I've been a right eejit, huh? You'd think I'd a learned by now, hi. I missed everything . . . everything. I was for me life, thinking you'd see through me, find someone else, someone better, but I never thought . . . I shoulda known. Sure, I did know. Haven't I been turning myself into him fer ye? I shoulda known ye'd fall for him. He's just like ye, so he is. He's everything I'm not. Sure, an' I'm a loudmouthed scrapper with a dirty mind and manners, and he . . . I can't blame ye. Haven't I been there myself? I know ye love him, Angel. I know ye love Asher." He squeezed his eyes shut, grinding his teeth. "Didn't I always know. I didn't need Vince te point it out, but now I can't ignore it." He glanced up at Angel, whose posture said it all.

"Wh-what? You think . . . You think I'm in love with Asher?" Incredulity laced Angel's voice, and his face was a mask of shock. Then he started to laugh. "You're teasing, right? God, Connor, don't do that to me. You'll have me going mental. You . . . Wait. You don't really . . . Con? You don't really think it's true . . . do you? Tell me you don't really think I'm in love with Asher."

"I'm noticin' yer not denyin' it. Are ye shocked? Are ye? Did ye not think the funny little Irishman had eyes in his head, had a heart te break?"

"You do, don't you? You do believe it. And you think I don't take you seriously? Do you honestly think I'm laughing behind my hand at you? That I'm having this great mental love affair with Asher—" He cut off, his eyes flying wide. "Or do think it's more? Do you think I'm cheating on you, that Asher's cheating on Erik? If you do, you truly are insane."

A worm of doubt began to burrow into Connor's righteous anger, sowing seeds of doubt. Angel wasn't acting guilty. Sure, Connor had expected him to deny it, but either he was a damn good actor, or . . .

"Yes, I love Asher. He's my best friend and has done so much for me. I look up to him, admire him, sometimes envy him because everything comes so easy." He got up and started to pace. "I can't believe this. I can't believe you'd actually . . . And you're growing your hair to look more like Asher? That's insane, *insane*, Connor. I love you because you're you, not because you look like someone else, anyone else."

He continued to pace, his face growing paler with two red spots on his cheeks, a sure sign he was angry as hell. Suddenly, he stopped and turned on Connor, his eyes blazing. "Okay, you want the truth? Here's the truth, the absolute truth. I adore Asher, and yes, there are times when I get a bit obsessed by him. I am attracted to him, and don't you dare tell me you're not! He's wild and crazy, says what everyone else is thinking and just doesn't give a damn. He's beautiful and fascinating and so many other things, I *know* you notice and appreciate, but I'm not in love with him. I've never been in love with him, and the fact is, he scares the crap out of me. Being his friend is more than enough for me. Besides . . ." The expression in his eyes turned from anger into something very different but burning every bit as bright. "I can't be in love with Asher because I'm in love with someone else. Although right now, I have no idea why."

Connor's thoughts were mush. He couldn't string together words that made sense even to him, so he remained silent. He rolled over on his side and pulled the pillow to his face, half wishing he could just smother himself and be done with this whole thing. Dammit, this wasn't solving anything. "If ye don't know why, then we have a problem, Angel. A bigger one than I thought."

"Oh, for heaven sake, Con, I wasn't being serious. I was teasing you. Hadn't I just told you I love you? Con . . . I have no idea where all this came from. I . . . ." Angel flopped down on the bed, behind Connor, and started rubbing his back. "I can't lie to you, *caro*, I'm very angry right now. Angry you would think this of me, that you could believe I would do this to you. But I am more frightened. I can't lose you, Connor. You're my forever man. I love you more than I love life. There is no light in my heart without my shining star. I love you, Connor. With all my heart and soul, I love you. There's no room for anyone else.

"You fill my life with richness, my heart with love. My soul cries for you. I beg you, *mio tesoro*, do not do this to me. Don't turn from me. Believe me, please. I love Asher, and I will never deny it, but I'm *in* love with you. You are the only man I want, the man I want to share my life with, my eternity. I feel safe with you as I never have with anyone else. I don't know what else I can say to make you see."

Crumbling, Angel turned away, buried his face in his hands and began to sob.

Connor gathered his thoughts and raised himself on his elbows. "I'll not be lying te ye. Sure, I love Asher, always have, always will. Everyone Asher meets either loves him or hates him. I guess that's just him."

He sighed, gazing at Angel's back, the ragged rise and fall of his shoulder as he tried to stifle sobs "What does me head in is that ye're all over him, and not me. I have te fight fer yer attention, hi. That's why I tried to change—the hair, the sketchin'."

"You're crazy. I'm not more interested in him, I'm not," Angel said through tears. "We talk a lot about art because we're at the same school and he's helping me get better. You don't need to do things to get my attention, Con. All you have to do is smile or touch my hand. My soul is full of you. I know without looking when you come into a room, I know when you're looking at me, I know when you're pissed with me, but I never, ever imagined you were feeling . . . could ever feel like this. I thought you trusted me. I thought you knew I'd never betray you. I thought . . . I thought you . . ." He stopped and dissolved into racking sobs.

Connor broke and pulled Angel roughly into his arms. "Ah feck, me love. I've made a right balls-up of this, so I have. I've been going crazy, thinkin' . . . Ah feck, who cares what I was thinkin'? I was an eejit.

"Can ye forgive me? It's been twistin' me up in knots, so it has. Watchin' ye. Watchin' him. I'm just the biggest tool in the box. I just couldn't . . . I couldn't have this between us."

"I'm not in love with Asher, Con. I'm not, I swear. I'm in love with you. You're my world. Don't leave me, please. Please, believe me. I love you. I love you so much. If you want, I'll never talk to Asher again. I'll go home, back to the US, or Italy, or anywhere not to be near him. I just want to be near you."

Connor shook his head. "No. No, of course not. I'm a feckin' eejit, but not that much. I'll never ask ye te choose, *a stór*, never. And I'm damned if I could leave him behind meself. I'm the biggest hypocrite."

"Yes, you are, but I still love you." Angel sounded hopeful, a slight smile tugging at the corners of his lips.

"That's the problem, *a chroí*. I'm the wild one, the one who weren't never gonna make anything of himself. Who weren't never gonna have a family, a cozy life. I was gutter trash and thought it's all I'd ever be. And then you. When I first set me eyes on you, I was blown away. I was with Sean, and even then . . . You were pure, and innocent and . . . and . . . so feckin' beautiful. I never thought . . . And isn't that the problem. Ye *are* pure and innocent. You've not seen what I've seen. How dirty life can be. I think . . . I think I'm still waitin' for ye to wake up and realize what a crock I am."

"Yes, I am young and innocent. I've no experience of life, I'm not going to deny it. I've lived a sheltered life, and I've never met anyone like you . . . or Asher, or Erik, or any of them. You . . . swept me away, all of you. Since then, I've met new people, had new experiences, learned new things, been all over the place. But I'm still the same. I still love you. Oh, God, I love you, Con. Please believe me. Please . . ." Angel's eyes were desperate, magnified with tears. His lips trembled. In fact, all of him trembled. He looked very young and so, so scared.

Waves of guilt ran through Connor's body. He grabbed Angel held onto him tight, afraid to let go. "I love ye something fierce, *a chroí*. I'm a feckin' fool and I trustin' ye te call me on it whenever it comes out." He shut his eyes and rocked them softly until they both calmed down.

"I'm de biggest feckin' jackass fer upsettin' ye like this. Sure, I don't know how ye put up with me at all?"

"I don't . . . don't . . . know," Angel hiccupped with a little smile, "but I . . . I do because I . . . I . . . love you." His breath hitched with each word and he clung to Connor as if his life depended on it. "Don't leave me, Con. Please don't leave me."

"I'd sooner cut off me arm, so I would." He kissed Angel's forehead gently. "I'm sorry, *a chroí*. I'm so sorry."

Somehow, Connor's lips found Angel's, and before they knew it, they were kissing, deep and desperate, clinging to each other, drowning in a sea of fear and uncertainty. They were both still crying as they clawed at their clothes until they were naked and locked together, making love with a ferocity that was usually missing from their union. There was no gentleness tonight, no finesse, only desperation.

Billy hadn't slept very well. The day before had not been fun. First the flight, then missing dinner—except for some room service they'd both forced down—then the emotional and somewhat gut-wrenching talk with Connor. Thankfully, Vince had caught a few hours and seemed to be more relaxed this morning. With some coffee inside him, he was happy to be at his hubby's side as they walked the streets of London on a short tour, conducted by their resident Brits, Asher and Daisy.

One of the reasons for Billy's lack of sleep was worry about what he'd find in the morning with Vince, and with Angel and Connor. As it turned out, everything seemed to be calm. He was grateful it'd blown over and they could relax, at least somewhat, again. It would be awful leaving Vince behind for three months, but it would be easier if everyone else was stable. He prayed it'd be okay and Vince would be busy and active while he was gone. He let out a sigh and tugged on Connor's hair.

"When're you cuttin' this mangy thing? I love long hair and all, but holy crap. You need it trimmed at least."

Connor laughed and ruffled Billy's hair. "You first, me friend. I'm keepin' it for now. But we'll see about a short trim."

Billy laughed. "So . . . um. You two seem happy this morning. Things all right, Angel?"

"Fine, thank you," Angel said with a slight edge to his voice. "Why wouldn't they be?"

"Just a question. I know things were sucky yesterday with some of us. We're doing much better now, and we hope you are, too." He bit back a sharp retort to the unusually snarky

Angel. Besides Caitlin, Angel was the youngest, and Billy wasn't sure how he felt about him right now. He pushed it aside and called up ahead. "Erik! Where we heading now?"

"To some place I've never heard of and then a pub for lunch. I'm starved." He rolled his eyes and pretended to drag his feet. "Starving . . . tour guides . . . brutal . . ."

Asher laughed and cuffed his ear. "Philistine. We're going to the National Gallery. It's got the finest collection of Western European art in the world. I just want to show you a couple of paintings and . . ." He bumped Erik, who moaned and doubled over, pretending to be in pain. "Shut up, you goofball. We've been doing your touristy things all week. I want you to see these paintings. Even if you don't appreciate them, Angel will, wontcha darlin'?"

Angel froze, glanced at Connor, then nodded and smiled. "Sure. I want to look at Cezanne and Monet, in particular."

Asher's eyes lit up. He dropped back to fall in line with Angel and started chattering on about artists, paintings and all kinds of art stuff Billy didn't understand and had no interest in. What he did have an interest in was the look Angel gave Connor. It was almost as if he was asking permission. Connor hugged him tight and whispered something in his ear. Angel beamed and leaned into Connor's side, even as he threw himself into what sounded like quite a technical conversation with Asher.

Billy was pulled out of his ruminations when Nora fell in line beside him and Vince and put her arms around them both. "You're looking much better today, Vince, I meant to tell you earlier. Looks like the pills did the trick."

Vince nodded. "They did, thanks. I needed to clear my head. I think I kept Billy awake, though." He pouted, which Billy took advantage of to kiss him.

"I didn't mind a bit. Coffee can fix a bad morning of little sleep sometimes. I've done it a lot. Do you like art, Nora?"

"Yes, some of it. I like landscapes, some sculpture. I like to design rooms, décor, things like that, too, more of a hobby, but I enjoy it. I'd love to help with the nursery if you need advice at all. With Daisy's input of course, as their ma."

"That would be great," Daisy chirped. "We could get some swatches for the soft furnishings and pick up some catalogs. You and Vince could Skype me, so I still feel I have some involvement in the whole thing."

Joey kissed Daisy's hand. "We'll have to fix up our place nice too. They'll be ours sometimes. Hey, maybe get a bulk discount?" He grinned, then turned to Daisy again. "Hey, will you guys' parents be seeing them too? I mean they are kind of dicks, but the twins will be their grandbabies."

Daisy stopped and put her hand on her stomach suddenly. "Oh . . . wait up a second everyone."

Nora rushed over. "What is it, dear? Is all this walking too much for you?"

"No, no nothing like that. I think . . . Oh, my God. Vince, Billy, quick, come over here." When the two men rushed anxiously and attentively to her side, she grabbed their hands and pressed one of each, flat against her stomach. "There. Did you feel it? Did you? Oh, my God, there . . . then." She gazed in joyous wonder at Billy and Vince. "Did you feel the babies?"

Billy and Vince both smiled, tears in their eyes. "Our babies! Omigod, I felt them!" Billy declared.

"So did I!" Vince added.

"Quick, get a photo of this moment, someone. You'll never forget it, and you won't want to, trust me."

Connor held up his phone, as did Erik, and they took photos of the three of them with huge smiles on their faces.

Daisy beamed. Motherhood seemed to agree with her wholeheartedly. She held Billy's and Vince's hands. "More of that to come. Just wait until near the end, Vince. It'll be a soccer game in there, I'm sure." She laughed. "Can we find a spot to sit down for a second?"

"There's not really ..." Asher began, then he rolled his eyes and scowled. "Oh, all right, let's find a café and have something to drink. But you are *not* to feed Erik too much, or he won't eat his dinner," he scolded while Erik rolled his eyes and pretended to faint through starvation."

Billy and Vince escorted Daisy to the café, helping her up the steps, with Joey watching over her as well. It had to be such an odd feeling for him, but he took it in stride, waiting his turn and letting his friends become parents first.

Billy knew Joey wasn't ready to start his own family yet, but he and Vince were. Now, though, he had to wonder about that decision. Vince hadn't been himself lately, and damn the tour, if things got too bad, he was ready to bail, permanently. So far, he'd only shared his concerns with his parents, who were fully supportive of them both. They were excited to become grandparents and he knew they'd help out as much as possible.

The café was not too crowded. It wasn't even noon yet. The ten of them spread out around a table that took up most of the back wall of the room.

A cheery waitress greeted them. "Hi! What can I get you lovely people?"

Everyone took their turn placing orders and sat back to wait.

Billy was on cloud nine. He draped one arm around Vince and one around Daisy. "That ... was amazing."

"There will be many more times, daddies." Daisy beamed. "I've been reading. It's a bit early to feel the babies, but I guess because there are two of them, they kind of fill me up more than one would. As they get bigger, we will be able to feel them actually turn over, and see elbows and feet sticking out."

Billy and Vince hung on her every word. Some of the others, particularly Asher, looked slightly nauseous, but fascinated enough to not be able to look away.

"Ah hell, Daisy," Asher said. "That's not conversation for the dinner table."

"We're not having dinner, remember," she said with a smirk. "You insisted."

"Just stop talking."

"Sure, an' weren't you the one after telling us what a beautiful thing it is. Don't ye be wantin' to feel yer niece and nephew wriggle about in her?" Caitlin grinned at him and he made a face at her.

"No, I do not. Not now and not ever, thank you very much."

"Don't you ever want to be a father, Asher?" Nora asked, smiling.

He shook his head instantly. "Not a chance. Can't think of anything worse."

Erik tutted and shook his head. "Just as well, this superstar's never seen himself as a daddy either." He laughed. "Just gonna have to be content with being an uncle to these two. Oh! Con meant to ask, how's our house coming along? I miss it already."

"Aye, it's grand, so it is. Here, I took some pics. This countertop is a thing of beauty." He scrolled through his phone for a moment, then passed it to Erik.

Erik and Asher examined every photo, exclaiming over most of them. When they were done, the phone was passed around for everyone to see. When it got to Billy, he leaned into Vince to share. "Love the color. Oh, wow, that window gets me every time, I swear. When did you pose for it, Erik?" he joked.

"Ha, ha . . . I might've, in a past life or something." Erik grinned. "Are they nearly done, Con?"

"Aye. I've got some finishing up to do. Then we call in the assessors again. Sure, an' I'd like te see them find anything te complain about. The place is a work of art, so it is. Vince and Billy's place is next on me list. Sure, ye're all keeping me busy. Maybe I should write up a schedule with some time for me-self."

"Oh? Having trouble, brother?"

"No. Nothin' I can't handle, darlin'. Just would be nice te have more time to spend with me fella." He winked at Angel and held him close.

Their snacks and drinks arrived, to a sigh of relief from Joey, who took a long drink. "I gotta admit, I'm looking forward to the gallery a little. Maybe our two art majors can teach me something."

"Joey, I've been offering to teach you something for years. Unfortunately, every time I mention it, Daisy hits me," Asher piped in.

"Asher, one of these days, that mouth of yours is going to get you into trouble."

He laughed. "As if it hasn't already. I am what I am, sis. Can't be anything else."

"You could try being it a bit . . . less."

"Yeah. Sure."

Still chuckling, Connor stood. "I need to take care of some business. No more room for me beer." He looked around.

"It's near the front." Billy pointed to a wooden sign hanging from the ceiling. "See the signs?"

"Cheers, sham." He kissed Angel softly and walked briskly toward the front of the pub.

Connor tucked his shirt back in and checked himself in the mirror as he washed his hands. He opened the top two buttons of his shirt and smoothed the collar. The walking had warmed him, and he wanted to look good for his man, too. He was still thirsty and ambled up to the bar.

"Pint o' black darlin', if ye please?"

"Coming up, love."

While he waited, Connor's gaze roamed the pub and came to rest on what he could have sworn was a priest, in a full black robe. He seemed to be talking earnestly to a smartly dressed businessman. Connor studied them both thoughtfully.

The suited man seemed oddly familiar. Once his beer was delivered, he took a route past the priest's table and studied the other man more closely. He took in the tall man's legs, which looked muscular under the gray suit fabric. His hair was in a ponytail, and he was a redhead, too—dark red auburn. He was clean-shaven and very attractive. He looked . . . *Oh, my God.* Connor nearly dropped his beer.

"Holy . . ." He covered his mouth as he realized at last why the man was familiar. He backed away, but the priest reached for him.

"Are you all right there, young man? You looked as if you were going to faint for a minute. Would you like to sit down? Pull up a chair for the man, Shaun."

Connor froze. He could barely believe it was Shaun. He looked so different—the suit, the hair, the face. But the eyes and build were him all right, and the eyes were trained on him, as were the priest's.

"Shaun. What the feck are ye doin' here? Beggin' yer pardon, Father."

He stared at the chair and leaned on it for a moment, before taking a seat closer to the priest.

"Might I ask what the feck is goin' on here?"

"I'm sorry, son, I don't understand?"

"Shaun . . ."

"Ah," the priest said, nodding his head. "You two know

each other?"

"Sure, ye could say that."

Shaun smiled. He reached out and put a hand over Connor's. Connor pulled it away quickly.

"How are you doing, Connor," Shaun murmured. "Ye look grand. Word had it you'd moved to America, permanent like. Doing all right for yourself. I heard ye got yerself a fine Italian boy."

Connor felt his face burning. He was angry, embarrassed, ashamed, and . . . curious? Why was Shaun even here? How did he know so much about Connor? Why did he care anymore? Wasn't he supposed to be in jail or something? Connor's head swam with questions.

"What I'm up te's got feck all te do wid ye. Ye should be in jail for what ye did te Angel, so ye should. Ye're nothin' but piece o' scum for what ye did, and I shouldn't even be talkin' to ye. I wished ye dead, and I still do."

"Now, now. There's no need for that," the priest interjected with a firm voice. "Shaun and I have been working together since his release and he's come a long way. If he's hurt you in the past, then I'm sure he's very sorry. We've been working on helping him take responsibility for the things he's done. He's doing very well, aren't you Shaun?"

"That I am, Father. Holdin' down a job, cooperating with me probation officer and the good father here. Becoming a model citizen, I am. You'd be proud of me, Con."

Connor smiled sardonically as he looked his ex up and down. "Ye might clean up nice, Shaun, but ye're still a load o' shite underneath. Me an' Angel won't be forgetting what you did, not in a month o' Sundays." He glanced at the priest. "Beggin' yer pardon, father, but this one's got the cheek of the devil, so he does. He could talk the knickers off a nun. Beggin' your pardon, Father, but he's a manipulative bastard, and I wouldn't believe a word out of his mouth." He gave Shaun a narrow-eyed gaze.

"Shaun's been very honest about his past. He hasn't tried to hide his previous misdeeds, and he's been honest about his current struggles, too. I can assure you he's doing very well. I can understand, if you've known Shaun in the past, then you may well be skeptical, but Shaun truly is a different person these days. I can personally vouch for that."

"Legit, Con, and it's all down to you." Shaun dropped his gaze and stared at his hands, which were nervously fiddling with a beer mat. "I'll no lie te ye. In the beginning, I hated ye. I trashed the hotel room and ran out on ye. I thought I'd get away with it if I ran. I went home, but the Garda were waitin'."

"I know," Connor said, glaring.

"When I did me time, I signed up for a program, a church program. I started at home, but I got an offer of work through the church here, so when my probation allowed, I transferred. Been here for the last couple of months. I'm truly sorry. I thought we had something good going, and I know it was all on me that it didn't work out." He sighed and shook his head.

"I know I was a bad 'un, Con. What I did was fecked up and unforgivable. I'll not ask that ye forgive me, but I have turned me life around, I swear. I counsel troubled youngsters, help out at fundraising events, help the father at the church. I'm one of the good guys now, Con."

It was all a lot to swallow. Connor knew Shaun was a smooth talker, and he still found it hard to believe anything he said. The fact he had a priest convinced didn't stand much stead with Connor. Priests had fallen for Shaun's charm before, and he didn't know this one from Adam. He could be working some scam with Shaun, for all Connor knew.

He stood and glanced over his shoulder. "If ye have turned yer life around, I'm glad fer ye. Good te meet ye, Father. Just be careful wid him, eh?" He hesitated. Something in him wouldn't let him just walk away. His eyes met Shaun's. Damn, they were still beautiful. If he were really being honest . . . No. No, he had Angel. "I have to go."

Shaun jutted out an arm. "Wait? Please?" He took out a business card. "Me number. I'd be made up if ye'd call. For sure. No strings. Just talk."

Con glanced at the card and snorted, but he tucked it away in his pocket. With a final glance at the priest, he backed away and returned to his friends.

Erik was the first to notice. "Damn, boy! Where were you? What hole did you fall in?"

He took his seat next to Angel. "Awae wid ye. I got to chattin' with the waitress, so I did. Broke her heart, poor thing. You know what a charmer I am." He chuckled, but his hand shook as he lifted his glass and half emptied it in one chug.

"Con? Are you okay? You look like you've seen a ghost."

Nora nodded. "Aye, you look a bit peaky at that. Did ye sleep well last night?"

"I slept fine, thank ye." He sniffed his plate of spud skins. "Think I'm after being faint from hunger. We've a long walk ahead."

"Aye, ye have little legs, Uncle Con. Ye be the shortest one, bar me. Angel's after being small, too, but he's got lovely long legs, so he has."

"I'll thank you to keep your eyes off my legs." Angel failed entirely to stifle a grin and sound severe.

"I thought you only had eyes for mine, Cait," Asher said, clutching at his heart. "Don't tell me you don't love me anymore or I'll die, so I will." Caitlin laughed and Asher tickled her. "Tell me you love me best. Go on. Tell me you love me better than Angel, or I'll tickle you until you're sick."

"Help . . . Help . . ." she gasped, but this time she was all alone because everyone was laughing too hard to help. "All right . . . All right, I love ye best. I love ye best, Asher. Would ya stop now? Stop . . ."

Asher released her and sat back grinning. "Told you."

"Well, so much you know, I had me fingers crossed, so I did. And I don't love ye best. I love Angel best, so there. He's pretty and sweet and he isn't mean te me."

Asher feigned shock. "I am *so* not mean to you."

"Aye, ye are Asher Von Nordgren. Ye're a mean man, so ye are, an' to a sweet little girl like me an' all."

"Right. Sweet. Yeah." He grinned and ruffled her hair. "I'm very sorry for being mean to you, Caitlin," he said solemnly. "If I give you a crisp, will you forgive me?"

She contemplated. "Make it all yer crisps and bit o' yer sandwich and I'll t'ink about it."

CHAPTER NINETEEN

Trafalgar Square was packed with sightseers, and it made Asher nervous. Ever since the incident with the press, he'd been wary of crowds. At least they were outdoors, and they didn't have to actually push past people. Still, his heart was racing and his mouth dry by the time they reached the steps of the gallery, where the crowd thinned. True, they had to climb over bodies on the first two steps, but then they were free and clear. If he just kept his focus on the cool, and more importantly deserted, portico, he'd be fine. He swallowed and wiped his sweaty palms on his trousers.

Erik turned from four steps above and grinned, saying something about it being his show so he'd better make it interesting. At least he assumed it was along those lines. He hadn't really heard. The sound of his heart was too loud. He forced himself to smile, and Erik seemed to buy it because he turned away and disappeared through the doors.

"You okay?" Angel asked, making Asher jump. "It's just that you've gone from being really excited about everything to looking like you don't really want to go. Don't do this for me. If you're tired or something, we can go back."

"I'm not doing it for you. I want to. I just . . ." Licking dry lips, Asher shivered and shook his head. "Silly, really. I'm freaking out with all the people. I don't normally, but after the crazy freak show with the press . . . I guess I'm just nervous when there are too many people."

"Well, you can be sure there won't be too many people inside. For reasons that escape me, tourists don't seem to be as interested in paintings as pigeons."

Asher smiled, the tension releasing him. "Thanks, Angel. You're a blast of fresh air."

When Asher reached for Angel's hand, he was a little surprised when Angel snatched it back, but hey, paintings were awaiting.

"It'll be fine, Ash . . . I know it." Joey added, slapping him on the back as he passed with Daisy.

Asher nodded and straightened his back. He grinned at Angel and caught what seemed to be a slightly off expression as Connor slipped his arm around Angel's waist and he laid his head on Connor's shoulder.

"Are you ready for me to show you why I keep telling you I'm not worthy to be called an artist?" Angel asked, his voice light.

Connor groaned. "Would ye stop now? Have I not told ye a million times, hi? Ye're everything an artist should be. Ye're goin' te a fancy school and the beautiful things you make put me childish scribbles te shame, so they do."

"Yeah, I'm a student, and that's the point. I'm a student, not a real artist."

"Everyone's a student, Angel." Asher smiled. "Especially artists. We're always learning. Let's go see the masters."

As soon as they passed through the doors, Asher made a beeline for Erik, grabbed his hand and drew him into the hall. No one, no matter what they felt about art, could deny the National Gallery was beautiful. Light, bright, and airy, it sported a domed glass roof and uplifting décor. The paintings were displayed in the best possible setting and effect. Like a kid in a candy shop, Asher didn't know where to turn first. They spent almost twenty minutes in the first room as he and Angel got absorbed into each painting, discussing everything from brush strokes, to setting, to colors, to style, and back to shading and perspective.

Most of the others wandered off after a few minutes and had viewed all the paintings before he and Angel had finished with the first one. The only person who stayed close was Connor, and it made Asher smile. Connor and Angel were so much in love, it was beautiful. Connor was insecure, though, and he never ventured far from his beautiful boyfriend.

Erik, on the other hand, he thought with amusement, was the complete opposite, so confident and secure it would never occur to him that Asher might betray him, and with good reason. Even as the thought crossed his mind, he smiled and sought out his husband with adoration. He was going to have to watch himself. Couldn't let Erik get the impression he was worshipping him too much, or the man wouldn't be able to get his head through the door. Erik glanced up and flashed him a wink, which made him blush and turn quickly back to the painting they were examining.

"I really want to see the Monet and Cezanne," Angel said.

Asher checked the floor plan. "Okay, let's go there now, and then we can find the restaurant and get something to eat before Erik passes out."

"Ha, ha, husband. I won't pass out, yet. I'll live, I think. I'm a big guy, it takes a lot of food to fill me up." He pulled Asher into a hug.

"Word." Billy chimed in. "This guy used to out-eat us all at my parent's house. My parents were always saying they wondered where you put it all. Not even in my worst growth spurts did I eat as much as you could."

Erik laughed. "Like I said, I'm a big boy." He patted his tight stomach. "Gotta feed me." He tipped Asher's face up. "Or I'll have to pillage and eventually plunder. I love to plunder . . ."

Erik brushed a soft kiss across Asher's lips that made him shiver and bite back a sigh. Even he knew there were places where PDA's should probably be kept to a minimum.

Instead, he rubbed his cheek against Erik's shoulder. "Save the plundering for when we get home, Viking." He grabbed Erik's hand and towed him through the gallery.

Vince took in the artwork quietly. He wasn't particularly interested in the paintings, he just loved being anywhere with Billy, savoring every moment until their forced separation, which was imminent. He'd tried to tamp down his feelings, to deny them, but he knew it was coming and couldn't help but work himself up over it. All he could do was hang in there and drink in every moment he could with Billy and Daisy.

As they passed from one room to another, he watched Angel and Connor hold onto each other as tightly as they were. Last night must have been difficult, but he was glad they seemed to have worked through it. He'd felt so guilty about how much what he'd said had hurt Connor. He shouldn't have said anything, but he couldn't help himself. He'd been so out of control lately. Maybe it would be better when he got home and had projects he could take charge of.

"You okay, baby?" Billy asked, his voice sweet and not probing at all. "You look lost in thought."

"Sorry . . . just out of it again. I've got so much on my mind, it won't stop. I thought it would after last night, but . . ." He shook his head.

Billy kissed him softly and held him in a warm embrace. "I wish I could help you, sweetie. Just lean on me."

I would if I could, but you won't be there. He pasted on a smile. "Always." He put his head on his hubby's shoulder and they caught up with Connor and Angel. "Hey . . . you guys loving the art?"

Connor snorted. "Well, I'll not be sayin' in all truth that I'm getting the kick out of it me fella here is, but it's grand to see him gettin' himself so excited." He laughed and shook his head, loosening some of the hairs in his braid. "Although I'd give me left nut to get a bit o' that talent in me own stuff."

"Your own stuff?" Billy laughed. "Angel, why didn't you tell us you were tutoring Connor on art," he teased.

"He's being silly, Billy. He tries to draw houses and plans and gets angry and frustrated when he doesn't think they're good enough. They serve their purpose, and his true artistry comes out when he's got a knife or a chisel in his hands. You should see the newel post he's carved for Asher and Erik's house, and the mobiles he's making to go over the babies' cribs. He's a true artist with wood. He just won't admit it's art at all." Angel tugged on Connor's braid and kissed him.

"He's got this silly idea I'm comparing him to Asher all the time. Of course, he's not going to compare with Asher when it comes to art. None of us can, not even me . . . ever. Just like none of us can compare with Erik's singing, or Vince's cooking, or your drumming. But I don't freak out and try to sing him to sleep or force feed him lasagna or bang around on dustbin lids. It's just . . . silly."

Connor smiled and pulled at his hair. "Aye well, ye've got me there. Just don't ye be puttin' down ye're own talent." He paused and laughed. "Though I've yet to see ye try to paint with a roller, and I'd be after quaking in me shoes if I saw ye with a chop saw in yer hand."

"Wouldn't even try," Angel said, kissing him again. "I'm a disaster at anything like that. Can't hammer a nail in straight to save my life, and once I went straight through a water pipe when I was trying to hang a painting at the villa. See . . . we're perfect. I paint the art and you can make the frame and knock in the nail to hang it on. Perfect compliments. Actually," Angel laughed, "Forget about the nail. You can build the whole house."

"Speaking of houses . . ." Vince began. "When are you

guys thinking of building and where? Is it gonna be completely custom? Did you buy a lot yet?"

Billy laughed. "Sorry, when he's awake, he can't stop his mouth running away with him. He took over for me today," he joked, tugging Vince closer.

"We haven't really talked about it yet," Angel said. Then, with a guilty start added. "Well, actually, Connor's been talking about it a lot, and I've been too far up my own arse to listen. When we get back, maybe we can look at it together. See if we can't turn your sketches into something more three dimensional."

Connor let out a small gasp and smiled at Angel. "Really? I mean . . ." he glanced at Vince and Billy, then back at Angel. "Ye're still wantin' te do it that way, to wait? Te build our own place. Ye wouldn't be wantin' somethin' quick and needin' work?"

Connor looked so cute, peeping through his red lashes with his emerald green eyes. He acted and thought of himself as older, but he was only twenty-two, a mere child to most people.

"Of course. We can stay at the little house until it's ready. There's no rush. We can take our time, let your creativity work overtime. You can create us a perfect nest, with a beautiful garden where our children can play."

Vince thought Connor would burst, his face blushed to such a deep red. But it had been a long time since he'd seen him smile so wide. It brought him a lovely, warm feeling that maybe things were back on track for the couple and looked better than ever before.

"Our children? Ours?" Connor repeated, with his hands on Angel's face. "Sure it's grand te hear ye say that, macushla. After . . ." He shot a look at Vince and Billy. "Well, I thought I'd screwed me chances. It's grand, so it is, grand. I love ye, *a chroí*, and I'd be honored te have children wid ye, hi."

Vince had thought Connor couldn't have smiled wider, but he'd been wrong.

"I hope they have their father's eyes," Angel murmured, "because they're the most beautiful eyes God gave to any man . . . or woman for that matter."

Connor leaned in and kissed him deeply. "I love ye so much."

Billy rubbed Vince's chest. "Gawd, that's the sweetest thing ever, isn't it?"

"Yeah, it is, baby." Vince let out a sigh of relief. Nothing had been said so far, and he wouldn't stir a hornet's nest, but he had to let them know it was all good. After they broke the kiss, he put a hand on Angel's shoulder. "Hey, cousin?"

Angel turned to him with a huge smile on his face and eyes so bright they seemed to be brilliant blue rather than their usual icy color.

"I-I just wanted to apologize for how I've been lately and for scaring everyone to death or making them pissed off at me." He blushed and glanced between them. "You two look amazingly happy, and I'm thrilled to death. I guess I'm just a crazy old nutjob of a married man, father-to-be student." He laughed, hoping they would, too.

Angel didn't laugh. He put his arms around Vince and hugged him close. "You're way more than that, Vince. You're my family. I've known you all my life, and I've never seen you so happy, or so stressed. Chill out. Don't take all the weight on your shoulders. You can shout at me and piss me off as much as you like, if it helps. I'll always be here for you, no matter what. You're family, *cugino*." He stepped back and grinned at Vince. "So you're not getting rid of me no matter what. When we go back home, I'm going to look after you, whether you want me to or not."

Vince smiled and hugged him again. He breathed another sigh of relief and tried to stop a couple of tears, but they came anyway. Angel would understand. "Of course I want . . ." He stepped back and patted the boy's face. "I'm . . . just so relieved you're still speaking to me after last night. Family is everything, isn't it?" He swallowed hard. "I'd love to have you look after me. I need tending to."

Billy hugged Vince from behind. "I couldn't think of a better person to hang with. Him and Connor both." He smiled at both the men. "I'm sorry too, for last night, Connor."

Connor shook his head. "It's on me, shams. Shoulda dealt sooner, hi. But it's all good."

"I'm sorry I upset you all. I didn't know . . . I mean I didn't . . ." Angel stopped. "I still don't really understand, but I kind of do. I never meant . . . Ah hell, it's just all so — "

"Hey, don't ye go takin' on so. This is all on me, so it is. I was a damn fool, and everyone could see it. My insecurities almost ruined it all, an' I'll not be lettin' that happen again. Sure, an' I'm glad Vince was after showin' me what a feckin' eejit I was."

Vince laughed. "Well, I didn't put it that way, exactly." He cleared his face and took their hands. "Look, the point is, we're good. No more missed signals or drama or weird looks, okay? We're cool now, and yes, Angel, you're right. I do need to chill out. I'll miss Billy to death, which means I'll need you even more. Con, you too, buddy. You've become dear to me, too. I need you both." He held their hands tighter and felt a knot in his stomach. Why had he caused such a scene? Too late now, the deed was done. He just prayed it stayed good for a long time.

"We're here for you. When we go back, you can help us look for a good place for our house and help plan it, too. With all the decorating you're going to do with the girls, then helping Connor's sister and her delightful daughter settle in, you won't have time to miss Billy too much. It's only three months, and before you know, it will all be over, and he'll be home. God, by then it will be coming close to the time for the babies. How exciting. Make the most of your youth and freedom."

Connor couldn't honestly say he had any great love for art, and having already spent the best part of an hour in the gallery, his attention was wandering. He knew Angel had particularly wanted to come to these rooms, and some of the artists' names were familiar, but only because Angel had spoken of them. Overall, he was uninterested and bored.

The gallery was a beautiful place, for sure, but it was beautiful in a simple way that didn't detract from the glory of the paintings. As a craftsman, Connor found himself drawn into a different kind of artistry, that of the perfectly executed architecture—the finely crafted joints, simple lines, smooth curves, and inlaid wood floor. He appreciated the colors that fed into but didn't clash with those of the paintings on the walls, the deeply matured shine on the parquet floors, even the way the coving cut up the vast dimensions to make the room seem more cozy, less imposing.

He was examining the joints on one of the chunky wooden benches when he caught the name of the band being mentioned by two strangers standing in the corner. He smiled to himself. Fame was a beautiful thing. Straightening, he noticed the security guard seemed to have his eye on the same two people, and a small prickle of concern ran down the back of his neck.

As he watched, the two strangers began to walk toward Erik and Asher, who were deep in conversation, with Angel at their elbow. The others were strung out, either looking at paintings or waiting idly for everyone else to finish. Something was up.

As he hurried across the room, a second security guard appeared and hurried over to the first, bending to speak quietly to him, too quietly for Connor to hear.

"Hey, Angel," he called, but before he could say another word, one of the two strangers took out a notebook and hailed Erik.

"Mr. Von Nordgren! A word if you don't mind, about the fight and your new marriage?"

"Shit," Erik mumbled so softly, Connor barely heard him. "No comment on the fight, and fine," he said louder. "Thanks," he added as an afterthought.

The man frowned, not even making a note. "But what about the fight? Did you know the young man? What did he do? How long have you known your husband? Let me get a photo of you both . . ."

Obviously, the man was a pest, big time.

Erik shielded Asher with his body. "No pictures, and I'm not answering any of your questions!" He glanced at the security men, but the room was suddenly filled with a bright light — a flash bulb that had come from the second reporter's camera.

"Dammit! I said no pictures," Erik roared and tried to rush forth, but Asher stopped him.

"Chill it, Erik. You know what happened last time. Come on, let's move on. We've done with this room. Maybe we can just go find the restaurant now. Surely they won't follow us there." Asher's voice was strained, but he seemed calmer than Erik, at least for the moment.

Connor raced to Erik's side. If there was going to be a fight, he'd be next to the big man when it went down for sure.

"I got yer back, sham. Best if we get the hell out while we can, hi."

Erik clapped Connor's shoulder. "Thanks, man."

But the situation wasn't getting better. In fact, it got far worse. Like a swarm of bees on a pot of honey, people seemed to crowd the room, surrounding them. They weren't reporters, not all of them, but they were worse. They were the curious, the gawkers, and the pointers, and here they were . . . in a fishbowl.

"Oh shit," Erik grumbled, his hand desperately gripping Asher's.

Angel appeared at Connor's elbow, and Connor hugged him briefly. "It's gonna be fine, darlin'. We need to get the hell outta here, big man. Sooner better than later, hi." He didn't want to scare the others, but he was a scrapper, a gutter rat, used to summing up odds, assessing situations, and this one didn't look good. There was too much potential for it to go bad real fast.

"Vince," Angel called over, "Get Daisy out of here. We'll take care of Erik and Asher. Just make sure the babies are okay."

Vince nodded. As all the attention was focused on Erik and Asher and the others had been at the entrance anyway, it wasn't difficult for them to slip out. Connor could see Daisy wasn't happy and fought them all the way, but they finally disappeared, and Connor heaved a sigh of relief.

The relief was short-lived, however, because more people were hurrying into the room, and what had previously felt like a lot of space had shrunk. Camera flashes were going off and people were shouting. Someone was waving a microphone in Erik's face, and it was all Connor could do to hold him back.

A glance over his shoulder made his heart fall even further. Asher was backed against the wall, his eyes darting from side to side, looking for a way out that wasn't there. Connor recognized the wild look. It had been there shortly before Asher flipped out all those years ago when Connor had crossed the sea seeking to save a relationship and almost finding himself catapulted into one himself. It had also been there at the rehearsal dinner. It wasn't good news.

Despite everything, he couldn't help the flood of emotion that passed through him on seeing his friend's distress. "Erik." He put his hand on Erik's shoulder and spoke softly. "Ye've got a bigger problem, sham. Yer man's not doing good. He needs ye." But Erik wasn't moving, what the hell was he doing?

"Get out of my face right now and leave my friends alone! You come any closer and I'll . . ." Erik growled. His Nordic blood had to be at the boiling point right about now.

Connor half expected to hear a battle cry and see axes start flying at any moment. When Erik started trying to push through the crowd instead of turning to take care of Asher, he almost lost it. Feck, the man was a selfish bastard.

"Dammit," Angel cursed at Connor's side. "Billy's right, he's a fucking meathead. Help Erik. I've got Asher. We've got to get him out of here, and now. Don't bother trying to reason with them or even talk to them. Just get the hell out, no messing around."

Leaving Connor at Erik's side, Angel ducked behind him, into the tight little circle that was the only free space in the room. Asher jumped when Angel touched his arm and stared at him wildly.

"It's okay, Ash. It's me, Angel. I know this is scary. Fuck, it's scaring the hell out of me, too. Let's get out of here, okay. Never mind about looking at the paintings, we're just going to get out of here. All right?"

For a moment, Asher looked blank, as if he had no idea who Angel was, then he swallowed hard and nodded, clinging to Angel's arms. "Angel, I-I can't . . . I . . . There's no . . . Please . . ."

"I know. Come on. Come with me. It'll be okay." Continuing to speak calmly, he drew Asher away from the wall and put his arm around him, drawing him into his side, trying to screen his face from the reporters who were still pretty much all focusing on Erik. Angel couldn't really hear what they were saying, and he didn't care at all.

Connor glanced over his shoulder. "All right?"

"No," Angel answered. "We've all got to go. We've got to go now."

Connor quickly scanned the area for a way out. "Where to?" he snapped.

Erik's ice blue eyes met his. "Over there . . . The next room over has a stairwell. If we can reach it, we can get downstairs and out. Damn, where are the cops? Too many donut shops here, too?" He stepped behind Connor and put his hands on his shoulders, effectively using Connor as a battering ram and his body as a shield for Angel and Asher.

Before they made it too far, the crowd closed around them, crushing them. Asher whimpered, and Angel tried to press him closer to his side, hiding his face against his shoulder. Security surrounded the dire scene and tried to reach them through the zombie-like crowd of reporters and onlookers.

Finally they broke free of the crowd and raced through to the next room, where they met more security who escorted them to the stairwell. They did a marvelous job at holding back the crowd, who had followed and were getting scarier by the moment, and much louder, especially in the acoustics of the stairwell, where everything was amplified. The yelled demands for questions got worse and worse.

They met Nora and Caitlin on the first landing, down a short flight of stairs. From there, the stairway turned at right angles and a longer set of stairs dropped them to the ground floor. Nora had her arms around Caitlin's shoulders and held her near as they all grouped together.

"Sure, an' I don't know why ye won't just let me at 'em," Caitlin growled. "They're after being way over de line here. Will ye look at what they're doin' to me friend Asher?"

Of course, everyone had to look, and the weight of their stares, along with the baying of the crowd pressed against the glass doors, was too much for Asher. Angel saw his composure crack. His gaze darted everywhere as if searching for a way out but unable to find one. Shaking his head convulsively, Asher sat down and covered his face with his hands, rocking.

It was terrible timing, because one of the reporters broke away from the security guard, pushed through the doors, and came rushing down the stairs toward them. At the same time, a door opened at the bottom of the stairs and two men walked in. Whether they were reporters or not, the effect was the same. They were trapped. All they needed was a reporter to catch on to what was happening with Asher, and it would be all over the news in an hour.

Without thinking, Angel grabbed Asher's hand and dragged him to his feet. Taking his life into his hands, he sped down the stairs towing Asher, heading for the disabled toilet he'd spotted at the bottom of the stairs. Thank God they didn't fall. The two men thankfully didn't say a word, simply stared at them and moved aside.

Connor was shocked by Angel's sudden departure, and his heart flew to his mouth at his headlong descent. He was sure Asher was going to fall and send them both crashing to the bottom of the stairs. He heaved a sigh of relief when they disappeared into the toilet. Part of him was glad because he knew the crowd was far too much for Asher, but why did it have to be Angel again? Was he the only one who could think? Or care? Why did he have to be the one Asher always turned to?

The gut-wrenching conversation from last night still played out in his head, of the jealousy he'd thought had left but which was still twisting his gut. Angel had done so well with avoiding Asher's hands, until now. He pushed the thoughts aside impatiently. Would his insecurity never let up? This was an emergency. There was no room for the green-eyed monster right now. None. What mattered the most was safety. Yes, that was it.

"We've got to go, Erik . . ."

"I know, buddy, I know." His voice had a rare note of fear to it as they were being encroached upon again.

"Do you think someone should call the police?" Nora asked nervously.

The door opened again below them, and they all turned nervously toward it. The relief was palpable when they saw a familiar fluffy red head. "Guys, this way."

The small crowd who had gathered around the exit moved aside as they thundered down the stairs.

"Don't ya dare be takin' me out of here without Angel and Asher," Caitlin complained, struggling wildly. "Dontcha be leavin' them behind."

"No one's going to be leaving anyone behind, Caitlin," Nora snarled. "We just need to get somewhere we can think and calm things down."

"I won't be—"

"Angel," Erik called, knocking loudly on the door. "I hope you can hear me. Stay there until we come back for you. Don't come out, whatever you do."

Erik grabbed Caitlin's hand and dragged her out the door into, surprisingly, a large, spacious, and very tempting smelling restaurant. All around, people had stopped eating and were staring at them. Billy had brought not only Vince and Joey but also several police officers, who surrounded them and escorted them quickly through the restaurant and out of the building. There was more press outside, news teams by the look of it, but the police were very efficient and practically manhandled them through the crowd, around the corner, into an alleyway, and through a door into what appeared to be some kind of workroom. Paintings were stacked in racks, and there were all kinds of art materials lying around as well as computers, desks, papers, and abandoned coffee cups.

The police remained outside, leaving them alone. Daisy was waiting anxiously. "What happened? Is everyone all right? Where's Asher?"

"We're fine, Daisy," Nora said, putting a hand on Daisy's shoulder and easing her back into the chair she'd been sitting in. "It got a bit scary but . . ."

"They left 'em behind, Daisy," Caitlin wailed, throwing herself dramatically into Daisy's arms. "Sure, an' they pushed 'em in the toilet and left 'em behind."

"Hush, Caitlin. Don't be silly," Nora muttered. "Asher wasn't doing very well with the crowds, Daisy. Angel took him into the disabled toilet to calm him down when it was all getting crazy. Erik told them to stay there until we can go back."

"You left them in a toilet?" Daisy was clearly appalled.

Connor stepped in to assure her. "Sure it was a madhouse, darlin'. Ye know Asher's been deadly feared of crowds this last few days. It was bad. We didna know what we'd be after finding through the doors, hi. He was freaking bad, and no one wanted this in the papers tomorrow."

Daisy stared at him coolly, then turned her glare on Erik. "So let me get this right. Asher was having a panic attack, and to avoid bad publicity, you threw in a toilet and left him there?"

"Angel's with him," Erik shot back.

"Oh great," Daisy said tight-lipped. "That makes all the

difference. At least Angel gave a damn."

"It's not that we didn't give a damn—"

"Can it." Daisy got to her feet and headed for the door.

"Erik had to be holdin' off the press, Daisy, and findin' us a way out," Connor chastised. "So don't ye be jumpin' down his throat, hi." He shot her a look which she returned with the coldest glare he'd seen for a long time.

"Thanks, bud, I appreciate it," Erik said, dropping an arm over his shoulder. "Trust me, Daisy, that wasn't the time or the place to deal with his meltdown." He huffed and turned from her.

"Ssh. Ssh it's okay." Angel stroked Asher's back, feeling very anxious himself. What the hell was he supposed to do now? He'd been terrified this would happen, ever since the day at Asher's house before the wedding. What if... What should...

Asher, rather than calming down, seemed to be getting worse, and Angel had the feeling things were just spiraling out of control. All he could do was hold on to Asher and rub his back and hope the shaking and weeping would stop soon.

When Erik banged on the door, it made things a whole lot worse, because it scared Asher, who pushed Angel away so hard he almost fell, and he began to claw at the door, trying to get it open.

"Gotta get out, gotta get out, gotta get out," he said over and over.

"No, you can't. We have to stay in here. It's safe in here. Asher, stop."

He tried to drag Asher away from the door, but Asher fought back furiously, completely uncontrolled and uncaring of whether or not he hurt Angel. A flailing arm caught Angel on the side of the head, making him see stars.

If it came down to a fight, they were pretty evenly matched in size and strength—Angel's lack of height was made up for in bulk. He'd been working out with Connor and was stronger than Asher now. If Asher had been cool, Angel would have had no chance at all because he would have been no match for Asher's martial arts skills, but with his brain of-fline, Asher was acting on pure instinct and Angel was able to get the drop on him.

Angel threw his arms around Asher from behind, no longer trying to be careful, and pinned his arms to his side, swung him around, and slammed him against the wall, throwing his weight against Asher to pin him there.

Asher cried out and went completely wild. It was all Angel could do to hold him. He tucked his face into Asher's back to protect it as best he could and held on tight. He was taken completely by surprise when, only a few moments later, Asher went completely limp, and the weight of his body knocked Angel backward. He staggered and fell, twisting to avoid hitting his head on the toilet.

"Shit. Fuck. Shit. What the . . . Are you all right? Asher?"

Frantically, Angel crawled around to Asher's side. He was sprawled on the floor and seemed to have passed out cold. "Asher? Ah hell, now what am I supposed to do? How the fuck do I get myself into these situations?" A thought oc-curred to him and he groaned. "Oh no, what have I done? What have I done now?" He squirmed at the memory of Con-nor's face when he thought Angel was in love with Asher. He'd been trying hard, and now, less than a day later, he was locked in a toilet with Asher and Connor was out there think-ing who the hell knew what. "Great. Just great."

Asher stirred and moaned, drawing Angel's attention back to him. Angel sighed. Was this the way it was always going to be? Was Asher always going to be drawing his attention back to him? No. No, absolutely not. He was absolutely not going to let that happen, because he loved Connor, and he would do anything . . . *anything* to keep their relationship safe.

"Asher, come on, wake up. Wake up, Asher." Seeming to respond to the sound of his voice, Asher opened his eyes and stared at him with wide, dazed eyes. "Asher. Ash, it's me, Angel. You fainted. Are you okay?"

"Erik," Asher whispered, turning his head.

"No, Erik's not here. We got jumped by the press, remember?"

"Yes."

It sounded as if the word had been spoken automatically, with no thought behind it at all. "Asher, look at me. Look at me. Are you okay now? Are you . . . here?"

"Here," Asher repeated in a toneless voice.

Angel's heart sank. A whole new set of problems were presenting themselves. Now what?

"Okay, look, sit up. Come on, put your back against the wall. That's right." He propped Asher against the wall, wedging him into the corner so he wouldn't slide down. They were half under the wash basin, with the handrail for the toilet pulled down in front of them. Hurdles, in case Asher freaked again and tried to make a run for the door. It would give Angel time to catch him . . . maybe.

Heart pounding like he'd run a marathon, Angel pressed his body against Asher's as the tremors gradually eased. Asher was very cold, and Angel put his arms around him, drawing his head onto his shoulder. He was surprised to find Asher was crying. "Shit," he swore softly, as Asher put his arms around him and pressed his cold cheek against Angel's own.

"It's okay, Asher. It's okay. All over now. It's okay. We're safe. We're okay. Everything's okay," Angel cooed as Asher held on tight and shuddered with his sobs. "Calm down,

Asher. It's okay now, just calm down."

"S-sorry, Angel," Asher whispered.

Angel almost fainted himself, with relief. "It's okay. It's going to be okay now."

"Yeah."

Asher raised his head, and Angel winced. Makeup had run down his cheeks, and it looked like he was bleeding black blood from his eyes. The wildness had died to a kind of hopeless helplessness and he was weeping uncontrollably.

"It's okay, Ash. Just calm down now. It's okay. It's over."

"What happened?" Asher whispered, making an effort to get himself under control.

"We were mobbed by the press. They came from everywhere. It was scary as shit. The security guards tried to control the situation, but it got completely out of hand. I . . . You weren't doing so well, and I was scared so . . . so I . . . I thought it would be better if we got out of the way."

Asher looked around. "Toilet. Good choice," he said in a whispered attempt at his usual sarcasm.

Poor as it was, it made Angel smile with relief. "Yeah, not exactly the Ritz, but the best I could do on the hop."

Asher licked his lips and smiled. "It's good enough." The smile grew warmer and he hugged Angel tightly. "Thanks, Angel. You're a real friend. I'm so lucky to know you."

Angel froze when Asher kissed him, but it was just an Asher kiss that meant nothing more than Asher expressing his feelings in the only way he knew how.

"Come on," he said, deflecting attention from his discomfort, "let's get you cleaned up."

With the assistance of handfuls of toilet roll and paper towel, they managed to scrub Asher's face clean of makeup, and by the time they were done, he was calm again. Producing a pencil from his back pocket, Asher used it to retouch more than Angel would have thought could have been achieved with just one black pencil. When he was done, he looked himself again. There wasn't much they could do about the black streaks on his white shirt, but apart from that, he was pretty much back to normal.

"What now?" Asher asked after a while. "I'm not going to sit in a toilet all afternoon."

"Erik said he'd be back for us as soon as it was safe."

Asher looked angry. "Safe? How stupid is this? Safe? What the fuck. No one's going to hurt us. They're the press, not a firing squad. There's nothing to be afraid of."

Angel kept quiet, knowing Asher was speaking to himself. "Do you want me to take a look around?"

Asher gave him a hard look, then shook his head. "I'll do it."

"Wait . . ."

But it was too late. With a shaking hand, Asher carefully cracked open the door. There were a couple of people climbing the stairs ignoring them, but otherwise, the hall was empty.

"They've gone. What shall we do?"

Angel squeezed past him. "Do you want to wait here while I take a look around?"

Asher stared at him, clearly torn between his pride and his fear, but he finally nodded.

"Okay," Angel said. "Go back in and lock the door. I'll be back in a minute."

Angel was surprised when he walked through one of the doors leading off the hall to find himself in a restaurant. People were eating and drinking, chatting and laughing as if nothing had happened. Ha, for them nothing probably had. No one glanced at him, well apart from the two girls in the corner who sighed and whispered, as he walked through to the outside door and peeped into the square outside.

"Damn." The square was full of people, even more than

before. Some of them were obviously reporters, and there were police trying to break up the groups and the crowds. Just great.

A shout of his name caught his attention, and he turned to find Connor and Nora hurrying toward him with Caitlin in tow. In the crowd, the little family stood out but not in such a way as would catch the attention of the reporters. They, like Angel, were not important enough to warrant notice.

Connor hugged Angel tightly, but quickly. He stepped back and took Angel's face in his hands and brushed back his hair. "Well, ain't ye a sight for sore eyes. Missed ye, *a chroí*."

His happy face melted away, though, when he saw that Angel had lipstick on his lips — in Asher's shade. He stared at it for a long, hurt moment. Crazy scenarios ran through his head. The lipstick itself wasn't smeared, which meant Angel hadn't tried to wipe it off, and it wasn't a rushed kiss. It looked planned, almost planted there. By choice. Angel's choice. After all they'd said just last night, how could this be? Or was he just being stupid, making something up in his head again? He shook his head and used his thumb to wipe the lipstick off Angel's lips.

"Quite a sight," he repeated, keeping his voice low as he wiped the color onto his wrist. "Have a hard time, did ye?" He had to remain calm and steady or else risk a meltdown right there.

"What?" Angel asked, confusion clear in his tone, but he shook his head, brushing it off. "Asher's better, but he's not up to this. He's really fragile. You've no idea how scared I was. It was hell in there. I had to . . ." Angel faltered.

You had to kiss him to make it all better? Connor fought the words in his head. They were too mean, too sudden. He didn't know all the facts, and he wouldn't do something stupid based on an assumption. "I'm sure ye did what ye could, hi." He pursed his lips and brushed his thumb over Angel's lips again. "Sure, an' I didn't know ye were after wearing makeup now? Asher's shade, too. Suits ye fine." He gathered up his strength, trying to keep his voice calm.

Nora cut in. "Let's go get Asher, okay? You two look like ye need to talk, but in private later, okay. Let's go get 'im out." She led them inside but hesitated outside the toilet.

"I'll go in." Connor offered.

"No," Angel said with a frown. "I don't think it would be a good idea, do you? He's freaked out enough as it is." He turned his back on Connor and directed his words to Nora. "We can't bring him out here. The minute he sees all those people he's going to freak again. I can't risk it. If he gets away from us and runs, I don't know what would happen. It has to be controlled. Where are the others?"

"Don't worry, dear," Nora said in a soothing voice. "There's a way to get from where we are to where they are through the backstage, so to speak. Asher won't have to go outside."

Angel nodded to her and knocked on the toilet door. "Asher, it's me. It's okay. Connor, Nora, and Caitlin are here. They can take us to the others without going outside. You're going to be okay. Let me in."

There was a pause that was just a little too long for comfort. Then the bolt slid aside, the door cracked open, and Asher peeked out. "Angel?"

"Yes. Connor's here, too, and Nora and Caitlin."

The door opened wider, and Asher's gaze scoured the empty hall and flickered over Connor and the others and then . . . He frowned. "What's wrong? What's happened?"

"Nothing's happened. It's a bit crazy outside, but Nora says we can get to the others without going out there."

"Something's wrong. I can feel it. What is it?"

Caitlin stepped forward. "Don't ye be worryin' yerself now, Asher, darlin'. Yer man Connor here's after getting pissy with Angel again about somethin', but they're always at it these days. You be comin' out here and holdin' me hand, ye hear. I'm only a little girl, ye know. Scared witless I am."

Asher gave Caitlin a quick glance and grinned. "Witless? You? I don't think so. Come here then." His smile faded and his hand was shaking when he held it out to her. His gaze flicked between Connor and Angel and he shook his head, closing his eyes. "I'm sorry. I really am, but I-I'm not feeling too . . . good right now."

"Ah, darlin'." Nora hurried over and put her arm around Asher's shoulders. He half turned toward her and put his head on her shoulder. Caitlin threw her arms around his waist.

"I'm here now, darlin'," Caitlin said with all seriousness. "I'll take care o' ye."

"Sure, I think it's established that everyone's *helping*, Asher. Can we be after getting our arses the hell out o' here?"

This time, Asher didn't look up, but Angel did. "Not now, Con," he snapped.

Connor watched them, all of them. What the hell was going on? He shouldn't feel angry with Asher. How could he, when he could practically feel the pain radiating off him? The boy was a mess. And, of course, he needed help. And, of course, Connor couldn't be angry with anyone for wanting to help him. Of course . . . of course . . . But right then he hated Asher. He hated him so much he could taste it . . . and he hated the others, too.

Connor bit his lip. It wouldn't do any good at all to say a word to anyone, not just then. He led the way through a door into the corridor where a security guard was waiting and took them to the others.

As soon as they opened the door, Erik stood and took

Asher into his arms, holding on tight. "Thank God you're all right . . . well, you will be. Thanks for pinch-hitting there, Angel. I don't know what would have happened. It should have been on me, but I was looking for a cop or a way out or —"

"That's grand, Erik," Connor cut in, "but can we please get the hell out o' here. I could use a drink right now.

"Amen," Billy agreed wholeheartedly.

The ride to the hotel in the limo, sent by the music company, was extremely stressful. Asher, curled into Erik's arms, cried the whole way, and it seemed no one else really felt able to speak. The only sounds were Asher's quiet weeping and Erik's attempts to comfort him.

"It's going to be like this all the time, isn't it? Hiding, running, sneaking out the back door." Daisy laughed bitterly. "The cost of fame."

"Yeah," Billy said, holding on tightly to Vince.

When they got back to the hotel, Erik took Asher straight up to their room. Daisy went with them, saying she was tired. Joey followed soon after. Connor accompanied the others, who were too hyped to rest and headed to the hotel restaurant to eat.

Connor was restless. He couldn't look at Angel without seeing the smear of lipstick on his lips. Of course, it wasn't actually there anymore . . . He ambled up to the bar and glanced back at Angel, Nora, and Caitlin, who were sitting with Billy and Vince, all talking quietly. Angel kept glancing at him. Connor shut his eyes and turned to face the bartender. His mind was in flux again. He couldn't wait to hear from Angel what had truly happened in there. If he'd even believe it anymore.

Connor was no stranger to men lying to him. It'd be everything from their age, to being gay or not, to their jobs, or being interested, or just out for a drink and a blow job. But he thought Angel was different. On the other hand, he'd thought

Shaun had been, too. The man had taken his world by storm a year ago, and seeing him today brought a lot of it back. Their first look, first punch, which led to a first kiss and first fuck afterward.

More than anything, he wanted a relationship to work out. It was something he'd never had. Ever. Despite knowing and dating Angel over a year now, they'd been separated by distance for most of it. He wondered if now, being in the same house, same town, seeing each other without their masks, they'd discover they didn't want the future he'd dreamed of after all.

"Here's yer drink, love." The bartender broke his train of thought.

"Thank ye." He walked back to the table, glancing briefly at Angel before devoting his attention to the menu. "So, what looks good today?"

"Can I have chips, Ma?" Caitlin asked. "I'm powerful hungry. And the burgers in the other place were shite, so they were. Do they have any here?"

"It's not the kind of restaurant that sells burgers, hun" Nora smiled, although she seemed surprised to find that, although it was served on ciabatta bread with prime beef and a flourish, there was, in fact, a burger on the menu.

Billy and Vince had their heads together discussing the various options, which left Connor with little choice but to face Angel.

"You don't look very hungry, Connor," Angel commented. "What's the matter? Got a bellyache?"

Connor shot him a glare. "Sure, an' the only bellyache I've got is from swallowing bullshit, darlin'." He took a sip of his beer and sighed to himself. He thought about earlier, seeing Shaun and hearing how he'd turned his life around. If it were true . . . well. He dared not say anything. Angel would shoot him if he knew he'd spoken to his attacker, and Connor wouldn't blame him.

"Whoa . . . Con! Where'd that come from?" Vince asked. "What's happened? Something has, because you two look like you're about to go for each other's throats."

"Yes, Con. What has happened? Maybe you can fill me in, too, because I'm damned if I know." Angel shook his head and sat back, folding his arms across his chest.

"Let me be straight on one thing. I don't begrudge what ye did for Asher." He took a longer sip off his beer and glanced at Angel's class ring sitting on his finger, calmly, just sparkling in the daylight coming through the windows. It almost teased him, especially as the stone so closely matched his boyfriend's eyes. The eyes he'd thought he could look into and see nothing but love for him. It made him clench the menu.

"But what? What, Connor? What do you think we did in there? Do you think it was fun? Do you think we had a nice chat, or maybe a bit of hanky-panky? You have no idea. No idea what it was like. I have never been so scared. Can you imagine what would have happened if the press had worked out what was going on? Can you imagine what it would have done to both of them, Erik and Asher, if they'd got to him, if they'd put pictures of him like that on the news or in the papers? And what about Daisy? His family?"

Connor slammed his beer mug down so hard it shook the table. Thank goodness it was a heavy glass. He pointed a finger into Angel's face. "As a matter o' fact, I do know what it's like to help him through those attacks! I handled two so far, and it is damned scary. I decked him the first time to stop him from runnin' away. The second time you were there! It took me and Erik te calm him down. And no, it would break me heart if Asher or anyone was hurt because o' that. If ye think different, ye've got yer head screwed on wrong."

"Then what is this all about? What the fuck is it about? You say you understand, so what the fuck are you so angry about?

What exactly did I do?"

Like at a tennis match, all eyes turned back to Connor, and he exploded. "What did ye do? Sure, I don't know, but I'm hopin' ye can tell me." He held up his arm, and the smudge of lipstick he'd removed was still there. "Ye had Asher's lipstick on ye, on yer lips." He shook his head and closed his eyes for a second. His braid fell forward and he angrily tossed it over his shoulder again. He didn't want to see it, not now, maybe not ever again. "Sure, an' it must have been a trial keepin' Asher calm all on yer own. I see ye've found yer own method, and damn, I know how well ye kiss. How many times did it take to calm him, hi? How many?" he stared right at Angel now, trying to hide his hurt, and letting only the angry side show.

"What? You . . . what? You think I . . . You think I calmed Asher down by kissing him? Or not? Maybe you think I had sex with him. Do you? Took the opportunity for a bit of a fumble? Gay sex in a toilet? You're letting your clichés show there, Connor. How can you say that? How can you *say* it? I would never take advantage of Asher. He was in a terrible state. He fought me like crazy, then he passed out cold. I was scared shitless. I didn't know what to do. When he came 'round he didn't know where he was and I held him, that's all. I just held him until he came 'round and calmed down and was okay again. Then we cleaned him up and put his makeup back on, and yes . . . yes, actually now I think about it . . . he did kiss me. You know what Asher's like. He kisses everyone. It was one kiss. After all of that, one kiss."

"After last night, I woulda thought ye'd have more concern for me than te walk out o' there with lipstick on yer face. At the least, ye could have wiped it off." He balled his fists thinking about the previous night, and how desperate they'd both been to hang on. Angel was a young man, very young, and Connor was his first everything, just about. He said he wasn't in love with Asher, but it was obvious he'd do nothin' to stop his advances if he'd try anything, right?

"And ye never said ye wouldn't sleep with him. After everything we talked about, ye never said that . . ." *So young, so scared. He's got a crush, but it's more than a crush. He's not committed to me, at least not like I've heard it should be anyway.* Nora and Liam were committed, they were in love and married and had a baby, and . . . But Connor didn't feel it right now, right now he felt betrayed and angry. Not a good combination. He stood and rubbed his face.

"You're crazy. I didn't think for a single moment about having lipstick on my face. It was the last thing on my mind. Jesus Connor, I . . . I'd just picked one of my best friends up off the floor after . . . I was so relieved he was still . . . functioning. I didn't know how we'd be getting out of there. I didn't know if he'd . . ." He threw his hands up. "I'm sick of this. You're insane. I love Asher. He's my best friend, and he will always be my best friend. He'd done so much for me and if it hadn't been for him, we might never have met. But I'm in love with *you*, Connor. There are only so many ways I can say that, so many times. It's obvious you don't trust me. How anyone could believe for one minute after having seen the way Asher was this afternoon that anything sexy went on in that bathroom . . .

"I'm sorry, Connor. This is going too far. I love you. I love you so much, but right now I don't know if I can . . . How . . ." He paused and took a breath. "I can't live my life with someone who doesn't trust me. And I won't turn my back on Asher because you don't trust him. You'd better think hard about what you want, really hard, because I won't go through this again. You're all in or you're all out. When you've made up your mind, come and find me."

Throwing his menu onto the table, Angel got to his feet and strode from the restaurant. Dead silence fell in his wake.

"What . . . What the hell was that?" Billy gaped in shock. "I thought . . . you two . . ."

Connor slammed down the rest of his beer. "Aye, so did I, but I think he's proved something this afternoon, and there's no comin' back."

Billy seemed distraught, and Connor tried to calm him, but it didn't work.

Vince cupped his hands around his mouth. "Omigod, this is all my fault. I should've kept my mouth shut. I thought it was just something you needed to know . . . to not have it be hidden. I hid mine from Billy, and it was causing tension, so I told the truth." He took Connor's hand. "The truth is there, you just have to find it."

"Sure, 'twas nothin' o' yer doing, Vince. I'd have seen it sooner or later, and who knows where we'd be. Halfway through buildin' a house maybe. I don't know what I'm goin' te do wid him, but I know what I'm doin' now."

Billy leaned forward. "What's that?"

Connor dropped the menu. "Leaving. I'll see ye at the show."

Before anyone else could say a word, he bolted from the restaurant and out the door. His thoughts were a jumble, and he needed to talk to someone . . . anyone. He felt the card in his pocket from earlier. Shaun's. He tossed it in his head for a moment. Definitely not alone, but with the priest along . . . before he knew it, the number was dialed, and he waited.

CHAPTER TWENTY

The morning had started out so well — sex, breakfast, more sex, then down to meet their friends. After being sent out of Angel and Connor's room the previous night, Erik had calmed Asher down and they took it the rest of the way. It'd been wonderful. The entire honeymoon had, except for those kids and the fight, and . . . aw shit. What the hell was he thinking?

This whole fame thing had become a menace and he knew, now more than ever, he'd need security twenty-four-seven, for himself and everyone else. Always. They couldn't be alone, not like that, maybe ever again. It angered him and saddened him at the same time. He'd turned in his freedom and that of his family and his friends — their right to be out and about without being hassled.

He should have been the one taking care of Asher, but he'd felt such a strong need to physically save them all it overpowered everything, even his need to save Asher. But then he'd worry about the others . . . awww fuck. He was sick of all of it. He was grateful to Angel for what he did and would tell him the moment he saw him.

For now, there was silence, sweet, blessed silence. Asher was asleep at last. Deep sleep, from the looks of him. Maybe he could go down for a cigarette or two . . . or five. Daisy was right next door. Joey had calmed her quite well. They were only steps away, or a good, strong yell away. He left the room, with a note . . . and went down to the alleyway to smoke. He made sure there was a guard nearby. He figured he might as well get used to it.

The air was still clear and somewhat bright, but cloudier than before. It looked like rain later. No . . . rain in London? He laughed at the irony and lit up a cigarette. He looked around and noticed a familiar figure nearby, huddled over and sobbing. He had to see what was up. Approaching cautiously, he put a hand on the man's shaking shoulder. He recognized him right away. It was Angel!

"Angel? Hey, what's wrong? What's up, buddy?" He sat down on the stoop next to him, close but not touching

"E-Erik? I've lost him, Erik. I've lost him forever. My fo-forever man. He . . . he's gone and I don't . . . I don't know what I did or how . . . how I can . . . I can't make it better. I can't. He's gone forever. I've lost him."

Erik dropped his cigarette and nearly burned himself trying to pick it back up. "W-What? Whoa, what're you talking about? You and Connor? How on earth did that happen? Holy crap, what've I missed?" He rubbed Angel's back and handed him a cigarette. "Ssh . . . Just tell me slowly, what's all this about?"

Angel sniffed and scrubbed at his face with his hand. Taking the cigarette in a trembling hand, he shuddered. "He . . . he thinks . . ." He lit up the cigarette and took a deep drag. "He thinks I'm in love with Asher."

Erik had to stifle a laugh with the back of his hand before he realized this was no joke. "Oh shit . . . you're serious, right? What? Holy shit, I think everyone's been in love with Asher except Joey . . . and that's iffy at best. You're kidding, right? Pulling this extra-long leg?" He yanked at the leg of his jeans for effect. But Angel's mood didn't change.

"He . . . We had this long talk last night. Apparently, Vince had been talking in his sleep and told Billy he thought I was in love with Asher. So Billy told Con, and he kind of freaked out last night. He said . . . he said he's grown his hair to . . .

to . . . and he's been making all these sketches of houses. I thought it was because we were both excited about the idea of building our own, but it's all been . . . I mean the hair and the sketches . . . He's been trying to be more like Asher because he thinks it's what I want. He said . . . He said he thinks I'll leave him if he cuts his hair because . . ." He collapsed again into incoherent sobs, his cigarette falling from his fingers to hiss into silence in the curb.

"Ssh. Calm down, okay? First, just calm down." Erik glanced down at the extinguished cigarette and pulled out another one. "Here, you need to take a long, deep breath first, then we'll figure this all out, okay? I'm used to calming Asher down, which, as you know, is no picnic. At least you're not trying to claw my eyes out." He ruffled Angel's hair. "Damn, man. I wish I'd known. You guys are so great together." He handed Angel a fresh cigarette. "Deep breath."

"I don't know what to do, Erik." He took the cigarette, lit it and took another deep drag, held it, then let it out. "He's gone. He . . . Erik . . . he's not entirely wrong." Angel looked terrified, casting scared glances at Erik as he spoke. "I have . . . I can't pretend I'm not a little bit in love with Asher but . . . I swear to the angels there is nothing in it. I would never do anything with Asher, and he wouldn't want to. I love Connor and Asher loves you and I would never, ever admit to him or try to . . ."

"But why not? You know how Asher is. He's a flirt, He kisses everybody and speaks his mind. He wouldn't want you to be anything less than honest with him, would he?" He flicked his ashes onto the pavement. "Connor's always kind of reminded me of Asher. I suppose it's because of how wild they both are, speak their minds, are flirty and sexy, but are loyal to the core." He smiled at Angel. "I kinda already knew anyway."

"You did? Oh God, Erik, I'm sorry. I-I would never do anything to hurt you, either of you. I swear I won't — "

Erik took another drag. "Hey, take it easy, calm down now. It's okay! We know you wouldn't. Hey, I wondered myself for a time, since you two are joined at the hip. But at the end of the day, who's he coming home to? Me. Who's he making love to? Me. Does he talk about you? Hell yeah, and it wears on me, but only because he won't shut up about art, and well, he just doesn't hush sometimes. He drives me crazy, but I love him. I love him and he loves me. Like Connor loves you and you love him."

"Not anymore. I-I thought we'd got it sorted. We had a long talk last night and I told him he was being silly. I told him to get his bloody hair cut if he wanted to, and he didn't need to make silly sketches because he had his own way of being creative. He doesn't need to try to make himself like Asher, Erik. He doesn't need to. I love him for who he is, the way he is. I thought he understood. I swore to him I love him, that I'm in love with only him. No one else. I thought he believed me. I promised to pull back a bit and to think about Connor before I go off one on one with Asher and I did, I tried. It's so hard when I get excited about the paintings and . . . But I thought it was going to be okay."

Erik frowned. He hung his hands between his knees and turned to face Angel. "So what happened?"

"He thinks I kissed him. He thinks I calmed Asher down by kissing him. I tried to explain. He said . . . he said that before, when Asher had a panic attack, it took two of you to hold him and if I did it myself I must have . . . must have . . . I don't know what he thinks I must have done . . . did. It's just crazy. I don't know what I did, what I was supposed to do, what I can do. It's over, Erik. He doesn't trust me. He isn't ever going to trust me. It's over."

"Like hell it is."

They both jumped at the furious voice that spoke from the shadows.

"Ash?" Angel gasped, obviously shaken.

Erik was less fazed by Asher's sudden appearance. Maybe he was finally getting used to Asher's almost uncanny knack of creeping up silently on people.

"What the fuck! Why didn't you tell me? Why didn't you tell me last night, or today? That stupid, empty-headed, self-ish, self-centered, thoughtless, stupid Irishman. Where is he?" Asher demanded.

"I . . . he was in the restaurant with — "

"Right. Come on. Let's get this sorted right now."

"He'll have gone by now. It was ages ago."

"Then we'll go up to your room. Don't do this, Angel. Don't just give up. He's a stubborn fool, but he'll never forgive himself if he ruins this, and neither will you. He won't come back to you, Angel. He's too proud, too stubborn. If we don't do something he'll go storming off, and his pride won't let him come back. We have to find him and beat him over the head with his own stupidity. Come on."

"Asher, it wouldn't do any good."

"And sitting here in the gutter smoking until your lungs turn inside out will?"

Angel turned to Erik with pleading expression.

Erik shrugged. "What would it hurt to try? You know how he is, and Asher's right. Who better to help solve this than him? Connor won't believe you alone. Asher adds credibility to it all. Go on . . . go on wid ya." he winked. "Find that Irishman and pour your hearts out. I know he'll do the same. Just find him."

Connor walked into a crowded, smoky pub. Peering around, he spotted Shaun and the priest sitting at a table near the bar.

His heart felt like it'd been ripped in two, and not for the first time, he wondered what the hell he was doing here. He didn't want Shaun to see he was upset, so he did what he could to gather himself together and strode inside.

Just seeing Shaun again gave him chills, not only because of the attack but for their relationship and how different it had been with an older, more experienced man for a change. Thirty wasn't old to most, but to him it wasn't far short of a decade. He'd felt young and silly and allowed Shaun to take care of him like he never had with anyone else. And if Shaun was rough with him . . . well, he deserved nothing more. He'd loved their sexual time together and learned a lot. But right now, he was back to the hurt little boy who needed comfort, even if it came with a price.

He cleared his throat and approached Shaun's table. He greeted Shaun with a tilt of the chin and a muttered, "Shaun."

"Connor. Sit down, wontcha. I must say I didn't think you'd come. I don't deserve it, and I never thought I'd hear from you again. Sure I've missed ye something fierce. I'm so sorry, I was such a bastard. Sorry, Father, I got a bit carried away there."

"No problem, Shaun. I can tell this is something you're really passionate about. I'm not naïve. I don't expect you to turn into a saint."

After taking a seat, Connor slumped down in his chair and toyed with his hair, trying not to make it too obvious how nervous he was "I'll not lie te ye. Bein' here is as much of a shock te me and it is you. Thing is . . . there's unfinished business between us, and I wanted to talk. After . . ." He closed his eyes for a second. "Mind if I order a draft?"

"By all means," the priest said in a concerned voice.

"I'll get it, Con," Shaun glanced at him in a way that made Connor feel he genuinely cared.

It sparked a hope that, for the first time in days, he was

going to be truly listened to and not looked at with conde-
scension. Here, he wasn't the fool Irishman, the clown, the idiot, the one who puts up with everything and gets into fights.
Here, he was the young one, the one who needed to be cared
for, who was crying out for attention, who might actually get
some away from the dramas of the group he'd never quite belonged to. It felt good, damn good.

His eyes felt moist, and he blinked them dry as quickly as
he could. When the beer arrived, he drank enthusiastically,
pleased Shaun had remembered his favorite drink. He put the
glass down and pulled on the braid again. "Thank ye." He
caught himself speaking in a little boy tone. Shaun always did
that to him. Always.

"Don't think I'm not grateful, Con, but I have to admit I
was surprised to get your call. What are you doing here?"

Wow . . . how much to tell him? About Angel? About his
insecurity? About how he felt? It was a tough call to make. He
twirled the end of the braid around his fingers. "It's bin a
feckin' shite day, and I was after needin' an ear. Must be
feckin' desperate to look fer yours," he joked. Always the
joker, even now.

"We all have bad days Connor," the priest said in a kindly
manner, "and it's quite natural to turn to friends for help.
Have you known Shaun for long?"

"No, Father, not long at all, but I knew him well. We were
together maybe two months before . . ." He stopped himself.
No need to bring that up again. "No, not long at all. Sure, we
were close, though. Closer than most, I'd say. We were . . ."
He glanced at Shaun again and noticed a flush coloring his
cheeks. Beardless, Shaun looked so different, but just as handsome.

Shaun smiled, but it wasn't the smile Connor had grown
used to before the wedding. It was a warm, natural smile with
no hint of conniving or manipulation, no mockery or even

lust. It was just a warm smile, and it made him even more handsome.

"Sure I didn't deserve you, Con. I see it now. I tried to change you, to drag you down to my level. I was wrong. I'm glad I've got the chance to tell ye that, to tell you how sorry I am for hurting you. I never wanted that. You've no cause to believe me, but I loved ye. If I'm truthful, I still do."

"What?" Connor sat up in his chair, his eyes trained on Shaun's face. "I . . . dunno what te say. After all that happened, I'm not going to lie, I hated ye. Thought I still did. Life's . . . complicated, hi." He stopped.

How could he talk about Angel? Even saying his name was too painful right now. He wondered how Angel would react if he knew he was even talking to Shaun at all. He'd probably like to kill him. But it didn't matter anymore. He was dead inside without Angel, but being with Shaun lit a spark of something. Not attraction—not just attraction—rebellion maybe, a reaction against all the thoughtless, careless words he'd been subjected to by so-called friends.

"I'm sorry too . . . for things I did. Some of them." He flashed Shaun a cold glare, then dropped his gaze to his glass, at a loss of what else to say. Shite, he must have been crazy to come here in the first place.

"I . . . saw the band's doing well."

Ah . . . a new topic. "Aye, that they are. I'm made up fer them. They deserve it, so they do, hi. Fame has its price, though. Damn reporters just about drivin' us all to distraction. That's why I'll never be famous." He chuckled. "One o' the reasons. Sure, I'll be happy in some little hut with me tools and a workshop, carvin' chairs on de side of de road somewhere. Alone."

He had to face the facts. He was alone now, and dead. All he had was his woodworking. He'd wanted to marry Angel so badly it drove him to insecurity and jealousy, and now, he was truly gone. The thought tortured him endlessly. Angel would always be there in his thoughts, in his heart, just not in his home or his life. He fought back tears and took another drink.

"You'll never be alone, Connor," Shaun said, in a soft, sincere voice that threw Connor into a spin. "You were made to be loved. You'll always have someone loving you, so you will."

Connor was breathless for a moment, as he let the line sink in. Was this really Shaun? The one who was all for the groping and sexting and in-your-face randy-ness? People could change, right? Connor had never wept in front of Shaun, never, but he was dangerously close now. He was scared to death of it, despite what his friends, and Angel, had told him.

"Nah, not meant for lovin', hi. I had a good thing and screwed it the hell up. I wasn't good enough for him, and that's an end."

"You're being too hard on yourself. You always were. Your big problem is you're so insecure. You rely on other people to make you feel good about yourself, and even then, you don't. I was a bastard to ye, Con, but you made it easy for me. You've got a lot going for ye, so ye have. You're handsome, funny, strong, talented, and fearless. You don't need to be looking for relationships where you have to keep proving yourself. You need a relationship where you're made to feel you don't have to, you don't need to. You deserve someone who treats you right. One day you'll find him, and I envy that man. I truly envy him because, in different circumstances, it could have been me."

Out of nowhere, Connor found himself longing to hold Shaun's hand, to hold on tight. Those hands had held him and tickled him, and . . . so many things. The past was catching up with him. Was it possible? Could Shaun be telling the truth and be a good man? Maybe now? Now could be their time?

Angel didn't trust him, but Shaun did . . . and that was a huge bonus point at the moment. His finger twitched to reach out.

"We weren't good for each other, not then. Now? I'm a free man, by me own doing. I've scared him off, so I have, and he . . . we weren't in the right place. No more than we were." He bowed his head and twirled his hair, the hair he'd grow to hate.

"Easy there, lad. Shaun, get the boy a drink, a soft one now."

"But Father . . ."

"A drink, Shaun." The father spoke firmly, and when Connor looked up, he saw a flash of something that could have been anger in Shaun's eyes.

"Yes, Father. Coke, Con? No whiskey, by order of the Catholic Church." Shaun smiled, but there was a slight edge that puzzled Connor.

As soon as Shaun vanished, the priest put his hand over Connor's in a fatherly way. "It's clear you have a strong connection with Shaun, and I'm not begrudging you that or trying to get in the way of anything, but it's also clear you're in a bit of a state here, lad. Shaun's a good man, but it's not been easy getting the good to shine through. There was a fair bit of tarnish, if you know what I mean."

Connor smiled and nodded.

The priest continued. "There's still a good deal of tarnish, Connor. We're working on it, and Shaun's doing well, but just don't go expecting too much of him. People can change, but not overnight. I'd worry about you, in the emotional state ye are now, getting involved in anything too . . . intense. With Shaun or anyone else. A little discretion now."

Connor nodded. "Sure I don't expect anything, Father. Expecting's what got me here in the first place." He dropped his face into his hands. "Ah, but I've been a damn fool, Father. I had a good thing and I let it go. I'm not meant for a good 'un."

"Are you so sure it's over, Connor?" The priest asked. "It seems to me you care deeply for this person. Are you sure you can't make it right?"

Connor shrugged. "Shaun's right. I killed it off with me own insecurities and doubt. When there's no trust, there's nothin'."

"What did your man do to make you lose your trust?"

Shaun appeared and set a Coke on the table in front of Con. He must have overheard at least part of the conversation. "Aye, Connor. What'd he do? It's the Italian kid, yeah. Sure he's sweeter than honey. I don't credit him being a cheater. You're the slippery one."

"Slippery?" Connor's ire rose. "Sure, it wasn't me that had eyes for another man," he retorted, taking a sip of the Coke and grimacing. "Ugh. No offense, Father, but without whiskey it's pish." He pushed the drink away. "I thought I had a life with him, so I did. Was plannin' to marry him. What a damn fool."

"He cheated on ye?" Shaun sounded incredulous. "Now there's a thing. I never would have guessed."

"Well . . . not in deed, as far as I know, but in mind fer sure, hi." Connor felt his argument weaken with every word that came out of his mouth. What had driven them apart? It was him. It had all been him. "I thought . . ." He paused, glancing at the clock and wondering about Angel. Could it be? Maybe? No . . . even if it was all him, the marriage issues were still in play. Angel talked a good game about kids and all, but he'd still freaked at the mention of it.

"Ye ran out on yer man because he cheated in his mind? Gawd, Connor, I thought ye had more sense than that. I seem to remember it was somethin' we'd argued about ourselves. I was half convinced the only reason ye wanted to go to the weddin' at all was to see the goth boy ye had the crazies over. He's married now, isn't he?"

Connor frowned. "Aye. Just a few days ago. What has that got to do with anythin'?" He growled, his mind confused and angry.

"Hey, Con. I wasn't havin' a go at ye. I was just pointing out that these things happen. They don't mean nothin'. The things that mean something are the ones that get thrashed out in the early hours of the morning, after a bottle of the good stuff, and over breakfast, and when ye're cryin' in each other's arms. If yer man is turnin' his eye somewhere else he's a fool, so he is. It's what I did, and because of that I lost ye."

"It was hard, Shaun, that it was. Ye hurt me bad when ye did what ye did. Now look at ye . . . all pressed and proper. You'd be a fine catch for any man, and I hope he has sense to hang onto ye."

"Well, that's the thing, Connor. I don't want another man. I haven't wanted another man since I lost you. You've been on my mind all this time. This morning, when I saw you in the pub . . . I couldn't believe it was you, couldn't believe my luck. I-I never thought I'd see you again, but you were in my mind. You're the one I'm fighting for, changing for."

"Well now," the priest said, breaking the moment and sitting up. I think it might be a good time to be taking my leave. Remember what I told you, Connor. It's a difficult time for you, and you don't want to be bringing more complications on yourself. Shaun, you keep some things in mind, too. Consideration and thought for what others need and not what you want."

"Yes, Father," Connor said at the same time as Shaun. They turned to look at each other and grinned.

The priest smiled as he left, shaking his head.

Connor's mind was going in a dozen directions at once. He wracked his brain for how to fix things with Angel. There had to be a way. But what about Shaun? Was it even possible all of this was true? It certainly seemed that way. His heart wanted to believe it was, and in his current state, he'd believe almost anything.

He gazed into Shaun's eyes. "Do ye mean that? Do ye really mean it, Shaun? I won't be puttin' up with a sham . . ."

Shaun shook his head and moved in closer. He brushed a hand over Connor's braid. "I hadn't told you how much I love your hair, Con. It suits you . . . like you suited me."

Before Connor had time to react, Shaun clamped his hand on each side of his face and pulled him in for a kiss. Connor put up little resistance until Shaun put his hand on Connor's thigh and began to slide it upward.

"Stop it!" Connor shoved him back. "Kissin' ye doesn't give ye the right to put yer hands on me again!"

"I'm sorry, Con, truly I am. You've always been my downfall. You're so goddamn sexy. You were right to slap me. I'm my own worst enemy. Tell me I haven't blown it. I promise ye, if I can have a chance with ye I'll swear myself to celibacy if I have to, until yer ready. If you give me one sign I might have a chance, I'd be down on me knees. I've missed ye so much. I've dreamed of ye for so long. I dreamed that one day, if I got me head sorted, I'd make something of meself, and I'd come find ye and prove to ye I'm worthy of another chance.

"Well, I'm not, not yet. I'm not worthy by a long shot, but just for the chance, I'd do anything. I'd give ye the world Connor, you mean that much to me." Moving slowly, as if dealing with a skittish colt, Shaun reached out and touched Connor's hand, lacing their fingers together. "I wouldn't hurt ye for gold." Slowly and carefully, he moved closer, keeping his hands on the table, and gently touched his lips against Connor's.

Shaun's lips were sweet—soft and familiar—but it was the words that made his brain grind to a halt. Was he serious? Was this really a new Shaun? Could it be? The attempted grope rang true of the old Shaun, but could Connor forgive a

342

misstep one more time? Was Shaun worth another chance? Slowly, his mind began to clear of the fog that had enshrouded it since he'd walked out of the hotel. Memories reasserted themselves and he knew what he had to do.

"Shaun, me darlin'," he murmured, smiling sweetly as he covered Shaun's hands with his own.

"Yes," Shaun said, his eyes shining, eager . . . greedy.

Connor leaned in again to kiss him, but instead bit his lip and slapped him across the face. "Ye're full of shite, so ye are! Ye think I'd feckin' fall for it? Ye think I'm that stupid?" He shoved Shaun hard enough to tip his chair and land the man on the floor. On the way down he'd taken out an empty chair from the neighboring table, which was, fortunately, unoccupied.

"I'd be the biggest fool in creation to fall for yer bullshit again. Even with yer fancy talk and fancy clothes, ye're nothin' but a predator. Aye, that's what ye are. Do ye think I'd forgive ye for what ye did to Angel? Never. I don't care if I've fucked up with Angel or not, but he deserves better than this, than me letting a piece of shite like you back into me life, after what ye did te him. I'll forgive ye for a lot o' things, Shaun, but I'll never forgive ye for that." He slung his braid back and noticed a crowd had gathered. His gaze caught three familiar faces in the waiting area, all with mouths agape. Connor's jaw almost hit the floor.

"Connor! Holy shit! You decked him again!" Erik had a grin on his face a mile wide. "Way to go!" He high-fived him and shook his braid.

Connor couldn't help but grin, his mood instantly lightening.

"Connor?" Angel whispered. "Shaun? You were with Shaun?"

Connor's heart almost stopped. "Sure, it's a long story, darlin', but it's not what ye think." He glared at Shaun.

"Ye're a fecking crazy man," Shaun muttered as he picked himself up and headed for the toilets.

Connor utterly dismissed him from his attention, all of which he rivetted on Angel. "I . . . didn't tell ye. I ran into him earlier when we were eatin'. He had a priest with him, so he did. Father . . . whatever. He told me Shaun's been on a church program, that he's doin' well, changing himself. I wished him well and went on me way."

Erik put a hand on his shoulder. "So why are you here now? Talking to him again?"

Connor bowed his head, but then squared his shoulders and looked up at Erik, then at Asher, and finally Angel. "Because of what a damn fool I'd been." He rubbed his arms out of nerves and guilt. "I . . . needed to talk to someone who wouldn't judge me. I asked Shaun about the priest and he brought him here. He helped me, Angel. Put things in perspective, so he did. But then he left . . ." He shot a look over his shoulder at the table where he'd been. "Shaun was after spoutin' the biggest load of bullshit ye've ever heard. I told him I'd not forgive him for what he did to ye, Angel. Not ever. Even if we're not . . . anymore . . . I knocked him down fer tryin' it on, and that's what ye saw."

Angel stared at him, and Connor couldn't for the life of him work out what the boy was thinking. And then the damnedest expression came over his face and he turned around and walked away. "Angel?"

"I think you'd better come home, Connor," Asher said, sounding nervous.

People were congregating, as usual when there was a sign of excitement. In the distance, Connor heard the whine of a siren, and the last thing he wanted was to be arrested, or for Erik to attract too much attention. Connor nodded wearily.

"Although, you realize, of course, that what I really should be doing is getting your arse hauled off to jail for what you

did. It's where you belong, because you're criminally insane."
As they left the bar, Asher threw his arm over Connor's shoulder. "He's crazy about you, Connor, and you know it. You know he'd never cheat on you, with me or anyone else, and that's your problem. You just can't accept it. You can't let yourself believe that someone like Angel would possibly love someone like you, and so you're looking for ways to sabotage it. It's a load of bollocks. You've never believed you're worth anything, never, and it's crazy. Well . . . you'd better get over it because you're screwing with that boy's head, and trust me, I know what it's like to be screwed in the head, and it ain't pretty."

"Ye're right. I've never seen me worth his time. He's got his life, with his father and his money and friends. What the feck do I have to offer, hi? How long will it take him te work it out fer himself?"

"You're almost a lost cause, you know. No couple has ever brought each other as much pain as me and Erik, and trust me, there's so much I wish had never happened, but it's made us what we are. It's made us strong. No one and nothing is ever going to part us now."

Connor watched Erik over Asher's shoulder as his eyes widened and began to glisten. It made him smile.

"You have to work through these things. I'm telling you one thing, Con, Angel loves you with all his heart, and you'd be stupid crazy to drive him away because of your own insecurities. You know — well, I hope you know — there will never be anything more than friendship between Angel and me."

The words calmed Connor's soul. "There won't? I-I mean . . . He says he loves ye, and I know it's true. I want to trust him, but how can I, when his heart's with another man? He's always runnin' te ye, Ash, fightin' the world fer ye."

Erik drew level. "Angel told me that, yeah, he does love Asher. He has a crush, who doesn't?" He grinned and draped his arm around Asher's shoulder. "But he'd never, ever cheat on you. He calls you his forever man. I think you started that, right? Well, he means it. Yes, he's young and new to all this, but fuck, man, he's only a couple of years younger than us, and you know Asher takes everyone's breath away. He launches crushes with a flash of his beautiful eyes, you of all people know that, but nothing's gonna come of it. You've got to know that, buddy." He yanked on the braid again.

"Would ya stop doing that, ye tool?" He stroked his beard. "I need to stop beatin' meself up and tryin' to be someone I'm not. I see it now, so I do. Everything I've done these last few months is tryin' te compete with ye."

"Then you're an idiot. You can't compete with me. I'm way out of your league." Asher grinned and pulled him down to monkey-scrub his head. "Anyone see where Angel went?"

Erik pointed to his right. "Thataway. Come on, Red. You've got some 'splaining to do." He patted Connor's shoulders, and they all headed off back to the hotel.

As soon as they arrived at the hotel, Connor went straight to his room and found he was alone. His stomach knotted again, and he knew it was over. It hit him again as he walked over to the bed and sat down to think, to wonder about what might've been. He knew why Angel wasn't there. It had to be because of Shaun. Dammit if that guy wasn't going to cause him trouble to the end! He punched the mattress and cursed at it and himself.

"Goddammit, ye fecking eejit. Ye've lost him, and it's all yer fecking fault." He lay back and covered his face, finally allowing tears to flow. He grabbed the pillow and turned on his side to weep into it. The world had turned to shite, and he was dead inside again.

Connor was dozing when the door opened, and he came awake fast to see Angel standing in front of the window in the moonlight, just staring down at him.

"A-Angel?" His heart sprang to life again, and he smiled . . . cautiously. "I-I wasn't sure . . ." He bit his lip to stop himself from babbling.

A cool finger brushed over his lips.

"Ssh. Don't speak." Angel just stood there, in the middle of a great puddle of moonlight, his face catching the luminosity of the beams and turning into a real honest-to-God angel right there in his room. "I've been thinking . . . a lot. Actually, I've been thinking for weeks, months . . . whatever, but I've never acknowledged it. I don't know why. I've been talking about building our own house, having children but . . ." He shrugged. "Somehow, none of it has seemed real. I feel like I'm still only a kid, playing at being in a relationship. Well . . ." He reached out and took Connor's hand, raising him until he was sitting on the edge of the bed.

Angel's gaze scoured Connor's, then he finally smiled. "I don't want to play at it anymore, Con. I think that's part of the problem. I haven't been taking us, our relationship, seriously. I love you, but I've not committed to you. You care for me, but you're never sure about me. I don't know if this will make a difference. I hope so, but I won't know until I try. So . . ."

Angel took a deep breath and sank to the ground, kneeling in front of Connor. He reached out and took Connor's hand. "Connor O'Reilly, I'm a damn fool and damn lucky one at that, to have a man like you in my life. I thought tonight I'd lost you, and I can't bear the thought. When I heard what you said to Shaun, I knew. I knew you loved me, and I've always known I love you so . . . Would you please do me the honor of marrying me and making me the happiest man in the world?"

Connor's mouth flew open in shock and then into the biggest smile he knew he could ever make. He quickly wiped at the tears on his face, and all he could do at first was nod like an idiot, but words finally poured out. "Aye. If ye'll have me.

You're a damn fool fer that, but I'll not argue wid ye."

He threw his arms around Angel, and they kissed deeply, clinging to each other and weeping softly. Hopefully, these tears would be cleansing ones, washing away the fear and doubt. Only time would tell.

Angel had never been so happy in all his life. He'd been thinking about proposing for weeks, but it had seemed like there'd be plenty of time. Until tonight, he hadn't been sure he was completely ready. He knew a proposal wouldn't fix all their problems—of course it wouldn't. And he'd been very thoughtful about whether this was the right time, whether maybe he was just using it as a means of trying to convince Connor of his commitment. Then he figured . . . of course a proposal is meant to be a show of commitment so why not?

The thought of losing Connor had really brought home some harsh realities. A life without Connor was impossible to consider. And then it had come to him in a blinding realization. He loved Connor. He couldn't imagine a future without him. He wanted to settle down in their own home and have children with him. He wanted to marry him. He was ready to marry him.

They'd celebrated in their own way and were lying together, warm, comfortable and happy. "When are we going to tell the others?" he asked, suddenly bursting with the desire to do just that.

Connor peppered kisses along Angel's arm to his neck. "Whenever ye're ready, *a chroí*." He nuzzled his Angel's neck and fingered his hair. "Sure, I can't wait to tell 'em, hi."

"There's just one thing, Con. I love you. I adore you. I want to spend the rest of my life with you, raise children with you but . . ." He brushed stray strands from Connor's face. "I need to know you trust me. It's the most important thing in the world to me. I can't live in a relationship where I have to keep second guessing myself, proving myself, and worrying if every time I look at Asher, you'll freak on me. I won't give him up, but he doesn't compare to you in my heart. He'll never compare to you, and before you start thinking I'm comparing you unfavorably, let me tell you, no man will ever compare to you, because you're perfect for me."

"Aye, I trust ye. And I trust Asher. I shoulda known it was all a bit o' nothin' It's clear as day Asher only has eyes for Erik."

Angel kissed him. "Like I only have eyes for you."

Connor laughed, then let out a sigh. "I know what Asher's like. He's after kissin' anyone fer any reason. Terminal flirtin' he's got, so he has." He rolled to his back and laughed again. "I was such a jealous fool. I just hope ye trust me too, Angel, coz I'll square with ye, Asher's made me old heart flutter a time or two."

Angel laughed and tugged on Connor's braid. He had to admit it was looking a bit ratty. "I trust you with my life, Connor, and I always have. Promise me you'll only ever be yourself with me and never try to be anyone else again. If you want to cut your hair, do it. You're beautiful no matter how you wear your hair. Although I would miss tugging your braid." He demonstrated again, playfully.

Connor laughed as his head tilted to the side and held onto the hair. "Sure, I'm after thinkin' I'll cut it a bit. It's long enough te be getting in me way when I'm workin', and I don't appreciate munchin' on hair when I'm eatin', but I'll be sure te keep it long enough fer ye to keep tuggin' on it te ye're heart's content, *a chroí.*" He raised his brows playfully over those gorgeous emerald eyes. "The braid too." His chuckles turned to belly laughing, and that got Angel started, too. How could he resist? Connor was just so damn beautiful when he laughed. "God, I love ye, Angel. I always will, and I'm sorry fer bein' a pain in the arse, so I am."

"Everyone's a pain sometimes. Just don't make a habit of it." He smiled gently and stroked Connor's face. He let his fingers linger on the soft hair on Connor's chin. He loved Connor's beard, which he took care of better than his hair. "Now, I'm going to give everyone a ring and tell them to meet us for dinner in an hour. So you'd better get your braid ready for some tugging, because we're now on a tight schedule."

The message from Angel to meet them all for dinner was cryptic, to say the least. It said they had some news to share. Vince's hands shook as he held the phone and read the message again while awaiting his drink. He wished he'd never started the whole thing. He was so afraid it would be bad news, and it was his fault. Despite Connor saying it wasn't, it still was in his mind.

The restaurant was busy at this hour, crowded almost to capacity, and their table was crowded. He was having an impossible time hearing anything unless it was Billy.

"Hey, you awake over there?" Billy nudged him softly and took his hand. "It'll be all right. I've got a good feeling about all of this. Trust my instincts, baby. It's all good."

Vince loved how positive and optimistic his husband always was. Never doom and gloom, always sweet and outgoing and seeing the good side of things. He thanked God every day to have this wonderful man in his life and to be starting their family together. He held on to his hand tight and sighed.

"Can't help but be awake with how loud it is in here," he joked. "I hope you're right, baby. I do." His eyes caught sight of Connor's red hair and smiled. "Hey, here they are, and they look . . . happy." He grinned, hoping they were about to share good news, that it had all been ironed out.

"You guys look much better," Billy said, tugging on Connor's braid. "Lookin' like ye found the pot o' gold, me dear friend."

Connor smiled. "That I did, Billy. That I did."

Vince took Angel's hands. "Hey, cous. How are you two? More, how are you? I was scared to death earlier at the restaurant." He gazed anxiously at them both. Angel's blue eyes were shining.

"Don't look so worried, Vince. You did us a favor, honest you did. It made us both look at things differently, made me at least realize I was wandering down a dangerous track, assuming things would always be the same without having to work at it, or really face it. I have you to thank for forcing me to finally grow up. That's why I wanted to ask you a favor."

Vince's raised his eyebrows, but he grinned, weak with the release of pent up emotion. He was relieved he'd been a help, not a hindrance. He felt so insecure himself most of the time, but this sounded like it was headed in a good direction. "Anything, cous. You name it."

"I was just wondering if you'd be my best man. We haven't got a date yet, but I'll let you know as soon as it's fixed."

Words escaped Vince for a moment as he let the news sink in. "Best man? Angel? Omigod!" He covered his mouth, then grabbed Angel around the waist and hugged him. "You're getting married? Omigod, that's wonderful! That's awesome! Of course, I'd love to be your best man." He held onto Angel for a moment before releasing him. He was so happy, so very, very happy.

"Congratulations, guys!" Billy added and hugged Connor, and when Vince had finally let go, he hugged Angel, too. "That's terrific!"

"Hey!" The yell from down the table startled them. "Now everyone's heard the good news, can we please eat? People are starving down here," Asher blurted out.

Connor laughed and escorted Angel to his seat next to Joey and Daisy. He elbowed his own cousin. "Hey, Joey, would you be me best man, eh?"

"I'd love to! Thanks, cous! I'm so happy for you guys!" He hugged them both and then sat down to a toast to the happy couple, and finally dinner.

CHAPTER TWENTY-ONE

The atmosphere was so thick it could be cut with a knife, the excitement a tangible being, curling and twisting, whizzing round and round inside the enormous arena. Joey peeked out at the crowd. *How the hell many people are there out there?* The stage alone was bigger than anywhere they'd yet performed.

"Jesus," Billy whispered. "It didn't look so big this afternoon."

Joey simply nodded in response, since he couldn't form any words right then. Thank God he wasn't the singer. He could hear the people like the buzz of a giant swarm of bees, and he closed his eyes so he could pretend that was what they were, not a crowd of thousands, here for the sole purpose of watching him and his friends perform.

Oh, God. He sat down on a box, his legs trembling too much to keep him on his feet.

"Where the hell is Erik?" someone asked.

Joey looked up to see a man rushing around, flapping his hands. He dismissed the person from his attention and tried to control his nerves.

"You okay?" a soft voice above him asked.

He turned his face into the softly rounded belly that appeared next to him. The denim of Daisy's jeans was stretching tight now, and she had to leave the top button undone. He suspected this would be the last time she'd be able to wear them.

"Nervous as fuck." He gazed up at her.

353

Daisy smiled and stroked his cheek. "You'll be fine. We all will."

"Have you *seen* the crowd out there?"

"I've seen. They're just people."

"But . . ."

"Ride the energy, Joey, don't sink under it. Let it flow through you until it makes your fingers tingle . . . then play."

"You're a wonder, my love. You know I love you, right? We don't have the drama and action of the rest of the guys, no grand gestures, but I do love you."

"Joey, you're sitting here looking at me like that, with your cheek pressed against a belly in which someone else's babies are growing. How could you even ask me that? I know you love me, Joey. I have no doubt at all about that."

Joey smiled. Sure, he felt a small pang when she mentioned the babies, but that was only natural, wasn't it? It wasn't going to affect their relationship, sour the pure beauty of his feelings for the sweet and beautiful girl he'd happily die for. He kissed her belly gently and stood up, taking her into his arms to kiss her properly.

"Where the hell is Erik?"

"He's backstage with Asher," Daisy said, trying to soothe him. "Don't worry, he'll be here."

"There's five minutes to kick off."

"Then he'll be here in five minutes."

And he was. With no time at all to spare, Joey saw Erik racing from the backstage area, his eyes full of fire with not the slightest hint of nerves.

Then, somehow, they were all on stage, blinded by the lights, deafened by the roar . . . and they were playing.

Joey tried to do what Daisy had suggested, letting the energy pour into him and lift him. It worked, too. He knew the numbers so well his fingers glided and danced over the strings of his guitar, and he soared, his mind free to wander, to look back over on all the things that had brought them to this point, and the people who had traveled with them.

Beyond his Daisy, watching from the wings, stood the person foremost on his mind. Connor. His cousin, his friend, and the one he'd watched and listened to for years. This past year especially, after Connor had nearly given up on love altogether, Joey was happy he'd convinced the fiery redhead to not give up, and now here he was, happily engaged to be married to Angel, whom Joey also considered a good friend. Joey was thrilled to be best man for Connor. He could think of no one he'd love to stand up for more.

Next to Connor, of course, was Angel. They were such a cute couple. Angel could surprise him at times. He'd come out of his shell and grown so much in just the short time Joey had known him. He was thrilled to be able to welcome Angel to the family as Connor's husband.

Next to them were Vince, Nora, and finally Caitlin. Vince looked sad, but happy at the same time. Joey knew it would be incredibly hard for Vince to say goodbye to Billy again, but it was only three months and he'd have gads of support at home with the house and preparing the nursery for the children Daisy carried for them. He liked Vince a lot and wanted only the best for them.

As for Nora, she was so like her brother, except without the insecurity. She'd had to be strong as a widow and a single mother to Caitlin. He found her smart, funny, entertaining, and very pretty. She'd be quite the catch for a man smart enough and able enough to keep up with her.

Finally, Caitlin. What a handful! What her mouth didn't spill out, her attitude did. She was a force to be reckoned with and made no bones about it. Anyone who could give Asher a run for his money had his vote.

Ah, Asher. He was backstage, away from the crowds and the exuberance of it all. Joey couldn't blame him for staying out of the way after everything that had happened. He hoped things would get better for him, but at least he had a strong husband at his side.

Finally, Joey took in his bandmates. He was in the *zone*, playing his guitar with hardly any thought at all as his gaze shot to Billy, who pounded away expertly on his drums. He was wearing the red rose shirt and the special ring Vince had given him as a reminder that Vince was in his heart, always. The two were so in love it made Joey smile. He cared for Billy, too, and was damn sure he was going to keep a close eye on him this time.

Daisy looked beautiful, as always, with her long, light hair, and dark blue eyes. Her guitar jutted out a little, but that was to be expected. She'd keep growing and they'd adjust it as they went. He'd love these babies because they'd be part of her and the men who would be their fathers.

And then there was Erik. The wild man who'd talked him into joining the band in the first place. It was the best thing he'd ever done. He loved it, and now things were finally all in place. He'd watched Erik come into his own strength and prove his devotion and love to Asher.

Joey was so proud. So very proud of them all.

With a quick breath, his gaze flicked back to the crowd. Their chanting grew louder and his smile grew wider . . . as they played long into the night . . .

YOU MAY ALSO ENJOY THE FOLLOWING FROM EXTASY BOOKS INC:

Opening Act
S.L. Danielson and Cheryl Headford

Excerpt

Billy felt breathless as he struggled for words amid his dizzying onslaught of thoughts. Dammit! Someone has to look after these two morons. He moved their backpacks out of his way and ran after them as more yelling came from inside the pool room. The strong aroma of chlorine stung his eyes and nose when he entered. He fanned his face, trying to guard it from the fumes. Erik was looming over Asher.

"That's the last time you get on my case." Erik crouched and dove at Asher, knocking him down.

Before Erik could pin him, Asher rolled and popped up. Bouncing on the balls of his feet, he taunted Erik. "Come on then, big boy. If you think you can take me, you're going to have to do better than that. I'm going to enjoy this. You've got all the skill of a lumbering elephant. Keep blundering about like some stupid bull and let me show you how to dance."

Billy hung back. He knew how Erik was with revenge and fighting. Billy usually wouldn't interfere unless it got too rough. Water was dangerous, though, and the pool was rimmed with concrete. He stood and said nothing, ready to pounce into action at any second.

Billy knew Erik didn't like being called a bull or stupid. Erik did his best mimic of a twirl and stuck his long leg out at the last second, which Asher saw coming and gracefully avoided the clumsy attempt at a sweep, landing softly on the balls of his feet at the edge of the pool.

"Will you two please stop now?"

Billy's plea was sincere and drew Asher's attention at precisely the wrong moment. As he looked over and took his eyes off Erik, Erik grabbed the pool skimmer and swung it with all his might. The long handle caught Asher below the knee, swiping his legs out from under him.

Asher's legs buckled, and he toppled over, his head bouncing off the side of the pool before he disappeared with an enormous splash into the sparkling water.

"What the fuck?" Billy screeched loudly. "You've lost it, man. You . . ." He gaped at the water. "What the fuck's that?"

"What?" Erik followed Billy's pointing finger, to see the red fluid in the water.

"It's blood, dude," Billy gasped. "And . . . and he ain't coming up."

Almost before the words had left Billy's mouth, water overflowed the sides from the god-almighty splash as Erik's body hit the water. Hell. Billy's heart turned over. He wasn't the best swimmer and he started to panic. He didn't know what he'd do if neither of them came up. Fishing around in his pocket, he realized his cell phone was in his backpack.

Time stood still. The whole universe shrank to the size of the pool. Billy scanned the surface. After what seemed like hours but was only a few moments, Erik burst up near the edge and struck out toward him.

Kneeling down as close to the side of the pool as he dared, Billy reached out his arms until his hands touched sodden cloth. Struggling to get a hold of the stiff cotton of Asher's gi, Billy grabbed the collar and tugged as hard as he could. He almost fell over backward as Erik shoved up from below at the same time.

Asher struggled and coughed up water. Although it was a relief, it was also dangerous and almost dragged Billy into the water with them.

"Whoa, dude. Keep still. We're getting you out. You're going to be okay — don't pull me in with you."

Asher raised his head and peered at him through long strands of blue and black hair. Blood trickled from a cut over his eye. He nodded once and stopped thrashing. Billy panicked again but didn't have time to think about it. Erik gave one more heave, pushing Asher on top of Billy.

Limp as a rag doll, Asher rolled away from him and curled onto his side, coughing and gasping.

"Fuck, Asher." Erik erupted from the pool like some kind of water god. "I'm sorry, dude, I mean real sorry. I didn't mean . . . I mean . . ."

Billy looked up at Erik as he paused, unsure what to do. Water sloughed off his body, and his t-shirt clung to his muscular frame. He was beautiful.

"Erik . . ." Billy's words petered out.

Erik ignored him as if he didn't even exist. Erik fell to his knees on Asher's far side and bent over him. Billy would have killed to have Erik look at him the way he gazed at Asher. Right now, he felt very much the odd man out.

"Asher? Asher, are you all right? I didn't . . . I swear I didn't mean to hurt you. Please, Asher . . . Tell me you're all right." Asher rolled over onto his back and stared silently up at Erik. Erik stared back, his expression unreadable.

Pain lanced through Billy's heart as Erik dragged the hair out of Asher's face and brushed the still bleeding cut with one finger. Asher winced but didn't break eye contact. He raised his hand and tucked Erik's hair behind his ear, letting his fingers trail over Erik's cheek before it fell back to his side.

"Asher, I . . ."

Billy wanted to close his eyes or to run away, but he

couldn't. A self-destructive streak made him watch as Erik bent toward Asher, drawing closer and closer. They were going to kiss — Billy knew they were going to kiss. It would kill him, break his heart, but still he couldn't walk away. Erik stopped, hovering over Asher, barely six inches apart with their gazes locked. Billy didn't even glance at Asher's face. He was interested only in Erik's, which was blank of all expression other than the intensity of his gaze. Any minute now Erik would close the last few inches and . . . and Billy really had to move, had to run, had to —

"No! Fuck you! Fuck you, screwing with my head."

Erik got to his feet and ran. Billy, his heart threatening to burst from his chest, was torn. Should he follow Erik or . . . Of course he should go after Erik. He got to his feet. But . . . Asher wasn't moving. He just lay there, staring at the ceiling. If he had a concussion he needed medical attention. His hair was dark and all over the place, making it difficult to tell how bad the cut was or how much he was bleeding. With a sigh, Billy knelt down again and hunched over Asher.

Fuck, those eyes were weird. He wondered if Asher wore contacts and decided he must. No one had eyes like that — opalescent, pale lilac all the way from the pupil to the outer edge, which was dark purple. They were so strange, so beautiful. Billy shook his head. This wasn't the time to notice Asher's beautiful eyes.

"Asher? Are you okay? Can you get up? We need to get out of here. You have to get dry and —" He stopped as Asher's shining eyes swiveled and followed him. "Um . . . you er . . . Maybe I should take you to the hospital . . ." His words died in the face of the implacable expression in the dull eyes. He hung his head.

"Asher, I . . . He . . ." Billy let out a breath and felt obligated to warn Asher. "Don't get involved with him. Don't give him your heart or he'll crush it. He's not . . . He'll let you in, kiss you, hold you . . . maybe. He'll make you think he really cares, but then he'll get scared. Whatever happens between you can never be anything other than strictly between you. He won't come out. He won't admit to anyone what he feels about you. He'll keep you guessing, keep you hanging on forever. He . . ."

"You sound as if you know from experience." Asher's voice was roughened by coughing.

"I . . ." Billy's eyes widened, his heart pounding as he backed away a little. "I . . . no. No, I . . . I just know him. He's my best friend and . . ."

"It doesn't sound to me as if you're just friends."

"It's none of your business." Billy's cheeks burned, and he wished he'd never opened his mouth. He realized the full horror of the position he'd put himself in and groaned. He'd revealed the biggest secret he'd ever been entrusted with, the most important thing in the world to Erik and him, and he'd told Erik's worse enemy. Billy buried his head in his hands and moaned.

A gentle touch on his hand startled him, and he raised his head to meet Asher's gaze. Asher had raised himself onto one elbow, and blood ran down the side of his face in a thin trickle. If it hadn't been for the water it would have dried already. He tried to concentrate on the cut, on his concern as to whether or not it needed stitches, and whether he should take Asher to the hospital to make sure he didn't have a concussion. But it didn't work, and in the end, Billy stared into Asher's eyes.

"I know," Asher said quietly. "I'm not stupid. I saw the way you looked at him, and I saw the way he looked at you. Must be hard to feel that much and not have it returned."

Billy blinked. Asher sounded as if he understood — as if he actually understood.

"It is returned. He loves me." The words sounded hollow, and that shocked Billy. "He does love me. It's just . . ."

"In a different way."

"I . . . guess so."

"Yeah. Sucks."

"You . . . sound like you know from experience." Billy was

desperate to deflect the attention away from his relationship with Erik and to fill up the painful silences. "Yeah. Let me give you some advice. Walk away now before it completely crushes you."

Billy gazed into Asher's face, seeing something very familiar in the pained gaze. In that moment he felt a connection with the Goth boy, whose face was paler than ever, his eyeliner and mascara running down his cheeks, like a weeping angel crying tears of blackened decay. Angel? Maybe a fallen angel. Strands of turquoise hair stuck to his cheek, and Billy understood why Erik felt the urge to wipe them away. He shook his head.

"Do you think you can stand? I'll help and drive you to the hospital. Get that cut checked out."

"No, no I don't want to go to the hospital. I can manage. I'll drive myself home." Asher's chin jutted stubbornly, and he hauled himself to his feet.

Billy followed him up and grabbed for him, catching him around the waist when he swayed and stumbled toward the water.

"Easy. Look, put your arm over my shoulders and I'll help you." Asher hesitated. "Stop being so damn stubborn. Let me help you. I won't take you to the hospital. Just let me drive you home."

Asher stared at him for a moment and then nodded. "Okay." His voice sounded weak, but there was fire in his eyes.

Asher leaned on Billy, and they made their way out of the pool room. Their backpacks lay where they'd left them. Billy paused to scoop them up, slinging them awkwardly over his arm.

Asher swayed again when the cold air hit him, and it was all Billy could do to stop him from falling. Someone appeared out of nowhere and took the weight from Billy's arms.

"Erik? What the fuck?"

"I'll take him home. I did this. Come on." He manhandled

Asher into his arms. He gazed into Asher's makeup-streaked face. "You're coming with me whether you like it or not." The tone was adamant yet soft at the same time.

Billy tried to catch his breath. "Are you sure you want to go with him, Asher?"

Asher blinked blood, water, and hair out of his eyes, swiping at them weakly. Glancing from Billy to Erik, he seemed dazed. "I . . . Yeah . . . yeah, okay."

Without further hesitation, Erik held Asher to his side and walked them outside to his car. Billy followed closely behind them. He prayed that Asher wouldn't divulge what they'd talked about.

With a quick flip of the seat switch, Erik reclined the passenger seat and laid Asher into it as cautiously as possible. Taking advantage of Erik putting the backpacks into the trunk, Billy approached the car and belted Asher in. "You'll be fine. Take care of that head." His heart raced, and fear stifled his words. "You won't say anything . . . right?" he whispered.

"Not a word. I promise."

"All right, ninja. Let's go." Erik climbed into the driver's seat, and after Billy shut the passenger door with a sigh of relief, he watched them drive off.

ABOUT THE AUTHOR

S.L. Danielson began writing at the age of six. She knew it was her calling from the moment she put pen to paper. In her teens, she began writing alternative works and the genre stuck. She also wove more elaborate tales and finally, in her college years, began to weave her new love of male romance into long novels.

She is classically trained in business, accounting, and education, holding both undergrad and graduate degrees. Her other hobbies include painting, gaming, and spending time with her husband and two cherished cats.

Contact S.L. at:
ladyauthorsld@gmail.com
or follow her blog at:
www.sldanielsoncom.wordpress.com

Cheryl Headford was born into a poor mining family in the South Wales Valleys. Until she was sixteen, the toilet was at the bottom of the garden, and the bath hung on the wall. Her refrigerator was a stone slab in the pantry, and there was a black lead fireplace in the kitchen. They look lovely in a museum but aren't so much fun to clean.

Cheryl has always been a storyteller. As a child, she'd make up stories for her nieces, nephews, and cousin, and they'd explore the imaginary worlds she created, in play.

Later in life, Cheryl became the storyteller for a reenactment group who travelled widely, giving a taste of life in the Iron Age. As well as having an opportunity to run around hitting people with a sword, she had an opportunity to tell stories of all kinds, sometimes of her own making, to all kinds of people. The criticism was sometimes harsh, especially from the children, but the reward enormous.

It was here she began to appreciate the power of stories and the primal need to hear them. In ancient times, the wandering bard was the only source of news, and the storyteller, the heart of the village, keeping the lore and the magic alive. Although much of the magic has been lost, the stories still provide a link to the part of us that still wants to believe that it's still there, somewhere.

In present times, Cheryl lives in a terraced house in the valleys with her son and two cats. Her daughter has deserted her for the big city, but they're still close.

Website: http://cherylheadford.com/
Twitter: https://twitter.com/SevenPointStar